Praise for *I Will Leave You N*

"Ann Putnam's ironically titled *I Will* leave-takings that even Zoë—the app(anticipate over the course of a year th ... strain but not break the bonds of her loving family."

—Ladette Randolph, editor of *Ploughshares* and author of *Private Way*

"Exquisitely written, this luminous novel takes you to the deep heart of a marriage. Threatened by illness and arson, a family with three children and too many puppies ultimately finds the strength to go forward with wit and insight."

—Beverly Conner, author of *Where Light is a Place* and *Falling from Grace*

"Ominous and original, Ann Putnam's novel is characteristically lyrical and precise. It is at its heart a love story, where characters facing loss uncover the generative quality of love."

—Beth Kalikoff, author of *Dying for a Blue Plate Special*

"It's no surprise that Ann Putnam's most recent novel, *I Will Leave You Never*, features compelling characters in Zoë and Jay (among others) and lush, vivid writing. Fans of her short stories and her novel *Cuban Quartermoon* will, like me, rejoice that a new novel has appeared."

—Hans Ostrom, author of *Honoring Juanita*

Praise for Ann Putnam's *Cuban Quartermoon*

"An American scholar visits Cuba and becomes embroiled in the politics of everyday life in this poetic novel . . . despite the novel's breathtakingly evocative descriptive focus on the country and culture [of Cuba], the author never neglects the intricacies of her complex plot. . . . A story with sumptuous description and a gradually intensifying plot that makes for compulsive reading."

—*Kirkus Reviews* (starred review)

"The lush imagery and cutting-edge prose of this narrative masterpiece makes for a compelling and transformative read."
—Linda Patterson Miller, PhD, author of *Letters from the Lost Generation*

"In her rich and evocative novel, Ann Putnam renders the beauty, lure, strangeness, and intrigue of the island in sensuous detail through the eyes of a North American woman on a personal journey toward restoration and redemption."
—Sandra Spanier PhD, Edwin Erle Sparks Professor of English, Penn State University

Praise for Ann Putnam's *Full Moon at Noontide: A Daughter's Last Goodbye*

"Old age, death, and impermanence—it seems at first glance impossible to make a reader see these timeless and universal experiences with fresh eyes, but Ann Putnam's luminous prose achieves that miracle and more, transforming pain, suffering, and loss into a literary gift of beauty and redemption."
—Charles Johnson, author of *The Middle Passage*

"—this is a hard book because Ann Putnam has the courage to tell us the truth about aging and dying. But it's a gorgeous book, too, one born from the endurance of the human spirit and the capacity to love."
—Lee Martin, Pulitzer Prize Finalist Author of *The Bright Forever*

"From the beginning, *Full Moon at Noontide* seduced me. Then it sliced me open, slapped me in the face, made me cry, and enlarged my spirit. We stay with the story because it is beautifully written, and because it shows us that love—not—death can have the last word."
—Thomas R. Cole, PhD, author of *The Journey of Life: A Cultural History of Aging*

I Will Leave You Never

ALSO BY ANN PUTNAM

Full Moon at Noontide: A Daughter's Last Goodbye

Nine by Three: Stories (with Beverly Conner & Hans Ostrom)

Cuban Quartermoon: A Novel

I Will Leave You Never

A Novel

Ann Putnam

SHE WRITES PRESS

Published 2023
Printed in the United States of America
Print ISBN: 978-1-64742-424-4
E-ISBN: 978-1-64742-425-1
Library of Congress Control Number: 2022918835

For information, address:
She Writes Press
1569 Solano Ave #546
Berkeley, CA 94707

Interior Design by Kiran Spees

She Writes Press is a division of SparkPoint Studio, LLC.

for Ed

and for Christopher, Robb, and Courtney

Contents

Shelter Moon

It was the fall before the Millennium, and fears, if they had them, were apocalyptic: computers die, planes crash, banks fail, clocks stop, dogs howl, no water, no food—all distant fears they tabled for the moment as the Northwest drought kept on. The leaves swirled about the house, flickering against the windows and drifting into corners. The fog settled in after sunset and it was dark before dinnertime, the air heavy with the promise of the winter rains that still didn't come. It was almost Halloween, but there were no lighted pumpkins on porches, no ghosts and goblins tacked to front doors or swinging from the eaves. Everything was now combustible. And things once longed for—homecoming bonfires, or autumn leaves in wondrous mounds, and the very trees—were now a fiery blooming.

It had been three months of fires—fifty-one and counting.

Tonight, it would be a ghostly shelter of a moon, a lantern lit against the night. Zoë was sitting at the dining room table, watching out the cathedral window, waiting for it. By day, the blue heartbreak of the October sky made you feel that winter would never come, and you'd live forever in this strange sunlit peace. Night was another story. She had dialed 911 in a thousand dreams.

It was too quiet. The kids had all but abandoned the kitchen in favor of their homework, or so they said. Jay leaned over and put his arms around her. "All right. I'll do the dishes."

"Are you looking for extra credit?" Zoë stood up for a proper hug.

Jay gathered her up like always, rubbed his chin against the top of her head. She gentled into him, felt his warmth through his shirt.

"We could just stay like this and forget the dishes." He put his hand under her shirt and stroked her back, fiddled with her bra strap.

"You'll never do it one-handed."

"If I could, would I still have to do the dishes?"

"Yup." Zoë pulled away from him and looked out the window.

"Just enjoy your coffee," Jay said. "Your moon is almost here."

Then there it was, in the peak of the cathedral window, erotic and full to bursting, then all too soon a drowsy smudge of a moon. She closed her eyes and felt the warm coffee cup against her palms. She could hear Jay loading plates into the dishwasher. When she looked back up, the moon was gone. It would be a long night.

"Later?" she called out. But he was gone. "Please, later," she whispered.

She got up to finish cleaning the counters. She liked this part of the job. Making things smooth and shiny, everything all safe and tucked away. At least she could do that. She smoothed back her hair and tried to see beyond her reflection into the dark. Such dark hair and dark eyes. You'd think at least one of the kids would have taken after her instead of Jay, with his blue eyes and sandy hair. Whatever was out there, she would never see it.

Jay was asleep by the time Zoë finally climbed into bed. She liked the rippling moonlight across his face, coming in from the blinds. She lay her head on his pillow and listened to his breathing but shied from drawing him out of that deep place. She could touch his face or get up to lock the bedroom door and see if he stirred. The kind of privacy she longed for required a locked door. She was pretty sure the kids were all fast asleep by now. Lately kids had been in and out of their bedroom half the night.

Zoë was just getting up when she heard Jillie coming into the room, dragging her sleeping bag. She was breathless, trying not to cry. "I dreamed about that bad man again."

"No bad man, Jillie. There's no bad man. Come here, Sweetie."

Jillie slipped in between them quick as a flash. Soon she would be fast asleep, warm and damp beside her.

All this new thinking about kids in your bedroom. She was too tired to figure it out. Besides, Zoë liked it when everybody was a second away.

She lay there long after her daughter had crawled in between them.

"Zoë," Jay said.

"I didn't know you were awake."

"When am I ever going to love you?" He'd stopped reaching for her when she came to bed, ever since they'd kept their bedroom door open at night.

"The winter of our discontent," she said. Her desire was a stranger on a long journey. What with all these nocturnal goings-on, when did they ever have the chance? "Dry spell."

"Long dry spell."

"Long is what?" she said.

"Long is a week. Long used to be a day and a night. And it's not even winter yet."

"I remember everything we ever did," she said, touching him across their sleeping child. Jillie's hand was curled up under her chin, like she was lost in some fine thought.

"Let's try and get her to bed," Jay said.

"Okay. If we don't wake her up."

Jay picked her up softly and carried her into her room while Zoë watched from Jillie's door. She looked at him tucking her in, the way he touched her hair, like a benediction.

Zoë went to him and ran her hand under his T-shirt. "Now," she said. "Now is when to love me."

He took her hand and led her back into the bedroom. He closed the door and locked it. "We'll open it later."

"We won't fall asleep and forget, will we?"

"We won't forget," Jay said, easing her into bed.

"Let's open the blinds all the way and have the moon on us," Zoë said.

"So I can see you."

She liked the way she looked in the moonlight, the way he was looking at her. She liked the way his hands looked, his strong shoulders, the way he was kissing her belly, then down and down again. She shut her eyes and felt herself float across the sky. She tilted her head back and became a flickering heartbeat that moved down her body. Then everything rushed over her in a radiance that narrowed to a point of heat and light so fierce she cried out too late to cover her mouth, and now an aching warmth that grew again, only softer, softly, in widening little waves of heat and light deep inside, then quiet like a whisper, a gentle breath blowing out the candle they hadn't lit.

Then Jay pulled himself into her, his hands under her bottom, holding her there tightly and how small and lovely she felt, and she started to cry at how much she had missed this without even knowing it. They lay back without touching, the night casting shadows across them, across the covers in a tangle at the bottom of the bed.

"Can you unlock the door now?" Zoë said.

"To do that I would have to leave you."

Zoë felt the ache of tears behind her eyes and reached for him as he got back into bed. Then she sat up and closed the blinds. She lay back, spooned into him, and shut her eyes. Jay spread the covers across them and tucked his hand under her breast. She had not felt safe like this in so long. They lay quiet in the dream for a long time until she sensed something bright flicker across her eyelids.

"Jay!" she whispered, coming out of the dream. "The *motion light* just came on." She touched his chest. He startled up and reached around for the blinds. Zoë leaned over and scrambled for the phone. "I'm calling the police," she said tightly because her heart was in her throat. Just like in her dreams, the plaid coat sleeve, the dark, narrow cap, the gasoline can, the sudden flare of the match in the dark, the flames catching hold, rushing up. There he was. Just like she knew he would be.

But she dropped the phone and slid out of bed to scoop it up. Niki, the dog, was standing there, wagging her tail.

Then Jay started to laugh. "I don't think we need the police."

"Why are you *laughing*?" Zoë said from the floor. Niki was licking her face.

"Come here," Jay said, giving her a hand. "You've got to see this."

And there was the woodpile, undisturbed as ever, and Ruby, the neighbor's cat, perched on top, looking back at them in the moonlight.

She turned away and sat down on the end of the bed.

"Don't do that," he said, pulling her to him. "Don't cry. See? We were safe all along." Jay clearly wanted to drive the lesson home, but she had already lived it through to the very end.

"I *hate* him. I hate what he's doing to us."

Soon they discovered that the woodpile was a favorite sitting place for not only the neighbor's cat but for possums and raccoons and birds and whatever else was down in the woods at night, so the light was snapping on and off all the time, and no warning at all. But maybe that light would startle the arsonist into changing his mind and moving on to another house.

It was a terrible thought, God help her, to wish such catastrophe on someone else, but she swallowed it whole.

The motion light was only one of their precautionary measures, but it was the one Zoë counted on most fervently. In this strange season of drought, the woods rose up next to the house, tinder dry, the evergreen cool of summer now one more rustling threat. Any fire here and the woods would ignite. And the house! The house, where all those precious ones slept, wouldn't have a chance.

Every night on the six o'clock news there were reports from the Arson Task Force, who'd arrested no one, the Arson Hotline, the Arson Reward up to twenty-five thousand dollars now, and last week a helicopter with a heat sensor detector just like in the war. The news report always ended with the Arson Map, covered with little points of fire that now caught them in a web of flashing lights. Jay shook his head at the map and laughed out loud. "Hey, buddy, you've missed a spot. Burn *this*."

"So you think that's funny?" Zoë said.

"You gotta laugh at some of this."

Jay had installed the three new smoke detectors she'd bought, and two motion-sensor lights—one for the woodpile by their bedroom window next to the woods, and one for the back door of the garage, which was now kept locked at night. If the arsonist came their way, he'd either set the garage or the woodpile on fire.

The newspapers had warned people to remove all combustibles from around their houses, but that woodpile was enormous, and it seemed a lot of trouble to go to just to move it a few yards. Besides, the woods rose up a few feet from the woodpile and were so dry that whole side of the hill could be an inferno in a matter of seconds.

For weeks now, every night after work, Zoë had pulled the car right up against the sliding garage door, so nobody could lift it up from the bottom and slide underneath, like the arsonist had done just last week—slipped under the door and set the whole garage on fire. It spread to the house so quickly the sleeping people inside escaped with only their lives—everybody but the family dog, who got left behind.

"You can't put a lock on everything," Jay said. "You just do what you can then go live your life." But Zoë believed that there was always something more you could do. It made her weary, keeping track of everything. She didn't think Jay was worrying at all.

This arsonist was a regular Rorschach. Zoë hated how he'd already snaked his way into the house. Jay had finally banned all arsonist talk at dinner. Max had booby-trapped sections of the gully by looping Jay's fishing line from tree to tree so he'd get his ankles all tangled up and fall down forever. She had to admit it was pretty impressive for a nine-year-old. He'd inherited Jay's magical gift for figuring things out. Will kept his own counsel, too big-brother cool to admit he was afraid. He was twelve, after all. Still, he was the one who paced the house at night when everybody thought he was asleep. Jillie was sleeping on the floor most nights, in a sleeping bag at the foot of their bed.

Some nights Zoë dreamed she saw the arsonist standing by the woodpile next to the house just outside the bedroom window. He was watching the flame burn down toward his fingers. She could feel his concentration through the bill of the cap pulled down tight over his face. The wood glistened in the moonlight, soaked with gasoline from the can tucked under his arm. He looked up just then and saw her looking back from behind the blinds. Nobody said anything, nobody moved. Zoë always woke up before he could toss the match, knowing that the face was familiar, but couldn't bring it whole out of the dream. She'd look out the window, just to be sure she had only been dreaming, and there was the woodpile, silent and watchful as ever.

Coming home late from the movies, they'd seen one of the fires rushing up the side of the hill next to the highway, as they stopped for a traffic light. It was a rare night when they left the house. It had been lovely, except for the lateness, and all the times Zoë had tilted her watch to the light of the screen to check the time. It almost wasn't worth it. Too much worry for such a mediocre movie.

She could see the shape of a solitary, darkened house on top of the hill. Somebody should wake those people up! Didn't they know what was coming their way? Maybe they weren't home. And where were the fire trucks? He must have started it in the brush or grass at the side of the road, because a flickering row of low flames was beginning to take off up the hill. He usually targeted garages or sheds, a couple of churches, a house last week. So what was this hillside? Was he working his way up or down? The car was close to the flames now, which seemed to rise higher and higher in some kind of draft.

Cars were backing up in the opposite lane, slowing to see what they could see. How would a fire truck get through now? They'd have to come from the top and aim their hoses below.

The fire was terrifyingly close to the house at the top. It looked like it was feeding on itself. They could see plumes of smoke rising in the cold night, floating across the windshield. Where were the goddamned fire trucks?

Zoë wanted to speed home to the children and slam the door. But there they sat at the world's longest red light. Maybe the fire had done something with the signal.

Through the smoke you could make out several people standing out front in their robes and pajamas. She thought she could see a couple of kids. Those poor people. She was glad it wasn't her family. But at least they got out in time. Now they could see a man with a hose, spraying down the roof.

Zoë was glad the children were home in bed, and not seeing any of this, the babysitter keeping watch, or so they hoped. They'd told her it was fine to watch TV, but she should keep her ears open for any strange sounds.

"Like what?" she asked.

"I don't know, any rustling, or any crackling or hissing, I guess," Zoë said. It was useless. The arsonist never made noises as he was skulking around, putting his fires together. And by then it was always too late.

The babysitter looked at her wide-eyed. It was a wonder she didn't put on her coat and ask to be taken home.

"Oh, don't worry about it. I'm being melodramatic. Everything will be fine. The dog would notice anything going on." She wasn't sure of that at all.

"A whoosh. Listen for that," she said over her shoulder. She didn't know what she was talking about. Then she turned back. "Never mind. I'm sorry. I'm just scaring you for nothing. We're absolutely safe here. All precautions in place."

Now the flames seemed to shoot across the side windows, in some wild reflection or lurid photograph. There was nowhere to go, jammed in with all these cars. If it came any closer to the road, they'd have to jump out of the car on the driver's side and make a run for it. Any closer and the car might explode. So close, so close. Zoë shut her eyes and tucked down into herself. Jay was hunched over the wheel as though he were urging the car far and away, when of course he was sitting perilously, agonizingly still.

Finally the light turned and they were inching away from the fire, away from the smoke, away from peril that could make other people's children orphans, and never theirs.

Zoë looked back at the flickers and embers by the side of the road as they put distance behind them. She lay her head down and grabbed her knees. So easy to start a fire in the garage, so easy for the flames to leap from one rooftop to the other, so easy to simmer in an inexorable line of fire. At first, silent and deadly, before it ribboned along the edges of the roof of the house, then spilled over and slid down the wood siding, a golden sheet of flame, finally crackling against the windows until they exploded.

Everybody would at least hear that.

"We shouldn't have left them," she said from between her knees.

"It's all right, Zoë. We had a great time and everybody's really all right." Jay touched her back.

Then they said nothing at all as the car hurtled through the dark toward home.

Zoë was sitting on the edge of the deck out back, waiting for Niki to finish sniffing around, before she locked up the house for the night. Everybody else had gone to bed long ago. They had come through another week all safe. Still, she was listening hard. She could almost hear the molecules buzzing in the air, a little staticky sound—her own heartbeat or maybe her breathing.

Everything felt heavy and close. She could hardly see a thing. Then the moon came out from the clouds and she saw the white plume of Niki's tail before the moon disappeared again behind a thick band of clouds that drifted across the sky. She loved her Malamute wildness, her regal bearing. The clothesline that hovered above her had disappeared into the sky. Soon everything was covered with a low ridge of clouds. She began to shiver. It felt foggy, damp. She zipped up her parka and wished the dog would hurry up. The motion light that had snapped on when she stepped out onto the deck had long gone out. She wondered about the arsonist, if he was out here somewhere, or was it too cold, too damp? It was Wednesday night, anyway. He almost always started the fires on Sundays or Mondays. His work schedule, or maybe his horoscope, or voices in his head.

She heard it first like the low hum of traffic on the street below, though it was too late for traffic. It grew and grew like a plane coming in low for a landing until the sound was everywhere and she was inside the white-hot sound, in the leaves blowing everywhere. Then there it was, dark against the flashing sky. It swept across the trees, passed over the house, the clothesline strung across the yard, the deck where she stood, washing everything in ghostly daylight. And then it was gone.

"Niki!" she called. The dog was a dark shadow in the middle of the yard, looking up at the sky. She came right away, and Zoë grabbed her collar and felt her hackles at attention. Niki turned back to look at the loud noise and growled a low, unearthly growl. The light clicked on as they rushed across the deck. She slammed the door and locked it behind her, then leaned against it, still holding tightly onto the dog's chain-link collar. It was all right. This dog was bred for such pulling. "I'm sorry, Niki," she said, kneeling down and burrowing her face into her neck.

Inside, everybody was still asleep. How could they sleep through all that? Just proved her point that sleeping downstairs they wouldn't know a thing. Maybe they'd sleep through the fire alarm too. Jay rolled over, pulled the covers up over his shoulder. Jillie's legs were half out of the sleeping bag so Zoë tucked them back inside, zipped up the bag.

She sat on the edge of the bed and cracked open the blinds, and there was the woodpile, just a darker shape against the dark. She looked out at the trees. She wondered if the arsonist was out there in the woods right now. What a damaged childhood he must have had. She leaned against the windowsill, watching through the crack in the blinds, too tired to sleep. But when she shut her eyes, she felt sleep coming, so she lay down on her back with her hands at her side, closed her eyes and listened for her breath, slowly, deeply, then deeper still. She gradually began to see the outline of some of the trees beyond the woodpile, tangled and strange. And beyond that just a hint of a flickering blue light, way back in the woods. The longer she watched, the more it seemed to flicker and pulse, flicker and pulse.

It felt peaceful to lie there with her eyes closed, watching the blue light. Why hadn't she seen it before? It was beginning to fan out, like a growing flame. She watched it take shape, first into a rectangle, then peaking into a roof, and now she could see the moon shining down on a house, far back in the woods. Why hadn't she ever noticed a house back there before? The moon danced and throbbed and drew her on. The wind made a silvery tremor in the trees. She knew she was dreaming, but it didn't matter. She could see a chimney now, a back door, an upstairs window.

She was watching the window, watching the little boy who was looking out the window too. The little boy was watching the tiny cold flames at the edges of the window grow and grow until the whole window was so frosty you couldn't see a thing. Then he rubbed a spot in the center of the window with the sleeve of his pajamas so he could keep watch over the little roof in the backyard under which the dog lay sleeping a cold and dreamless sleep.

Zoë could feel the fierce cold of the window too. Her fingers ached with it. She knew he liked the way the frost felt hot. Liked the way it burned his hand when he held it there, so that when Dad held his hand over the stove for turning it on without asking, he could pretend it wasn't hot at all, but only very cold, so cold it burned. He liked the burning cold. He liked to watch the match burn down close to his fingers before he dropped it onto the stove. He liked the clean way the little blue flame of the gas stove pulsed and burned. He liked to turn on the stove when no one was home and watch the cool blue flame and feel how hot it was. He liked the snow in the same way, the way the snow muffled everything in a roaring stillness. He liked to listen to the snow falling, liked the cold feeling that could cover the hot feeling when Dad held his hand over the stove. He liked the way fire made everything pure and clean, like the falling snow outside his window where he watched, dreaming this.

Scarecrow Man

"That man watches me when I get the mail sometimes," Jillie said one day, putting the mail on the kitchen counter.

"What man?" Zoë felt a flash of heat rise up her neck, over her face.

"That man in the Turners' old house."

"What do you mean he watches you?"

"From the window. He talked to me once."

"Jillie! You know better than that."

"But he's not a stranger. He's just new."

How long had he lived there anyway? It couldn't have been very long. She'd never really known the Turners, but during the summer a big Allied moving van parked in the driveway and then the next day, the Turners were gone. It wasn't a very neighborly part of the neighborhood. The yellow house across the street from the Turners had been empty for months, and now an older man lived there. Zoë didn't know him either. Something about that turn around the corner by the mailboxes and then the rush on up to their house on the hill kept her distant from the neighborhood below.

Then one day a brown van was parked in the Turner driveway and she knew somebody was home at last. She'd seen him getting the mail, as she drove by. He wore a baseball cap, with a dark brown ponytail down his neck. She'd remembered the strange dog that stood beside him, its black and white markings familiar enough to startle her. It wasn't a Malamute exactly but almost. Maybe part wolf or German shepherd. He must keep that dog inside all the time, or maybe it was fenced in the backyard that spread far out, before it dropped off into the woods.

A week before Halloween he'd hung a scarecrow from the eaves above the front porch. It was a regular scarecrow, all right—khaki pants, plaid shirt, a belt virtually cutting the poor guy in two, cornstalks for hands and feet, arms held out by a broom handle. But it wasn't just hanging from the eaves, it was hanging by the neck. A faceless, fleshy dummy with its head lopped over, a noose around its neck. It gave her the chills. He looked crucified, with his arms outstretched.

It was there every morning on her way to school, and every night on her way home, days before Halloween and days after. The head at that angle was an affront to the universe, the arms a salute to all the earth's dark forces. She had just finished teaching Toni Morrison's *Beloved*. Baby Suggs's sermon caught in her throat every time: "And, oh my people . . . [white folks] do not love your neck unnoosed and straight." And Sethe's lament: "Boys hanging from the most beautiful sycamores in the world. It shamed her—remembering the wonderful soughing trees rather than the boys." She hated him for putting up such a terrible thing. She would never forgive him.

For that and for watching Jillie from his window. What did he think he was doing anyway? She couldn't look at the scarecrow without dread. Still, she couldn't take her eyes off it, either. She thought it was some projection of the man and what life had done to him. "There's something wrong in there," she told the kids. "You guys skip that house this year." She didn't care what she sounded like or what kind of example she was setting. On those chilly October mornings when she drove down the hill on her way to school, the house looked haunted in the fog hanging over the giant firs in that gray-green light. It was an optical illusion, of course, but there were lots of those that fall. The kids called him Scarecrow Man. That was okay. Scarecrows only looked scary. After all, they were just straw and air. Better than Hangman any day, which is what the boys down the street called him. She'd never call him Hangman in front of the kids, though that's what she called him in her head.

Then one day coming home from school, Zoë noticed the brown van wasn't in the driveway. So, as she was getting the mail, she reached into his mailbox and pulled out an envelope. *Roy*. His name was *Roy Leland*.

On Halloween night, hellfire flashed against that front window. It was only a red strobe light and strips of red and orange crepe paper blowing in the wind from a fan he'd no doubt set up. The Grateful Dead blared from a loudspeaker set up on the porch. It was terrible. It was sad. Somebody trying too hard. At the very least, the guy had a bad sense of timing, considering all the fires. People had already started to talk. His trash cans overflowing, an old lawn chair, scraps of wood, the detritus of his life propped against those big cans. It broke every safety rule they'd been given. Jay was right. You want something to burn, buddy? Burn this. But somebody was the arsonist. He had to live somewhere.

Every kid in the neighborhood wanted to visit that house. On the porch he'd put a pumpkin with a face carved from an Edvard Munch painting backlit by a candle. Not a crooked, toothy smile or even a demented grin, but a scream, a giant, oval, orange scream. Was he trying to scare all the kids off or beckon them in?

"Where's your pillowcase?" Zoë said, watching Jay put on his rain parka and wool cap.

"What pillowcase?"

"For all the candy."

Jay laughed. "Oh, that's right. I'll go right up to that man's door and say 'trick or treat.' Ya think?" He turned back and kissed the bridge of her nose.

"I should go too," she said.

"Probably nobody should go. You know what Will would say if he saw us creeping around behind him."

"But you said it was a good idea anyway," Zoë said. "All things considered."

"Yeah, probably. But you're better off staying inside. You sound terrible."

"It's not really raining yet. Maybe it won't rain. You know how strange everything is. And it's Sunday anyway. Arson night."

"Not every Sunday now."

Jay put his hand against her forehead. "Did you take your temperature?"

"I'm okay. I can tell when I have a fever."

"There is just no reason for you to tag along."

"Okay, but the kids better not see you."

Somebody had spray-painted that man's driveway again, and who knew what else? Too much mischief out there for those kids to go it alone, no matter how insistent Will was that he could take care of everybody. There was a humming in the air if you listened for it, a pressure behind the eyes you couldn't rub away—a barely suspended sense of danger. The fire in the window, the scarecrow, the blaring music could conjure evil spirits out of the air, or out of their dry, earthen graves.

"I'm glad you're going, though," she said. "I don't really feel so great."

She grabbed the comforter around her as she watched out the front window. Niki stood beside her, and nosed the window, her hackles up. The kids were almost all the way down the hill. Then she watched Jay slowly angle his way down after them, tucked back into the dark.

She would never forgive that man, though, for hanging the scarecrow. What was Halloween anyway? No All Saints' Day here. No Day of the Dead in America. Kids didn't give it a second thought. You could dress up as a wraith or skeleton and enter Hades if you knew you'd return to the morning, sun on your face and rapture in that pillowcase full of forbidden treats tucked under your bed. No sweetness and death. No sugar candy skeletons and skulls. Or smell of vanilla and wilting flowers in the sun.

Zoë could see the kids standing by the mailboxes under the streetlight as other kids flocked to that door. They made the kids promise to stick together, only go to the places they'd been to before, and skip the Ferguson house, where the tough boys lived with the dad who beat them. They were probably the ones who'd spray-painted Roy Leland's driveway. And never stop at the Scarecrow house. Zoë didn't want to alarm Jillie, but didn't want her striking up a rogue friendship with him either, because she was as curious as Max, and felt no threat at all. But Will knew. It would have been an insult to him not to believe he wouldn't keep to the rules.

Adults stood in a circle outside the fence, looking on, watching their kids rush up to the door, drawn in by the melodrama, by the promise of a real scare. Zoë could imagine it—the ghosts and goblins, devils and demons approaching the house in clumps. But the bunnies and princesses were holding tight to their parents' hands and looking on from outside the fence. There was a certain poignancy in his efforts, though. In all this time Zoë had never seen another car parked in his driveway, or anyone going to the door except these children now, lured by the pyrotechnics coming from the crepe paper, fans, and strobe lights. Good thing Jay was out there.

The kids had moved on down the hill and out of sight. She could see Jay standing in the middle of the road looking at that house, then turn the corner and disappear into the dark. He'd say he was just out for a stroll, as he kept watch over those three heads all in a row as they went up each porch into the light, then down and back into the dark.

Jay stopped and waited. The Ferguson house was next and they knew better than to ever stop there. Jay would not be seen if he could help it. As he waited, a song kept going through his head. Jillie sang it often as she was getting ready for school.

This is the way you brush your teeth,
tie your shoes,
make your bed.
This is the way you look both ways,
so early in the morning.

He found he was humming it. He hoped they were looking both ways now and forever. He felt a rush of pride and fear. Jay himself worried more than he let on. Something about this arsonist had thrown him off kilter. He felt a new tightness in his throat, imagined he was coming down with a cold that never came. In his dreams he burned his arms grasping to rescue them just as they vanished into a rush of flames. He always woke with the sting of hands fallen asleep. He would do anything to save them but wondered if he would be strong enough, if it ever came to that. He knew he'd postponed his annual physical three times now. Just like a man, Zoë always said.

He couldn't see them on the road anymore. He wasn't ready to let them go, but he imagined it anyway. But instead of the house below the Fergusons, there they were, coming fast back up the hill. Will had his arm around Max's shoulder and Max was holding Jillie's hand.

"Dad! You and Mom *promised*," Will said. Then softer, "What are you doing out here?"

"Yup, we said you kids could go out on your own. You're *on* your own."

"But you're *here*."

"Oh, not really. I just felt like a walk to see what's what."

Jay was caught and he knew it. Still, he could tell something had spooked them.

Jillie dropped Max's hand and rushed to her father and buried her face in his parka.

"What happened, guys?"

Jillie looked back at her brothers standing shoulder to shoulder.

"Daddy," she said, and started to cry.

Jay knelt down and scooped her up. She wrapped her arms around his neck and dropped her pillowcase.

"Guys?" Will's Groucho moustache and eyebrows were now dark smudges and for a moment, Jay thought he'd been beaten up. Jay's werewolf mask was hanging by the elastic down Max's back. His face was pale in the streetlight. Jillie was still a princess, but she'd lost her aluminum foil crown. Jay wanted to gather them all under his rain parka and never let them go.

Max was the one who told. "Benny Ferguson jumped out from the bushes and screamed at us. He said the Scarecrow Man's house was a Death House and that the scarecrow was really a dead man. A man that he *killed*. He said if we ate his candy we would die. He said we would all die tonight anyway because we lived so close."

Benny Ferguson was fourteen and bullied all the kids as they walked up and down the hill to the bus stop. He wasn't any taller than Will and only a few pounds heavier, but he made up for his size in a meanness the kids could never understand. His flat, cruel eyes always frightened them.

"I tried to keep everybody safe," Will said. "But he was hiding in the bushes like he was waiting for us."

"You did fine, Will. Everybody *is* safe. You know their dad doesn't treat those boys very well. And they've got no mom. He's just a bully. Let's come on home and go out for ice cream."

"But we didn't even stop at the Scarecrow house at all," Jillie said. "We just slowed down a little bit before we went down the hill. That man wouldn't do bad things." Jillie wriggled out of Jay's arms.

"Kids all right?" said an older man who'd come out of his driveway into the street. "Will Merwin," he said, extending his hand. "I saw that boy jump out at them."

"They're gonna be fine," Jay said, taking his hand. "I'm Jay Penney. This is Jillie and Max. And this is Will. He's Will too. Nice to meet you."

"Great kids," he said. "You're awfully lucky."

"I know I am. But thanks."

"I don't know why he'd go to all that trouble, considering all the fires these days. He's a strange one, all right."

"They skipped it, thank goodness." Jay saw the kids exchange some secret look. "Nice to meet you, Will. Better get these guys home."

When Jay finally climbed into bed, he turned to Zoë who was half asleep on Nyquil.

"I met the new neighbor."

"You *met* him? The Scarecrow guy?" She sat up.

"The old man in the yellow house. Mr. Merwin. He was alarmed at the decorations and came outside. He said he saw what that Ferguson boy did to the kids."

"I think he's a nice man. Sometimes he waves when I stop for the mail. Great shock of white hair."

Jay was shivering and Zoë wrapped her arms around him. "You're not coming down with this, are you? Don't do that."

"Nah, I'm okay. I didn't take very good care of the kids, though. You want them to grow up brave and strong, but mostly you just want them to be safe."

"But they *are* safe. They're all tucked in fast asleep."

"I should have said something to that Benny Ferguson. I should have gone to the door and called him out."

"What would that have done?"

"Probably made things worse."

"Go to sleep, Jay." Zoë lay back down and put her hand against his chest. His breath was too hard, too fast for sleep. "Want some Nyquil? Sweet, dear Jay."

"He had the best treats of anybody," Max reported the next day after school. No razor blades in the apples or rat poison sprinkled over the popcorn. But big Hershey chocolate bars shiny in their wrappers, three to a kid. The word had gotten out. Jay just looked down the street and shook his head.

October turned into November and still the rains did not come. These November nights Zoë had gotten into the habit of slipping out onto the back deck after everybody was asleep to sit on the chair she'd hauled out of the garage. Niki came out with her and lay beside her, keeping watch over the woods, sniffing the air. Coyotes howled in the gulley and the fur on her neck stiffened. The children fled the woods before dusk now, rushed up the hill and into the lighted house, and locked the door. You'd never hear the striking of a match. You'd never hear the roll of newspaper soaked in kerosene flame up. You'd see it first.

So here they were, keeping watch. At first she wondered if she were a little crazy, but then the habit became so familiar it came with a comfort of its own. If she tried to explain it, it would sound perverse, so she kept this ritual secret. That was part of its pleasure, shielded from judgment and the necessary explanation. She looked into the woods. She would stare him down, whoever he was. He would never get her family.

Sometimes coming back into the house and turning on the bathroom light, she'd wonder why the lights seemed so piercingly bright. Then her vision would narrow and blackbirds would skitter across her eyes, and she'd remember what it was, and get the Tylenol for the headache to come.

Days, then weeks, of silence from this arsonist and still she kept the appointed vigil. She began to long for it. Now she waited for eleven o'clock, when she could go outside alone, sit in the deck chair, look out into the woods, shut her eyes, and listen. Then she could hear things she couldn't with her eyes open. Something brushing against the bushes, a snap, then a whir of silence as though he'd caught himself and stepped back, as though he knew she was up here, waiting. It was all right. It was a strange comfort. It calmed her to be out there where he might be.

But finally the winter rains came and brought them to safety from fires that could rise up out of the woods. And with the rains, talk of the arsonist fell off the back pages of the paper. If the Arson Task Force was still at work, they were doing it without the benefit of news coverage. Thanksgiving was just around the corner and there was so much to be thankful for. They had made it through the fall, made it through the cluster of fires. She had wished for rain so extravagant you couldn't imagine anything being that dry ever again.

Now here it was. Her sojourns outside these days were quick, just standing under the eaves of the back door and listening to the rain patter against the last of the leaves. They hadn't had a hard wind-storm yet to finish the job. If it weren't raining she'd step out onto the deck and search for the low-hanging moon just above the trees, black and skeletal in the moonlight. He was still out there, though, she knew it. Whatever was coming was just around the corner now. The air bit through her thin coat, nipped at her bare legs.

"Mom!" Will said as she came back inside. "What were you doing outside?" She had her coat over her nightgown. She had frightened him.

"Why aren't you asleep?" she said. "You've got school tomorrow."

"I don't know," he said, opening the refrigerator. "I just like to check on things." It was a wonder they hadn't run into each other before now. She knew Will sometimes wandered around at night, though he would never talk about it.

Will closed the refrigerator door.

"Not hungry?"

"I don't know." He pulled himself up on the counter and sat down. "Mom? Why were you outside?"

"I don't know either."

"Yes you do." He wouldn't let her go. He knew her as well as anyone, maybe even better than Jay.

"Well, I like to say goodnight to the sky sometimes. Or the moon if it's out." She couldn't explain how this going outside had become an incantation against unspoken things, as close to prayer as she could get these days. This benediction cast a net of safekeeping over them so they would all cross over to safety in the morning. And other, stranger things.

"But it's raining out."

"Oh, I was just standing under the eaves. I like to listen to the rain in the woods."

Will just narrowed his eyes and looked hard at her. "It's gonna be okay, Mom."

Tears filled her eyes. "I know it will. Thanks."

"Okay. I'm going to bed now."

"Sleep tight." *My precious boy. Firstborn of my heart. My precious, lovely boy.*

The Other Shoe

Zoë leaned over and felt her shuddering heart against her legs. She could hardly breathe. She hadn't known she'd be sick until she found herself running down the hall into the bathroom. She looked at the giant polar bear she'd jammed in the corner of the stall. She leaned over to see who was in the stall next to her, but that stupid bear was in the way. The blood rushed to her head and she sat back up. The spinning wouldn't stop. She shut her eyes. She could hear someone in the next stall rustling with the toilet paper. She didn't know what she'd do, if that old woman had followed her. The minute she'd seen her in the gift shop, she'd grabbed the bear and run down the hall, past the patient information desk, past the cafeteria. She'd know her feet anywhere. A walking skeleton in black orthopedic shoes. Zoë shoved that polar bear back up against the door—he was taking up half the stall—and leaned all the way over. It had been a strange day.

The waiting room had no clocks. Of course, when you're waiting between one thing and another it's best to lose track of time altogether. But she had her wristwatch, which she was trying not to look at every five minutes. She didn't want to lose track of time completely, but she didn't want it gathering forces behind her back, either. What if something had happened and they were figuring out how to tell her? Or what if they'd opened him up, taken one look, and just closed him back up again. *Jay. My God.*

—

"What's that?" she'd said, pulling her hand out from under the covers. It was their first night back home in Illinois for Christmas. Her father had been ill and it seemed best for them to make the long holiday journey.

"What?" Jay'd said.

"That lump. How long has it been there?"

"What lump?"

"There," she said, pointing under the blankets. She couldn't touch him.

"Oh, that. I've always had that."

"No you haven't."

"Sure I have."

"Then how come I never noticed it before?" She turned on the light by the bed and just looked at him. Her heart thundered.

Jay tried to pull her toward him but she shrugged him off.

"Okay," he said, rolling back over.

"Jay?" she said to his back.

"What?"

"How long has that lump been there?"

He just sighed and rolled over. "Turn off the light, okay?"

Zoë lay propped up against the headboard in what had been the bedroom of her childhood. They had opened the drapes to watch the falling snow, and so she lay watching the snow come down into the shaft of light from the streetlamp in front of the house. She couldn't stop thinking about it.

The kids were all asleep in their sleeping bags downstairs in her parents' family room. She got up and felt her way down the stairs to the basement. Jillie was half out of the sleeping bag, her leg hanging over the side of the couch, her teddy bear fast in her arms. Zoë picked her pillow up off the floor and slipped it back under her head, tucked her leg back inside the sleeping bag, kissed her damp forehead. Will was on the couch across the room sleeping like a soldier, neat and tidy as always, his arms across his chest just like Jay. Max had burrowed so far down inside his sleeping bag she could only see the top of his head. How could he breathe down there? She pulled the flap down so he could get some air.

They had argued the whole two weeks that Christmas about what was or wasn't a rather large lump in Jay's left testicle. It was all she could think about. At least she'd stopped thinking about the arsonist.

"But if it was always like that, how could I not *notice* it?"

"Forget it, Zoë. You think everything's cancer and it never is, and this isn't either." It was Christmas Eve and they were out walking in the snow. Everybody else was fast asleep. It was near midnight and the street was deserted. They stood with their faces upturned to the snow, and watched it fall into their eyes.

"Don't spoil things, Zoë. It's Christmas Eve, for godsake." He looked so sad, so pained. She'd never seen that look before.

"Okay, but tell me one last time why I shouldn't be scared shitless."

He sighed, shoved his hands in his pockets, and plunged ahead through the falling snow. Finally he yelled over his shoulder, "Because it's nothing."

That was okay with her. She let out a long breath. You got a headache? It was a brain tumor. Nasty bruise on your shin? Leukemia. Swollen glands? Hodgkin's disease. She was an expert at catastrophizing. And that's what she was doing now, besides ruining Christmas.

"Okay," he finally said, turning around. "Just for the sake of argument, suppose there was something wrong. It wouldn't be something you'd have to worry about anyway, because it's an organ outside the body. I'll get it checked when we get back. So you can stop this any time now." He ended the argument by scooping up a handful of snow and stuffing it down her neck.

"Oh no you don't!" she said, turning to run. But she lost her footing and fell into the snowdrift made by the snowplow.

"Got you now." He grinned at her and leaned over. She yanked his leg and he fell into the snowdrift too. They couldn't stop laughing. Jay rolled over and kissed her.

"*That* felt good," Zoë said. "I wish we could stay out here forever." They lay there a little longer, watching the snow come down in the light of the streetlamp across from the house. They were both in love with snow and with this moment outside the argument—and didn't want to go back in, where it might all start up again.

Then they looked up and there was Will, watching them from the upstairs window. They waved up at him and he disappeared.

"We're probably embarrassing the hell out of him," Jay said.

It was strange thinking of Will watching them. Was he making his nightly rounds here as he'd done at home during the arson months? Had he found his parents missing and gone looking for them, like a mother hen, counting her chicks? Zoë wondered what he was worried about now.

"Let's not go in yet," Zoë said, looking at the sleeping house.

"Gotta pee," Jay said. "I'm going in." He turned to kiss her.

The snow was falling on his beard, his cap, covering his shoulders like a blanket. Zoë knelt down to tie her boot. When she looked up he was gone, and what she saw was the snow spinning in the shaft of light, spinning emptily upon itself. She stepped into the light as the snow fell all around, and this time the snow on her face felt hot like ashes. She thought of the fires. She thought of the little boy in her dream.

—

They held their uneasy truce the rest of the vacation with the promise that Jay would see a doctor when they got back to Seattle. The night before the appointment with the urologist, Zoë waited until everyone was asleep, and snuck outside and unlocked the garage where they'd stored their old college textbooks. Her computer had frozen, so no luck there. What a mess. Everything everywhere. She made her way to those cardboard boxes stacked against the wall and found the old medical guides from long ago. She sat on the floor of the garage in her old ski parka and boots, her back against the hot water tank. She flipped to the index and ran her finger down the list of *T* words. The first four books jumped safely from *temperature* to *tetanus*, or something like that. No *testicles* heading at all, which she took as a good sign. Anything really important would have its own listing. How serious could a testicle be anyway? About as serious as the punch line to a bad joke. Besides, as Jay kept pointing out, it's not like your liver or pancreas or heart, not something you couldn't do without.

But at the bottom of the box, she found an old edition of *The Better Homes and Gardens Medical Guide*, a wedding present from a great-aunt long ago dead. *Mr. and Mrs. William Jay Penney*, she'd written in long, lavender script. And there it was. *Testicles—disorders of.* Two categories. Something called a *hydrocele spermatocele cyst*, which sounded horrible, but was really only a benign little marble of fluid, about as harmless as something you might step on walking on the beach. Pop! And it would vanish into a watery blot on the sand.

The other category was the one she'd been hoping she would never find. The words lifted off the page and hung there flickering. Her hands were shaking. She could hear the freezer humming. She shut her eyes and took a deep breath. She heard somebody open the front door and call, "Mommy where are you?" but knew no one would find her here. She looked down at the book again. The words had settled back onto the page where they belonged. She read on and this time the words stayed put: *Tumors of the testicle are surprisingly common, and highly malignant, spreading rapidly throughout the body once they infiltrate the lymphatic system or the blood. The treatment is almost always surgery followed by radiation or chemotherapy.*

There wasn't any point in knowing any more. She put the books back into the box, jammed it into the corner, and made her way through the golf clubs, bikes and tools, old mattresses and lawn furniture to the door. She couldn't get out of there fast enough. She turned out the light, locked the door behind her, and stepped onto the back deck. The motion sensor light snapped on as she crossed. She stepped out of the light and waited until it went off. She sat down on the step and looked out into the woods. So here it was after all. Something as bad as arson. Something that could devour her whole family.

Zoë looked at her watch again. It was getting late. She was beginning to hate that waiting room. It was clear what they were up to, making it look like a hotel lobby. A room perfectly designed for killing time when all you can think is: *How much longer can this go on?* She'd been watching a woman with hair like dandelions gone to seed, wearing a pink smock. She was sitting behind a big oak desk, her hand resting on top of a sturdy black telephone perched innocently enough in the center of the desk. When it rang, she'd know who had or hadn't come back from surgery, and so which one of them she'd summon over for the news.

Jay was somewhere deep inside this maze she'd gotten lost in once already, and the only connection between them now was that phone, and the woman with dandelion hair. She couldn't stand to just sit there watching the phone, but didn't want it ringing behind her back, either. She finally put her watch in her back pocket.

She looked across the lobby. There was somebody going home, all decked out in civilian clothes, getting a final ride out the door. Zoë watched her as she sailed past, holding a pot of flowers in her lap, concentrating on those double doors just ahead. Saw the way she gripped the arms of the wheelchair as she tried to lift herself up, saw how much that simple gesture cost her, and Zoë knew that although she had to stop thinking about what was happening in that operating room, it had already changed everything.

She fished her watch out of her pocket. Almost four o'clock. The kids would be home from school now. Or rather home with the neighbors. Jillie was safe and sound with her friend Hannah, and Max and Will were staying at Aaron Wellington's house. She should give them a call. They'd be expecting to hear that it was all over and done with. They'd be expecting to hear something. It wasn't possible she could have forgotten her cell phone today of all days.

The phone had rung seven times. It was a simple operation, the surgeon had explained, and should have been over an hour ago. "We'll go in through the abdomen. We'll make an incision right here," Cobb, the urologist, had told them two days ago, as he pointed to Jay's groin. He had been sitting on the examining table wearing a sheet, looking so healthy and fine. She could see the golf tan line on his ankles. "We'll go in and pull it out through the incision and take a look. But I must tell you, there's a high chance this is a malignancy." The doctor had scooted back over to his side of the room. "Any questions?" he'd said to nobody in particular. He'd picked up Jay's chart and scribbled something at the bottom.

She looked at Jay. He didn't even blink. It was all happening to somebody else. Jay had never even caught a cold that she could remember. The whole family could come down with the flu and he'd be the only one left standing. So he'd run to the store for more cough syrup and juice and popsicles and chicken soup and ice cream, keep the house running, the movies going, and never even so much as sneeze.

So she was concentrating on that phone. Her call would come any minute now. When it rang again everybody in the room looked up. The dandelion woman looked at Zoë and squinted, then turned and looked just beyond her.

"Mrs. Coates?" There was no need to say it twice. Zoë saw a woman in sweatpants and tennis shoes flinch and drop the magazine she wasn't reading and startle toward the desk.

The dandelion lady lowered her voice and said something Zoë couldn't hear. Mrs. Coates looked like she was going to cry. She brushed her hair from her eyes with the back of her hand and sat back down. Zoë's heart was frantic inside her chest. She thought she was ready for this, but she wasn't. She couldn't do this after all. She untucked the leg she'd been sitting on, so she wouldn't run away, and ran down the hall.

"You can't sit there," someone said. Zoë looked up at the woman behind the desk and dropped the pamphlet she'd been reading. *Living with Cancer* glared back up at her from the floor. The woman looked at the pamphlet on the floor and back up at her.

"I've gotten lost," Zoë said, getting up off the end table she'd sat down on by mistake. She picked the pamphlet back up and set it on the table. "How do I get back to the main lobby?"

"See the sign?" The lady behind the desk pointed a long, red-tipped finger at the shiny blue arrow painted on the wall.

"Thanks," she said, turning to go.

"Don't you want the pamphlet?"

"Oh, no. No thanks." She turned and followed the arrow back toward the lobby, but sat down in an alcove on the way to catch her breath. Something about that pamphlet had shaken her. She remembered another pamphlet from three or four months ago. It had been lying on the back seat of Jay's truck. She'd been waiting for him to run an errand and looking for something to read. It was a pamphlet on testicular cancer. Testicular cancer! She'd never even asked him about it. But what if she had? What if she'd picked it up and said, "Jay, what's this? Why do you have this?" The thought of it made her angry. She felt better. She'd take anger over fear any day.

"We've been calling you," the dandelion lady said, as Zoë came back into the lobby and took her seat.

"Oh," Zoë said. She couldn't slow her breathing down.

"Your husband's in recovery and Doctor is coming out to see you." She looked at her oddly.

Zoë looked over the lobby. A shockingly old woman in a strange blue raincoat and moon-silver hair had come in, but her own chair had not been taken. It was hers by certain rights they all understood. Squatter's rights she'd give up in a second.

She looked out the window. The cold January rain that had drummed against those windows all day long had turned to snow. Enormous, wet snowflakes coming down on everything, melting into the pavement, but beginning to cover the grass and shrubs in white. When had this happened? She sat on her hands, watching it snow. She wouldn't run off again.

Then there he was, Jay's doctor himself, striding into the lobby in surgical greens, wrinkled now like discarded wrapping paper. He took off his surgeon's cap, wadded it up, and sat down in the chair

next to her. Zoë couldn't look at him. She was watching his hands
with that cap. She wanted to know Jay wasn't dying but couldn't ask.

"It was malignant, wasn't it," she said.

"Yes it was, just what we thought." She was watching his dark eyes
flicking behind those black-rimmed glasses.

"Is he going to die?" she said from someplace else, looking down
that road as far as she could go.

He cleared his throat and looked everywhere but at her. "No, no,
no. He's going to be fine. I mean as far as we can tell. Of course
there are no guarantees. But I must tell you, it was a complete
malignancy of the testicle, so we won't really know where we stand
until we do the CAT scan tomorrow. If it's infiltrated the lymph
system, that would be another story. But I'm sure we got it all.
Locally, I mean."

"That's good news, then, isn't it?" She couldn't remember anything
he'd just said, but she grabbed onto the *got it all* and hung on like
crazy.

"That's always good news," he said, putting his hands on his knees.
She could tell he thought his job was done now, time to throw those
surgical greens into the hamper and make his afternoon tee time. Of
course, it was winter, and no time for that.

"But he's okay *now*, isn't he?"

"Oh yes."

"Is he awake now?"

"He was still in and out the last time I checked." He waved the surgical cap in the air. She was finally able to take a breath. She looked
out at the snow. Everything would be all right now. He was alive.

"Does he know?"

The doctor just looked at her. "I really don't know. I haven't spoken
to him yet."

Then something occurred to her that she hadn't thought of before. She cleared her throat. "Would this be like a woman losing her breast?"

Cobb shifted his weight in the chair. "Not at all. No more than a woman losing an ovary. Remember, he's got two."

Had two.

Three days ago, when the doctor mentioned the possibility of a prosthesis, they both had laughed. She'd pictured Jay in some kind of padded jockstrap. Of course, three days ago all this was happening to somebody else.

"We would go in through the abdomen, through the same incision we use in removal," he went on. She looked at Jay. He had a funny look on his face she couldn't name.

"After we remove the testicle," he said to their uncomprehending faces. "We would *implant* it." She was still trying to understand this operation wasn't going to be some surgical shears and a couple of snips. And it had sounded so funny when he described it. What would you do? Pick a size? Gosh, Jay, whadya think? A golf ball or a baseball? Then she noticed how quiet Jay had become. Shut up, Zoë, stop talking and shut up.

But now, after this chance was gone, she wondered if maybe they should have given it some thought. She wondered if this funny little absence would show. She wondered if he'd feel like a walking punch line. How would he feel in a locker room? How would he feel with her?

"If there was some concern, Mrs. Penney, I wish you'd have said something before. You can't really go back in now." He was looking out the window, wadding his cap into a ball.

"I didn't mean that exactly," she said, trying to explain what she didn't understand herself.

"Well. He should be in recovery about an hour. Then they'll take him to his room. You can see him there." He stood up and stuffed the cap into his pocket. He wanted to finish this but Zoë needed him to tell her again Jay would be all right.

"Why did it take so long?" she said. She wanted to tug his sleeve, grab an arm, and hold him there.

"Oh, well. It didn't really. There was a backup in the holding area so the surgery was late." She watched the back of his green pajamas turn down the hall and disappear. The last time she'd seen Jay he was almost gone himself, as they wheeled him down the long hall and into the surgical elevator while she watched from the doorway of his hospital room. He'd tried to wave goodbye, but couldn't get his arm off the gurney. "Goodbye, goodbye, goodbye," Zoë said, and went down to the lobby to wait.

There was an hour to go before Jay would come back, so she sat watching the snow. It was coming down hard now, spinning beneath the light from the lamppost outside the hospital entrance. It was so strange and lovely. Snow on this hilly city put a silent stop to everything. You stayed home from work, safely tucked inside with your hot cocoa, watching it snow from the picture window, or you got your old parka from the downstairs closet and slipped on your boots if you could find them, and went for a walk.

It was completely dark now, the way it turns dark in winter, all of a sudden. If she were home, she'd be starting dinner and the kids would be spilling in and out of the kitchen. The thought came to her like longing. She'd be standing in a room full of light and steamy smells and listening to them talk about their day. Max would be sitting on the counter describing how the substitute bus driver got lost and took a wrong turn and drove into the shopping center instead of school, and Will would be standing by the refrigerator eating a peanut butter and honey sandwich, explaining in between bites how somebody, it certainly wasn't him, had hidden a *Playboy* centerfold behind the map of South America and how it unfurled when the teacher flipped the map over. And Jillie would be curled up in the living room in the big chair by the window watching *Mister Rogers*, rubbing her cheek with the satiny edge of her baby blanket. Of course, they weren't really home at all, but staying at a neighbor's today, and maybe through the night.

Nothing changes, nothing has changed. Somebody else could have her chair. She gathered up all those unread books and her purse, and wandered down the corridor toward the cafeteria. She hadn't eaten anything all day. Maybe she was hungry, it was hard to tell. She could smell the cafeteria all the way down the hall. She turned the corner and there it was. This was not the inner sanctum where doctors sit around like on TV and discuss their patients' chances and tell dirty jokes. Here you can get your food and if you have someone to talk to, you discuss what to have for dinner tomorrow or why the heating bill was so high last month, or whether to keep on with your kid's clarinet lessons when he keeps leaving it on the school bus. Here, you could eat your sandwich and pretend that everybody you loved was already here.

But it was too early for dinner and way too late for lunch. Nobody here but an old woman sitting back near the window, her head turned toward the snow. Zoë recognized the blue raincoat. She'd been waiting in the lobby too. Who was she waiting for? A little grandchild? Great-grandchild? An aged husband? She was all dressed up for a journey somewhere. Hospitals must be haunted with spirits who couldn't let go, angels in waiting if you could only see them.

She looked back out at the snow. She hadn't wanted anybody coming with her today. Not even her best friend, Meghan, though it turned out Meghan's grad student was defending her dissertation that day and there was no way to reschedule at the last minute. That was all right with her. She wanted to pack herself up tight, button her lip. Conversation with anyone would be too risky. Even with the beloved. Better to keep things fastened down, cross your arms, and look past anybody hoping for a little conversation to pass the time. She sat down with her sandwich and cup of soup at a table across from the window and watched the snow falling into the ground lights aimed at the sky. She didn't feel like eating anything after all.

The old lady in the blue raincoat had turned back around. She seemed to be staring at her. That color was odd—lavender or purple, but not quite—and shocking next to the drawn white face and the moon-silver hair. It was the color of those little flowers down in the woods. Periwinkle. She thought of conflagration, and all the dark things igniting and rushing up the side of the hill to the house. Right now nobody was home to catch it. And Niki! How could she get out in time? Of course Niki was at the neighbors' with the kids. She didn't know why she thought of that—the arsonist had gone silent for weeks.

Vincristine. It was a cancer drug made from the periwinkle plant. Not that Jay would need something like that. But she read it somewhere and apparently had tucked it away just in case.

Now the old woman was doing something with her hands. They were talking in midair, like she was signing. She was looking right at her. Zoë's heart slipped out from under her. Now the old lady was pulling herself up by the edge of the table and heading her way. Zoë fumbled in her purse so she wouldn't have to look up. The old woman seemed to stop for a moment just as she passed her table, and Zoë heard her whisper something. The old woman's coat touched her wrist, sending shivers up her arm. She shut her eyes and kept her head down. *Go away. Go away. Pass me by.*

When she looked up, she could see the old woman disappearing down the corridor that led out of the cafeteria. Her heart faltered then slid back into time. But the lights had turned painfully bright, and blackbirds gathered at the edges of her vision as before. She pushed her tray across the table and started to cry. The snow kept on.

A man and woman came into the cafeteria, picked up some sandwiches, and sat down a few tables away. They began talking in earnest whispers, then grew still and sad, or so it seemed. It would be nice to have someone here, though, someone you wouldn't have to talk to, exactly, but who'd just sit here nice and quiet and not ask you any questions, just hold your hand. Suddenly she knew she ought to be in Jay's room even if he wasn't there. That old woman was probably only talking to herself. She was just a crazy old lady anyway. She brought no message from the other side.

Zoë was sitting in an old brown vinyl chair, waiting for Jay. This room was exactly what it seemed. Linoleum floor, pale green walls, two white beds with sheets tucked tightly under the mattress, a TV set suspended from the ceiling. She looked at the two empty white beds. Soon Jay would be in one of them. She knew she had to say it once before he came back, but the word lay secret and dangerous on her mind. *All right. So Jay's got cancer.* She expected the floor to give way but the room didn't even quiver. The word came out flat and undeliverable.

Do they tell you the instant you're awake? Or do you trace the shape of the pain with your hand and wonder if you could feel the pulsing absence? She didn't want to be the one to tell him. Ah, but didn't they know it all along?

Then there he was, flat out on the gurney, his eyes half open as they wheeled him into the room, positioned the gurney, and in one smooth motion, rolled, then lifted him onto the hospital bed. He winced as they set down his legs.

"Hi there," Jay said out of the corner of his mouth. It sounded thick and cottony.

Zoë couldn't say a thing.

"Welcome to the Millen . . . ium," he tried to say. You could tell he'd rehearsed it.

She wanted to touch him, but was strangely shy of it. She should have leaned over and kissed him, maybe climbed up into the bed with him. But she couldn't, so she stood by the bottom of the bed and touched his foot through the sheets.

She was watching the nurse change the IV and hook it to the metal stand that had wheeled in with him, while another nurse put the blood pressure cuff around his arm and pumped it up. Zoë watched the bulb rise, bob for a moment, then sink to the bottom. Someone else came in with a hypodermic needle.

"Oh, you don't have to leave," the one with the needle said. "I'll be done in a minute." So Zoë turned toward the window and watched the snow still coming down.

"You were right," Jay said, after everyone else had gone.

"Yeah, but I didn't want to be."

"You better sit down," Jay said, and pointed to the chair. So she pulled it up as close to the bed as she could without touching it. She was afraid of the needle in his arm and the tubing connected to the bottle hanging from the metal stand, and the catheter tube going into the yellowy bag by the side of the bed.

"They got it all out," Jay said.

"I know they did. The doctor talked to me."

Jay shut his eyes.

"Are you okay?" Zoë asked.

"Yeah, I'm okay."

"It's snowing, Jay. It rained all day, and then about four o'clock it started to snow. I think that's a good sign." But he was gone. Gone somewhere she couldn't get to. His head was turned away and his mouth was open. She thought he looked dead.

"You sleep. I'm staying." Besides, the roads would be terrible if this snow was really going to hang around. Everything would get canceled anyway. She'd already called her neighbor, and the kids were fine for the night. Even the dog could stay. They could all have a sleepover.

It was almost seven when they brought his dinner. Zoë motioned for them to set it on the tray for later. No point in waking out of a sound sleep for green Jell-O and beef broth. Besides, this way he wouldn't have to think about any of this. There would be time enough for that. And she wanted to take a good look at him before they began to watch each other for signs of evasion or fear. So she just sat in the chair by the window and watched him sleep, his eyelids as fragile as tissue paper.

Outside, all the lights had come on. On the rooftop below, someone had traced an enormous message in the snow—a message someone could read from a hospital bed that said *I love you*.

She kept her eye on the IV drip. They were going to keep it in all night just in case. In case of what? she wanted to know. So the night nurse explained the convenience of having a needle already in place, so that if something happened, they wouldn't have to bother finding another vein, in the event of, say, a drop in blood pressure, or other dangers she did not name.

They dimmed the house lights, and nearly shut the door. Zoë settled into the old brown vinyl chair for the night. She had no desire to climb into the empty bed across the room. No desire to get inside those white sheets, and besides, she couldn't even sit on the bed without paying for it. So she just pulled her coat around her shoulders, sank down into the corner of the chair, propped her feet against the window ledge, and listened to everything grow quiet. Sounds drifted under the door, muffled and secret. It was a strange sort of underworld where voices wound in and out of rooms and nurses floated around corners as disembodied as wraiths. Zoë watched out the window for a long time, watched the snow bury the sign that said *I love you.*

"He's all right, isn't he?" she asked the third time somebody came in to take his blood pressure. He lay so still.

"He's fine, luv. We always do this the night after surgery," the nurse said over her shoulder. She'd brought in a pillow, and so Zoë curled up in the chair and tucked the pillow into the curve of her neck. For the first time all day, she began to feel sleepy. It must have been well past midnight. Soon she was in a dream and she remembered it because she startled right out of it when the nurse came in again. She was being examined by her gynecologist, who had covered her with a white sheet. Everything was hot and white because he had pulled the sheet up over her face. But her arms were either tied down or paralyzed, because she couldn't pull it from her face. She could hear the instruments click when he twisted and tugged at something deep inside her. He had discovered an enormous growth and was trying his best to pull it out. But the twisting and tugging went on and on and made her chest burn.

"Why does it hurt in my chest?" she asked. She could feel his voice hot and white against her face before she could hear it.

"The tumor has long, twisting roots that extend to your heart. That's why you feel it way up here." His voice became reedy and thin. She could hardly hear it now.

"Can you get it all out?" It felt like she was shouting, but also that it was coming from far away.

The doctor put his hand on her throat. "My dear. It is growing even now. It reaches up to here." She felt something tighten around her neck. She thought it was the doctor's hand but he said no, it is only death, please relax. The doctor pulled down the sheet and brought his face an inch from hers. He had put on a surgical mask and she could only see his eyes. "This may feel like a dream because I have given you an anesthetic," he said, "but don't be fooled. You may expect what you like. It is nothing like that."

She tried to scream but couldn't, and then there was the nurse touching her arm and saying, "Are you all right?"

"You really should go home," she whispered, taking off Jay's blood pressure cuff and disconnecting the IV. "He's doing quite well." But it was four o'clock in the morning and there was no point in going home now.

So she settled into sleep again and dreamed of the moon shining down on that strange house in the woods, the peaked roof, and that little boy's face in the window, his eyes so wide and sad, and now she could see they were gray. "I must be dreaming in color," she said in the dream though it may have been out loud, because she came awake to the melting snow hanging in wet clumps on the shrubs, and the rooftop, which had once held the message written in snow, now dull and sleety in the early morning light.

Will this waiting never end? It was the afternoon of the second day, and they'd taken him away again and left her waiting. But this time they'd rolled him out sitting in a wheelchair, a bedsheet draped over his legs, his feet in blue paper hospital slippers, rolled him down two floors for the CAT scan, which was going to tell them whether or not any of it had gotten into the lymphatic system. If it had spread, it would look just like an approaching enemy, little white blips on the screen as the radar hand swept a fatal circle, or like the Arson Map that had circled their house with little peaks of fire.

She couldn't stand waiting in that room any longer. So she took the elevator to the first-floor gift shop she'd remembered seeing somewhere along the corridor that led out of the main lobby. She'd wanted to greet Jay with a present, because after this test was over, which would be read by radiologists tomorrow, he was coming home.

But the gift shop was full of female things—perfume, ceramics, jewelry—things for babies. Nothing you'd give somebody like Jay. Then just as she turned to leave, she saw what she'd come here for. Behind a rack of get-well cards, propped up against the far wall—a giant polar bear with a zipper up its stomach. At first she thought it was some kind of joke, a polar bear with an abdominal incision, then realized it was one of those pajama stuffers little girls use for sleepovers, where you unzip its tummy and store your robe and slippers and nightgown, and then use it as a giant pillow. She picked it up off the floor and inched around the card rack. On the way to the counter, she saw the other thing she'd come here for even though she didn't know it—an extra-large, lacy blue nightgown—and pulled it over the bear's fat body.

"Both of these, please. I'm buying these together."

"Will this be all?" Zoë wanted to tell the salesclerk how funny it was going to be, that the bear was for her husband, who was coming home today. But she'd already been given a funny look and just then the joke became a little bulky, for there were no bags large enough to put it in. As Zoë leaned over to sign the charge slip, she noticed the old woman in blue out of the corner of her eye. She would have known her anywhere, even though all she saw was the back of her blue raincoat. Zoë fumbled for her credit card, and spilled her purse all over the counter. The old woman had disappeared. So Zoë threw the wallet, credit cards, the kids' pictures, and all the change into her purse, grabbed the bear, and reached out to the door. There was the old woman waiting in the corner where the bear had been.

She couldn't find the way to the elevator, so she rounded the first corner she came to, and saw over her shoulder that the old woman had come around the corner too. Zoë was running now, down this long white hallway, past arrows and signs she could not interpret. Ahead she saw a woman's bathroom. She flew through the door and into the farthest stall, slamming the door and jamming the lock shut. She leaned against the stall, hugging that bear, and listened for the sound of an opening door. Nothing. Only a strange stillness and what sounded like the hum of heating pipes. She shut her eyes.

She began to laugh because the bear took up most of the cubicle. Then she heard the swing of the door, the sound of shoes on the linoleum, and the snap of the lock in the stall next to hers. She didn't dare take a breath. Somewhere far away, she saw a white-coated arm point to a radar screen and someone invisible whispered, *See there? And there? And there?* Then the screen began to fill with tiny, pulsing nodes of white-hot light until the whole screen shrieked on and off like a strobe light in that awful neighbor's Halloween nightmare. She felt a hot rush up her neck and over her face and thought she might pass out. She sat down on the toilet hugging the bear, and tried to breathe.

Zoë had to know for sure if the old woman had followed her into this last end. She knew what she would see if she looked. Two brittle legs tottery in black orthopedic shoes. Or worse, nothing at all. She took a deep breath, leaned all the way over.

Oh! Oh, I love you, whoever you are in the stall next to mine!

Because there they were, two enormous calves, no ambiguity here, thinning only slightly into a set of ankles jammed into a pair of high-heeled, black patent leather shoes. She laughed out loud. There was no death lady, no pale horse or pale rider. She really had been a little crazy today, she thought, as she left the bathroom hugging that bear. The old woman in blue had either gone around some corner for good, or she had never really seen her at all.

The year had safely turned and the only apocalypse now was this one.

Captain Ace Bandages

After saying for certain he wouldn't go, Jay changed his mind and said, "All right, I'll go to the damned party. I'll hate it, though."

"It will be good for us," Zoë'd said about a hundred times. It was their first time out of the house together and not such a bad way to get used to being in the world again. But it was a costume party and that had been part of the problem all along. Even under ordinary circumstances, Jay would balk at a party like this. But once he'd figured out his costume, he'd changed his mind, though Zoë knew it was only for her.

Jay got the idea for their costumes from the movie they'd rented a couple of nights ago. It was one of those sex thrillers set in a hospital where somebody kept slashing up patients while they slept. They had laughed through the whole thing. For two whole hours they didn't think about anything but how funny that terrible movie was, and with the bottle of wine they'd emptied between them, they kept the party going.

Jay had wound Ace bandages and athletic tape over his long underwear, and gauze around his head. Then he'd made red slashes on his legs and arms with some old red nail polish. Jay thought it was pretty funny. Zoë thought, well, whatever helps, and didn't say anything. But it was strange. He'd be the patient; she'd be the nurse. He was wearing their nightmare. Then she remembered the polar bear in the blue nightgown, and the lady in periwinkle blue. That wasn't so funny either.

The kids had laughed like crazy when they saw Jay come up the stairs. "It's Mummy Man!" they cried. Their dad up to his old tricks. Good as new. They couldn't stop touching him.

"What's all the red for?" Max said. "It's *shiny*."

"It's *blood*, Max," Will said.

Jillie was on the floor turning circles on her bottom. "What's the blood for?" she said from the floor.

"Mummies can't bleed."

"Mom? What are you?" Max said.

"I'm the nurse. Can't you tell?" Zoë took the cap out of her pocket and pinned it on, did a star turn for good measure.

"But what does he need a nurse for? He's already *dead*!" Jillie exploded.

Will gave her a harsh look and she tucked her head down.

"I didn't mean that," she said, tears filling her eyes.

Jay looked like he was ready to bolt downstairs and unwind the joke. What had he been thinking? "This is ridiculous," he said, taking the stairs.

Will grabbed his arm. "Dad! Wait. You're Captain Ace Bandages! He's a cool superhero."

Jay turned back around. "You're kidding me. There's a Captain Ace Bandages?"

"Yeah. That's one of The Living Mummy aliases. He's not dead, he's alive! He's got rock-hard skin that nothing can touch. It's impervious to germs."

"*Impervious,* huh?" Jay couldn't stop the smile. But he clearly saw the gift that was offered and stepped back up. "Thanks, kid. You're right. This is a great costume." Zoë saw the tears in his eyes.

"They gave me five dollars for my *Captain Ace Bandages* comic at the comic store. He can be burned though," he started to explain, then took it back. "But not really. You can't hurt him no matter what."

"Remember, you're in charge, Will. Call us if—" Zoë stopped herself. If what? If you see the arsonist setting the blaze? What was she doing? Only teaching them the world was a dangerous place, and they would never be safe.

"Bye, Mom, bye, Dad," they shouted, as they raced down the stairs, the dog beating them to the bottom.

Zoë and Jay stared after them. How glad those kids were to be on their own! Maybe they weren't such bad parents after all.

Zoë tried to park close to the house, but there were cars everywhere—in the carport, on both sides of the street. She could see about a dozen people through the big kitchen window. It looked hot in there.

"Want me to drop you off and go find a place to park?"

"I'm not an invalid. I can walk."

"I know that. Just don't rip your costume." They'd be lucky if the costume lasted half the night.

They weren't early, that was for sure, but they found a spot down the street and hoped they weren't blocking anybody's driveway. The night felt cold against Zoë's bare legs. As they turned the corner, they could see their breath in the light from the streetlamp. Stars nodded and winked from some secret place. She was glad she'd never had to find her way by those configurations. It felt strange walking down the street in their costumes under that vast, unreadable sky. She wondered briefly where the arsonist was tonight. They wouldn't stay late, and Will and the dog were on guard.

—

She felt admonished some way. She looked at Jay. She wondered if it hurt to walk this far, though far wasn't even a block.

They didn't recognize anybody through the kitchen window, but besides Meghan, they really only knew the hosts, so no need for medical explanations. Zoë'd begged Meghan to come, even without her date.

"We'll be your date," she'd said. "We'll pick you up."

"I'll drive myself so I can ditch if it's ghastly."

Zoë's heart tightened. What was at stake here, anyway? It was just a party.

"I feel like an idiot," Jay said.

"Ah, well, there is that." Zoë ran her hands over her little makeshift nurse's dress and cap. She knew her part.

A banner hung from the front of the carport. BE THERE OR BE SQUARE: THE FOURTH ANNUAL KGB, shorthand for the Krumrine Grub Bash. Zoë took a deep breath and ducked under the banner now beginning to sag. The host met them at the door wearing a white coat and mad scientist glasses, with eyeballs popping out of the frames.

"Hey, it's Mummy Man!" Scott said, shaking Jay's hand. "We didn't think you guys were coming."

"Zoe talked me into it," Jay said. "Besides, I had to return the robe." Scott just laughed. They'd borrowed his robe for the hospital, since Jay had never owned one. "Actually, I'm Captain Ace Bandages."

"Well, *okay!*" He couldn't figure it out. "We really thought you guys weren't coming. Peggy's around here somewhere. I'd let you be *my* nurse," he said, kissing Zoë's cheek.

They walked into that hot yellow kitchen crowded with couples: Raggedy Ann and Andy, Laurel and Hardy, Sonny and Cher, Fred and Ginger, a couple of ex-presidents and wives, Roy Rogers and Dale Evans, and one garbage can, standing in the center of the room, holding a bottle of beer. He banged it on his aluminum chest.

"I'll go get us some wine," Jay said and disappeared. Zoë looked around for Meghan.

The garbage man waved at Zoë from across the room, and inched his way over. "Hi there," he said, offering her the bottle of beer.

"Oh. Okay, thanks."

"Well, when you're done you can deposit it inside this great-looking garbage can," he said, pointing into the can.

"Oh, thanks but no thanks." Zoë backed up and turned to find Jay.

"Who are you? Why have I never seen you before?" he said with a wink, then turned himself around and headed out the kitchen door.

"Who was *that*?" she said to Scott.

"Larry Radabaum. A guy from work. He's okay, he just got divorced. He's a little drunk."

"And a little horny." Scott just laughed.

"Hey, so how did you like the robe?" Scott said to Jay who'd reappeared with two plastic cups of red wine.

"Would it hurt your feelings if I told you I never wore it?"

"Would it hurt your feelings if I told you I've never worn it either?"

Jay laughed. "Hey, I think I look pretty good for a guy just out of surgery." He undid the robe and handed it to Scott.

"Where'd you get the beer? I thought you wanted wine," Jay said, handing Zoë the cup.

"Somebody just handed it to me. It isn't even cold." She set it down on the table.

They inched their way through the kitchen and out to the rec room where they could sit down. Jay eased onto the couch, stretched out his left leg. Most everybody else was still in the kitchen so they had the couch to themselves.

Jay just sighed. "I don't know about this."

"Come on, Jay, we just got here. We'll have fun once things get going."

"Hey, I'm here, aren't I?" He put his arm around her shoulder, tweaked her makeshift cap. "My little nurse."

"See? We're having fun."

"I feel like a fool," he said, looking down at the red gashes all over his legs. "I don't know what I was thinking."

Soon other people drifted into the room. They didn't know any of them but the white-haired lady dressed like Little Bo Peep. She was their hosts' neighbor from across the street. She sat down next to Jay and her hoop skirt popped up in front of her.

"Oh dear. This wasn't such a good idea." She scooted forward and pulled the back of the hoop out from under her, then edged back against the couch. "There. I'm Molly."

Zoë smiled at her. "We remember you from last year." Molly was a gardener and wanted to talk about the best time to put out bedding plants, once you were sure winter wasn't coming back. But it was always tricky. You could go all winter without a bit of snow and the first of April could be thunder and hail, and so much for those frail green promises.

Molly and Jay talked on. Zoë got up and made her way to the dining room where the food was being spread out on the table.

"Zoë? Hey, it's Sandy Fischer." She recognized the voice of one of Scott's friends they'd known from before.

She was wearing a black dress with layers of fringe that bounced whenever she moved. She was drinking white wine out of a Dixie cup.

"So what are you teaching these days?" Zoë knew she would ask her that. She was a professor too.

"A couple of lit classes, and a writing class with mostly second language students." It felt good to be talking shop, so she must have gone on about it. She didn't know how much Sandy was listening anyway.

"They come into class with such hopefulness it scares me. I wasn't exactly prepared for this quarter. They just sit there and look at me, you know? They don't even talk to each other." Jay's operation had coincided with the beginning of the term and she'd been running uphill ever since.

Sandy kept stirring the wine in the Dixie cup with her forefinger then tasting her finger. "So what's Jay doing these days? Still counseling those juvenile delinquents? I'm kidding. They're not juvenile delinquents. Are they?" She laughed and turned her head to find him. "He's coaching, like wrestling, right? Is he around?" She'd always had a thing for Jay. Wait till she saw him dressed as a bandage.

"He's . . ." Zoë couldn't finish. But Sandy didn't notice. She was already pretty far down the road.

Then somebody tapped her on the shoulder, and she sauntered off, her back swaying, or maybe it was just the fringe. Zoë grabbed a beer from the ice chest, put it against her face, shut her eyes. Then she went looking for Jay.

She found him on the couch by himself. Sidelined. Benched. Zoë thought he looked completely miserable. He'd unwound his bandages and was sitting there in his long underwear and running shorts. The Ace bandages lay in a pile by his feet. So much for Captain Ace Bandages. She'd forgotten the food. She was wondering why on earth they had come. This wouldn't have been fun even in their other life.

When she came back with the food, there was Meghan, her head on Jay's shoulder, her hand on his arm. She looked up sharply and withdrew it.

"Thank God you're here. Nice costume."

Her old standby: *Rosie the Riveter*—her blonde hair pulled back in a red bandana, red lipstick, denim shirt rolled up at the sleeves.

Meghan kissed Jay on the cheek, and Molly kissed him on the other cheek.

"We're cheering him up," Meghan said.

"I don't suppose you want any of this food with all this cheering up."

"Just another beer, please. I'm going to need it. They're going to have a *dance* contest," Jay said grimly. "I'm the judge. Molly and me. Bet you can't guess why we're the judges and not the dancers."

"Okay, why are you the judges?"

"Molly's had her hip replaced and I'm sick."

"You aren't *sick*, Jay," Zoë said, handing him her bottle of beer. Meghan took the plate of food and picked up a meatball on a toothpick. "What kind of dance contest is it anyway?"

"I don't know. I'm just the judge. Me and Molly."

"Okay, I'll be the judge's assistant." They'd all three be judges. But it turned out that everybody was already paired with somebody, so Jay and Molly were a couple, and Zoë was a couple with Larry, the divorced garbage man, and Meghan declined. She'd be leaving soon. Zoë just stood there.

The lights dimmed and Frank Sinatra began "My Funny Valentine." Meghan stood up and took Jay's hand to help him off the couch. "He promised me a dance," she said.

"Only if it's a slow one." Jay pulled her close.

"Best kind," Zoë said.

Meghan wrapped her arms around his neck, lay her head on his shoulder.

Zoë felt a rush of heat flash across her face. Zoë wasn't in a costume. She was playing herself. She didn't want to be anybody's nurse, but there she was. Why hadn't she come as Marilyn Monroe? She even had the wig and the dress.

Jay stepped back and felt Meghan's biceps, then wrapped his arms around her waist. "All that riveting. Look what it's got you."

"You, of course." Meghan looked over at Zoë and shifted her gaze. Something had happened. Zoë didn't want to know what. She turned around and headed to the bathroom, her eyes full of tears.

When she came back, Meghan had gone. Scott was flicking the lights on and off while Frank Sinatra sang "New York, New York," and everybody began drifting into the rec room.

"Dance contest! Dance contest!" he shouted.

"Come on, Zoë, you'll probably win," Jay said, giving her a pat on her little nurse's bottom. Larry walked over and took her hand. He'd taken off the garbage can and was standing there in the middle of the room in running shorts and a T-shirt.

He was tall like Jay. Her chin hit him in the chest. The music began with a polka, and they two-stepped around the edges of the room until they collided with another two-stepping couple. Then the music changed to a tango, and they slouched across the room, shoulder to cheek. He dipped her low at each turn. "I like the way you dance," he shouted.

"Thanks," Zoë shouted back as they wove in and out of sliding couples. She saw Jay leaning toward Molly. They were both laughing at something. Well, good. Her white hair caught the light. She was beaming. Then Scott dimmed the lights and they began to slow dance to Nat King Cole. "Embrace me," Scott sang out over the dark, hot room—and that's what the garbage man did. Pulled her up close. Zoë could smell his aftershave, his shampoo.

The lights came up slowly as the music wound to a close. Zoë looked over at Jay. He'd stopped talking to Molly and was staring at her with a look she didn't know. She took her arms from around Larry Radabaum's neck. Jay? She wanted to grab Captain Ace Bandages and run for the door.

Then Scott flicked the lights on and off. The contest was over. "Who will win the Dancing Foot Award?" he shouted, holding up a giant, size twenty, red high-top tennis shoe. "Judges! What's the verdict?" Molly handed Scott a piece of paper.

"Aw, *favoritism*!" he yelled. He wadded up the paper and threw it at Jay. "The winner of the First Annual Dancing Foot Award goes to Larry Radabaum and Zoë Penney!" Since everybody was a couple except for the winners, they awarded two prizes instead of one. Zoë let Larry take the Dancing Foot and she would take the consolation prize, an old book with a black dusty cover, which she handed to Jay.

"Read the title," Scott said, grinning like crazy.

Jay opened the book to the title page. "You're kidding," he said with a laugh.

"Read it!"

"Okay. What I've got here is the 1936 edition of that bestseller *Sex and Revelations: A Safe Guide for Marital Health and Happiness*." Jay shot a look at her. "Okay, Zoë, so which do you want—health or happiness?" What was he trying to say? Some dark thing that went too fast for her to catch.

"Both," Zoë said, trying for a laugh that snagged in her throat.

"Yeah, both," he said back to her. "If that's possible." He put the book down, and edged off the couch. Nobody was paying any attention to him now. Zoë watched as he made his way down the hall toward the bathroom and into the dark.

Scott wound his way through the rec room but still had to shout. "Phone's for you. Take it in the bedroom. You might even be able to hear in there." Zoë couldn't get there fast enough. Then she sat down on the bed and counted to four. It was all coming true.

"Will? What's wrong, Sweetie?" She was almost shouting.

"We heard something outside."

"Like what?"

"A bang or a crash or something." She wanted to ask if they smelled smoke but stopped herself.

"Jay? The kids heard something outside," she said, handing over the phone. "Should we call 911?" she whispered.

"What exactly did you hear?"

"Like a branch or something crashed down on the house. And Niki's acting really funny. She's lying by the back door sniffing and sort of growling. She never does that."

"Is it windy?"

"Yeah, kind of. But something really did hit the house."

"Probably don't need to call 911. Captain Ace Bandages is on his way home. Be there in twenty minutes. And thanks for the call. You did fine, kid. Okay till then?"

"Okay already."

Radium Man

"**B**asically, we're in the second stage," Frankel was saying. "There has been some metastasis through the lymph system—the CAT scan showed that. So you'll need to have the lymphangiogram after all." He was looking at Jay but was talking to them both. Charts and files were jammed into folders and lay heaped on his desk. He was holding one of them. He looked too big for his office. Like he'd have to duck to get out the door.

They were down in Radiation Oncology, in a tiny cubicle on the bottom floor of the medical complex. They'd been demoted to the basement, which Zoë did not take as a particularly good sign. This was where the cobalt and X-ray machines lay in wait beyond the heavy doors marked with skulls and crossbones. But in this little office, surrounded by heavy concrete, they were as protected from those X-rays as Superman from kryptonite. Zoë wondered if Captain Ace Bandages was impervious to X-rays. She most devoutly hoped not.

They'd begun this whole thing on the seventh floor, on Urology, a long week ago, and now here they were on the very bottom floor seeing this new doctor, the radiation oncologist, who would coordinate the final diagnosis with the final treatment. She pulled her coat around her shoulders.

"Yeah, it can get chilly down here," Frankel said. "I know you must have a ton of questions. So shoot." Zoë liked him. There was no tension here, as she'd sensed in Cobb, the urologist. And he could say the word *cancer* like it was an everyday sort of word and nothing to fear. "I'm Joe Frankel," he'd said, stretching out a paw of a hand as they'd stepped into his office.

She looked over at Jay, who was sitting with his elbows on his knees, fists under his chin, looking at the floor. He'd pushed his chair back as far from the doctor's cramped desk as he could get. "How exactly do they give this test?" she said, determined this time to ask everything. Jay just sat there.

"It's not as complicated as it sounds, but it gives us a refinement of what we learned from the CAT scan. Basically, it's a matter of transfusing a special blue dye through the lymphatic system."

Jay looked up.

"How exactly do they do that?" Zoë asked.

"Sure." He looked at Jay, then back at her. "They insert the dye through the toes. But it isn't nearly as bad as it sounds. And it isn't all that uncomfortable. But we'll need to readmit you, just for the day."

Jay shut his eyes.

"They use needles for this, right?" she said stupidly. She looked over at Jay, tried to signal him with her eyes. Aren't there a million questions here? Please say *something*.

"Oh, they're small needles. You'll feel like a pin cushion for a couple of hours, that's all."

Jay looked up. "After this dye test, when will radiation start?" He was snapping the band of his wristwatch.

"Two weeks."

"Two weeks?" Zoë said. "Why so long? If you know the cancer's in there, why would you wait at all?"

He smiled at her compassionately. She knew he could see how

scared she was. "We need to wait for the incision to heal. The radiation slows down the cell replacement process, so we need a little more
time."

"But won't two weeks make a difference in how far it spreads?"

"I don't think so. Really, what we've got here is a fast-growing
cancer, as you know, but it's on a predictable course. It's showing
up right where we'd expect it to, so once we get the lymphogram
done, we'll know right where to focus. And for the most part, it's a
radiation-sensitive tumor. We're lucky there too."

But none of this had felt like luck. They'd wanted a little luck three
days ago, waiting for Frankel to call. Jay had answered the phone
from the couch where he was stretched out, watching TV. The dog,
lying as close to Jay as she could get, sat up when Jay reached for
the phone. She'd been on duty ever since he came home from the
hospital. Zoë got up and left the room as fast as she could. She didn't
want to know what she already knew. But she stood in the hall and
listened anyway.

"Oh," Jay said into the phone, as he sat up. There was a pause that
went on forever. "Uh-huh, I understand." Another long pause. "Well,
thank you, Doctor." He sat there rubbing his forehead with his empty
hand. The dog licked the phone.

"It's not in the lungs yet, even though it's practically everywhere
else," he called after her as she made her getaway toward the bathroom. She couldn't hear any more.

"Well, that's good, Jay," she said, shutting the bathroom door. She
splashed cold water on her face, and tried to slow down her breathing.
She came back in and sat down on the floor and buried her face in the
dog's fur. It was all coming true.

"They're gonna give me chest X-rays every two months now,

because that's where it's supposed to go next—if they can't stop it, that is."

"What do you mean by everywhere else?" she whispered from the floor, where she sat hugging the dog.

"The lymph system up to my neck. I'd say that's our apocalypse," he said over his shoulder on his way to the kitchen. "Our very own year of the Millennium."

And they had wanted a little luck sitting on those hard plastic chairs by the magazine rack, waiting to be called in for the first of their many appointed hours with Dr. Joe Frankel. Zoë took a deep breath and looked for an escape route. She could see the double elevators out in the hall. She'd concentrate on that. No windows to escape through down here. This place was bathed in an unholy light. You just wanted to keep your eyes shut.

But she wanted a sign for luck. Some image she could carry back with her out of this terrible place. So she tried not to look through the open doorway at the old man they'd just wheeled down for treatment. An IV had rolled down with him. Maybe he wasn't old—it was hard to tell, the way he sat hunched down into himself, the way the light fell so heartlessly on his bare white head. She could see his shoulder blades through the pale, thin hospital gown. He was wearing black street shoes and black socks pulled halfway up his frail, white calves. She wondered how much he'd had to fight his nurses to wear those shoes. She shut her eyes and dressed him up in a tartan plaid cap and matching lap robe. There you go, that's better. Bet you're warmer now. It's cold down here. She tucked the blanket around his legs, adjusted the cap. Maybe she even kissed his forehead for luck. She wondered if Jay would lose his hair.

"We'll do the radiation in two halves," Frankel was saying. "Six weeks groin to chest, two weeks off, then six weeks chest to throat."

"That's a lot of radiation," Zoë said, calculating that, even with time off for good behavior, it added up to over sixty treatments. "What are the side effects?"

"Nausea, diarrhea in the first half, sore throat, hoarseness maybe, difficulty in swallowing in the second half. Really not too bad. Most people tolerate this very well."

"What about hair loss?" she said, thinking back to the old man. He was probably a young man when he checked into this place.

"Just body hair. You won't go bald, so don't worry about that. At least not from radiation." Frankel smiled, inviting them into the joke, a place neither Zoë nor Jay wanted to go.

"What about over the long haul?" she wanted to know, sure their greatest weapon now was knowing all they could.

"Well. We don't always know about that. But there can be side effects, sure. Damage to the kidneys, pancreas, maybe other organs along the radiation route. Maybe cancer somewhere down the line. That's remote, though."

"My God," she said. "Why would anybody agree to this with side effects like that?" She was ready to grab her coat, grab Jay by the sleeve, and make a run for the elevators.

"Because he'll die without it."

So there it was. She slumped back into her chair. What good was knowing any more? She knew they'd have to trust this man no matter what. That cancer was moving through him even as they sat in that basement office. It was radiation or nothing. Those two weeks stretched out dangerously in front of them. She couldn't wait for it all to begin. Overhead, the bar of fluorescent light flickered and pulsed.

She could hear the hum of the waiting machines beyond the heavy doors.

Jay himself had said nothing. He was looking out the door.

"So how are you feeling generally?"

Jay took a deep breath that came out as a sigh. "Okay."

"Getting around all right?"

"Yeah. It only hurts getting up out of a chair."

"Fine. Well, the incision looks good. Your color's good. Eating and sleeping okay? Everything pretty much back to normal?"

"Sure." Jay kept looking toward the door. Zoë could tell he just wanted to get out of there.

Just for a minute, though, she was sorry she was there. She knew what the doctor was asking, and wondered what Jay would have said if he'd been alone. She wondered if he would have told him how they'd slept like spoons yesterday, his arm over her shoulder. "Hey, Zoë, look at this," he'd said, and like a magician's trick there it was, as he slid back the covers. They'd looked at it proud as new parents. "At least *that* still works."

"Do you think it's all right?"

"I never thought to ask," Jay said. "But why not?"

"We can be careful."

"Fine. Well, that's about it, then," Frankel said, shaking their hands again. "Stop at the desk and set up an appointment for the lymphogram and I'll see you in two weeks. Hey," he said, stopping Jay at the door. "Don't you worry. Either of you. Remember this course of treatment has a good cure rate."

At the desk, the receptionist was writing out an appointment card for a tall blonde woman who wore a stack of thin gold bracelets. They tinkled as she put the card in her purse. She was wearing a powder-blue suit, matching blue spiky heels, and big, loopy gold earrings. Dressed to the hilt. Well, why not? It was just her way of holding on, like the old man with the street shoes and socks, who'd refused the blue paper hospital slippers.

The receptionist looked up at Jay and then at her. She'd come on while they were with the doctor and didn't know which one of them was the patient.

"We need to schedule a lymphangiogram," Zoë said, letting that word just roll off her practiced tongue.

"Whose patient are you?" she said to both of them.

"Frankel's," Jay said.

"You'll need to plan on checking in for the day," she said, looking back at Jay. "The test will take about four hours."

The blonde woman put her braceleted arm around Zoë's shoulder. "My dear, it isn't so bad. You can read or listen to music. It doesn't really even hurt. You'll be just fine."

The blonde woman smiled at Zoë, then turned on her spiky heels and walked toward the elevators as if she knew they would turn to watch. Zoë wondered if she was their good luck sign. She wondered what kind of cancer she had, and hoped it was radiation sensitive too.

He'd been inside for over an hour, but today was nothing to worry about. They were just going to take some X rays and give him a tattoo. She was sitting by the magazine rack like before, because from there she could see the way out of here. Just *Reader's Digest* and a few copies of *Outdoor Life* and *Better Homes and Gardens* and some ancient issues of *Time*. No copies of the *New Yorker* or the *Atlantic* down here.

There wasn't really a skull and crossbones on those double doors, but Zoë also knew those X-rays were full of death as well as second chances. She was thinking about that little click you hear getting your teeth x-rayed, and though you know it's only dental X-rays and nothing to be afraid of, it's the seconds that go by after you hear the click that make you want to slide out from under that lead apron and bolt from the chair. But you hold your breath and sit perfectly still with that cardboard wedged between your teeth and feel the hum go to the bone.

Anyway, today it was just X-rays, not *radiation,* though she didn't exactly know the difference. They hadn't even given him any radiation sickness pills yet, so what was there to worry about? They called today *mapping day* because they were going to mark the path the cancer was taking with little pinpricks of indelible blue dye. Next week that constellation of tiny blue stars, nothing but a stony hieroglyph to the uninitiated, would light the way for all those X-rays. Well, it was going to save his life.

At least you couldn't tell who was a patient down here and who was only waiting. No visible line between those in another country and those who had crossed over to safety. Still, she wondered. Maybe they were looking at her, wondering the same thing. But then how could something this deadly be so silent and so clever for so long? Sooner or later something would have to show. A sudden thinness, a certain angularity in the face, something in the eyes you couldn't exactly name, which, thank God, she had never seen.

She looked at her watch. *Oh, please, haven't you learned anything?* Still, how long could it take to get a couple of X-rays and a tattoo? Zoë felt sick all the time now. Not really sick, but just an unforgiving wildness in her stomach that didn't get better but didn't really get any worse. Maybe she was getting an ulcer. She fixed food all the time, but she couldn't remember actually eating it.

Somebody dropped a magazine. It was the kid sitting two chairs down from her who'd come in about ten minutes ago. He must have been eighteen or nineteen. He was wearing a wool stocking cap and a green parka, which he began to unbutton. The boy took out a big, red, western handkerchief, and wiped his forehead. Zoë leaned forward to ask if he was all right, and he just folded over like a rag doll, hitting his cheek on the carpet. She knelt down beside him and touched his face. It was soft and damp, like a little boy lost in sleep. His eyelids fluttered when she touched him. His cap had slid off and there was his head like a baby's, smooth and white. "Help me," he whispered. She thought of the little boy in her dream whose gray eyes had said *help me* too.

The new receptionist came rushing over with her hand over her mouth. "Oh no," she said, and ran to get the nurse. In a moment they had him sitting back up and were wiping his forehead with a damp towel.

"Can you stand?" the nurse said, touching his arm. He just sat there propped against the wall, shaking his head. His face shone with sweat.

"You should have him lie down when he first comes in," the nurse said to the new girl. "He faints sometimes, so get him inside right away and don't make him wait out here. He gets so nervous." They were getting him to his feet. "This is Michael, so make a note by his next appointment, so you won't forget." Then they each took an elbow and walked him down the corridor toward the double doors. He shook his head all the way, like he'd gone swimming in the creek and gotten water in his ears. His face was chalky white save for the single red mark on his cheek where he'd hit the floor.

"Here," Zoë said to the receptionist. "He'll need this," and handed his cap to her. Her hands were shaking as she took it.

Zoë couldn't stop trembling. She looked around the room. She'd concentrate on somebody else. Someone new had come in and was sitting in the far corner of the room. He had his hands jammed into the pockets of his jeans. He was wearing a red, plaid flannel shirt and a baseball cap pulled low over his forehead. The high cheekbones, the gaunt face, the deep-set, fierce, gray eyes. Then she looked away when she saw he was staring back. A waft of cold air from the vent brushed over her. The head lopped over, the noose around the neck, that salute to the darkness, the fire all around. She felt dizzy, leaned over, and put her head in her hands. There was no death lady in blue, and no Hangman either. No prophecies of disaster. She would not believe in such things. Only an arsonist now and then.

Just then Jay came through the double doors and stopped at the desk to make the next appointment. Zoë got up and took his hand.

"Jay, look at that man in the corner. Who is that? Is that Roy?"

"Who's Roy?"

"Our *neighbor* Roy. The Hangman. Is that possible?"

Jay turned to look then turned back to the receptionist who was handing him his appointment card. "Let's get out of here," he said, tossing his jacket over his shoulder. Then they were waiting by the elevators. She took his hand and they stepped into the elevator, watching the panel of lights flicker from *B* to *LL* to *L* to *M*, and as they waited for the doors to open, she saw the number seven, where it had all begun a hundred years ago. They didn't say anything. They both wanted to get above ground.

"Did you get a good look at him? He was wearing that baseball cap he always wears. It had to be him."

"Everybody wears a baseball cap down there. This is *radiation*." Jay laughed. "Really. What are the chances?"

"But did you see him?"

"No. Not really."

Zoë just narrowed her eyes. She knew what she had seen. She would watch out for everything now.

Then they were rushing down the freeway across the bridge toward home. The wind had churned up the lake, pounding the waves into a fury, and driving the rain hard against the windshield, though the wipers tried heroically to beat it back. The bridge felt like it was swaying but it was just the wind blowing across the lake in hard, steady bursts.

"But it took so long," Zoë finally said.

"Yeah, well they had some trouble."

She felt something turn over inside. "What kind of trouble?"

He didn't say anything. He was leaning forward, trying to see out the windshield.

"What did you mean they had some trouble?" she said again cautiously. Jay was looking over his shoulder, changing lanes. He pulled into the right lane, and now was hugging the shoulder.

"They couldn't figure out where to put the damned dots." He was practically shouting.

"What do you mean?"

"I don't know, Zoë."

It seemed like the car could float across the pavement and over the side.

"I was just lying there on that table, and they'd go out and look at the X-rays, then they'd come back in and say we need some more pictures. What was I supposed to say, *no*?"

The waves were crashing against the bridge and spilling over onto the pavement. "Jay?" She held his arm. She wanted to shut her eyes but could not.

"I must have had fifteen X-rays and I don't know what for."

"But this is supposed to be an exact science! My God, Jay, they have to know what they're doing *exactly.*" She should have just shut up, but she kept thinking of those fifteen X-rays on top of the sixty scheduled ones.

"Was Frankel there?"

"He was off today. I know they know what they're doing, but it was weird. They were playing tic-tac-toe all over my body." He started to laugh.

"What can possibly be funny about that?"

"Oh, it just is."

Zoë turned from him. She blinked back the tears, held her stomach. What she'd counted on couldn't be counted on after all. Now what did they have?

"You can laugh at anything," she said, rubbing his leg. She couldn't stop touching him.

His hands were tight on the steering wheel. "What else is there to do?"

She looked back at the lake as they turned off the bridge. It looked more dangerous than ever. She thought about the bridge that had sunk during a storm last year. They were lucky to get across today. It had been impossible to see. The spray from trucks in the other lane had hit the front of the car like a giant wave, dissolving what was in front of them. They drove off beneath that heavy, weighted sky sinking all around, and the sound of the frantic wind.

She knew something was burning because of the smell. *It's all right*, she said in the dream. *You can go back to sleep.* Not like all the other nightmares of fires and screams in the night. This was the smell of a candle blown out, the sweet, smoky smell from a stone fireplace, the bonfire of wondrous leaves caught into piles and nothing to be afraid of—and there! The rustle of leaves kicked about by children in green rubber boots—but wait! Not leaves. It was the night wind through the cornhusks of the Scarecrow's hands and feet. Then the Scarecrow swayed in the breeze and inside the rustling sounds were wind chimes that shivered in the air, a sound inside a sound. She opened her eyes and there he was, waiting inside his shadow in the corner of the bedroom. He was watching with a half-smile or maybe not, his intention was unclear.

"Oh, it's you," she said, tucking her surprise under the pillow.

He nodded and looked back, but it was a trickster's smile. Because just then she saw him reach inside his pocket for the match.

She woke herself up saying, "He's in the bedroom now."

"Who is?"

"Go back to sleep," she said, touching Jay's chest.

But she watched where his shadow waited, until first light.

It was a clear Sunday morning and the kids were already up and watching cartoons, while Zoë and Jay were sleeping in, or so they said. The dog was sitting in the middle of the bed staring at them. They hadn't known she was curled up in the closet when they'd locked the door and gotten back into bed. But she always stayed discreetly tucked in, until they were through. Then she jumped up on the bed, inched her way up between them, and stuck her nose under Jay's chin.

"What do *you* want?" Jay said, rubbing the top of her head. Niki jumped off the bed, grabbed her leash from the corner by the door, hopped back up and dropped it onto Jay's chest, and sat there panting.

"Is that just a little *hint*?"

"Let's take her down to the lake," Zoë said. "A walk would be good for us. Will can keep an eye on Jillie."

She looked at the day through the blinds and tried to imagine those forsaken trees sunstruck and flickering with green. She could see the blue, piercing sky behind those dark, bony sculptures. Today was a reprieve from the certainty of winter and they needed to be in it.

"We'll be back in an hour, okay?" she told the kids.

The sun was on the water—a wintry blue, but with light enough for a late January day. They set out on the trail that led around the lake, Niki leading the way. She was leader of the pack, her tail erect and full, pulling that sled across those long miles of Arctic drifts. For as much as they had tried to train her to heel, she loved the pull of that collar around her neck. She kept looking back to see that they were both all right, and following close behind. Zoë slowed her step to keep pace with Jay. But Niki urged them on.

They passed a group of bikers in green, fluorescent jackets and black helmets, and a couple of joggers here and there. But no dogs today. No cats either, crouching in the drainage ditch, waiting till the coast was clear. Just a bird in a bare tree branch here and there. It felt good being outside. They'd lost their perspective, that's all. The day stretched out ahead, fearless and full of light. There would be many such days. A whole string of them. She took Jay's hand. They smiled at each other and walked on.

Up the trail they could see something fluttery and white in the middle of the trail. Niki flattened her ears, lowered her head. Zoë pulled the leash up tight. Then Niki edged back close to her. "Good girl, Niki," she said, and kept the leash taut. Then the fur behind her neck stiffened and she strained at the leash. "Now stop that. That's just a sea gull." She'd protect Zoë from that gull, who just sat there, resting in the middle of the trail. When it finally noticed them, it tried to flop its way off the trail onto the grass, dragging one of its wings across the asphalt.

"Will it be okay like that?"

Jay looked at her then back at the bird trying to get out of harm's way. Zoë could see its chest heaving, and imagined its heart beating furiously inside that white, feathered breast.

"I think you need both wings if you're a bird," he said, as they watched it drag itself down the slope toward the lake.

Niki just stood there watching after the bird. She wanted to run after it and chase it down to the water. They walked on. Zoë looked back one more time. There was the gull, looking like it might tip over, staring out at the lake from the edge of the grass.

Zoë wondered how that sea gull got its wing broken. Did it fall out of the sky, or was it hit by a biker zooming on ahead, helmet down and taking no notice of something so small and white? She thought about Pecky, Max's yellow parakeet, and how wild and glorious he was when they'd let him free. How he sometimes crashed into things and slid down the wall behind the couch. How safe he was sitting back on his perch, pecking at his reflection in the mirror. There was something to be said for keeping birds in cages. She had never sorted it out.

They could take Niki home and come back with a towel and a cardboard box and try to scoop it up, but if they brought it home, Niki would never let it alone. She didn't know if there were any bird rescue hospitals around here. Well, they'd walk to the mile marker and turn around and see if it was still there when they came on back.

"Don't worry about it, Zoë—too much is going on already." She thought of what tomorrow would bring. Jay would go back to the hospital for the first of those sixty radiation treatments. She let go of Jay's hand and let Niki pull her on ahead.

By the time they'd turned around and come back to where they'd seen the bird, it was gone. They walked down the hill to the lake.

There were a few ducks floating innocently enough, but no gull in sight. They sat down on a bench by the shore and watched the sun on the water. She thought of the summer to come, and how they'd just have to hold on until then. They'd get Jay out on the lake in his boat, get him in the sun, and then maybe everything would be all right again. She didn't trust those X-rays.

In the distance she could see clouds gathering. Niki sat between them while they watched the clouds drift in from the south, watched the light drain out of the sky. She couldn't look at him, couldn't take his hand. It frightened her how much was changing already. She didn't know whether she was holding tight or letting go.

The last thing they gave Jay after they'd mapped him up was a bottle of pills for nausea, which he'd carried in the pocket of his jacket ever since. Zoë had offered to pick him up at school and take him down, but he said he'd be fine. You wouldn't get sick from just one treatment, anyway. So she came straight home from school and met the kids at the bus stop. She was going to make him a good dinner even if he didn't feel like eating.

"Dad isn't home yet," Will said, coming into the kitchen.

"He had to go back to the hospital. Radiation started today, remember?" But he knew what was up; he always did. He just stood there by the refrigerator looking completely stranded. She pulled him into a hug, which he tolerated for about two seconds before he wriggled out of it.

"What's everybody doing?" she said.

"Pecky's flying all over the rec room. They're trying to catch him."

"They need any help?"

"Nah. Pecky likes it."

"Is Max okay? It scares him if he crashes."

"They're laughing their heads off, Mom. You can stay here."

He knew what she was doing. "Okay," Zoë said. "So how was school?"

"Good," he said, standing in front of the open refrigerator. "There's nothing to eat in here."

"Sure there is." Zoë pulled out the jelly and peanut butter and handed him the loaf of bread sitting on top of the refrigerator.

His back was to her as he spread the peanut butter and jelly onto the bread he'd laid out on the counter. "Is Dad gonna be okay?" he said so quietly she almost didn't hear him.

"These are just X-rays, Will. It just takes a couple of minutes." But Zoë knew what he meant. He meant will he be okay forever? It's what he'd wanted to know three weeks ago when she'd come into his bedroom the night after the operation and tried to explain as casually as she could what had happened, what was going to happen now. But after just a few sentences he'd said, "I don't want to talk about it," and turned toward the wall.

But Max had listened to every word. "Did it hurt when they took it off?" he'd wanted to know right away. "Our science teacher said you get it from chemicals and X-rays. So is that how Daddy got it?"

Zoë tried to explain how they didn't really know, but that he was going to be all right, because he was going to have treatments to cure it.

"What kind of treatments?" Of course he'd wanted to know that. He wanted to know everything.

"Well, these are a different kind of X-rays. Healing X-rays." What did she know? That these healing X-rays would make him better by first making him sick? She tried to explain that a certain amount of radiation might give you cancer, but a different amount could cure you and the doctors knew exactly which amount was which. She thought about those extra fifteen X-rays and wanted to know which was which too.

"Can I get it?"

"Oh, Max, come here." Zoë drew him into a hug, kissed his head. "Children don't get this."

"I mean when I grow up." She had no idea about the hereditary possibilities.

"I won't get it," Jillie had said. She knew what part of her father's anatomy was in question. "Those flowers are for my daddy," she told one of the neighbors who had come outside when the florist's truck had pulled into the wrong driveway. "He got something cut off his leg," she told the neighbor, protecting his modesty even so.

Zoë was watching for Jay out the window every couple of minutes now as she was finishing up with dinner. She'd made a big pot of chicken noodle soup, put some biscuits in the oven. She could see the fog drifting in from the lake. It was six o'clock, long ago dark, and beginning to rain. You could barely see the streetlight at the bottom of the hill.

Even from the kitchen she was listening for Jay's Volkswagen to round the corner, listening for the gears to shift as it made a run for the hill, rocking like a rowboat in rough water, as it took the bump in the road, high centered, just before it rushed on ahead, then slid on into the driveway. On any other day Will would be in his room with the door shut, doing his math homework to the tune of whatever was coming through his earphones. But here he was, sitting on the arm of the chair by the window. They were both pretending they weren't waiting for the headlights of that car coming up the hill.

"Hey, kid, what're you doing?" Zoë said, coming into the living room.

"Our neighbor's dog's out there playing with Niki." She could hardly see them. Just two dark shapes drifting over the lawn.

"We better get her inside and towel her off. It's starting to rain." She didn't want Niki playing with that dog. He was always fenced in so he'd probably gotten loose somehow.

She looked again. She couldn't tell who it was. Dogs were always getting lost and finding their way up the hill, then couldn't get themselves turned around and back home without a little help. Will called Niki in and cleaned her up. Then he went back into the living room and took up his looking post.

"It's just an X-ray, Will. It won't even hurt."

He was hunched over, watching down the road. Niki was sitting next to him, her nose against the window. Zoë began to rub his shoulders and he leaned into it. They didn't say anything. Then he reached over to hug the dog and Zoë went back to the kitchen. She knew how to listen for that car everywhere she went. She stirred the soup again, took the biscuits out of the oven.

The phone rang behind her back. Will ran in and got it on the third ring, before Zoë had had time to put down the soup ladle and turn around.

"It's okay, Mom, it's okay. It's for me." He knew what she was thinking. Then she turned the burner on low and headed toward the hall. She'd heard that longed-for, familiar shift of gears, and now tires sliding into the gravel in the driveway.

"Dad's home."

"I gotta go," Will said, and slammed down the phone. Zoë stood in the hall, listening for the car door, footsteps on the gravel, footsteps on the porch, the creak of the front door, then only silence. She stood at the far end of the hall, waiting in the dark. She'd forgotten to turn on the lights.

"What are you doing, Mom?" Will said, coming up next to her. "Why are you just standing here?"

She didn't know. What was Jay doing out there? Maybe he'd gotten sick and couldn't get out of the car. Maybe he was taking some of those pills, just to be sure. Maybe he just needed a moment to steady himself.

They stood in the hall listening to the growing, darkened silence.

Then the front door opened, and she heard it shut and knew Jay was in the hall. But she could only see a shadow. The dog started to growl.

"Jay?" she said. Then Will screamed. It was a tall, familiar werewolf standing by the door, with his arms outstretched. Will ran down the hall to the thing coming toward him, then rushed back.

"Aaarrrgh" it said, lunging at them. "R-a-d-i-u-m M-a-n!" he growled, as he gathered them up in his arms. The dog jumped up between them and licked the werewolf mask. Then Will snatched it up and raced downstairs. "Aaaargh," he growled as he disappeared down the stairs. "R-a-d-i-u-m M-a-n." The dog raced down after him. Zoë and Jay stood there in the darkened hallway, listening to the kids downstairs with the mask. Rich, steamy smells floated down the hall from the kitchen.

"Smells good," he said, pulling her into him. "Hey, you're in the dark here." He reached over and flicked on the lights. "I'm *hungry*." So they called everybody up for dinner. Radium Man was home.

Side Effects

It was a cold, cloudy Friday in March, and Zoë had missed Max and Jillie's bus by half an hour. She always tried to spare them that long trudge up the hill on those dark, wintry afternoons if she could. Will was usually home by then, off the middle school bus and through the shortcut over the top of the hill.

She knew Jay wouldn't be home for a while, because Radiation was always behind schedule on Fridays. In an hour or so he'd walk in the door, roll his eyes, and say, "Sorry I'm late," give them all a big hug, then collapse on the living room couch in front of the TV. He was never very hungry on Friday nights, though he tried to keep up appearances. "Thanks, that was so good," he'd say as he took his half-finished plate to the kitchen. Sometimes they'd just let him sleep through dinner altogether. He'd sleep half of Saturday, and then by Sunday begin to feel like himself again, just in time for it to begin all over again on Monday.

They'd more or less divided his body in half, and in another week, they'd be finished with the groin-to-chest half. Then after a two-week break, they'd begin the chest to throat half of the bargain. It was all routine by now, so Fridays were nothing to worry about.

Zoë pulled into the driveway and found them huddled together on the steps of the front porch like three little orphans.

"Will climbed on the roof," Jillie said, opening the car door for her mother.

"*Will*," Zoë said, looking at him hunched over, retying his shoelaces, so he wouldn't have to look back at her.

"The door's stuck again, Mom. The key won't turn. I was just trying to see if I could get in a window. I didn't get hurt or anything." She could see it. The slow-motion fall off the roof, the thud that would stop her heart forever, the wide-staring eyes.

She started to speak sharply then caught herself. He was just a kid. Kids were always falling off things. Tree houses, roofs, bunk beds. She rubbed her forehead. Letters in the mailbox, phone calls, sirens and brakes, planes low overhead—steely reminders of their fragile lives.

"Why didn't you get in with the back-door key?"

"It's not there."

"Sure it's there—you just have to feel around for it. Well, let me try the front door."

Zoë turned the key but the lock wouldn't budge. She jammed her shoulder against it, trying to get the lock to pop open. Lately that door had a will of its own. There was Niki, looking at her through the window, wagging her tail. "Come on," she said to the kids. "We'll get in the back with the spare key."

"It's not *there*," Will said, scowling at her. "I already tried that."

The kids followed her through the passageway between the house and the garage and up the steps to the back door. Piles of leaves made slick spots on the brick passageway.

She ran her hand over the ledge by the back door for the key that was always supposed to be there no matter what. "Okay, the key's not there."

Will smiled at her. She could hear Niki whining by the back door, her tail banging against the wall.

It was beginning to rain. In a little while it would be dark. She thought about Jay coming home so late, the roads slick with rain, those radiation sickness pills in his coat pocket. Maybe this time he'd get sick and have to pull off the road. Nothing to do now but wait for Jay, so they piled into the car and drove to Happy Burger. She gave the kids money and they went on inside. She'd sit here and enjoy the quiet.

Then the kids piled back in and they all sat eating dinner watching the Happy Burger lights flash through the rain on the windshield. Nobody said anything. Nobody wanted to wait in the driveway in front of that dark, empty house.

Finally Will said, "I think Dad's home." So he took all their empty cups and sacks and put them in the Happy Burger trash can. He was wet climbing into the front seat. It was an effort to start the car. Is this what it would be like without him? Sitting in the Happy Burger parking lot in the rain watching it grow dark, afraid to go home?

But there Jay was, on the front porch fiddling with the lock as they pulled into the driveway. He turned and waved into the headlights of the car. The dog rushed out to meet them, wagging from side to side, as she scooted down the steps and jumped into the car the minute Max opened the door. Jillie grabbed her backpack from the car ledge and slid off the back seat. The dog jumped from the back seat to the front seat, then hopped out of the car and dashed up the steps.

"Where were you?" Jay said.

"Happy Burger," she said, putting her arms around his waist. "That stupid door locked us out again."

"I'll get it fixed," he said. He could always get that door open.

They all went inside and turned on the lights, and everything was all right again. She imagined their house from the outside—an empty, sorrowful place miraculously brought out of the dark.

Will and Max headed downstairs. Jillie went into the living room to hug the dog, who was sitting in the middle of the couch. "Get her off there, Jillie," Zoë said. "Daddy wants to lie down." The dog scooted off and Jay settled down to watch the news.

"My head hurts," Jillie said. She was sitting on the floor by the couch.

"Come here," Jay said, and Jillie curled up on top of him, tucked her head under his chin. Jay stroked her hair. Zoë thought Jillie was maybe coming down with a cold or something. She didn't want Jay getting it. Well, what was a cold anyway? A cold was nothing. Then he said, "Let's go downstairs and get your jammies on. Me too."

"What's that smell?" Max said, coming into the kitchen. Zoë had been heating up some leftover vegetable soup for Jay. The soup was boiling over the side of the pot onto the burner and pooling onto the stove.

"Damnit!" Zoë said before she could stop herself. She tried to shove the pot off the burner with her bare hand but not quick enough to stop the red welt that instantly bloomed across her palm. She turned off the burner with her other hand and let the cold water run over her hand up to her wrist. Her whole arm throbbed.

"Mom, you're getting a blister already," Max said, hugging her around the waist. "You need ice."

He got an ice cube out of the freezer, wrapped it in a dish towel, and handed it to her. "Thanks, kid," she said.

Then he went to the cupboard and grabbed a can of vegetable soup and stuck it under the can opener, wriggled it around under the blade until it caught, and pushed the lever. It turned smoothly and popped right open. Max could do it like no other. He got a small pot from the cupboard and began heating up the soup. "I'll keep watching it," he said. "I can help clean up the stove later."

She watched him stirring the soup and felt tears slip down her face. Will wasn't dead on the ground, or Jay sick in the car, and they weren't locked out of house and home. She wasn't responsible for everything. She'd forgotten that.

Then Max turned around and looked at her. There was some mournful secret gathering behind his eyes.

"What's wrong, Sweetie?"

"Something's wrong with Pecky," he said. "I think he's sick."

"Like what?"

"Something's growing on his beak. I'm scared he's got cancer on his beak or maybe his throat."

"How long have you been worrying about that?"

"I don't know."

"I don't think *birds* can get cancer, I really don't."

"Come on, Mommy," he said, tugging at her hand.

Zoë pulled him into a hug and kissed the top of his head. "Maybe he has a cold or something. I think birds can get colds. I just don't think Pecky could have cancer. You shouldn't worry about stuff like that."

Pecky did look funny. His beak looked almost deformed—like somebody had given it a good tweak. She wondered how long it had been like that. "Hey, Pecky, what's up?" He blinked, then closed his eyes and began rocking, like he could hardly stay on his perch. She could see that the bottom of the cage was wet with droppings.

"He never looked like that before. He was like this when I got home from school."

Well, she'd have to find a vet that treated parakeets. Niki's vet didn't.

—

Darla Farkus, Birds and Exotic Animals. She called first thing Saturday morning, bundled the cage up in towels, and set off down the hill. Max sat in the back seat holding the cage in his lap. She could hear the bird scrambling against the newspaper on the bottom of the cage when they turned a corner, so she slowed way down.

Bells tacked to the top of the door jangled when they walked in.

"So where's the bird?" the vet said. She looked at Max standing with the toweled cage against his chest. She lifted a corner of the towel. "What's the matter, birdie, are you *sick*?" The bird skittered over to the opposite side of the cage.

Dr. Farkus led them into the examining room. Zoë had never quite seen hair like that. Long brown ponytail and a tuft of red hair on top. She looked like a cockatiel in a lab coat. Max set the cage down on the stainless-steel examining table. "I'm gonna turn out the lights so I can get him out of the cage without freaking him out," she said, reaching for the light. The room went dark. They could hear the creak of the cage door, a couple of squawks, then Pecky's toenails scrambling against the newspaper on the floor of the cage. Then the beating of wings.

"Oh shit! Don't anybody move. I don't want anybody stepping on that bird." She slid her foot across the floor and reached for the light switch. The fluorescent lights overhead flickered and took hold. There was Pecky, sitting on top of the light.

"I gotta go and get a stool," she said as she left the room, her lab coat whipping around the corner after her. Zoë and Max just looked at each other. But there was Pecky, safe after all, on the edge of the light.

"He's really scared, Mommy." He'd tucked into himself as tightly as he could. He sat there blinking at them.

Doctor Farkus came back with a stool, climbed up, threw the

towel on top of the bird, and wrapped him up. They could see him struggling inside the towel. *Bok bok!* he said through the towel.

She turned him over in her hand. "Your bird's got scaly face. Pretty funny name, huh. It's caused by these teeny tiny beak mites you can't even see. I'd recommend an injection treatment. It's the quickest way to get rid of them." Pecky was trying valiantly to turn his head and bite her thumb.

"Now stop that," she said to the bird. She handed him to Max. "What this is," she said, preparing the syringe, "is a systemic insecticide." She was waving the needle in the air. Max backed up. "Come here, little birdie."

"Will that hurt?" Max had tucked the bird safely under his chin.

"He won't feel a thing. Here," she said, scooping the bird out of Max's hands.

The bird fluttered against the vet's closed hand as she plunged the needle into his heaving chest. He barely squeaked. Zoë could hardly watch. She'd tried to turn her head but was too late. Standing up close, Max didn't miss a thing.

"Where'd he get beak mites from?" Max said.

"You brought him home from the pet store like that."

"Is it from cancer?"

"No, no, no. What a biza*rre* idea," she said, holding onto the *r.*

"Wow. He's really, really *thin*," she said, turning him over. "And he's dangerously dehydrated. I'm going to have to plump him up. Didn't you notice the bottom of his cage is just soaked? He's probably not eating either."

She imagined Pecky hopping around the cage connected to an IV stand thumping along behind him. The vet took a syringe and plunged a needle into his chest for the second time. Pecky lay limp in her hand.

"Don't worry, it's just saline. He'll perk up here in an hour or so. But you've *got* to get him to eat. Listen. A bird can starve to death over a weekend. You know the saying eat like a bird? Well. Human beings would *burst* if they ate like a bird. What do you feed him anyway? Store bird seed, probably."

"Well, yes," Zoë said.

"No, no, no, no. I'll give you some samples of what he should be eating." Zoë sat down on the chair in the waiting room and held the cage in her lap, while the tech put the special bird food into plastic baggies. Okay, she was buying the works. This bird wasn't going to die on her watch.

"Obviously more's going on here than scaly face. I'll run some tests."

"What kind of tests?"

"Blood sample, stool specimen. It's a good thing you got him in here when you did. I'll get the lab results back on Monday, and if there's an infection you'll need to give him antibiotics. But in the meantime, you gotta give him Kaopectate for the diarrhea. Every coupla hours."

"How exactly do I do that?"

"With an eye dropper, of course. What did you think you'd use, a *spoon*? Ha ha ha."

"I didn't know you could do that for a bird," Zoë said, suspicious now of everything. "How much will all this cost?"

The vet just looked at her. "Do you wanna lose this bird or what?" she said, putting the bird back in the cage. He staggered across the newspaper to the corner, where he sat weaving back and forth, his chest heaving. Max put the towel over the cage, picked it up, and headed for the car. Zoë scrawled out the check and grabbed her purse. They couldn't get out of there fast enough.

Once they got the bird home and the cage back up on top of Max's dresser, Pecky seemed no worse for wear. He began to bat his bell around the bottom of the cage, then hopped back up onto the perch and dropped his bell into the seed cup. *Bok*, he said, stroking himself in the mirror. Then he climbed on top of the bell like he always did, and pretended he was hatching his egg.

"She was *on* something," Zoë said to Jay that night. "Or she was crazy."

"Pecky seems okay. His beak looks pretty funny, though. I never noticed that before."

"Well, don't say anything to Max."

They lay there watching the moonlight filtering through the open blinds, listening to the low, mournful wind. Niki jumped up on the bed to say goodnight. She burrowed her nose into the crook of Zoë's neck, then turned around and slid off the bed onto the floor. Zoë could hear her pawing her blanket, heard her sigh, and knew she had settled in for the night. Jay lay still for a long time but Zoë could tell he was awake.

"What are you thinking?" she said.

"Nothing."

"Come on, *what*?"

"Oh, on Friday one of the technicians said to visualize the X-ray machine as the sun. Just give me the real sun and my boat on the water."

"Maybe you should close your eyes," she said, moving over.

"Yeah, well I tried shutting my eyes. I figured I'd better keep them open. Be sure they don't mess things up."

"Are you still worrying about that? My God."

"Nah, it's okay."

"Maybe I should go with you. Two sets of eyes are better than one."

"You don't have to do that. You couldn't watch anyway."

"I'd go if you asked me to."

"I know you would." She could feel him smiling in the dark. He knew how glad she was not to go down there. Jay knew what that did to her.

"Every night before I go to sleep, I send good images into you, you know what I mean? My images are from the moon, though, not the sun."

"I wish you wouldn't do that."

"Why not?"

"I don't know. It feels funny." He shrugged away from her. "There's nothing you can really do, Zoë."

"But there's *always* something you can do."

"Leave it alone, okay? You know how you are with anything medical."

She put her head on his chest. "That's not medical. That's like prayer." All right. She didn't have to tell him these things.

They lay there listening to the wind.

"You're warm," he said, touching her face. "Anyway, what I was really thinking about was fishing."

"That's exactly what you should do. Think about fishing and summer." She knew he hadn't really been thinking about fishing. But she'd never know what.

"Better than thinking about that radiation machine. It could never be the sun even with my eyes closed."

"Tell me about summer," she said, as she turned back over and snuggled down into the pillows. She wanted a bedtime story where everybody lived happily ever after.

"Okay," Jay said, then that long silence he always took before he said anything important. "Here's what I was thinking." His voice grew softer. "I'm out in the boat, watching the downrigger release and that fishing line just takes off and I know I've got something big on the line. I keep seeing that moment just before I start to reel him in, when he could be the biggest sockeye I've ever caught. It's that moment when anything's possible, you know?" And then he was asleep.

She liked lying there, listening to his slow, steady breathing. She tried to breathe with him, but her heart always went too fast. She would suffocate going that slow. She lay there watching the moon float up through the branches of the trees. Monday radiation would begin all over again. There had been no fires for weeks now.

"That bird is *sick*," the vet said over the phone Monday afternoon. Zoë had been opening a can of tomatoes when the phone rang. She'd set the cage on the bird stand in the kitchen so she could keep an eye on him while she made dinner. She'd rushed home from classes about two to give the bird his next dose of Kaopectate. And there he was, back up on his perch, which she thought was an encouraging sign. But now he was opening and closing his beak in a weird kind of way. His chest was heaving. It looked like he was trying hard to breathe. Max had gone from school to Cub Scouts and he'd be home any minute. She looked up at the bird again. He had dark, wet circles under his eyes.

The vet went on. "It's a strep infection, just like I thought."

"But a couple of days ago he only had beak mites and now he's half dead."

"Well, birds carry around strep germs all the time," she said. "Then when they get weak it just takes over. Now you gotta keep that bird *warm*."

"Okay," Zoë said. Pecky was still all puffed up. He looked hot, not cold, but what did she know?

"The temperature in the cage must be *exactly* eighty-five degrees. So you'll need to keep a thermometer in the cage. And I'm putting him on erythromycin, so you better get out here before I close up. Every four hours he gets three drops. You'd also better be giving him that Kaopectate if the diarrhea hasn't stopped. You could keep him here overnight if you don't think you can handle all this."

"We can handle it," Zoë said, and hung up the phone.

"How's Pecky?" Max said, dropping his backpack on the floor. He put his finger in the cage. "Mommy, he looks *worse*." Max tried to stroke him, but instead of nuzzling up to his finger like usual, the bird just blinked and closed his eyes again.

"He's got strep throat, just like you had. But the doctor has some medicine that will fix him up."

Max had climbed up on a chair and was taking the cage down. "Pecky, you're gonna be okay," he said, hugging the cage. "Can I pick him up?"

"You'd better let him rest, Sweetie. We need to get the cage real warm. Do you still have that weather thermometer in your room?"

"Yeah but it broke."

She stirred the spaghetti sauce again, and put the lid on the pot. Steam rushed out from under the lid, and she turned the heat down.

It was dark now, and you could see a star here and there. It would be cold tonight. If she could do anything, she could keep things warm. She found the heating pad under Will's bed but couldn't find the cover. Oh, well, she wasn't wrapping the *bird* in it. So she tucked the edges of the heating pad around the bottom of the cage and set it on the bathroom counter. Then Max put the towels over that.

"We don't want it to get too hot," she said. "We really need a room thermometer." She wondered if an oral thermometer worked the same way. At least she didn't have to take the bird's temperature. It was tricky enough holding the bird and prying its beak open with one hand while she put the drops of Kaopectate in with the other.

"Hey, what's all this?" Jay said, peering into the bathroom. It was getting on to five o'clock. She was sitting on the edge of the toilet seat, scrounging through her purse for the car keys.

"Hi, kid, how's Pecky?"

"He's really sick," Max said. Jay bent over and peeked into the opening she'd left in the towels. Pecky was still sitting on his perch, but he'd stopped rocking. He blinked at them through the towels.

"What's going on?" Jay pulled Max into a hug, touched Zoë's face. "Where are you going?"

"I've got to get a room thermometer for the cage. We're supposed to keep him warm, but we don't want to cook him, for godsake. I'll get it when I pick up the erythromycin."

"For the bird? You're kidding." She nodded, rolled her eyes. "Well, let me go," he said.

"Jay, you don't have to do that. You just got home. You stay here and stir the spaghetti sauce."

"Hey, it's Monday, remember? I'm good on Mondays."

By the time she'd finished telling Jay how to get there, Max had disappeared. She found him sitting in the rocker by the living room window in the dark, watching the lights from the Volkswagen fishtail down the hill. "Is Daddy coming right back?"

"Oh, there's not that much of a rush, Sweetie. The important thing the vet said is to keep him warm, and he's nice and warm now."

So she went back into the kitchen to finish dinner. They'd just have to guess at the temperature for now. Then it was after six o'clock and dinner had long been ready. Jay still wasn't home. She was trying not to watch the clock. Then, like the thousand times before, they heard the car pulling into the driveway and everything was all right again.

"Are you okay?" she said, sorry as always to have asked that.

Jay came into the kitchen with a grocery bag in each arm.

"My God, what did she sell us now?"

"I thought we needed some ice cream. Pretty damn depressing around here."

"Did you bring the medicine?" Max said.

"I did." Jay reached into his coat pocket and brought out an orange bottle and a medicine dropper. Max took the bottle and went into the bathroom.

"Can we give it to him now?"

So Zoë picked up the bird with one hand, held its beak open with the other, while Max put three careful, orange drops on the bird's tongue. Will and Jillie unloaded the sacks—three different kinds of ice cream, chocolate sauce, marshmallow sauce, peanuts, bananas, raspberry jam, a small jar of cherries—and spread it all before them on the counter. Supplicants all, they gathered around with their soup bowls in hand, and made their dinner. They'd have the dinner warming on the stove for dessert.

Something was out of place. Zoë sat up and tried to think of what it was. She slept on the edge of sleep these days, her senses so keen she could hear through walls. But she didn't know what had wakened her. There was Jay, his face buried in the pillow. She thought as long as she was awake she might as well give the bird another dose of antibiotics, so she headed down the hall toward the stairs and the upstairs bathroom. She could see the moonlight coming through the window by the landing. There was Max sitting on the stairs against the wall, holding something in his hands. She sat down beside him.

"I kept checking on him, and he was doing okay, but then he was lying on the bottom of the cage. I picked him up and petted him but he died, I think."

Zoë turned on the light at the top of the stairs. The bird was just a tuft of yellow. He was already fading. His head hung loose over the edge of Max's cupped hand.

"Let's put him back in the cage for now, Sweetie, and go back to bed. We'll think of what to do tomorrow."

They carried the bird back to the bathroom. She touched the bars of the cage, which felt almost hot. Maybe they'd heated him to death. She picked up the thermometer off the floor of the cage. It did feel awfully hot in there. The thermometer said ninety-two. She turned off the heating pad.

Max put him inside the cage. He looked strange, lying on the newspapers. "I better cover him up," he said. Then they turned out the light and shut the door.

She walked him back to bed and tucked him in. She thought sleep was surely finished for the night until she woke up and saw that Jay wasn't there. But she couldn't climb out of the dream. She kept seeing Pecky lying on the newspapers, staring back at her, from eyes rising out of those wet, dark circles. It was awful to just put the bird back in the cage on those dank newspapers.

She walked down the dark hall toward Max's room. His light was on. She could hear Jay. She stood in the doorway and watched. There they were, sitting on the bed, tucking cotton balls all around the bird who was lying in one of Jillie's old shoeboxes. Max laid Pecky's little bird bell beside him, then closed the top. He'd drawn a row of yellow flowers all around the name he'd printed on the top of the shoebox. It said *Pecky Penney* in yellow and green letters.

Zoë watched out the front window while Jay and Max buried

Jillie's shoebox in Ferny Land, the little hill just beyond the edge of the lawn with the wooden marker the kids had shaped like a cross, where they buried all the pets most loved then lost. She could see them clearly in the moonlight, even as the moon was disappearing into the trees. She looked at Jay out there in his parka and pajama bottoms. *So this is death*, she thought. No wonder dying is so hard. No wonder every living thing fights the dying of the light. And now this strange, blue, moonlit peace.

Two nights later, she dreamed again of the bird. They'd rushed it to Jay's hospital where two white-coated men had laid it on a stainless-steel table under a single, flickering light. They watched from the corner as it turned from yellow to white feathers and air. Then they looked and it was gone. "I saw it fly up," Jay said. All Zoë knew was that the table was empty now. She couldn't tell whether it was death or resurrection.

The Devil and Willie Nelson

The telephone rang in her ear, a heart-stopping sound Zoë knew right away. *Who died?* she wondered from the heavy, dreamless place she'd come from. Her heart was pounding as she reached for the phone, which she'd managed to knock clean off the nightstand. It fell in a jumble and clatter onto Niki, who was curled up beside the bed. She yipped once, jumped up, and stood there looking at Zoë.

She fumbled for the receiver somewhere on the floor. Jay was safe because she'd touched his shoulder before she reached for the phone; he didn't even stir. Jillie was safe and sound in her pink and white bedroom, and Max in the room down the hall. It was Will who was gone. Adam Wildermuth's birthday sleepover.

"Can you come and get me?"

"Are you sick?"

"Just come and get me, Mom. Everybody has to go home." The clock on the nightstand, which she had not managed to knock over, said quarter after one.

"What is it?" Jay asked from someplace far.

"Go back to sleep. It's nothing. Will wants to come home."

"I'll go," he mumbled.

"Go back to sleep," she said, touching his back as he rolled over. It was Friday night, and the end of the usual battering week of radiation.

The depth of his sleep frightened her. He went so far away she was always a little astonished when he came back.

There was still one police car in the driveway when she pulled up in front of the house. Its red light flashed across the porch. Mrs. Wildermuth was standing in the driveway in the flashing red light, holding her bathrobe across her chest. Before Zoë had a chance to get out of the car, Will rushed across the lawn and slid into the car, slammed the door, and pushed down the lock.

"Let's *go*," he said, sliding down into the seat. Zoë turned the car around in the middle of the street. Other cars, other parents, began pulling up as the police car began to back slowly out of the driveway. Neighbors peered through darkened windows or stood in clumps on their lawns, looking across the street.

"We need to go *home,*" Will said. He sat hugging his knees.

"What happened?" Zoë said as coolly as she could. She reached over to touch his shoulder. "Is everybody okay?"

"I don't want to talk about it."

"I mean nobody's *hurt.*"

"Nobody got hurt except for Mrs. Wildermuth, but she's okay now."

Zoë could see that, but she couldn't imagine how Mrs. Wildermuth had gotten hurt. Any sensible adult in the same house with a seventh-grade sleepover would have been fast asleep buried in pillows at the other end of the house.

It had begun to rain, and Zoë flicked on the windshield wipers. They swished back and forth like a silent metronome, beating time to the tires whirring through the rainy night. She switched on the radio, thinking if they just drove a few blocks, Will would calm down enough to tell her what in God's name had happened. She wasn't going to force him. He'd been so quiet the last couple of months. Nothing dramatic, just lots of time spent in his room with the door shut, hardly saying anything at dinner, just eating his food and excusing himself when it wasn't his turn at the dishes. There was a new edginess to him, a sort of vague, free-floating anger. Well, he was approaching puberty—who could blame the kid for being jumpy? Plus, everything else that had been going on.

The road glistened under the streetlights as they drove up the long hill home. The windows were beginning to fog up and she cracked open a window.

Will shot her a glance. "Don't do that," he said, shaking his head.

"Okay," Zoë said, sending the window back up, and flicking on the defroster. "We're almost home." She was trying to get a good look at him without notice. "You'll feel better when we get home."

"I was scared, but I'm not now."

The gravel crunched under their wheels as they pulled into the driveway. The living room light was on. She could see Jay sitting on the couch by the window through the half-closed blinds. The dog was sitting on the couch next to him, nosing the blinds. Will dashed out of the car and into the house.

"Lock it," he said from the couch as Zoë came in the front door. He was already sitting close by Jay, who was sitting on the couch with a towel over his lap.

"What's going on?" Jay looked pale and tight around the eyes.

"Were you sick?" she said, sitting down. Zoë felt a little sick herself.

"I'm okay," he said, rolling up the towel. "I woke up and you weren't there, so I came upstairs to see what was going on. I just got a little dizzy. I thought I heard the phone ring."

"The sleepover was canceled," Zoë said, looking at Will sitting there hugging his knees again. "Adam's mom got hurt some way, and everybody had to go home."

"Will?" Jay said. "What the hell happened?"

Will eased back into the couch, took a deep breath. He was in his own living room now, lit up against the night. "It was my fault. It was the present I got him."

"What do you mean?"

"The Ouija board."

"How could a Ouija board hurt Adam's mom?" Jay wanted to know.

"We wanted to see if it really worked." Will tucked down into the couch, rubbed his eyes.

"The Ouija board?" Jay said, trying to follow him.

"Yeah. We tried it out after the movie."

"What movie?" Zoë was beginning to get an idea of what had happened. "Something scary, I suppose."

"Yeah, *The Exorcist*." Jay and Zoë just looked at each other. When Will was in the third grade, he'd slept with a Bible across his chest for weeks after he saw *Dracula* at a friend's house. He was afraid to go outside after dark, because he thought the bats they sometimes saw circling the trees just at dusk were vampire bats.

"We turned off the lights and lit some candles and Adam got some incense out of his sister's room."

"Mr. and Mrs. Wildermuth were *home* during all of this, weren't they?" Zoë said.

"Oh, sure. No. Mr. Wildermuth wasn't there. And his sister wasn't. But his mom was. Then we started burning the incense." Will took another deep breath, and stared across the room at the darkened front window.

"Then you played the Ouija board?"

"Yeah, we started out asking it stupid questions like are Adam's eyes brown and stuff like that. A lot of the answers were *right*, and it kind of freaked us out. Then Adam asked, 'Is Satan in the room?' and the pointer went to *yes!*" Will leaned away from the window. "Can you close the blinds all the way?"

Jay reached up and flipped them shut.

"Everybody started screaming and the candle went out. Then we saw Adam's mom running down the hallway into the rec room, and she opened her mouth to yell at us but then her eyes rolled back in her head and she fell over and slid down against the door, and we thought Satan had gotten her."

Jay looked down at his lap. She could see him trying to stop a smile.

"We couldn't get out because she got jammed against the door, so we dragged her over against the wall and ran upstairs to the phone. Adam called 911 and then the police came and the aid-car and then we all had to go home."

Jay pulled Will into a hug, but she could see he was trying hard not to laugh.

"Well, I don't know what to say." He cleared his throat and leaned over. "You want anything to eat?'

"No thanks," Will said, as he put his head back on the cushions, closed his eyes. It was over. He was safe. He'd confessed and been absolved; he'd told everything and the house hadn't split in two. The dog lay curled up on the floor next to him, her head on his foot. He reached over to pet her.

"Well, I feel like I need something in my stomach," Jay said, getting to his feet. Will gave his dad a funny look as he watched him walk down the hall toward the kitchen, the towel slung over his shoulder.

"Did you take one of those nausea pills?" Zoë said after him.

"I did."

"Maybe I should take one," Zoë said absently.

"What do you mean?" Jay said, coming back into the living room. "Do you feel sick?"

"Nah. You know. All this drama. Do you feel better now?"

"I do."

"Do you mean your radiation pills?" Will said.

Jay laughed. "Yeah, I guess you could say that." The dog got up to follow him into the kitchen.

"Mom, is that blood?" Will said, pointing to a dark stain on the rug. Zoë touched the spot and her fingers came away wet. She looked at Jay down the hall in the kitchen spreading peanut butter on a piece of bread. She turned to Will. Her heart was a knot in the center of her chest.

"It's *dog* blood, Mom. That's where Niki was sitting." They were both thinking the same thing: it wasn't Jay. And why would he be bleeding anyway? They looked down the hall. There was Niki, standing by Jay, waiting for her part of his peanut butter sandwich.

"When was she in heat last?"

"I don't know, a long time ago," Will said.

"When was the dog in heat?" she shouted after Jay.

"I have no idea," he said through a mouthful of peanut butter and bread.

"She'd better not be in heat," Zoë said, going into the kitchen. She lifted her tail. "Oh God. How long has this been going on?" It was one more of those things she was always supposed to keep track of. It suddenly occurred to her in a wild rush that she couldn't remember when *she'd* last had her period. Stress could do that to you. Her breasts ached. *Oh shit*, she thought. *Oh shit.*

Jay pulled up the barstool by the counter and began to laugh. It was nice to hear.

"Find the doggie bag in the pantry, Will. Get out Dad's old

underwear and the Kotex. And don't *anybody* let her out. I suppose she's just been strutting her stuff all over the neighborhood."

Will came back in a minute with a pair of Jay's old, stretched-out jockey shorts and a jumbo Kotex pad. He knew the routine. He jammed the pad into the crotch of the shorts, then put her back legs through the leg holes, her tail through the schnitzel, then pinned the waistband with a big baby diaper pin.

The dog turned around to get at the shorts sliding down her haunches, sniffed, then remembered the routine too.

"Better pin that tighter," Zoë said. So he pulled the waistband tighter and pinned it again.

"Okay, Will," she said, steering him toward the hall. "It's after two in the morning. Better get to bed."

"Can I sleep on the floor in your room?" he said under his breath.

"Sure." Zoë put her arm around him as they started down the hall to the bedroom downstairs. She was glad he had something to think about other than the Devil. But as they neared the uncurtained window by the landing, Will ducked behind her. The light from the bathroom downstairs lit the rhododendron outside the window in shadowy light. Something rustled the rhododendron bush outside the window as they went down the stairs, and it shivered.

Will yelped and raced down the rest of the way, jumping the last four steps in one leap.

Zoë stopped and stared into the dark. A dark shape stared back. It pressed its dark nose against the window and made a dark sound. Well, no arsonist had a nose like that. It was only a dog. Everything was basically all right. "Go home!" she shouted, banging the glass with the palm of her hand. It skittered away and disappeared into the dark.

Finally they were all settling in for the night once more. Zoë had gotten one of the night-lights out of Jillie's room and plugged it in near where Will was tucked into his sleeping bag at the foot of their bed, the dog in her underwear curled up next to him, glad for company on the floor.

"Goodnight, Will," Zoë said. "Sleep tight."

"Sorry, Mom. Sorry for all the trouble." Then he sat up. "Goodnight, Dad."

But Jay didn't answer.

"You stay away from that dog out there," she said to Niki, and gave her a pat. "That shadow was only Rambo. He probably came down the hill."

Then she leaned over to hug him goodnight and for once he hugged her back. "There isn't really a Satan, is there?"

"No, of course not." Zoë sat back down on the floor to pet the dog and wait for him to relax into sleep.

In a minute she could hear him breathing and knew he'd fallen asleep.

Will was never sure whether the Devil had been in Adam Wildermuth's rec room that night because, for four nights in a row, he slept on the floor by the end of the bed, curled against the dog. And Zoë, who had said there was no Satan, dreamed of Satan as an old man in periwinkle blue who lived at the Theodora Rest Home where she'd driven Jillie and four of her classmates in December to play Christmas bingo with the old folks.

He looked a little like Willie Nelson, with his ponytail and guitar. He was just a wizened-down little old man who smiled at her when they came in the door, but when Zoë smiled back, his eyes turned red just like in the movies. She knew it was a dream, but she was afraid anyway. Then he struck a chord and raised his guitar high over his head and the room went dark. All she could see were his red eyes.

She couldn't find Jillie anywhere. She reached through the dark but it was like pushing her hands through warm water. The red eyes were laughing. Give her *back*, she said with such force she knew he would have to do it. And sure enough, the lights came back on, and there was Jillie, after all, in the corner of the bingo room, and there was Roy the neighbor, with his arm around her, looking across the room at Satan with such fierceness she couldn't breathe.

Zoë sat up, trying to catch her breath. Something was hurting her. She leaned over and grabbed her knees. Light was coming from somewhere near the floor and she couldn't tell whether she was still in the dream. But there was Jay, turned away on his side, and Will asleep on the floor, one arm half over the dog's back, and Jillie and Max asleep down the hall.

Stay away, she said to Roy. *Don't you go near Jillie. And stay out of my dreams.* Then it occurred to her that she didn't know whether Roy had saved Jillie or caught her at last. It seemed like he was trying to tell her something. Roy could be the arsonist. But he just as easily wasn't. She thought she might be sick. She got up and went into the bathroom. Blood was trickling down her legs. Her belly was a circle of pain that drove into her back. At least she wasn't pregnant. She leaned over and tried to breathe. She sat down and listened to what was coming out of her. When had she had a period like this? Maybe it was an early pregnancy and this was the end of it. She flushed the toilet so she would never know, put on the largest pad she could find, and leaned over the sink until the dizziness passed.

A Grief So Like Fear

They'd made love that afternoon and Jay had taken her to dinner. They were celebrating the coming of their first baby, and the cessation of the morning sickness that had plagued her for over three months. They'd gone to bed early, but near midnight she woke with something tugging at her, at first under her belly button, then it moved down and pulled lower and deeper. She could feel it all the way around now. She pressed her fingers into the small of her back. What it might be she would not countenance.

She got up to go to the bathroom. It hurt to stand up. She sat down on the toilet and thought for a moment it was a urinary tract infection. She got those all the time. She leaned over, put her elbows on her knees, her head in her hands. It was easing off a little, she was sure of it.

But even in the bathroom, lit only by the night-light, she could see the dark stain on the toilet tissue. She stood up and turned on the light. The water in the toilet was bright red. Blood was trickling down the inside of her thighs. She dug through the cabinet underneath the sink for a pad and held it between her legs under her nightgown. She knew now that this pain wouldn't go away. She held it there as she made her way back into the bedroom.

"Jay? Can you wake up?" His head was turned to the side, his mouth open in sleep.

"Okay. I'm awake." But he was asleep again.

"I think I might be losing the baby."

Jay sat up. He touched her face. "God, Zoë. Really?"

The pain was coming in waves. She could feel her womb tighten into a hard knot. "Oh," she said. She felt a rush of heat spread over her chest and across her face, then a cold sweat. She couldn't stop trembling. Jay left the room then came back.

"I'm taking you in."

"I don't think I can walk."

"I'll carry you."

So he gathered her up and carried her down the hall, then eased her onto the couch. He slipped her coat over her shoulders as she lay down. A rush of nausea spread over her chest and caught in her throat. Zoë drew her legs up and turned away. Jay rushed back to the bedroom to get his wallet and keys and pull on his jeans. Then he picked her up and carried her to the car.

"It's a good thing you came right in," the nurse said as she was settling Zoë into the bed. She'd helped her out of her coat and bloody nightgown and into a hospital gown, then lay her back onto the bed while the other nurse slipped a pad under her bottom.

"Am I bleeding a lot?" It frightened her not to know.

The nurse looked at her quickly, then smiled and patted her arm. "Oh, this happens all the time. We know what to do. I just need to get an IV going. Your blood pressure is pretty low."

But her veins kept collapsing, and they couldn't get the needle in. The two nurses tried both arms and the back of both hands. She was already bruising. "We're so sorry, but your veins keep rolling."

Jay winced every time the needle wouldn't go in.

"We've got to get this in pretty soon," the nurse said, as she tapped the inside of Zoë's arm then placed a warm compress over the intractable veins. "Let's see if this can pop them up." After a few moments she tapped the inside of her arm again and then prepared the needle. "Okay, here we go." Zoë turned her head, shut her eyes.

"Sorry. No go."

Jay came straight off the chair where they'd made him sit. "Can't you get somebody who can *do* this?"

"We're paging Dr. Chin."

"I hope he's the *acupuncturist*," Jay said sharply.

"He's the *anesthesiologist*," the nurse bristled. "She may need a D & C anyway, so it's good to get a line going."

"How long before he gets here?"

"Any minute, Mr. Penney, don't worry. We can turn this bed on its end, if we have to. Then we can get her legs above her heart so she won't be so shocky. Just if we need to. We don't need to right now." She stroked Zoë's arm. "I'm going to keep trying." Then the tapping on the inside of her other arm, the warm compress for a moment and the needle going in and slipping off.

"Please stop," Zoë said. She was crying.

The nurse didn't say anything. She looked at Jay, then went out into the hall so strangely lit and quieted for the night.

"I'm really losing this baby, then," she said as the nurse came back in.

"We don't know that for sure."

"How can I not be with all this blood? I'm scared about the blood."

Jay was standing at the end of the bed as out of the way as he could get and still touch her through the sheet.

"Maybe you'd like to go outside for a minute," the nurse said. "I need to check her and change the pad."

"I'm staying."

Zoë didn't want to see how much blood there was as the nurse lifted the pad out from under her. She just wanted someone to tell her. Standing at the foot of the bed as the nurse lifted the sheet, Jay could see everything.

"That's a lot of blood," he said without meaning to. "Doesn't she need a transfusion?"

"It's not as much as it seems. Don't you want to sit down?"

Zoë had her eyes closed but she could feel how anguished he was. "Jay, sit down," she whispered.

"We're giving you a morphine injection. You'll feel better right away."

Zoë couldn't stop the tears running down her face. "Why can't I stop shaking?"

"It's just your body fighting off the shock," the nurse said.

Faces appeared then disappeared. Everybody floated rather than walked. It was better to keep her eyes shut. She couldn't be dying, could she? If she opened her eyes, the room swirled around her. Where was Jay? There. He was back now. She could feel his warm hand through the sheet. She could shut her eyes as long as he held onto her.

"Oh yes. That's better now. The needles don't even hurt. You can keep trying." She let go of the bed railing. "Jay?"

"I'm here," he said, patting her leg.

Suddenly the room went end over end. Her bed was on a disk that had flipped over and she was upside down, then violently uprighted. She grabbed hold of the side of the bed, and vomited onto the floor. Her heart was pounding. She could feel it in her ears.

"She's having a reaction to the morphine. We'll give her some Valium. Here, Sweetie, this will make you feel better."

"You said that already," Jay said. His face looked pale in the hospital light. He'd thrown on a sweatshirt and you could see his pajama bottoms below his jeans. He was wearing loafers but no socks.

"Mr. Penney, you should sit down."

But he wouldn't.

"Dr. Chin will be here any minute," the nurse said again. And then there he was, in his green cap and scrubs, striding into the room like he'd just come from surgery. He ran his fingers over the inside of her arms, the backs of her hands, flicked the inside of her left arm with his finger and thumb, rubbed her arm with alcohol, then just slid that needle into the vein smooth as could be, taped it down, and connected it to the IV tubing. He adjusted the flow rate, and turned on his heel and was gone. He hadn't said a word.

"Jay?"

He went to the side of the bed. "I'm here." He put his face against hers. "I'm never going to leave. You should try to sleep now."

"No more baby," she whispered.

"Just you. You're the only one I want." He touched her face, then stepped back to let the nurse by.

She tucked the pillow under Zoë's cheek so she could lie on her side and lifted the IV line over the top of the bed rail, put the call button by her other hand. "There," the nurse said. "That IV is really going. All that good stuff going into you. You're all right now, you know."

"What do you mean she's all right *now*?" Jay said.

"Just her blood pressure. That was the only worry."

Jay sat down and put his head in his hands.

There were tears down his face, which he did not wipe away. His reserve was all gone. "I think it was my fault," he said. "It was my idea. I shouldn't have asked you."

Zoë reached for his hand. "My dear, sweet Jay. I don't think so. I wanted it too. I wanted it so much."

But when Dr. Silverstein came to check on her and tell her the D

& C was scheduled for nine, Jay followed the doctor to the doorway. "Could I have done this? I'm worried that I did."

"Oh no, Mr. Penney. Intercourse doesn't cause miscarriage. Sometimes these things just happen. It's fairly common."

"Not to us," Jay said, and turned back to the bed.

The IV was hydrating her and keeping her blood pressure up, and between the morphine and the valium she was tucked into a cocoon of warm surrender, with only a little halo of pain in her belly and lower back. Yet she couldn't let go into sleep. It was about six in the morning and still dark. Jay had dashed home to let the dog out.

Just a night-light in her room so she could sleep and the hall half-lit. Her door was left partly open, which she took as not a particularly good sign. She could hear everything. First, she heard carts being wheeled down the hall and wondered why breakfast was so early. Then she heard a baby cry and knew those weren't food carts. They were the little isolettes from the nursery going to the mothers who wanted the night off to rest up for the hundreds of sleepless nights to come. It hadn't occurred to her until now that she was on the obstetrical floor. At least she didn't have a roommate. Imagine a roommate with a baby coming for its early morning feeding.

"There's a good-looking guy outside who wants to see you," the nurse said. "He's been just down the hall the whole time." Zoë had come awake instantly. One moment she had died, then, in an instant, she was wide awake and there was Jay, coming toward her, looking fresh and rested, if that was possible. He'd changed his clothes, washed his face, combed his hair. He was wearing his pale blue denim shirt, khaki pants.

"Hey," he said, kissing her on the forehead then on the mouth. "My best girl."

"You've got socks on," Zoë said, touching his arm.

"Socks *and* shoes," he said, pulling up a stool.

The woman in the bed next to her in the recovery room was throwing up in a basin as the nurse held up her head.

"Glad that isn't me," Zoë said. "When can I go home?"

Jay got up and pulled the curtain. "This afternoon. They said you did fine. Everything's okay now."

"It doesn't hurt anymore," she said. She looked at her name on the hospital ID bracelet, the blood pressure cuff flaccid around her arm, the oximeter over her fingertip. "Still wired for sound though."

Jay looked at the monitor. Blood pressure 110 over 65, pulse 88, sats 97. "Heart's too fast. That's for me, isn't it? Your fast beating heart is for me."

"My one and only," she said. He looked so strong. She couldn't imagine being without him.

She lay in bed that first evening home with the television on, while Jay sat at the foot of the bed and rubbed her legs through the blankets. They didn't mention the baby. They had no name for what they had lost.

Magic So Fierce and Fine

"What was that!" Zoë said, sitting up. "Jay?"

"What?"

Will hadn't moved, but the dog had jumped on the bed.

"Something crashed into the window," she said, peeking between the blinds. You could see the outline of the trees in the woods just beyond the bedroom window. They listened to the silence. It was just beginning to turn light. "It's too loud for the arsonist."

"Maybe we dreamed it," Jay said. She could tell he was being pulled back into sleep and was trying to fight it off.

"Well, the dog didn't dream it," Zoë said, scooting her off the bed. She moved close and lay her head on Jay's pillow, listened to the day begin.

"There!" A giant crow was teetering on a branch ten feet from the house, looking back at them. Niki was back up on the bed.

"What's going on?" Will said, half out of sleep.

"Just a dumb bird," Jay said, lying back down. "Go back to sleep." But that dumb bird crashed into their window every couple of minutes for almost two hours, until the early April sun warmed up the morning.

"Drunk," the neighbor said. She was standing in her backyard looking at the picked-over elderberries. "Drunk on these berries.

They get to fermenting in the sun and birds get drunk on them." Her dentures clicked as she talked.

"But why do they eat *your* berries and then crash into *my* window?" But Mrs. Morgenstern was already headed inside, leaving the answer behind her. It had been three days in a row of this crazy, early morning wake-up call.

The kids stood on the deck and looked out over the woods in silence.

"Birds can't get drunk," Max said at dinner. "Nobody in my bird books said that."

"I don't think birds can get drunk either," Jillie said. She'd slept through every early morning bird thump so far and was feeling left out.

Will just stared down into the woods safely from the kitchen window. You heard strange things in those woods at night—sometimes a coyote howl, as plaintive and eerie as an abandoned baby's, or low, secret rustlings through the ferns and blackberries, or whirring leaves and shuddering branches as possums crawled from one tree to another, turning the branches weighty and dark, or bats that flickered through the treetops just at dusk. The kids only reclaimed the woods in the daring of summer light.

But the dark bird, the *ravenevermore* as the kids called him, was something new. A great big glossy crow sitting on the branch near the bedroom window every morning at dawn but mysteriously hidden by day.

"Maybe he's trying to build a nest under the eaves and just keeps missing his foothold," Zoë said to Will. But Zoë knew Will never forgot how Adam Wildermuth's candle had gone out, or how he kept his eye on those woods. The Devil had many manifestations.

In between the window and the blinds, Max had propped up the giant yellow bird he'd painted in memoriam. "I really miss Pecky," he said. "I miss him all the time."

"I know you do," Zoë said and pulled him into a hug. "But this is just a wonderful picture. It helped to make it, didn't it?"

"I cried when I was painting it. Then I felt better. Maybe it will scare that crow away."

But the bird kept on, and they covered their heads with their pillows. It was Zoë's migraine nightmare come to life.

"Maybe it *likes* my picture. Maybe it thinks it's its mate," Max said, taking the picture down.

"You may be right," Zoë said. "The picture is so good it's probably attracting the bird."

One night they let all the kids sleep in the bedroom. Everybody brought in their pillows and sleeping bags so they could hear the bird smash into the window. When the bird first hit the window, Jillie and Max sat up and then instantly fell back to sleep. But Will got up and sat on the edge of the bed and stared at the crow who perched on the branch, staring back—a black phantom barely visible in the thin, pale light.

"That bird must be brain-damaged by now," Zoë said to Jay at breakfast. It seemed as important to explain this mystery as it would the others to come. The slugs who were eating the computer paper by night, disappearing by day, were a mystery. Cancer was a mystery. Radiation was a mystery. That spring they all wanted the explanation, not the extravagant, fierce magic of the mystery left untouched.

"Maybe it's mating season and he sees his reflection and thinks it's another bird," Max said. He still couldn't decide whether he wanted another bird in that birdcage he couldn't bear to put away. "I don't want the bird to get hurt," he said. "We need to stop him from doing that."

So they finally nailed an old white sheet over the bedroom window. The next morning they slept through till the alarm rang at seven, and knew they'd outsmarted that crow.

But the morning after that they woke at five to the same crashing sound, only now it was more muffled, more distant. They thought he was smashing into the sheet, but he'd just moved up to the big kitchen window right above them. They couldn't put sheets over all the windows. It would be like living inside a shroud.

Zoë thought about the days of the fires and how they had dreaded any thump or rustling that came from the woods. But those days seemed far away now, as they were replaced by other dangers more intimate and terrible. These fires came from inside. And Jay was paying all hell to put them out. Not that you'd notice unless you knew what to look for. But there it was—his face sharper now, and pale in the early spring light, a tiredness around his eyes, less laughing.

They had just made what seemed to be the first sure turn into spring, those early days of April, when the bird woke them to falling snow. They would have missed it had they slept until the alarm. They opened the blinds all the way and from the bed watched the snow drift down in lacy patches. They pretended it was not a cold, dark morning with the promise of spring betrayed, but a Christmas to be unwrapped all over again. Then Zoë remembered the hospital snow and felt a sudden ripple of panic. So she slid on top of him, feeling the full length of him so warm and strong. So much health in him, cancer notwithstanding. Then they made love while the snow drifted down, over the trees, the grass, over the black bird perched some-where outside, waiting.

Rambo, the rottweiler from up the hill, began circling the house every time his owners let him out, whining and pawing at the windows, and one time sticking his head through the downstairs bathroom window somebody'd left open, and scaring Jillie half to death as she got out of the shower. She looked up and there was his big black head and long pink tongue halfway through the open window. So, a week later, when Jillie mentioned the dog outside, of course Zoë thought it was Rambo.

"What's that dog doing out there?" Jillie said. Zoë was in the kitchen putting dinner together while Jillie was watching for her daddy's car to come up the hill. It was Friday, the last radiation day of the week, and beginning to get dark.

"What dog, Sweetie?" Zoë said, coming into the living room.

"That dog on top of Niki."

Zoë rushed to the window and banged on the pane. "Stop that! Stop that!"

"There's a dog on top of Niki!" Will yelled from the kitchen window to Max who was outside in the backyard somewhere.

Then they were all lined up watching out the front window. Anybody could see it was too late to do anything, for there stood Niki, regal and still, one leg still caught in Jay's underwear. She didn't even turn her head when they shouted out the window, as an oddly familiar black and white dog pumped up and down in short rapid thrusts. Zoë would have had to tear them apart, and truth to tell, she didn't have the nerve to go near either one of them at a time like that. She thought of the garden hose, then remembered it was somewhere in the garage for the winter. She could feel a cool breeze through the house from the back door, and knew it didn't matter anymore who had left it open.

The dogs were circling in little hops, waiting to become disconnected. Niki whimpered every now and then. Zoë remembered all those jokes in high school about a couple doing it in the back seat of a car then getting stuck and needing the fire department to get them apart.

"Is Niki pregnant now?" Max said, as he watched the two dogs hopping round and round.

"I don't know. God, I hope not."

"That boy dog is the father," Jillie said.

"That *dog* is Roy's dog," she said aloud, without thinking. It made her shiver. It made her feel a little sick. Well, there it was.

"Who's Roy?" Will asked.

"I mean the Scarecrow Man."

She'd never said his name in front of her children before. She hadn't wanted Jillie, especially, to feel the familiarity. But she hadn't wanted to demonize him either. Or maybe a little. Just enough for them to keep their distance.

They stood at the front window watching those dogs and everybody got strangely silent. There was nothing to say. There was everything to say. Either way, it was too late for anything. They watched the dog drift back down the hill and disappear into the coming dark.

"Get her inside, Will." Zoë sat down and shut her eyes.

"No," the vet said over the phone, "there is no early pregnancy test for dogs, and no, we don't perform canine abortions. But we could do a hysterectomy."

"That seems so drastic," Zoë said.

"Then I'd recommend we just wait and see. It might not even have taken. There really is only a small window of fertility."

"How small a window?"

"Four to seven days or so."

"That seems like a pretty big window to me."

"Well, let's just see what happens."

Wait and see? Wasn't that what they were doing all the time now?

There should be a morning-after pill for dogs. This kind of thing must happen all the time—dogs making a break for it and getting knocked up.

She didn't want anything from Roy's dog inside Niki. She thought about Roy. What were the chances he was the arsonist? There hadn't been a single fire in months. But all those fires, and that awful scarecrow on his front porch. That's why he'd gotten into her dreams. But she knew the real danger was the terrible thing happening inside Jay, that dark thing there and there. No morning-after pill for that.

The next morning was a Saturday. A cold, sleety, unforgiving morning when you knew spring would never come. Zoë tried the doorbell, but couldn't hear any ring, so she knocked, at first gently, then a little harder. She wrapped her shawl more tightly around her shoulders, wished she'd thrown on a coat. She was only going down the hill, a two-minute walk, to say just one thing even though it was too late to say it.

At least the Hangman was gone. She didn't know whether the wooden flowerpot by the door had ever been there before. The soil looked rich and dark, and ready for a spring planting. She wanted to think of it as a sign of redemption. The dirty brown van was parked aslant in the middle of the driveway, no expectation of any visitor. The garbage cans were stuffed and running over with cardboard boxes as always. She looked at the curtains hanging unevenly from hooks in the wall, could see a rustling, the flicker of a hand, then the door opening a crack.

"Your dog got out. He was in our yard. He . . ." She couldn't think of the word. *Molested? Attacked?* "He assaulted our dog."

"*Assaulted?* You mean they got in a fight?"

"Not exactly a fight. My dog's in heat. So will you please keep your dog fenced in?"

"I guess I could ask you to keep *your* dog fenced in," he said in a low, tight voice.

Roy stayed halfway inside the house while they talked. Zoë tried not to look inside but couldn't help it. She couldn't see a thing. Then there he was, nosing Roy's hand. His black and white face, amber eyes so familiar, so strange. Roy turned and said something, and the dog sat down and stared out at her. He gave off a low growl. Roy told him to cut it out. She's a friend.

"He dug his way out," Roy said through the half-opened door. "He dug a hole under the fence."

Zoë just stared at him. "You're right," she said after a moment. "My dog got out by accident too." She wanted to take a step back but wasn't sure where the porch was. She didn't dare look away. He was taller than she'd thought.

"Your dog has been drivin' him crazy, you know," he said with a half-smile. Even so she could see that his mouth had too many teeth. His long, thin face, his high cheekbones, his deep-set gray eyes, the thin brown hair in a ponytail as before. But without the baseball cap she could see he was balding.

Then Zoë was gone, half running up the hill.

"He's a good dog!" Roy shouted after her, as she made her way home.

They were all sitting around the dinner table, just finishing up. It was already late. The cake and ice cream were hiding in the outside refrigerator, but Zoë kept trying to sneak looks at Jay to see if he was up to all this. He was quiet as usual for a Friday night, but she thought she could see dark circles under his eyes, though it may have just been the fading light. "It's getting dark in here. Somebody turn on the lights." She hadn't meant to sound so urgent. Max got up and flipped on the lights and Jay bloomed into health.

He was well into the chest-to-throat phase and Zoë had long ago stopped asking him how things went. He just showed up, offered his body to the Radiation God, that big, humming bullet of a machine, shut his eyes, and got the hell out of there, careful not to look at anybody too closely or overhear too much conversation. But the days he had to wait too long must have been terrible. It was all the other people you couldn't help noticing—the ones wheeled in from upstairs on gurneys or in wheelchairs, the ones who'd already lost their hair, the ones who looked like death camp prisoners. She was always ashamed at how grateful she was she didn't have to drive him.

But it was getting harder and harder to make it to Friday. Mondays were good days, full of the energy stored up from the weekend off, but by Friday morning Jay could hardly get himself out of bed. The alarm would ring and ring and she'd be the one to reach over him and shut it off. He was sleeping through the bird thumping against the upstairs window now, just a sleepy, distant reminder of things gone crazy inside and out.

Still. Tonight they were painting the town red, so to speak. "We're celebrating," Jay said, and went outside for the Rocky Road ice cream and cake and brought it in. Jillie and Will grabbed the blue and white ice cream bowls and passed them around. Max had gotten the jar of caramel syrup from the pantry and set it in the middle of the table. Jay reached for the carton of ice cream and dished everybody double scoops.

"Let's toast," Jillie said. So they all clinked spoons and dug in.

"What are we toasting for?" Max said. Zoë and Jay looked at each other and tamped down their smiles into mysterious airs. "Just life. To life."

"And magic," Max said. "Magic that doesn't hurt."

"You mean no black magic," Will said too earnestly for the moment.

Then Jay sat back and began rubbing his neck. It was all in slow motion. It was over in an instant.

"What's wrong?" Zoë said, getting up.

"Pressure," he said. "Like my throat's closing." She could hardly hear him. He was getting sweaty, turning chalky as he spoke.

"Put your head down. Go get a cold washrag, Will."

"Oh," Jay said, "I feel awful." His hands gripped the side of the table.

"Does your chest hurt?" she said, leaning over.

He reached toward her. "I'm gonna pass out." His forehead hit the edge of the table with a smack as he slipped through her hands to the floor.

"Somebody give me the *phone!*"

By the time the aid-car made its uncertain way up their hill, Jay was already sitting up against the dining room wall, holding an ice bag over the goose-egg beginning on his forehead.

It was the ice cream, the medic said.

"How could ice cream do something like this?" Zoë practically shouted at him. Then she thought she saw that wizened-up old Devil, perched like a sleek black crow in the corner of the room. She thought she heard him whisper something. She thought he whispered *gotcha*.

Zoë knew what he meant. *You better be ready because from now on anything can happen.*

"Didn't anybody tell him not to eat cold things during radiation to the throat?" the medic said, packing up.

"It seems like an easy thing to tell a guy," Jay said from the couch. The ice cream sat melting in the carton in the middle of the table. The half-eaten bowls of ice cream lay abandoned on the table, or spilling over onto the tablecloth. Jillie stood on a chair, dipping her fingers into the carton and licking them like frosting. The dog stood with her paws on the kitchen counter, licking the cake they had forgotten.

So now they knew that second-phase radiation could trigger esophageal spasms in the presence of cold things, contractions so intense you could pass out thinking you were having a heart attack. Especially if you happened to be worn out or under stress.

But hey, who was under stress around here? Look how jolly they all were. Zoë herself was doing fine, by day. It was only the things that came into her dreams that frightened her.

"Is Dad gonna be okay?" Will asked that night at bedtime, back now in his room and trying his best to hold on to his dignity.

"He's already okay," Zoë told him. "He wasn't in danger for a minute, even when he fainted. It was just the radiation."

"And it will get rid of it?"

"That's right."

"And it won't come back?"

It took effort to say it, but she did. "No. It won't ever come back."

She said goodnight and went to leave.

"Could you leave my door open?"

"Sure. Goodnight, Sweetheart."

"Too many things going on," he said and shut his eyes.

She turned to go but looked back and thought she saw Will holding something over his chest. Probably a Bible. Made her wonder if they should be going back to church. She left the door all the way open, switching on the light as she turned down the hall. It seemed like nature had just gone crazy that month. Dogs in heat, birds drunk on elderberries, slugs on computer paper, and savage, mutinous cells so tiny they could only be seen by a microscope. Maybe it was just a spell they were under, a spell you could throw off if only you knew the right incantation.

Sleep was a far country, and so she lay in bed and thought of the little boy in the house in the woods and wondered if she could dream him again. It had been a long time. Why not? There were mysterious powers at work these days, floating through the air on the slip of every breath. She always began with the moon, which tonight was so high in the sky it looked almost like morning. She looked for the flickering blue light and there it was. She could see him looking out his bedroom window at the old doghouse out beyond the clothesline that hung low and icy in the moonlight. She thought she saw the black bird perched on it. The dog had stopped barking and pulling on the rope that tied him to one of the metal posts that held up the clothesline. He'd disappeared inside the old dog house that had come with the house they'd rented last summer. The little boy was hoping the dog had just curled up into the wool blanket he'd smuggled out to him a couple of hours ago to keep him from howling.

Dad had said, "You listen real *good*, boy," grabbing his shirt collar, "'cause I'm gonna blast that dog if he don't shut up." But it was too cold to do more than threaten to go outside with the shotgun, so Dad had only reached for the channel changer and leaned back in his chair. The boy stood in the hallway looking at the back of Dad's chair, looking at the back of Dad's head, stood looking at the front door. The lock to the back door had gotten jammed some way, and could not be opened.

"*Piney's* a stupid name for a dog," Dad had said that morning when he'd brought him to the front porch. "Why'd you name him something stupid like that? Well, he can't stay in the house. I don't care how cold it is. He's somebody else's dog anyways. Look," he said, grabbing the dog's collar. The boy had made a floor for the doghouse out of some old cardboard, then he'd found an old rope in the shed and tied it in a big loopy knot around the dog's collar, then tied the other end to the metal post, so he couldn't run away. He didn't ever want to lose that dog.

The Sky Is Falling

"So, who do you think you'd have married if you hadn't married Jay?" Meghan was saying. They were halfway to the cabins, beginning the long drive around the north end of Crescent Lake on their way to the ocean. Zoë looked over at her and began to laugh. Meghan kept her eyes on the road. Every now and then a logging truck loomed around the corner, making a wide-angled turn. They felt the car shudder every time one of them barreled past.

"I have no idea. I never really thought about it." She knew what Meghan was doing. Reminding her of her very own solitary self.

"You've never thought about it? *Never* thought about it?"

"No," she said. "I got married my last year of college. I wasn't ever with anybody but Jay."

"Not even in high school?"

"Oh, well sure, in high school."

"I'd have married Denny Reagan," Meghan said, braking for the next long curve, as the road wound its way around the lake.

"Denny Reagan! Then you'd be *Meghan Reagan*!"

The tires hit the gravel at the side of the road and Meghan braked almost to a stop.

"I'd better slow down," she said, pulling back out onto the road. The sun was coming through the fir trees alongside the road in patches. It was like driving through sunspots. A golden green everywhere.

"Prelapsarian," Meghan said.

Zoë leaned her head back on the headrest, felt the sun on her face. She was trying hard not to think about everybody back home.

"If you'd married David Bowie, you'd be *Zoë Bowie*." Meghan was smiling, her gold loop earrings catching the light. She was good at bringing Zoë out of the dark. She was the best.

It was fun to be in the car with Meghan, think about wacky things, laugh like mad. Jay'd had to practically shove her out the door. He'd said it was just what the doctor ordered, her doctor who'd threatened her with antidepressants, if she didn't snap out of it. *Find another doctor*, she'd put on her TO DO list. Still, she couldn't shake this vague sadness and fear.

"Jay's going to be all right," Meghan said. "You believe that, don't you?"

Zoë didn't say anything. She wouldn't cry. She wouldn't do that to Meghan after all this work setting things up.

"And we're not going to talk about *work*." Meghan's office was just down the hall from Zoë's. Some days they did nothing but talk about work. Now this hiatus—the days before finals and nothing to grade—*reading period*, when all their students were supposed to be studying furiously but God knows what they were actually doing. Well, work talk was banned for the weekend, along with every other dark and complicating thing.

It was night by the time they got to the resort. *I wouldn't have married anybody else*, Zoë said to herself, as they settled into their little cabin tucked safely in the trees on a cliff above the ocean. *Kalaloch*. A Pacific Northwest Indian name. She liked this place already. But it was late, and though she knew the ocean was out there, she couldn't see a thing.

"I wish *we* were going off for the weekend."

"Me too," Jay had said, as he drew her into a hug like always. "But I'm glad you're going." He kissed the top of her head, slipped his hand under her sweatshirt.

She lay her head on his shoulder, hugged him tight. "I'm sorry about everything. I can't believe what I said to you."

"So long ago I forgot all about it."

"Not so long ago."

"I'm just sorry to put you through all this."

She could see tears in his eyes. "Don't. Please don't," she said and kissed his face. They stood there in the middle of the kitchen, holding on. Then she whispered, "Jay?"

"What?"

"They're coming!"

"What's coming?"

"Sides!"

"They'd better not be."

"Oh yes they'd better." And she raked her fingers under his arms and down his sides. It always drove him crazy. He couldn't stop laughing.

"All right for you!" And he pulled her to him and tongued her ear. Then he caught her arms and held them behind her back. "Double chicken wing. I've got you now."

It was his favorite wrestling hold. Hers too. He'd taught her the double chicken wing escape. She could never do it though.

"All right, all right. You win," she said, leaning into him. He wrapped his arms around her, then gentled her breasts.

"So don't even think about Monday. Monday is going to be fine. That's why you're getting away."

She could feel his warmth, breathed in his smell. "*Old Spice*, huh? Is that for me?"

"Didn't want you to forget me."

"So tell me, kiddo," Meghan said from the other side of the wall.

"I'm going to sleep now. I'm asleep already. I'll think about it tomorrow, as the saying goes."

"I'm sorry," Meghan said softly. "I was just trying to get us back to when we didn't belong to anybody but ourselves. Know what I mean?"

Zoë rolled over and tucked the blankets around her chin. But she didn't go to sleep. It was only a double bed, but it felt too big, forsaken, tenantless. She propped up both pillows against the headboard in the middle of the bed, and stretched out. She wasn't going to sleep next to any empty place. She listened to the wind in the high fir trees and tried not to think about anything.

She didn't know quite when she fell asleep but knew the instant she woke up she'd slept through the whole night, and no bad dreams. She wanted to see the ocean. A whole day stretched ahead and she didn't have to plan it around anybody. Not even Meghan, who was still asleep. The kids seemed far away. So did Jay. The morning was hers, a present to be unwrapped. She opened the curtains and sat down by the front window. She watched the shadows on the grass retreat into the woods as the sun rose up over the treetops and spread over the ocean below.

By eleven the day was warming up and they'd packed up their stuff and headed for the beach. The breeze was cool coming off the ocean as they walked through the tall grass to the path that led down to the beach. They took off their sandals and walked in the cool morning sand. They found a large piece of driftwood, propped their beach bags against it, and spread their towels over the white sand.

"I just want to lie in the sun and not think about anything. I want to lie here all day," Zoë said, stretching out.

"Well, that's what we came here for. To do nothing. Or anything we want." Zoë could hear her rustling through the beach bag. Out of the corner of her eye she watched her settle down with a book propped up on her bare, tan belly. Meghan always committed every inch of her skin to the sun. She'd tied her hair back with a red scarf.

Zoë pulled her straw sun hat over her face and looked up at the sky through the latticed little cupola she'd made for herself. She breathed in the dry straw smell, the little breath of cool air fluttering under the brim of her hat, her coconut suntan lotion—and closed her eyes.

She wanted to store up as much sun as she could. It felt safe lying on the sand under the sun, as though the ground wouldn't give way, or the sky come falling down. All these months she'd waited for the phone call in the night, the house in flames, blood clot in the heart, the meteorite from a starless sky.

The sky is falling, the sky is falling, Henny Penny cried, jumping up from under the acorn tree where she'd been scratching around in the leaves. How the kids loved that book, partly because the sky had not fallen after all, and because it said their name. Henny Penny, Ducky Lucky, Turkey Lurkey, Meghan Reagan, Zoë Bowie. She had been running around all spring just like Henny Penny. Some dark, soundless thing had fallen out of the sky, that was for sure.

The sun was hot and getting hotter. She could feel sun prickles on her legs and arms, felt the sun penetrating her bones. A sun-deprived person gets depressed, thinks crazy thoughts. Even the dog, with all her Arctic fur, sought out the sunspots on the carpet. That's what Jay needed, a whole summer of sun.

They'd told Jay to make the radiation machine into a sun, but he could never conjure up the sun in that cold, despairing place. The heat from the sun was better than the dark fire of radiation any day. There had been too much worrying over fires and cancer cells anyway. It was all too complicated. Whatever was happening to him was invisible to the eye, unthinkable to the mind, and an affront to the heart. Well, on Monday, they'd find out whether any of it had worked.

Will's science teacher kept telling the class how dangerous radiation was, had assigned the kids the nuclear holocaust movie *The Day After* but said to watch it with the family, thank God. Will couldn't see how something that could make your hair fall out and peel your skin off could also make you well. It was just one more mystery that assaulted him.

"It's like X-rays out there. You can't see it or feel it or taste it or smell it," somebody had explained in the movie, "but it goes right through your bones." Rayed and X-rayed, Jay had his own nuclear nightmare. He knew what radiation sickness was. Hair falling out in private places, nausea, sores that didn't heal. One morning during his shower, all his body hair just washed down the drain. He kept his hair though—his sandy blonde, wavy hair, which caught the sun in any light. She was glad the kids got Jay's hair. Her own dark, thick hair was a different kind of nightmare. That's why she always kept it short and to the point. Had anybody told them what would happen if the radiation didn't work? Her heart felt tight, fluttery. She snapped the rubber band on her wrist.

"What did you do that for?" Meghan said. "Didn't that hurt?"

"Well, of course it hurt, that's the point." She rubbed her wrist. "I'm breaking a thought circuit."

"What were you really doing?"

"That's what I was really doing. It's something I learned in biofeedback."

"You're kidding," Meghan said, rolling over onto her stomach. She propped herself up on one elbow, shaded her eyes with her hand.

"When I get a thought that drives me crazy, I snap myself and after a hundred snaps my wrist is so sore I'm not going to think about *that* anymore."

"So what were you thinking about?" Meghan sat up.

"Oh, I don't know." Zoë nestled into a gentle curve in the driftwood. "Just that Jay has this big CAT scan on Monday to see how things are going."

"I didn't know that."

"I wasn't dwelling on it. It just sort of pops up every now and then."

Meghan was rubbing coconut oil onto her legs, then wiped her hands on her belly. She was already turning brown. Zoë looked at her white legs, which weren't turning anything, so far, thanks to her SPF 45 sunblock. Meghan screwed the bottle top back on and stuffed it in her bag.

"Pretty funny, huh. Jay gets cancer and I'm the one who winds up in therapy. Well, biofeedback, anyway. But you had to see this psychologist before the insurance would pay for the sessions." She didn't want to talk to anybody. She just wanted to learn how to relax a little. Or keep her heart from skipping beat after beat until she thought her chest would burst from all that unsung breath and blood.

She'd waited for that psychologist in a tiny office with no windows. There on the bookshelf by her chair was Virginia Woolf's *The Waves*, and she remembered thinking, *Okay, maybe this won't be so bad after all*.

"I see you have a book by Virginia Woolf," she said first thing after he sat down.

"Oh, those aren't really my books," he said, picking up a manila folder with her name on it.

"Then this isn't really your office?"

"No," he kind of snorted.

"And you aren't really the therapist?"

"Heh heh heh. You have quite a sense of humor there," he said, sitting back, crossing his legs. "Tell me what brings you here."

"I thought it might help me feel more relaxed," she said, looking at the bookcase full of somebody else's books. She wanted the therapist who owned *The Waves*.

"So. Tell me what seems to be making you tense." He tried to smile, but only got the lower half of his face going.

She took a deep breath, looked at his doughy face and the long strands of black hair combed over the top of his head and knew she wasn't going to tell him anything. He cleared his throat, and crossed his legs the other way. You could see a stretch of white skin above his black sock. She thought of the Devil sitting in the corner in her dream.

She was watching his pant leg creep up his fat calf and wanted to scream, *You are making me tense!* "No, really. I just need to learn some relaxation techniques to help me sleep better." She knew she had to say something so this would be over, but she couldn't think of a single thing to say.

"But he kept at it, you know? He *knew* there was something I wasn't telling him, which of course there was." They were both sitting on beach towels, leaning against the log. The tops of Zoë's knees were turning pink.

"I'd have gotten up and walked right out," Meghan said.

"I know you would have, but I just sat there. He got it out of me, though. I was crying by the time we were done. He got this smug look on his face, like he'd *won*. I wanted to smack him with Virginia Woolf upside the head."

"But did you feel any better talking about it? Getting it out, I mean?"

"No."

"I didn't think so."

"But the biofeedback technician was great. She taught me the trick with the rubber band. And the cobalt blue shield you conjure whenever you need to feel safe."

She taught her deep breathing, showed how you could do the whole routine in ninety seconds without anybody taking one look at you and crossing to the other side of the street. She showed Zoë how to focus on one perfect image as she breathed in and out. And it was always this—lying in the sun listening to the ocean, or floating on the waves.

"So sometimes I get myself to sleep thinking about a place like this, and now here it is."

"What's that all over your elbow?" Meghan said, touching a black splotch on Zoë's arm.

"Hey! you've got some on your feet."

"So do you!"

They looked at the sand. They could see little dabs of tar bubbling up out of the sand here and there.

"Should we move?"

"I think it's everywhere. Let's wait and see if it gets worse."

"Oil spills," Zoë said. "Toxic waste." She thought of the article she'd read that spring about salmon in Puget Sound swimming around with tumors all over their bodies. She thought of the fishing they were going to do this summer to get Jay well.

"How do we get this off?" Meghan asked. "Don't we need turpentine or something?"

"What if we can't?"

"A thought for your rubber band."

—

It was past time for lunch, so they opened the lunch basket and took out the sandwiches they'd bought at the deli on the trip up. Meghan lifted out the bottle of wine she'd put in the cooler, and twisted open the cap. She held it up. The bottle was sweating in the sun.

"I read somewhere that drinking in the sun makes you drunk. It goes straight to the brain, or something like that," Zoë said.

"I read that drinking makes you drunk."

"I mean more drunk than you'd be if you drank in the shade."

Meghan took a long swig, grinned, and wiped off the top. She passed the bottle to Zoë and she took a swallow too. Then Meghan got out the Dixie cups and poured them each a cupful.

They sat cross-legged in the sun eating salami and cheese on thick slices of French bread, passing the wine back and forth. The Dixie cups had tipped over into the sand long ago. Meghan took off her scarf, shook out her hair, and stretched her arms up to the sun. Then she unfastened her top and lay on her stomach, trying to even out her tan. The tops of Zoë's legs were getting red so she turned over on her stomach, too, and pulled her straps off her shoulders.

"God, I hate having to hold my stomach in all the time, you know?" Meghan said, propping back up.

"Why do you think I'm wearing a one-piece? Twenty-seven months of stretched-out skin."

"Why twenty-seven months?"

"Three kids. Nine months times three."

"Oh. Sure." Meghan lay back down, tilted her hat over her face.

Zoë pulled out the suntan lotion and made an *M* on Meghan's back and rubbed it in circles.

"That feels good."

Then they both sat up against the driftwood, watching the ocean slip from shore then gather itself back up, that easy rhythm like breathing or a heartbeat.

"My turn." She handed the suntan lotion to Meghan. She drew on a big creamy Z. "Z is for *Zoë. Zoë* is Greek for *Life.* That's you."

Zoë felt tears gather in her eyes. She shaded her eyes and watched the sun turn the water into stars. It hurt to look at it. "I just want enough life to go around."

"There is, Zoë."

"I know." She put her arm around Meghan, lay her head on her shoulder. "Thanks."

Meghan patted Zoë's knee and leaned back. "It really is great not to have to hold in our stomachs."

Zoë pulled her hat down over her eyes. "Did I tell you the dog's pregnant?"

"What happened?"

"What do you mean what *happened*?" Zoë laughed out loud. "What do you think happened?"

"I mean, did you plan it or what?"

"No." She laughed again. "We didn't *plan* it. This guy's dog knocked her up."

"What guy?"

"Oh, just that crazy neighbor with the Halloween stuff."

"You don't have to tell him, do you?"

"I already did."

"What did he say?'

"That it was my fault for letting the dog out."

"God, Zoë, don't talk to him again."

Zoë had to laugh. "We had her all cooped up in the house wearing Jay's underwear with a Kotex stuck in the crotch like always, but she got out anyway." She shook her head. "You know. Life."

"God. A pregnant dog." Meghan lay back down and folded her hands over her belly. "I remember this girl in my seventh-grade math class who got up to do a problem on the board and her Kotex fell out and this kid named Dickie Gardner stepped on it and it stuck to his shoe. He walked to the front of the class before he saw it."

Zoë started to laugh and knocked the bottle over into the sand. She wiped off the sand and took a long drink. "In seventh grade I knew a girl with three nipples. She went to the doctor because she thought it was a growth."

"Where was it? In the middle?"

"No," Zoë said. "Under her arm pit."

Meghan was laughing so hard by now she motioned for the bottle and raised it to the sky. "Yes," she said. "Oh, yes." She took a long swallow. "Almost gone," she said, passing it over. "My mother sent me a birthday card once and it showed this woman with *three* giant boobs, and when you opened the card it said, '*Nobody's Perfect!*'"

Zoe took another swig. Her tongue felt numb. "I always wanted really big broobs."

"Big what?"

"Boobs."

"Well, I hated mine so much I slept on my stomach all ninth grade."

"I think you're very Marilyn Monroe–esque," Zoë said.

"I think you're very Audrey Hepburn–esque."

"We're Laurel and Hardy," Zoë said.

"Then I'm Laurel and you're Hardy."

"I'm Abbott and you're Costello."

"Okay," Meghan said. "I'm Gertrude Stein and you're Alice B. Toklas."

"I'm Thelma, you're Louise."

"I'm beer, you're champagne," Meghan said.

"No you're not," Zoë said. "You're Cabernet Sauvignon. You're the finest wine there is."

"Want another swig?"

"You finish it," Zoë said. Her office was two doors down from Zoë's, but she could hear Meghan every time she laughed. She never told her how that laugh kept her going all winter. "I love you, Meghan the Pagan."

"I love you too."

Zoë looked down the beach. She felt hot, a little vague. The afternoon sun was making the water shimmer. A solitary heron touched down on the sand bar far out from the shore. A man and woman were coming down the beach, walking ankle-deep in the surf, the cuffs on their trousers rolled up. His hand touched her neck, pulled her to him. He kissed her hair, and she tightened her arm around his waist.

"Honeymooners," Meghan said. "You can always tell. What do you think happens? Why don't people married a long time look like that?"

"Some do," Zoë said, imagining her arm tightening, the kiss on her hair.

"You and Jay do." She tilted her head back and took a long swallow, letting the last few drops slide down her tongue. "Well, that's that. Wish we'd brought down another bottle. I know. I've already had too much."

"I won't even be able to climb back up to the cabin as it is," Zoë said.

"Can I tell you something?" She leaned over and hugged her knees. "That night at the party when Jay and I were slow dancing? I kissed Jay on the mouth."

Zoë took in a quick, sharp breath. A hummingbird fluttered in her chest. She looked at the couple far down the beach. "So what did he do?"

"He said thank you."

Zoë laughed, but it caught in her throat. "He would say that, wouldn't he?"

"I love him too," Meghan said. "Not like you'd think though."

"Enough love to go around," Zoë said. But there wasn't. Not anymore.

In the distance she could see several hot air balloons drifting high over the water. "I always wanted to ride in one of those," she said, watching them float away. Everything was in slow motion. The edges of the afternoon were softening, slowing down. She looked over at Meghan, who lay on her stomach, her mouth open. Zoë propped her sun hat over her face.

Jay had ridden in one of those last year for Father's Day. A sunset balloon ride with a champagne twilight dinner, the ad had said. But dinner was a couple of wieners roasted over a propane flame, and a bag of Doritos. They had apple juice, not champagne, and they never got higher than the treetops.

She could feel the sun growing hotter, could feel the sun burn her legs and chest. She threw a towel over her legs, lay back down, put the straw hat over her face, and breathed in the salt air. She was sleepy, getting sleepier. She was going to a safe place. She closed her eyes and watched the clouds floating across her straw, latticed ceiling, felt the drowsy swell of the waves. She was watching a solitary cloud sweep across the sky, coming closer and closer, until she could see it wasn't a cloud at all, but a white, hot air balloon drifting high over the sand. The balloon was high above the ocean now. She watched it until it wasn't a balloon anymore, but just another cloud. She woke with dry, salty tears streaming down her face.

The sun was shimmering over the water. She could hardly look at it. They sat there without speaking while the tar bubbled up in black, shiny blotches here and there. The broken world.

"I'm going for a walk," Meghan said.

"Well, don't step in it."

Meghan didn't answer, didn't turn around to wave goodbye.

Zoë watched her sway over the white, white sand, her long blonde hair tied back in a red scarf, her red and gold sarong caught up in the breeze. Two golden retrievers were playing tag just at the edge of the water, their ears flopping in the wind as they ran, back and forth, back and forth across the sand. How she loved her. How suddenly she hated her. Zoë should have been Marilyn Monroe that night and never, not ever, the nurse.

It was getting late. She'd been covered up with her beach towel and sweatshirt for an hour or so, but Meghan had come back from her walk and was baking her front side again. The wind was picking up. She could tell the afternoon was over.

"I hate lying on my stomach," Meghan said. "You can't read without getting a neck cramp."

"It's the front side that everybody sees anyway."

"Just never turn your back."

"Well, I must have turned my back. That's when all this stuff happened."

"So if you'd been watching some way, you could have stopped it? You know that's not true."

"I'm going on up," Zoë said. "I'm going to take a shower." She gathered up her towel and bag, then stood there in the cooling sand holding her sandals, looking up at the cloudless sky.

It was dark by the time they'd finished dinner and walked back to the cabin from the lodge. They couldn't see the ocean, but could hear it as they walked along the gravel path. They settled in and Meghan built a fire while Zoë locked everything up tight. Meghan knew just how to crisscross the kindling, where to light the newspapers, how long to wait before putting on the log. Zoë watched the first sparks take hold then spread like little rivers of flame that pooled at the edges of the wood. She wondered which the arsonist loved best—the suspense of waiting for it to ignite—or the blaze itself. It was nice not to think of him. So why was she? She snapped the rubber band on her wrist.

They were sitting in front of the fire, working on the other bottle of wine. It felt cozy and safe, tucked away on the edge of the bluff overlooking the roaring ocean.

"I'm glad I came," she said to Meghan. "Thanks for doing this for me."

"Hey, it was fun for me too. It's good to get away once in a while—from the men, I mean. You know me and my boyfriends. We should do this again. And not wait so long this time."

"We should," Zoë said, settling back on the couch, closing her eyes. She was missing Jay already. "Pass me the wine, girlfriend." They'd abandoned the glasses long ago.

"Almost gone," Meghan said.

"Do you miss being married?" Zoë asked.

"To Steve?"

"Well, who else then?" Zoë laughed.

"No, I don't miss being married to Steve."

"I didn't mean to joke about it."

"Good guy, bad marriage. You know we weren't getting along, and I thought, *Why am I doing this? Why am I sticking this out, with no kids to worry about?*"

"But you did."

"Theoretically."

"What do you mean?"

"It was somebody else. The reason was somebody else."

"How come I didn't know?"

"Same reason I didn't know about the CAT scan or any of the other things you've been going through. All I can do is watch you snap your rubber band and try to read your mind."

"Why do we do that, do you think? Keep things to ourselves? Aren't women supposed to tell their best friends everything?"

"That's why we've been such good friends," Meghan said. "We're the same that way. We really can read each other's minds. God, I think I'm drunk. Glad it's all gone." She turned the bottle upside down and not a drop left. "I'm sorry I said anything about the party."

"It's okay," Zoë said, and surprised herself that she meant it.

"It was the first time I'd seen him since the hospital, and I felt so awful thinking maybe . . ." Meghan shook her head, smacked her forehead harder than she'd intended.

"Ow!" Tears came to her eyes. "I'm so stupid. Of course he's not. He's going to be fine."

Zoë looked into her wide blue eyes with the golden flecks she'd always loved. And knew she'd kissed him only because she'd run out of time. Or so she thought.

"You and Jay. It's like loving the same person twice over. I can't explain it."

Zoë wanted to gather her up and never let her go. So she asked, "If anything ever happened to me, you know, theoretically, would you look out for him?" But what she wanted to say was, *If anything ever happened to* him, *would you look out for* me? though to admit it would be a betrayal.

"I know what you meant," Meghan said. "I already am." She took Zoë's hand, rubbed her palm, the inside of her wrist. "No more rubber bands. Your wrist is bruised." And she kissed it.

Then she got up to check the fire. She was kneeling by the hearth, pushing the logs around with the poker, but the fire just flamed up briefly then flickered down. "My true love," she said so softly Zoë almost didn't hear her. "He was married too."

The fire was dying but neither of them tried to save it. The room had turned chilly and Zoë got up to get the comforter. They could hear the wind in the trees, could hear the darkness coming on. It settled things and tamped down their words into a silent telling. They watched as the light drained out of the sky.

They watched the fire for a long time. It took a long while to die completely out. "Hey, did they ever catch that guy who set all those fires?"

Zoë's heart closed like a fist.

"No," Zoë said. "They never did." She looked out the window at her reflection staring back at her. Anybody could be out there looking in. She got up to pull the curtains shut and saw Roy's long face, high cheekbones, in the corner of the window. She saw his shadow against their porch light, the shadow of his dog at his side. She saw his brown van parked crossways in the driveway and the Hangman on the porch, the Halloween strobe light against his front window. She sat down and pulled the comforter tight.

The last smoky tendril rose up and disappeared. She shut her eyes. She could still smell it and that's when she knew there had been another fire. He was just getting started again. She couldn't tell how she knew but she did.

"Does he still give you nightmares?"

"A little."

"Do you still have those dreams about the little boy in the woods?"

"I know his father beats him, and he has a dog," Zoë said. "It's always so cold. The dream is always the same, but then it kind of grows. Am I making all this up in my sleep then? Or are the dreams just happening?"

"You've asked your dreams to tell you things. You know your dream is real because you know you're inside it when it's happening. It's called 'lucid dreaming.'"

"I like dreaming about him. In the dream I want to help him. It's sad. But it's like writing a story. Lucid dreaming, huh?"

"Maybe. I think so."

"The arsonist is back."

"God, Zoë. How do you know that?"

"It's strange, but I do. He did something awful."

"But you can't know that."

"Some way I do. I kind of dreamed it outside of sleeping."

"You've got to stop thinking about it."

"I know I do."

"Maybe you should tell somebody. About that neighbor, anyway?"

Zoë felt her heart collapse. She could never tell anyone about him. She didn't know why. Yet how could she not? The bottle of wine lay on the floor next to their overturned glasses. Zoë closed her eyes, took some long, slow breaths, could feel her legs and arms getting heavy. They could still hear the night wind through the trees.

"You really love him, don't you," Meghan said.

Zoë couldn't say anything. She just kind of nodded and pulled the comforter back up.

"With Jay it was you, you know. It was only ever you."

She'd had a comforter down in the family room, but it still felt chilly. They'd been watching TV, nothing special, just a Saturday night and too tired for anything else, when Jay started to cough. Zoë looked at him bending over, watched his shoulders jerk each time he coughed.

"Why are you coughing?" she said.

Jay just looked at her. "That's a weird question."

"You don't have a cold, do you?"

"I'm coughing because my throat tickles, and *no*, I don't have a cold."

"Maybe you're allergic to something."

"Well, it *is* pretty dusty around here."

"Well I'm sorry my housekeeping isn't good enough for you."

He just glared at her.

They were coping in their usual shameful manner. Anger was the easiest emotion of all. "If it spreads, it will show up in the lungs next," Frankel had said in January, when he'd put Jay on the every-eight-weeks-chest-X-ray regimen.

But Jay couldn't stop coughing. He got up to get a glass of water.

In the lungs in the lungs in the lungs was what Zoë heard every time he coughed. But she knew only too well that passing one test only meant having to go through it all over again. The checkup rhythm took them to the edge every two months. Catastrophe or reprieve, the disaster was real either way. As for Zoë, there were too many days left to worry about them all, but that's what she was doing, all right, one by one.

Jay came back into the room and sat down. But the coughing didn't stop, just slowed down.

"I really wish you'd stop that," she said.

"Really."

"Yes, really. I wish you'd cut it out."

He coughed again. Just to make her mad, she thought.

"I hate it when you cough like that so just cut it out."

"*You're* the one who should cut it out."

Zoë stood up. All of a sudden, she was shouting. "I counted on you," she yelled at him. "I counted on you to be stronger than me! You watched it grow and you never did anything about it. So don't you keep on coughing, goddamnit, because I'm afraid to love you anymore."

"Well then don't." He turned to get up.

"Stop it stop it stop it!" she said, picking up the pillow and raising her arm to hit him with it. But her arm came down with the pillow and her elbow struck the side of his face.

"Oh!" he said, doubling over.

He just sat there with his head in his hands without saying anything. Zoë was crying by then. It felt like the end of something.

"I feel so fragile," she said, reaching for him.

But he turned away from her and stood up to leave. "We're all fragile, Zoë." She just sat there and let him go. Sat there and let him go down the hall past the hall light and into the dark.

She couldn't sleep. She was listening for the ocean, but could only hear the wind, now just a whispering at the edge of the windowsill. Her rubber band had fallen off somewhere in the bed, so she tried snapping her wrist with her finger. Finally she just let the scene play all the way out. It was the last time she'd gone with Jay to the doctor.

"The CAT scan will tell us how well the treatment's working," Frankel was saying again. He looked at Jay, then at her. She thought he was measuring his words.

"What if we find out it didn't work?" she finally said. Jay gave her a there-she-goes-again glance and looked away.

"Oh, I think we'll find it worked very well," Frankel said.

"But what if it didn't? I mean what I'm getting at is, are there other things you could do? You wouldn't just quit on us, right?"

"Of course not. But remember, those cells have just been getting whacked with X-rays."

She snapped her finger against her wrist. She hardly felt a thing.

She'd gone almost the whole day without snapping her rubber band more than a couple of times, gone a whole day without thinking in that tragic way. Well, tomorrow they were going home, and she'd lost her rubber band. The next day was Monday, CAT-scan day. She wondered what they'd done to bring this on. "Nothing," she said out loud.

She knelt on the bed in that tiny bedroom and pulled back the curtain. The moon was floating over the fir trees high on the bluff. She turned on the light and caught her reflection in the mirror above the dresser. In that half-light she could see shadows under her eyes. When did that happen? She pulled on her sweats, put on her parka, and headed for the winding path down to the beach.

She stood at the top of the path in the tall grass, watching the moon drift across the sea toward the horizon. The beach stretched out on either side then vanished into the dark. It was easy making her way down the path by moonlight. She stood on the shore and stretched out her arms, turned her face to the sky, then closed her eyes and listened to the whispering sea. She could feel the water seep through the soles of her shoes but just stood there in the wet sand and listened.

Little waves lapped and drew back, foaming in the moonlight. A gust of wind sent wreaths of sea-foam rolling across the beach. She felt the salt spray on her face, watched the sea-foam sail down the beach. This ocean, the moonlight, the sea-foam. It would be enough, she thought. Her very own life.

Then the moment passed, and the terror returned. She looked down and saw that the surf had come up to her ankles. She walked back up the beach and found a piece of driftwood to sit on. She heard something rustling in the tall grass against the bluff but knew nobody was there. Her ankles and feet were wet and beginning to get cold. She looked out at the sea again. The moon path had disappeared. The sea looked dark, angry, too wide to imagine. She thought about sharks and eels with great snapping jaws, undiscovered sea serpents, a leviathan of biblical proportions, a weighty final darkness. That's where Jay would be. Lost somewhere out there beneath the vast, empty sky.

She looked up at the moon floating into the clouds. "To whoever might be listening," she said out loud, "I've come empty-handed." She held no offering. Could she call it forth? Speak its name? She was afraid of hymns sung off key, words in the wrong order. So she would go silent before it. Just to speak its name would be a prayer, but she knew no one to call by name. Her silence would be as close to prayer as she could come.

Monday

He wasn't actually late. Okay, he was a little late, and Zoë thought he'd be here by now, but she wasn't really worried, even though she used to worry all the time. She'd never wait like that now, and that's not what she was doing. She might glance out the window, if she were going past it anyway, but she wouldn't just stand there. Maybe she should have gone with him, been there to hold his hand while the doctor delivered the news, but somebody had to be here for the kids, start dinner, keep things together.

"Anything happen while I was at the beach?" she asked Will, who'd been trying not to look like he was waiting too. She'd gotten home late last night and hadn't really caught up with the kids.

"There was another fire," he said under his breath. His eyes were unblinking, his hands cold when she touched them.

"Where was it?" she said before she could stop herself.

"Lynnwood."

"Well that's not really around here," she said, though of course it was.

"It was a retirement place. A couple of people didn't make it out in time." Will caught the terror in her eyes.

"Shit, shit, shit," she said, and reached to hug him, but he ducked out and went into the living room to stand by the window. He knew way too much. He shouldn't be tracking stuff like this. She followed him, putting an arm around his shoulder, which he permitted.

"I'm really sorry about those old people," he said under his breath. "I'm pretty sure they're okay now though."

"Me too." She looked down the hill. A flush of anger stopped her very heart. She could feel it gallop to catch up. She could see Roy's fence and his driveway, but there was no van in the driveway. She couldn't see the house itself or the porch from here, though she knew it well enough. She'd smell the fire before she ever heard it. There would be enough time. She should tell somebody about that van.

"Dad's gonna be okay, right?"

"He's got really good doctors, Will. The best." She had no idea if that were true. She'd had her doubts ever since they'd gotten the radiation tattoos all wrong.

"Well, he should be home by now. I know what today is."

Poor kid. He was the one who never wanted to know anything and always did. He wanted to stay in his room and not watch for that little blue car to turn the corner by the streetlight, then race on home.

"Don't worry, okay? You know how sometimes his appointment is late. I think we should go ahead and eat dinner. I'll go heat up the chili. That sound all right?"

"I really hate this," Will said, his eyes filling with tears as he turned toward the stairs.

She knew better than to go after him. A year ago, she would have, but he had declared himself in so many ways these past months. He was changing fast now, and he knew it.

She thought about what it would be like if sometime Jay didn't come home. What if it were all over in a flash and there was no waiting anymore, no long, drawn-out dying? She'd be weightless without the pull of him. She wondered if he'd ever imagined what it would be like without her, some night when it was dark way too soon and the streets were slick with new rain and she was late by an hour. Would he be weightless too?

But what if he got a bad report or maybe a terrible report? What if the radiation hadn't worked? What if he was trying not to cry and driving too fast or maybe too slow coming home on the freeway in that little car, not remembering his seat belt, or maybe just driving around because he couldn't figure out how to tell them?

It was after six thirty now and they'd finished dinner. She couldn't eat, though, sitting next to that empty chair. She tried not to look at the phone while she was cleaning up, but there it was. She didn't know whether she wanted it to ring or not.

"I want Daddy," Jillie said, and started to cry. So she scooped her up and took her into the living room. Jillie crawled into her lap, pulling her blanket after her. "Here, Mommy," she said, rubbing Zoë's cheek with the satin ribbing of her blanket.

"Thanks, kid."

But after a few minutes Jillie said, "I'm going downstairs now. Tell me if Daddy comes home, okay?"

"You bet." She watched Jillie make her way downstairs, her blanket trailing behind her. She was changing too. Zoë knew how hard she'd been trying to give it up. But not tonight.

Maybe he was just caught in traffic. That was a pretty scary phrase if you thought about it. Caught in traffic you'd be safe, anyway, not hurtling through the windshield toward some apocalypse.

If something were really wrong, though, somebody would have called her by now. She went into the bathroom to wash her face, stare at herself in the mirror. She wondered how she'd look going to the hospital. Crazy. Wild-eyed. Mascara smudged under her eyes, old T-shirt and sweater, chili stains down the front. Ah, the widow's entrance, and all eyes turn.

At quarter to seven the phone rang. She rushed past Will to the phone. He stared at her from the half-open door to the fridge. She wanted something to happen.

"Is Will there?" said a tiny female voice.

"It's for you." Zoë handed him the phone. He gave her a funny look and turned his back.

She shouldn't have run to the phone. She should have let Will answer it. There couldn't really be anything wrong. But why couldn't there?

Then it was seven and he still wasn't home. She was sitting at the top of the stairs. Niki'd been lying by the door, her nose against the crack, sniffing now and then. Zoë leaned over and hugged her great furry neck. "Don't worry," she said to the dog, who licked her ear. She wanted her to roll over so she could feel the puppies, but the dog was concentrating on that door.

Then she did. She rolled over on her back and Zoë put her hands on her belly and felt those tiny pushes against her palms. *Do you know what this is, Niki? Do you know your babies?* She yawned. Upside down like that, she looked like an alligator.

If something really had happened, she'd know it, wouldn't she? Maybe the doctor told him he only had six months and he'd been driving around trying to figure out how to break the news. But six months is a long time, if you count it in weeks or days, or hours. He could come home any time now. She could take it.

No matter what, he could have at least called. He ought to know by now she'd be going crazy, waiting like this. But maybe he couldn't call. What about that? She didn't want to watch out the window anymore. She didn't want to see that he wasn't coming and that the road by the mailboxes was empty and no car lights anywhere.

So she'd just sit here by the door on the top step with the dog, and shut her eyes and wait for the sound of his car. First she'd hear it coming up the hill, the way it grumbles when he changes gear over the bump, which high-centers the car and wipes out your field of vision, then the wheels on the gravel as he slides into the driveway, and then she'd hear the car door slam, his shoes on the porch, and finally the click of the doorknob.

She remembered waiting when she thought the very worst had happened and he came home all right. They'd just gotten married and he'd been coaching a double basketball game and she waited and waited and still he didn't come. She watched the street from their tiny apartment window for his car lights coming through the dark. At midnight she'd heard the wail of an ambulance shattering the air, its red lights flashing across the apartment window. She threw her winter coat over her nightgown and went running down to the street corner. She just stood there under the streetlight with her hands stuffed into her pockets, looking up the road.

Zoë had said she'd never wait like that again, but right now that's just what she was doing. But look how well she'd waited! She couldn't wait like this much longer.

But then that little car was rounding the corner by the mailboxes, just sailing up the hill, then over the bump in the road like a little rowboat in the wind, and he was honking the horn as he glided into the driveway, and then the tires were splashing up the gravel as he bounced to a stop, and even from here she could see that the car was full of a thousand bright and shining balloons.

A Dog Sled Team

"**A**re you sure this is gonna be big enough?" Jay said, reaching for the hammer.

"Very funny," Zoë said. The whelping box Jay was making on the floor of the bedroom looked like they were trying to whelp a horse, not a dog. Zoë was reading out loud while he pounded away. "It says you need to leave room for the owner to get in if she needs help."

"That would be me, I suppose. Pass me the beer." He took a swig and passed it back to her.

She took a swallow and set it on the floor, where she was reading *The Complete Guide to Canine Midwifery*. "She's got to have plenty of room to lie down. We don't want her squashing the pups. Isn't that right, Niki?" She reached over to pet the dog, who was sitting next to her, staring at that box. "This is for your babies." Niki looked at Zoë suspiciously. She didn't like all this pounding.

"This is a really big box. How many does the vet think she'll have, for godsake?"

"He thought he felt six, but maybe more."

"Did he say what the pups might look like? I mean since the father is of dubious origin."

Zoë just looked at him. "God, Jay." She couldn't get the image of Roy out of her head. The baseball cap, the ponytail, the fierce eyes. And his dog that was almost Niki but not quite.

"I told him about the neighbor's dog. The vet said the pups would be beautiful. I said thank you."

"Could be worse. Could be Rambo the rottweiler."

"My turn," Zoë said, reaching for the beer.

"It's all your turn, you know."

"I love those puppies already. No matter who the father is. He doesn't have any rights, does he?"

"Guess how much I know about canine custody law?"

"Nobody can prove who the father is."

"I really wouldn't worry about that one."

"I'm not worried. I'm just hoping everybody'll be okay."

"Zoë, don't. Don't start worrying."

"I'm not. And the box isn't too big."

Jay stood up and measured the side boards again. "Four by five is a bedroom, for godsake. Well, for a small child. Is this going to stay in our bedroom for real?"

"But she'll want to be with us."

Jay began to laugh. "Okay, if you say so. It's pretty funny though. I mean don't dogs do this on their own all the time? Come here."

"Why?"

"Because."

"Come and get me."

"Okay for you," he said, wrestling her to the floor. He pinned her arms behind her back and began kissing the side of her neck.

Delicious chills rushed down her neck and chest. He helped her up and drew her to him.

"Double chicken wing? Is that all you've got?"

"Don't you dare," he said, catching her hands so she couldn't rake his sides.

Zoë leaned into him and kissed him on the mouth. "I don't think you taught your wrestlers the kissing part."

"We're lucky, aren't we," Jay said.

"All these puppies coming our way," she said, but she knew what he meant, and reached to kiss him again.

"What are you guys doing in here?" Max said, drawn in by all the laughing. "I brought Dad his Pepsi."

"Max, hand me that towel," Zoë said, pointing to the beer foam on the carpet, next to the beer bottle they'd knocked over. She soaked it up and threw the towel in the sink then set the beer on the counter.

"Here," Max said. "Pepsi is better anyway."

"Ah, thanks, my beautiful boy." Jay snapped it open and took a long swallow. "You're right. Way better."

Then he set the Pepsi on the counter and went back to pounding. He'd already cut the four-by-five pieces of plywood, and was nailing them together.

"What are these boards for?" Max said, pointing at four strips of plywood stacked in the corner. He sat down next to her and Zoë showed him the diagram of the whelping box with the newborn pups snuggled under a sort of guardrail.

"That's so if the mother lies down against the side of the box, a puppy won't get wedged in and maybe get smushed." She didn't want to say *smothered*, though that's what she meant.

"Niki wouldn't do that."

"No, of course not. She wouldn't mean to. This is just to make sure."

"Oh," he said, thumbing through the book. She wished she hadn't shown it to him. She'd practically memorized the "Difficulties and Dilemmas" chapter—uterine inertia (primary and secondary), prolapsed vagina, prolapsed uterus, uterine torsion, ruptured uterus, emergency C-section, all described in uncompromising detail and listed in ascending order of catastrophe. Oh well, dogs do this in nature all the time.

"What's this?" Max said, pointing at a drawing that looked like a black baby dinosaur.

"Oh, Max, don't look at stuff like that." But he read on anyway, this kid who'd been reading since he was four, who always had to know everything.

"It's called a *mummy*. It's a dried-up baby that comes out with the alive ones. That's terrible."

Jay stopped pounding and was standing there with the hammer in his hand just looking at her. "A *mummy*?" he mouthed.

"It's okay, Max, that hardly ever happens. Here, give me the book. We don't need to know all this stuff anyway." She put the book face-down on the dresser.

Max lay down on the floor next to the dog, draped his arm over her neck. "I like to feel the babies when they move around. I wish she'd roll over."

"Well don't push on her, and don't go poking around," Zoë said.

"I wouldn't hurt her."

"I didn't mean you'd hurt her, Sweetie. The book just says dogs get kind of funny before they have their babies. Hey, kiddo, go get some newspapers and you can shred them up for the box. Daddy's almost done now, except for the guard railing."

"So she can make her nest."

"Pretty soon now. The vet says she'll have the babies next week. He thinks there'll be six of them."

"I want to see it," he said, "so if I'm asleep or *anywhere* you gotta call me."

"You won't miss it, Sweetie."

"Okay," he said, giving Niki a last hug before he headed out.

She watched him run down the hall. She wished them all safe passage. She wanted this to make up for Pecky. But of course loss was loss and nothing would make up for that bird. If she'd learned anything these last months, it was that.

"Well, Zoots, how do you think we'll like sleeping with half a dozen dogs?" Jay said, finishing up for the day. "Where do you want it?"

"Over next to the closet, I think. We won't even know they're in here, Jay—they sleep practically all the time."

He just looked at her. "Right. Just like the kids always did."

"Well, like they were supposed to."

Jay rolled his eyes, tilted the can, and finished the last swig.

"You don't really think she needs all this stuff, do you. You're just going along to humor me."

He looked at her and smiled.

"She can't just give birth under the house or in the woods. She'd want to be with us. She's always been with us."

"Christ, Zoë," he said, beginning to laugh. "You gotta lighten up." She knew he was thinking about the motion sensor lights and the locked garage and moving the woodpile, which of course never got moved after all.

"I just don't want her to get anxious, you know? She needs a safe place so she won't get jumpy and try to move the pups. I'm just going by what the book says, Jay."

"But who's the one who's anxious around here?" he said, pointing to the dog, who'd gone to sleep rolled over on her back, her rounded belly and eight swollen teats going up and down with her breathing. Little waves rolled across her pink, taut belly and little droplets of milk bloomed from some of the teats. Niki's ears were twitching as if she heard something in her sleep. Jay stood up and Zoë put her arms around him. They stood there, watching the dreaming dog. "To life," he said.

"L'chaim."

"We aren't Jewish."

"Wish we were. They have prayers for everything. So do Catholics."

Jay reached down and touched Niki's belly, then gathered up his tools. "Better get to the store."

Zoë sat down on the floor by the dog, put her hands on Niki's belly, and felt the babies nestle against them.

Bags (paper and plastic), towels, alcohol, heat lamp, rectal thermometer, petroleum jelly, spare rectal thermometer, clock, clamps, white thread, scissors, nail clippers, surgical gloves, nasal aspirator, vet's phone number, vet's emergency phone number—it was all there, laid out according to expected order of use, on a table next to the closet by the whelping box.

Zoë was in the rocker, keeping watch over the dog, who was sitting in the middle of her whelping box looking back at her, panting up a storm. She'd found her in the hall stretched out, her belly rigid and hard. Niki'd begun digging around in the shredded-up newspapers last night, and toward morning they'd heard her roaming around the bedroom, then digging again.

Jillie had brought her little rocker in next to Zoë's, and together they watched for telltale signs—howls, yelps, pacing, squatting. They didn't know what they were looking for. If a new mother didn't know to tear the sack off right away, that first little guy might need some help before she figured it out.

So they spent the afternoon rocking away, waiting for some moan or cry to tell them what to do. But all the dog had been doing for the last hour was sitting there in the middle of the newspapers, panting. Will and Max were down in the gully in the tree house, but Zoë had promised to call them the minute something began to happen. Jay was out in the garage trying to figure out what to get rid of so they could finally get the car into the garage for the winter, something he valiantly tried to do every summer, though the car hadn't spent a winter in the garage for as long as Zoë could remember.

"That's okay," Jillie said, patting Niki on the head. She'd gone over to check on things, offer her some water and moral support.

"Mommy, there's a stuffy in Niki's bed."

"No there isn't," Zoë said. "You didn't put something in there, did you?"

"Uh-uh. She's playing with it."

"I don't think there ought to be anything in there with her, though. You'd better take it out."

"Mommy! Come here!"

Whatever it was, Niki was licking it and nosing it around.

There had been no moan or cry. No sound they ever heard that would tell them what had happened, not knowing that Niki did not and would not make even so much as a whimper.

She had just stretched out her neck and had her baby right there on the newspapers just as they'd planned it—a perfectly formed black and white little pup, who lay motionless in the center of that big whelping box while Niki licked and licked it. Zoë picked it up. It lay still in her hand.

"Get Daddy," she said to Jillie, who ran down the hall.

"Daddy!" Zoë could hear her scream all the way through the house and out the door.

Jay rushed into the room, then Max and Jillie, and then Will, who stopped just outside the door. Zoë handed the baby to Jay, while Niki tried to stand up to nose at it. Jay cupped it in one hand, while he held the pup's mouth open with the other. He put it up to his mouth and breathed, while he pressed the pup's sides with his cupped hand. In, out; in, out; in and out; breathe, little guy, breathe. Jillie was crying. Niki sat back down.

Jay looked at the kids and laid the pup in the towel-lined cardboard box. They looked down at it, waiting for it to wake up.

"What should we do?" Zoë said.

"I don't think it's dead," Jillie said, leaning over to touch it.

"It is though," Max said, pulling her away. Will had vanished from the doorway.

"I should call the vet."

She looked at Niki who was sitting down now, her eyes shut, stretching out her neck in that funny kind of way. It was what they should have seen before and did not.

Jay climbed into the whelping box, patted Niki's side, and lifted her tail to try to see what was going on.

"Do you see anything?" Zoë said, leaning over too.

"It looks like a green bubble. It's the sac. I'm gonna tear it open and get this pup out." Niki looked around at Jay. Then there was the pup on the newspapers for a moment before Niki turned toward it and then all they could see was the back of her head as it moved up and down.

"She's licking off the sac," Jay said, "and biting the cord. She knows what to do now."

"Is it okay?" Zoë said.

They could hear little squeaks as she nosed it around in the newspapers. The pup was lifting its wobbly head, as Niki licked it clean.

"Look," she said to the kids. Niki had turned away from the pup to finish off the placenta.

Zoë picked up the baby and it squirmed in her hand.

"Jillie, get the towel. We need to dry it off." Jillie took a corner of the towel and patted the pup's back, and Zoë turned it over and saw that it was a boy, and like the book said, Jay and Zoë tied the remaining cord with the white thread.

"It's a baby boy, Niki," Jillie said.

They went to set him in the little cardboard box with the towels warmed now by the heat lamp, and remembered the pup they'd put there what seemed a long time ago. But the box was empty. Max was gone too.

She looked down at Jay sitting by the whelping box. He looked exhausted. "Go get Will," she said to Jillie. "He needs to see everything's okay now." Niki looked exhausted too. She was panting, so Zoë put the pan of water in front of her. She just turned her head and kept on panting. Then there was Will, standing just inside the door.

"Look in the box, Will." He went over to the cardboard box, put his hand out, then pulled it back.

"Can I touch it?"

"You can pick him up if you want. Niki won't mind."

He put the pup against his cheek. "It's soft," he said. "It's like a little mouse." The pup tried to wiggle out of his hand. "I better put it down now."

Max came in just then, his cheeks smudged with dirt and tears.

"I buried him next to Pecky. So he won't be alone." He wiped his nose on his shirtsleeve. "I wrapped him in a towel so he'll be warm."

"Thank you for doing that," Jay said. "That was really brave of you." She could see the tears in Jay's eyes for this child in the middle, who was so strong and so valiant.

Zoë wrapped her arms around him, kissed the top of his head. "Max, look in the box. Niki has a baby."

He turned around and knelt down by the cardboard box.

"It's moving around like it wants to get out. It's strong."

"You can hold him," Jay said. "Everything's all right now."

Max picked him up and the pup tried to climb up onto his shoulder. "We should name him Climber."

"That's a great idea, Max," Zoë said, though she wanted to say, *Please don't name him.*

Jay just looked at her and shook his head. Neither of them had really explained how all too soon these puppies would have to be given away. Good Lord. Or they really were going to have a dog sled team.

"I'm starved," Jay said, letting out a sigh. He was still sitting propped up against the side of the whelping box.

"Good job, Daddy," Jillie said, leaning over to pat him on the knee. Then she crawled into his lap. "Niki did the hardest job."

By now it was after six o'clock. They were all getting hungry, and since they figured Niki took about half an hour between births, they'd have time enough to dash down the street for pizza, anyway.

"I'll get it," Jay said.

"No, I'll go." If anybody needed to climb in that whelping box again, she wanted it to be Jay.

It was nice to get out of the house, take a deep breath. Things really were all right. Zoë came to the stop sign up the road and looked down at the lake and the sun glinting off the water. A few sailboats were scudding across the lake, their white masts bobbing in the sun. A seaplane soared overhead. She thought about that little black and white pup curled up against the towels in that cardboard box and couldn't stop smiling.

She looked at her watch, then turned into the pizza parking lot and went inside.

"Is the Penney order ready?" she said.

"Is Penney ready?" Kurt, or so the name tag said, yelled back through the delivery window.

"No," came a voice from the kitchen.

"Not yet," he said. "About five minutes."

Zoë sat down at one of the tables near the jukebox. The pizza parlor was practically empty. The sun was shining brilliantly through the window but she felt cold. The air-conditioning was pouring out of the ceiling vent, and so she edged her chair into the sun.

Suddenly she wanted to be kneeling beside that big plywood box. She got up and went to the counter. "I really need this right away," she said. "My dog's in labor."

"Her dog's in labor," Kurt yelled. "Hurry up with that pizza order."

Minutes later she was on her way home, hoping on the one hand she hadn't missed anything, and on the other that it was all over and done with and everything was still all right.

"Mommy!" Jillie said, "Look!" Now there were two black and white pups curled up against each other in the baby box. Niki was sitting up, smiling at her when she came in.

"Oh, what a good girl you are!" she said, leaning over to give her a hug. Niki sniffed at the pizza box in her arm.

"She's hungry," Max said. "Can we give her some?"

"I don't know. I don't remember what the book said about that. We don't want to upset her stomach."

"She loves pizza," Jay said. "She doesn't have to eat it if she doesn't want to."

But she did. Three pieces of Goofy's Family Combo Belly Buster Special.

Niki licked her chops, then lay back down and didn't have anything more to do with them until she had unceremoniously delivered four more perfect black and white pups.

Jay led Niki outside while Zoë put the newspapers into a big plastic sack, then spread a fleecy white blanket over the bottom of the box.

Niki came right back in, went over to her water pan, and drank and drank. Then the kids put the pups in the whelping box one by one, and Niki climbed in after them.

They watched them sniff and turn their heads as they wiggled across the blanket, their baby eyes shut tight, toward where Niki had lain down. Niki turned her head to watch the pups as they dug their back feet into the blanket, pushed up against her, and grabbed hold of a teat.

"Listen," Zoë said. They could hear little smacking sounds as those pups began sucking in earnest, stretching out their back legs. Then one by one they slid off the teat and curled up fast into sleep, their little sides going up and down. Finally Niki put her head down and closed her eyes, the first time that long day. It was the first day of summer.

The kids wanted to have a sleepover that night, but Zoë and Jay said no. Niki needed some privacy and so did they. Zoë wondered what it would be like sleeping in a room with six pups and a mother who'd just given birth.

"What are you thinking?" Jay said, as they curled down into the summer comforter.

"I'm too excited to be sleepy."

"I know."

"Do you think the kids are okay?" Zoë said. "Do you think Max is okay?"

"Yeah. He's a tough little kid."

"Listen. They're nursing again. I love that sound."

"Come here," he said.

Birds of the Air

It was late but still she couldn't sleep. She could hear Jay breathing. And the pups made a lot of noise, considering the fact they were supposed to be sleeping all the time. Somebody squawked every now and then, either wedged in a corner or sucked on by mistake. Niki was always careful not to step on any of the pups, careful not to lie on them, when she settled back down. Niki didn't need anybody's help.

Zoë was listening to the pups and watching the moon slip into the trees outside the window. She could hear Niki in the whelping box changing position every now and then. She was thinking about the first time they brought Will into her hospital room that early morning in December.

"Here's your baby," the nurse had said, handing him over wrapped up tight but for his head and one tiny hand. Zoë tucked his head into the hollow of her neck, rubbed her chin against the top of his head, smelled his baby smell. The whole universe was in that room, the sweet smell of him, the little smacking noises when she fed him, the way she knew just what to do. She'd have done anything for that baby, would do anything for him now.

She looked over at Jay, his face in the moonlight. He'd fallen asleep long ago. She was watching the shadows in the wind. The moon was gone and the room had turned dark. Somebody was wailing outside the window. It was the sound of grief filling the air. A sky full of babies lost in the night.

"What's *that*?"

"It's okay," Jay said. "It's just the coyotes." Babies had been born a couple of weeks ago and you could hear them yipping, and the unearthly cry of the mother. Then they heard Niki moving across the room. They turned on the bed light. Shoes were flying all over the room. Niki was digging shoes out of the closet. Then she tried to curl up into the empty space at the bottom of the closet, but it was too small for that, so she tried to crawl under the bed, just as she'd done a couple of days before the babies were born, when she crawled under the deck, and Zoë feared she was going to crush them. Jay was afraid he was going to have to rip up the deck to get her out. After an hour or so they finally coaxed her out with some bagels and cream cheese, and nothing, it turned out, had been squashed after all.

She must have known it was a den or a cave that would keep her babies safe, not some plywood box, however well constructed. She must have felt the pull of some earlier existence, some wilder claim. It was clear in that moment that she wasn't anybody's pet. She wouldn't acknowledge them or let them touch her until she had finally stopped circling the room and gone back into the box where she lay, keeping watch the rest of the night.

There had been another fire the night before last, but farther north again, this time in a dumpster behind a little church. Suppose there were a fire in the woods next to the house. The first thing Zoë'd hear would be the tree branches crashing against the window. The glass would shatter over everything and the smoke would rush in. How would she get all those puppies out in time? She went down the hall and got the large blue plastic laundry basket and set it in the corner by the whelping box. She could scoop them up into that basket in a couple of seconds and rush down the hall, calling for the kids as she raced. Why was she always alone in these melodramas?

The pups grew while they slept. They seemed bigger every morning. Niki seemed to enjoy getting out of the house, away from the kids, now and then. The pups began to take their first shaky steps, wobbling across the blanket, sometimes falling over fast asleep in mid-step, then one morning the first glint of a partly opened eye.

Days passed. Max was keeping a diary. Jillie was making a notebook of pictures. Will was off with his friends.

Early one morning, though, when Zoë looked in the whelping box, which Niki had always kept spotlessly clean, she saw a rust-colored stain where she had been lying. "Niki?" Her eyes looked funny. Zoë touched her nose with the palm of her hand. Hot. She felt something drop inside. The vet said to bring her over right away, so she woke Will and told him to look out for things, they'd be back soon. But Niki could hardly get to the car she was so shaky. Jay had to lift her haunches to get her inside.

"A hundred and four," the vet said, turning the thermometer to the light. "Acute metritis. A uterine infection," he added for their benefit.

"I know what *metritis* is," Zoë said, looking over at the vet standing beside the stainless-steel examining table with the thermometer in his hand. Niki lay on the floor, halfway under the chair where Zoë was sitting. Jay was standing in the corner with his arms crossed. They hadn't even tried to get her up on the examining table. She looked up at them mournfully.

Zoë got down on the floor beside Niki, and stroked her back. Jay sat down in the chair. She thought he looked pale and a little shaky himself.

"I don't understand how this could happen."

The vet, the one she didn't like, just stood there, holding that thermometer. "Well, it happens."

"But we brought her in for X-rays to be sure everything came out. She didn't want to leave her babies. She cried the whole way here. And now you're saying it didn't?"

The vet shifted his weight, rested his hands on the examining table. "Sometimes you can't know what's wrong until something shows up. We'll see what her labs say. I think maybe more is going on than infection. But don't worry."

"That's not very reassuring," Jay said from the chair.

"Well, it isn't always an exact science," the vet said.

Zoë wanted to smack him. She thought of the CAT scan so recent and so fine. But that was what? Two months ago? She couldn't remember. He'd never had that lympho-something. She remembered the woman with the golden bracelets that day down in radiation. "It's not so bad," she'd said. She thought about capillaries and small, invisible routes for cancer cells to burrow into, and shuddered.

But she took a deep breath and said, as slowly as she could, "So what do we do now?"

"We could try her on a course of antibiotics. We could even IV her. But I'll bet she's had this for at least a week, and she's already pretty shocky."

Niki struggled to stand up but her back legs gave out and she flopped back down with a yelp. Zoë's eyes filled with tears. Jay got out of the chair and went over and cupped her belly with his arms and lifted her up. She nosed his hand, looked at him. *Let's get out of here.*

"Look at her gums," the vet said. He leaned over and grabbed her snout and pulled up the side of her mouth. "You tell if a person's in shock by their color. On a dog you look at the gums."

They certainly did look pale, but then she'd never noticed the color of her gums that she could remember.

"I think she needs surgery right away."

"You mean a hysterectomy?"

"It's the only way to be sure we get out all the infection." He reached into his pocket for a doggie treat. He put it in front of Niki's nose, but she turned her head, backed up against the wall. Intelligent dog that she was, she couldn't be bought for a stupid dog biscuit.

"But what about the babies?"

"You'll have to bottle-feed them for a few days, then you can pretty well switch to pan-feeding. She won't be able to nurse them when she comes home anyway."

"Why not?"

"They'd tear out her incision."

So they left her there. There was nothing else to do. They watched her walk away on unsteady legs, no last-ditch lunges for the exit this time. She didn't even look back. They watched her disappear through those double doors into a setting they had always tried hard not to imagine. Jay put his arms around her and she softened into him. "It's okay. It'll be okay."

"Kiss me," Zoë said.

"Here?" The room was full of dogs and cats and their fearful, expectant owners.

"Yes." *Yes, yes, yes. Please, yes.*

So Jay kissed her, leaving a strange coppery taste on her tongue and she pulled back and looked at him. There was a tightness around his eyes. It seemed new. The room flipped over then righted itself. Then the strange taste was gone, but remembered like a bad dream.

"Your dog is in good hands," a woman said. She was holding a black and tan dachshund in her lap. "They do real good work here."

Zoë could only nod. She had no faith they did good work, here or anywhere. They headed for home, the back seat empty and stained with blood.

They passed Goofy's Pizza Parlor as they turned onto the street in front of the vet's office. They went on up the road, and there was the lake with the sailboats in the early morning sun, and a seaplane coming in low overhead, all just as before.

Jay was right. The whelping box was way too big. Without their mother, the pups had moved toward the warmth of their littermates and were now sleeping in a little black furry pile in the middle of the box.

"Where's Niki?" Jillie said. She was sitting by the whelping box in her pajamas, holding her baby blanket.

"She's at the vet's. You were still sleeping when we took her in."

"I know. But where is she really?" Tears filled her eyes.

"She just has an infection, Jillie."

"Did she die?"

"Oh, no. No," Zoë said, sitting down beside her. Jillie crawled into her lap.

"Everything's all right, Sweetie, you don't have to worry. Where are your brothers?"

"What will happen to the puppies without their mother?"

"We'll take care of them. It's just for a couple of days."

Jillie slid off her lap and reached in and took up one of the pups and it snuggled into her and purred. "Where's Daddy?"

"He went to do some errands. We have to get some things for the puppies."

"I want him to come home now. I don't want him to be gone."

"He'll be home soon. He just went to the store. Where are your brothers?"

"In the tree house. They told me to watch the puppies till you got home."

"Did you have breakfast?"

"I don't want any breakfast."

"I'll go make something and surprise you."

Zoë went on upstairs, and stood there by the refrigerator, leaning her head against the door when Will came in.

"How's Niki?" He put his arm around her shoulder. "It's okay, Mom."

"Thanks, kid. She's going to have surgery. So we'll have to feed the pups for a couple of days."

"Oh," he said. He clearly didn't want to know any more. "Jillie didn't want any breakfast." He turned to go, then looked back. "Mom? Is everything really okay?"

Of course Niki would be all right. Why not? It was just a hysterectomy anyway, not a heart transplant. Then she'd be home, and anyway the pups were doing fine.

But the next morning the vet called. Her labs had come back and they showed that she was in kidney failure.

"Kidney failure! How can she be in kidney failure?"

"I don't know what to tell you," the voice on the phone repeated. "Kidney failure is unusual in a dog so young. There isn't anything that can undo kidney damage. And they really don't do transplants in dogs, or even dialysis. Around here, anyway."

"But there must be something you can do."

"A special diet, antibiotics for infection, weekly urine specimens, check her temperature. And a kidney biopsy to tell us exactly how much—" The vet fumbled, as if he didn't mean to say how much time she had left, but he did.

They let you say stuff like that? Zoë wanted to scream. But instead, she just said, "Oh." But before she put down the phone, she couldn't help saying, "You really don't know anything at all, then, do you." Then she put down the phone. With a slam.

She couldn't stop thinking about how weary and slow Niki had seemed all the time she was carrying the pups. Maybe there had been something wrong all along.

She remembered the first time she saw her, in a little chicken wire pen, face half drowned in the big water dish she was drinking from. Zoë had picked her up and she'd peed all over the front of her sweatshirt. Niki's was the first face she saw in the morning and the last face at night. She lay curled up under her desk while she worked, followed her everywhere, and though she loved them all, she loved Zoë best.

"I think we should skip the biopsy," Jay was saying that night. "I mean why put her through that when they can't do anything for her anyway. You know how panicky she gets the minute we pull into that parking lot."

"We can't just give up on her."

"But I don't want her getting to the point where she loses her dignity, you know? I don't want to see her peeing all over the house, or bumping into walls. I don't want to see her in pain."

"So you'd go gently into that good night."

He didn't say anything. She could feel him staring at the ceiling. It was covered with stars. For their anniversary last year, the kids had painted constellations of stars on their ceiling with glow-in-the-dark paint.

But she knew why he'd said that. The next checkpoint was only a couple of months away, and he wanted to be ready for whatever might be coming around that corner. But she'd never give up, not until they'd tried everything, and even then she wouldn't give up.

—

They fed the pups over the next several days, three times by day, and once during the night.

Zoë slept half-listening for the six little complaints that came as regularly as clockwork at three each morning. "Time to feed the babies," she told the kids. In a minute they all padded into the bedroom and picked up one of the pups, each of whom had been named, generically speaking, the day of their birth. Zoë took Buttercup, the biggest girl; Will took Speck, with the white spot on his forehead; Max took Climber, who'd tried to climb up his shoulder when he'd first picked him up; Jay took Twinny and Spock, with the strange lightning bolt on his forehead; and Jillie fed Graylie, her favorite.

They showed the kids how to hold the pups on their lap, belly side down, then wiggle the rubber nipple against the inside of their mouth till they began to suck the baby bottle full of goat's milk.

"They're our babies," Jillie said, watching how the pups grasped the bottle in their front paws as they sucked away. "Can we keep them?"

"All of them?"

Of course she meant all of them. But even Jillie was a realist. "Or maybe two or one."

"We'll see," Zoë said, not willing just then to think more than a day ahead. She knew it would soon enough be time to let them go.

When the pups were done, they pulled the bottle away and heard a little pop when they finally broke suction. Then they put them over their shoulder and rubbed their backs until they burped. They each took a cotton ball and massaged their little bottoms until they eliminated, all things Niki had been doing all along. They held them for a little longer, as they fell back to sleep, curled up in their laps. Nobody minded the coyotes wailing in the gully or the night wind rustling the trees. They were safe inside where nothing could touch them. Then they put the pups back in the box and soon they found their way back to each other. In the morning it was like a dream, in the half-light, on the floor of the bedroom, with the puppy noises and the night sounds and the kids floating off to bed without a word.

On the morning of the third day, the vet called to say Niki could come home. Zoë and Will brought Niki home, black stitches criss crossing her shaved belly, exposing her swollen teats. She didn't look at them the whole way home. Just sat in the middle of the back seat with her head turned away in indignation.

"We're home, Niki," she said, as they drove up the hill. The mother quail, who'd made a nest for her babies in the bushes by the side of the driveway, scurried across the road in front of them. Zoë put on the brakes just in time. She disappeared into the bushes as they slid into the driveway. Will helped Niki out of the back seat and she climbed cautiously up the porch steps and headed through the door. She stopped at the top of the stairs leading down to the bedroom where she knew the puppies were, then began to edge her way down. Zoë grabbed her collar and led her back up.

"No, Niki, you can't have your puppies right now. They'd tear your stitches. You don't need to feed them anymore."

So they blocked off the stairs with the baby gate. But she wouldn't budge from her post at the top of the stairs. She just stood there, looking through the gate and wailed, her teats dripping milk onto the floor.

"Let's try to distract her," she said to Jillie. "Why don't you make her some dinner?"

So Jillie led her into the kitchen and filled her dish with the canned food they saved for special occasions, and topped it off with some leftover spaghetti sauce.

Jillie set the dish on the floor then got down and smacked her lips.

"I'll eat it up if you don't first." Niki looked at her suspiciously, then proceeded to eat it all and lick the platter clean.

"Maybe she'll settle down now," Zoë said, getting out the pan for the lasagna she was going to start for dinner. It was good to have her home, good to have everything all right again. She wouldn't think about this kidney thing. It was some kind of lab mistake. She could hear *Sesame Street* come on in the living room. Will had gone down to the tree house to find Max. Her boys of summer. They were pretty nearly finished. They'd stocked the tree house full of snacks not allowed in everyday light—Twinkies, Ding Dongs, Sno Balls, Doritos, a gallon of red Kool-Aid. Reading material—*Spider-Man* comics, Choose Your Own Adventure, *Lord of the Rings*—two sleeping bags and pillows for comfort but not sleeping, one chair never used. Jillie was jealous only in theory. There were too many blackberry bushes, too much invisible scuttling about.

"Mommy! Come quick!" Jillie yelled from down the hall. "Niki threw up."

Well of course she would. Too much excitement the first day home. They shouldn't have fed her so soon. But it turned out she wasn't sick after all. For there she was by the gate, pawing at her dinner, sculpting her dinner ceremoniously into a perfect mound, food for the pups she could not feed, remembering some primal signal from centuries ago, and placing it as close to her babies as she could get.

But in a week, the pups were slurping their goat milk and puppy chow all mixed up in a blender and set out in six little pie tins. Jay had made a feeding trough with a circle cut out for each pup's little food pan. They moved the pups out of the bedroom the end of that third week into the puppy run they'd made between the house and the garage, for they were finding a way out of the whelping box no matter what barricades they put up.

One day toward the end of the week, they put them to bed as babies, their ears still flattened against their heads, their droopy tails dragging behind them. The next morning when they came tumbling down the run, their ears stood at full attention and their floppy tails were now elegant little plumes.

They still heard the coyotes at night and worried that they would smell the pups and some night come creeping into the yard. Jay had put up wire fencing all around the puppy run, and they hoped for the best.

Each night Zoë stood outside the back door and looked out into the gully for their yellow eyes just at the edge of the yard. But tonight she went down to the puppy run to say goodnight. The pups spilled out of their boxes and down the puppy run the moment she opened the gate. They crawled into her lap, tugged at her sweatshirt, untied her shoes. But soon they settled back down. It was way past their bedtime. Inside, everybody was already asleep, all safe, all safe. Zoë could hear one long coyote wail floating over the trees. She thought about the mother quail who'd made her nest in harm's way, in the bushes at the side of the road, hovering in midair just above the road, beating her wings and shrieking *ree! ree! ree! take me! take me! take me!* as the neighbor's cat scooted out from under the bushes, the baby bird limp in her mouth.

She sat there on the floor of the puppy run for a long time, listening to the rustling sounds coming from the gully—possums or raccoons or the coyotes, or maybe the wind, and hoped the fence would hold. She thought about fire. No fence would stop that. She looked at the pups asleep in her lap and thought about the puppy ad she would place in the morning.

The Long Goodbye

He'd said her name a couple of times before she stopped dreaming and knew she was awake. He was sitting on the edge of the bed. "Jay?" She touched his back. "What's the matter?" Darkness hummed from the edge of the dream.

He reached over and turned on the bed light. "Look," he said, standing up.

She looked at him standing by the side of the bed in his boxers and T-shirt. "What?" Her hands were shaking.

"Look at my leg."

Even in that shadowy light she could see his right leg was swollen, nearly double the size of the other. She reached out to touch it, then pulled her hand back.

"Does it hurt?"

"I don't know," he said and sat back down and stared at that leg sticking out over the side of the bed. "It aches a little."

"Maybe it's a spider bite or something and you're having an allergic reaction."

Ah, the spider bite theory. It reminded her of the old athletic injury theory they'd held onto last Christmas, before the doctor's appointment which had put that theory to rest.

"Are you having trouble breathing?" Allergic reactions, anaphylactic shock, windpipe closing, emergency tracheotomy, aid-car

176

wandering all over the hillside trying to find their address, just like after the ice cream.

He took a deep breath just to make sure. "I don't think so."

But she knew the moment she saw that leg it was no bug bite. "We should probably get this checked out," she said as casually as she could. But she was moving fast now.

"Yeah, you're probably right," he said in a voice just as urgently casual. But he could only sit there, looking at his leg. He picked up the clock. Four in the morning, the hour of the wolf. "Here we go again," he said. Jay set the clock down hard on the nightstand. The dog, who'd been sitting by the edge of the bed, gave out a yip and jumped back, then lay down on the floor, wagging her tail. "It's okay, Niki," Zoë said. "I'll tell Will we're just going to get this checked out. We won't be gone long."

When she got back into the bedroom, Jay was still sitting there by the side of the bed, his pants down around his ankles. "I can't even get my sweats on."

"That's okay, it's the middle of the night. We'll just put on your running shorts." So she helped him into his shorts, first the swollen leg then the other. He stood up and pulled them the rest of the way. "Just put on your flip-flops." She could see that shoes would be even more impossible than the pants. She thought of some joke about elephantitis but decided against it.

Zoë had to loosen the left one so he could slip his foot in.

And so he walked carefully up the stairs out the door and across the driveway into the car.

He edged his way onto the front seat, but his leg was so swollen he could hardly bend it. She pushed the seat back as far as it could go, and he turned a little sideways to accommodate his leg. She knew it was a blood clot. She was sure his leg must be swelling even now, hanging over the edge of the seat like that. She worried it would dislodge and rush to his lungs.

Not a car on the road. Everything sleepy and dark, with just a streetlamp here and there to light the way. It was raining lightly, and Zoë flicked on the wipers. She looked over at Jay. He was watching out the side window. She turned on the radio and found some middle-of-the-night jazz. She couldn't think of a single thing to say.

Soon they turned off the highway onto the side road and saw the flags on top of the hospital flapping in the wind, lighted up against the night sky by a floodlight on the roof. They turned into the Emergency lane and Zoë pulled the car right up next to the double doors. The lighted entrance yawned back at them. Jay swung his leg out of the car, and just sat there on the edge of the seat.

"I *really* don't want to go in there." The minute she touched his back, though, he lifted himself up and dragged that leg with him through those doors, while Zoë just sat there thinking how she should have made him wait while she ran in and got a wheelchair—he shouldn't be walking on that leg—but she didn't, thank goodness she didn't.

She drove off to park the car. No problem finding a parking spot, that was for sure. She looked across the lot to the square of light Jay had disappeared into. She didn't want to go in there either. She wanted to go back home, crawl into bed beside Jay, and go back to the dream. Still, she walked right through the lighted double doors and over to the Triage Desk. Nobody in sight. Nobody anywhere.

She pushed through the swinging doors that said *No Admittance* into a silent, white corridor, heard the snap of the doors closing behind her. She walked past a dozen cubicles, half-curtained and still. No patients; no doctors or nurses; no aides or custodians. She stopped to listen, heard the clock hum, felt the molecules buzzing in her ears. Maybe the blood clot buried deep in that leg had gotten loose and gone straight to his heart. But it couldn't have been more than ten or fifteen minutes since she'd left him, and he was in a hospital for godsake, so why was she panicking?

Then Zoë heard a chair move and saw a tiny white-haired little nurse bent over some charts or papers, sitting in the nurses' station. "Excuse me," she said, and the nurse swiveled around.

They'd told her to wait for him on the seventh floor where they'd bring him after X-ray. So she went back out into the lobby, turned down the hall and found the elevators, pushed "seven," and waited. The doors slid open and there it was: *Oncology.*

What were they doing on the goddamned oncology floor?

"Excuse me," she said to the first nurse she could find. "I was wondering why they're putting my husband on this floor. He just has a blood clot."

"Well, we have other kinds of patients up here too. There's a TV in the waiting room if you like," she said, and went back to her charts. She couldn't just stand there, so she thought she might as well go down the hall and watch some television. She'd never watched TV at five in the morning that she could remember.

Zoë walked down that silent, dark corridor and turned into the waiting room, dark as well, but for the blue, unholy light of the television bolted high up on the far wall. She leaned back on the couch, shut her eyes. Then she heard somebody in the corner, somebody talking in low whispers on the phone. She was wearing sweats and running shoes. One of the laces had come untied. Zoë leaned her way a little, to see if that woman's misfortune was greater than her own.

A blood clot was a simple thing compared to what she overheard the woman in sweats say on the phone—that is unless the clot broke loose and traveled upstream.

Pretty soon it would be the morning news. Maybe she could catch a class or two of *Sunrise Semester* or something like that. The woman hung up the phone and disappeared into the hallway. Zoë picked up the channel changer, punched some numbers, and settled on *Sewing with Sylvia*. There was Sylvia herself, describing how to make heirloom baby clothes. She was demonstrating how to sew a band of lace onto the hem of a tiny white dress. She looked like she'd just come from the dentist. One side of her mouth went up when she smiled into the camera, and the other side went down.

She punched off the TV. Maybe Jay was in his room by now. She didn't want him to think she was keeping some kind of vigil, but she couldn't wait there any longer.

She thought about Sylvia and how brave she was to be on television like that. Sooner or later everybody was broken in some way. She wondered about those who slept even now behind those hushed doors, if any of them would be among the lucky ones to mow the lawn again, or buy a red scarf, or wash the dog, or walk down a tree-lined street some fine spring morning, *hello there, hello there, yes it is, it surely is*, or look in the mirror and not see the angry pink scar first thing forever.

Zoë found the door with Jay's number and peeked in, but there was only the waiting bed, with the sheet tucked in tight, so she sat down in the chair in the corner. Staring down at her was a giant clock bolted high on the wall next to the TV. She thought about turning it on again, but didn't want to hear any news today, thank you.

So she waited, watching the sun edge its way across the parking lot until she heard the gurney coming down the hall and knew Jay had come back. She shut her eyes and took a slow, deep breath before she floundered around trying to say everything right. She looked up and there was Jay, laid out on the gurney, hooked to an IV, all of it just as before. The bed came through the doorway and Jay looked at her, and looked away.

"I'll let you get settled," she said, and fled out of that room straight to the window at the end of the hall, where she stood looking out at that parking lot again, washed now in sharp, glaring sunshine. She didn't want to watch Jay being helped into bed.

"So who's your doctor?" she said, smooth as could be, slipping back into the chair by the bed.

"Dr. Salt, I guess."

"Dr. Salt! Don't you need a specialist or something?"

"How should I know? They only called him because he's in our files as the family doctor."

Ah, Dr. Salt, that strange, sad man whom she'd always thought looked a little like a thin-faced Hitler, with his square little mustache and dark, side-parted hair. Over the years he'd seen them through a couple of broken bones, a few stitches here and there, flu shots once a year, antibiotics every now and then. But he wasn't one of their many -*ologists* and she worried that they didn't have the doctor they needed for this new and dangerous thing.

"What exactly do they do for this?" Zoë said, looking up at the clear bottle of fluid hooked to the IV stand.

"Heparin."

"Do they know why this happened?" she asked, hoping for anything near the spider bite theory, or even the old athletic injury theory that had gotten them through Christmas.

Jay looked down at his leg propped up on a couple of pillows, bulging through the thin hospital sheet. "No."

"Do you think Dr. Salt knows enough about all this?"

Jay just sighed. "I don't know, Zoë. He's supposed to be in sometime this morning."

"Ask him if you need a specialist."

"Okay," he said, looking down at that leg. "I'm sorry about all this."

"Please don't say that."

She looked at the big clock. Seven thirty. She could hear the clatter of breakfast coming down the hall.

"I'd better get back," she said after a while. "I don't want the kids to worry. Jillie'll be worried anyway. I'll bring the kids after lunch. They need to see you're okay."

"Right," Jay said, trying to give her a smile.

"See you," he said. "Tell the kids I'm doing fine."

"See you."

She kissed him casually on the mouth and fled that room, and down the corridor and out into the sun. She couldn't remember where she'd parked the car. There were at least fifty cars waiting in that parking lot, the sun glaring off the windshield of every one. Then there it was, just where she'd left it a century ago. She looked back at the emergency room entrance. It seemed innocuous enough. It wasn't going to swallow them up in its tricky yellow light. She looked up at the flags on the roof of the hospital wilting in the windless morning.

Max was waiting in the doorway when she pulled into the driveway, Niki beside him, thumping her tail against the door. He looked like he'd just gotten up. "Where's Dad? I thought he was coming home with you." His eyes were wide with alarm and accusation.

"He needs to stay at the hospital for a little while. But nothing to worry about."

Then she gathered the kids into the living room while she explained what could not be explained—he'd be home in a few days, and no he wasn't exactly sick, he just had to rest. They'd all go see him after lunch.

"Is it cancer?" Max said. Jillie climbed into her lap. Niki lay down by her feet.

"Oh, no, it's not cancer," she said, remembering how those elevator doors opened up onto the word *Oncology*. What would the kids think when they saw that word? They knew exactly what it meant.

"Mom," Will said, "this shouldn't be going on." His eyes filled with tears. "I'm not going to do this. I'm not." He stood up, tucked his head, and bolted downstairs.

"I'll go tell him it's okay," Max said, getting up. But he turned back. "Is it?" Nobody said anything.

Zoë could feel the ache of withholding tears. How would she ever save them? "Of course it is, Sweetie."

"I'll tell him too," Jillie said. "I'll let him use my blanket."

Zoë watched her scoot down the stairs after Max, then leaned over, put her arms around Niki, and cried.

She'd brought the kids to the hospital after lunch to see that their dad was really all right. But she decided to take them home, then come back for dinner. She'd have a tray brought up for herself so they could have a little dinner date. Will was going to make everybody dinner. He insisted upon it.

"Don't set anything on fire," she said, then regretted it. "And don't go near the barbeque." The kids exchanged knowing looks Zoë did not want to interpret. Anything they came up with would be better than a dry hamburger on a stale bun in some hospital cafeteria. She couldn't remember what food was in the refrigerator or the pantry but there was always peanut butter and jelly.

Will told Max and Jillie to go outside and feed the pups while he got to work. He put on Jay's barbeque apron, which Jay himself hardly

ever wore. He smiled to himself. Something was just coming to him.
He looked in the pantry. Top Ramen and mac n' cheese was too easy
and too ordinary. Tonight needed to be special. He didn't know why.
Except that their dad was in the hospital. He wanted to make something adult, something from the olden days, though he wasn't sure
what that was, exactly, so he grabbed the big, old, red cookbook with
the white paint splatters. He couldn't remember why there was paint
on the cookbook but knew it was a good story. He felt powerful, magical. He would make something awesome.

He shut his eyes—he'd let fate guide his way—and opened the book.
Fish Aspic. Fish Aspic? What the hell was *aspic?* It looked like something
dead. Or some kind of organ. He turned the page. *Sauced Dove Breasts
on Croutons.* Who would eat *doves?* There was something really wrong
with these pictures. They didn't look like actual food. *Cornish Lobster
Pasties.* They looked like they might bite your fingers. *Crab Nut Mold
with Green Onion Medley.* Tentacles. *Lemon Trout in Parsley Jell-O.*
Dead fish floating in swamp water. *Viscous,* he was thinking, without
the word for it. Everything looked kind of greenish yellow. Or brownish
slime. Like somebody threw up and somebody else took a picture of it.
Their mom never made stuff like this. So why was the book so olden?
*Tomato Stuffed Eggs. Pork Stuffed Apples. Carrot Boats Stuffed with
Liver and Bacon.* Everything was stuffed with something.

He sat on the counter and looked down at the apron. *Dad's Cookin'*
in white letters. He thought about their dad having to lie so still in
that hospital bed. He didn't even look sick. Will turned the page. All
the eggs looked like eyeballs. He was beginning to feel a little sick.
He certainly didn't feel hungry. Nothing wrong with peanut butter
and jelly sandwiches. He could open a can of chicken noodle soup
and then get out the ice cream. Or why bother with the sandwiches
and the soup? Just go for the ice cream. He'd get out every topping

they had. They'd have dessert for dinner like they did when something really great happened or something bad. Chocolate sauce, caramel sauce, marshmallow sauce, butterscotch, M&M's, Redi Whip, gummy bears, chocolate chips, maple syrup—why not? He'd crumble up some Oreos for the topping.

He got out a dish for each condiment and spread it out across the dining room table, put out the bowls and the spoons, then set three gallons of ice cream—strawberry, chocolate chip, and French vanilla—in the middle of the table. He thought about lighting some candles but it was way too early for that. He'd put on some music but couldn't think what. He'd call them in to a great surprise. This would cheer everybody up. Especially Max. "I don't think we should leave him," Max had said just as they were getting on the elevator. "Dad's all alone." He looked like he was ready to cry. But it was good their mom was going back.

They sat in their accustomed places, but the dining room table seemed way too big. Too many empty chairs. So Jillie got Debbie, their mom's childhood doll, and propped her on a pillow in their mom's chair. Max put their dad's werewolf mask on his old Dapper Dan doll and set him at the head of the table. Then Will got up, put Dapper Dan in his own seat, pulled out the chair, and sat down at the head of the table.

Max started to say something but then became strangely quiet. "That's okay, Max, I need to sit here." Something was settling upon them. It was only for one night, out of a thousand nights past, a thousand nights to come. The kids ate quickly, and for once in their lives, passed on seconds.

It was late and the kids had long gone to bed. Zoë was standing by the front window, watching the moon float in and out of the clouds building in the west. Tomorrow it would rain. She walked out onto the back deck. The wind was almost chilly now, and she wished for a sweatshirt. But she still wasn't tired, and wasn't going to bed until she was so tired she couldn't keep her eyes open. She often was afraid of this sleepless dark. She thought briefly of the fires and was glad for the coming rain. She couldn't seem to remember when she didn't think of fire.

The pups were sound asleep in their little cardboard boxes. She wished for a lock on the puppy gate. She couldn't hear anything but the wind. No birds, no owls, no coyotes now for days. Then a howl that seemed closer than it had ever been, just at the edge of the yard.

She rushed inside and blocked off the kitchen with the baby gate, spread newspapers all over the floor, and brought the pups and their cardboard boxes in through the back door. She looked out the window. All she saw was her face looking back. She turned out the light. "Goodnight, puppies, you go to sleep now."

She climbed into that big, empty bed and wished for a kid or two. She took some deep breaths, and tried to put herself to sleep. She could hear the pups dragging their boxes across the floor, could hear their toenails sliding over the floor as they chased each other around the room. But by then she was too tired to do anything but lie there and hope the pups would settle down. She stayed curled up on her side of the bed as far as she could go and listened to the pups and to the wind, until she finally fell asleep.

In the morning, she came upstairs and walked into the silent kitchen. It looked like the morning after. Newspapers shredded and scattered all over the floor, puppy shit everywhere but on the newspapers, and there were the pups, lying in a heap in the corner of the room, sleeping it off.

Jay called her in the afternoon, sounding kind of funny. "The nurses keep coming in and looking at my leg. I'm lying here trying not to move, but I'm listening to everything. When are you and the kids coming down?"

"Do you think something's wrong?"

"The nurses don't think the heparin dosage is strong enough to be doing me any good."

"Did Dr. Salt see you this morning?"

"Yeah. I asked him about it and he said the dosage was fine. Are you coming over pretty soon?" Zoë had never heard him ask for anything in that way before. But the poor guy was lying there in bed trying to keep perfectly still so this little time bomb in his groin wouldn't go off and blow him to pieces.

So they all piled into the car and drove to the hospital. They walked in on Dr. Salt himself. He looked like he'd grown shorter since she'd seen him last. But then she'd always been sitting or lying down when he walked into the examining room.

"So I think we'll schedule the CAT scan for tomorrow," he was saying as they walked in.

"What CAT scan?"

Dr. Salt stared at them. "Is it all right to discuss this in front of the children?"

What was she supposed to say? *No?* She didn't know what was coming next, but sending them out in the hall might be worse than hearing whatever it was they were going to hear.

"That's okay, go ahead," she said, hoping Jay felt so too.

"All right," he said, then picked up the thread he'd dropped when they walked in the room. "Given your history, there's a good chance there's a cancerous node behind the vein and that's what's caused the blockage, but we won't know till we get the CAT scan results." He sat down in the chair next to the bed. His shoulders sagged. He did look a little bit like Hitler, only sadder, smaller. Jay's folder slipped off his lap and spilled out onto the floor.

"My husband is concerned about the heparin dosage," Zoë said to the top of his head as he bent down to pull things together.

"What?" He jerked his head back up and looked at her.

"Some of the nurses think the heparin dose is too low."

He scanned the files again, tilting his head to look through his half glasses.

"No, this is exactly on schedule for the first twenty-four hours."

First twenty-four hours?

"Excuse me, but what do you mean by the *first* twenty-four hours? This is his *second* twenty-four hours."

"My mom's right," Will said, scooting off the window ledge. She and Jay just looked at each other.

"Oh, that's right," he said. "Well." He looked at the charts again, fingered his glasses, cleared his throat. "The dosages are still correct. What I'm concerned about is something else. His blood sugars are sky high."

"What do you mean sky high?" Jay said.

"Over three hundred on the last reading. So. We've got to get them down."

"Down to what?"

"Somewhere around one hundred, one twenty at the most, so I'm going to give him a shot of insulin to lower those numbers." He fumbled around in his bag for something, turned around, and went out into the hall. They heard him talking to one of the nurses.

"One more thing," he said, coming back into the room, nodding in her direction. "You'll need to cut way back on fats. That's just like sugar for the diabetic."

"You think Jay's diabetic?"

"Yes I do. So. Instead of frying with oil, you should get some Pam."

"But I don't really ever fry anything anymore." She knew what was healthy. These last months, she'd become an expert.

"Well, you'll need to cook with vegetable spray from now on."

"But what about the CAT scan? What about the lymph node?"

"Now if you spray the frying pan with vegetable spray, it works just like oil. I've scheduled the Pam-scan for tomorrow afternoon. We'll know about all that tomorrow."

Jay looked angry, pulled himself up on the bed as far as he could without moving his leg. Dr. Salt turned toward the nurse coming in the door with a syringe. She gave them a funny look and handed it to him, then turned on her heel and went out the door. Jay and Zoë traded crazy glances.

"What's that for?" Jay said.

"Insulin. Like I said. We need to get the blood sugars down."

"I really don't want to rush into this insulin business," Jay said, holding up his hand. Dr. Salt looked startled, stepped back from the bed. Zoë could see that the syringe was shaking.

"All right, but I don't think things are going to change."

He fumbled around in his bag, then snapped it shut. "I'll see you in the morning," he said. "We'll check your sugars then."

The kids had been so quiet and so still Zoë had almost forgotten they were here. Jillie was in the chair sitting on Max's lap; Will was standing in the corner.

"Here, Will," Zoë said, handing him a twenty. "You guys go to the cafeteria and buy some ice cream, okay?"

"Maybe we should stick around, though."

"Nah, go get some ice cream." Jay looked at Will standing there with the twenty in his hand. "Come here." Will leaned over so Jay could wrap his arms around him. "We'll figure things out."

"Dad?"

"Tell me."

Will stood up, blinking back tears. "I'm okay, Dad." He touched Jay's foot through the sheet on his way out the door. "Come on, guys," he said, then turned back for a moment and waved.

Zoë's heart tightened. When had this happened? This strong, lean boy so tall now, his face becoming Jay's face before her very eyes. His lovely cheekbones, his golden hair, those blue eyes catching the light.

"Are they all right?" Jay said, wiping away the coming tears.

"They will be," Zoë said. "Because *you're* going to be all right." She sat down and lay her head on his chest. "That's all they need."

"Did any of that make sense?" Jay's eyes were hot and bright.

"No." She sat up and looked out the door.

"Do you think he was drunk?"

"Maybe he's on drugs." A nurse hurried past the doorway with something in her hand. "Well, he can't be your doctor anymore, that's for sure."

"But how can we get rid of him?"

"Can't we fire him or something?" She was ready to hire an ambulance and rush Jay to the medical center downtown where the real doctors were.

"I have no idea." He lay back and shut his eyes.

Visiting hours were over and it was time to round up the kids, who were probably playing chase in the cafeteria or down some forbidden corridor. So she kissed Jay goodnight and said not to worry, they'd think of something.

She rounded the corner and passed the little foyer on her way to the elevators. There he was, sitting at the table by the magazine rack, hunched over somebody's files, rubbing his eyes. What was going on here? Some slow, shifty senility you only saw now and then? She didn't care. All she knew was that she wanted to strike him in the chest or call him some terrible name. But she was too polite back then to do anything but frown past him on her way to the elevators.

"That doctor didn't sound very smart," Max said.

"No he didn't."

"I don't want him to be Daddy's doctor anymore."

"Me either," Zoë said. "Don't worry, kid, Daddy'll be all right. And we'll get him a new doctor."

She got the kids home, fed everybody leftover chili, and settled them down. Then she checked to see that they'd tucked the pups in all right. She let Niki out to say goodnight, then let her in again. Niki followed her to the little upstairs bathroom and sat down outside the door while she got ready for bed. She could hear the chink of her collar as she lay down and stretched out because she knew Zoë would be a while.

She thought of Jay, all alone in that room on the seventh floor, and what if Dr. Salt came back with a needle while he was sleeping? Or that clot! What if it came loose and went to his lungs or heart, and they called him in and he did something terrible? She knew she had to do something, but what could she do?

It felt hard to breathe. She turned off the bathroom light and sat down on the floor by the heat register and hugged her knees. She listened to the hum of the furnace fan. The dark felt warm and heavy on her skin. She took a deep breath and let it out slowly. She could hear Niki pawing the bathroom door. She could feel her heart skipping beats, listened for it to catch up. She began deep breathing again, saying her biofeedback mantra over and over—*all safe, all safe*—which did nothing to keep those images at bay: a black cast iron frying pan, a yellow can of vegetable spray, a milky white lymph node behind some plugged-up stretch of arterial plumbing.

He couldn't move that leg but he had to get out of there.

Will tapped lightly on the door. "Mom, are you in there? Are you okay?" She could see his shadow under the door. "It's dark in there."

"It's okay, Will. I'll be out in a minute." She could hear him leaning against the door. Then she tried to say the mantra again but the words had vanished.

"Mom?"

"Just a minute," she said through the door. She stood up and turned on the light. She ran cold water over her wrists, splashed some cold water on her face, buried her face in the towel for a moment and breathed in the clean, soapy smell.

"What are we gonna do?" Will said. He was sitting on the kitchen counter. His eyes were frightened.

"Please hand me the phone book."

Safe as Houses Out There

"Oh shit," she said under her breath when she came into the room two days later and saw that the other bed wasn't empty anymore. She'd liked the private room feeling. It was easier to pretend this was a budget motel in some strange country where they were only stopping on their way to somewhere else.

"Zoë, this is Mr. George Brazil," Jay said.

"Hello, Mr. Brazil," she said, and took his hand. It was papery and dry.

"He's in the plumbing and heating business."

"That's right," he said, blinking as though startled out of some dark dream. "Thirty-five years. I sold it to my brother's kid last year when the diabetes got so bad."

"He's having an amputation tomorrow. Diabetes complications." He looked at her as if to say, *Don't worry, this will never happen to us.*

"I'm so sorry," Zoë said, but she wasn't sorry. She'd conjured her cobalt blue shield and it shimmered before her. Arms, legs, feet, what did she care? As it turned out, though, it was only a couple of toes—gangrenous toes, three of them, two on the left, one on the right, and hidden away under the covers, thank God.

"Well, good luck tomorrow."

Mr. George Brazil nodded and closed his eyes. They'd already doped him up.

Zoë pulled the curtain around them, turned down the light, and edged the chair close to the bed. "So you like your new doctor, huh?" she said with a smile. Everything was going to be all right now. She knew it. The CAT scan showed no lymph node.

He couldn't stop smiling back at her.

"I don't suppose it hurts that she's completely gorgeous."

"No, it doesn't hurt. It never did."

"Very funny." She liked this easy joking they'd begun, wished she could keep it going until he got out of here. It was all up to her.

"Gangrene doesn't hurt either."

"God, Jay, don't go sardonic on me."

She leaned over and kissed him on the mouth. She eased back in the chair. Tonight she felt safe enough to say anything. So she did. "What did she say caused it?"

"She doesn't really know."

"But she's a specialist!" And then it was gone. Like that. No secret, safe place, no cobalt blue shield. She was left stranded in air.

"She said sometimes they never do figure it out. She just said they'd keep watching everything."

"But could it have something to do with *cancer*?" Zoë had to whisper that last word.

Jay looked away. "Maybe. Probably not though." He still couldn't look at her.

The thought grabbed at her heart and she felt suddenly, frighteningly dizzy. She put her head between her hands. She'd read somewhere that cancer could do this. But Jay's cancer was gone, for godsake, the *oncology* ward they seemed to be on notwithstanding.

"It's gonna be okay, Zoë," Jay said, touching her hair. Her face had unmasked itself in its terror and rage.

"This." She touched his leg through the sheets. "*This* is not okay." She looked at him fiercely. "Don't you ever leave me."

It had come upon them again so powerfully—all that was at risk, all they could lose—they turned silent before it. The lights outside had come on, erasing the dusky purple of twilight she loved. Zoë could see people making their way back to their ordinary lives.

"It's getting dark," Jay said. "I don't like you going out there in the dark."

"Safe as houses out there," she said, washed over with a sudden longing to be back in the world. She knew it wasn't safe out there either.

"Visiting hours are over," said the serene voice over the loudspeaker.

"I'm not a visitor," Zoë said.

"Neither am I."

"Wish you were. Wish we both were." Just then Jay's eyes filled with tears and he turned away.

Zoë looked up at the IV bag hooked to the stand by the head of Jay's bed so he wouldn't know what she had seen. The bag was collapsing in on itself. She tamped down the urge to rush out and get a nurse. She knew an empty bag wouldn't let air into the vein because she'd asked about it a dozen times. Still, she couldn't stop looking at it.

"I told the doctor about spraying everything with Pam and she just laughed," Jay said. Zoë let out a long breath. "She said fat is *not* like sugar. We don't have to spray anything with Pam. We could spray *him* with Pam, however."

"But what did she say about this blood sugar thing?" She would not call it *diabetes*.

"Yeah, they're gonna watch that too. She thought it might be a side effect of the radiation. She thinks maybe some islet cells in the pancreas got nuked along the way."

"So the blood sugar came from the radiation, then?"

"That's what she thinks."

"Well, that's a side effect they never told us about."

Jay looked toward the other side of the room. "Is he asleep?"

Zoë pulled the curtain aside and nodded.

He'd fallen asleep, poor devil. Having your toes cut off like that. There must be a nicer way to spend the day, though all things considered, it could be worse. But the man in the bed bore no resemblance to the George Brazil in the picture on the side of those plumbing repair trucks she'd seen everywhere lately—a fleet of strong, shining faces, flying down the freeway.

"What are you smiling at?" Jay said. "Time for a quickie?"

She began to laugh. Then she lowered her voice. "Did you ever see any of those George Brazil trucks?"

"Those what?"

"George Brazil Heating and Plumbing?" she whispered. "Those trucks with that picture of the repairman who looks like he walked right out of the fifties?" She leaned close. "I wonder if that's *him*."

She looked over at the old guy lying there with his mouth open, white, wispy hair, the sharp-angled cheekbones—and tried to see if he had ever been the man on the George Brazil heating truck, with his tanned, well-muscled arm carrying that heavy toolbox, ready to step out of the picture and come to the rescue.

Nobody came to see George Brazil, not that Zoë ever saw, anyway. He couldn't carry that toolbox now. After tomorrow he wouldn't even be able to carry himself. That night she dreamed of George Brazil. He put down his toolbox and held out his arm. She was surprised he was so tall. She reached up and traced *George* in the red script on his breast pocket. Ah, George. Come over here and unplug this drain, make us cool or make us warm, but make the pipes cool and smooth again.

PUREBREED MALAMUTE MIX / BLACK AND WHITE PANDA BEAR FACES. 6 WEEKS OLD. The moment she posted it, she realized what a contradiction it was. How can you have a purebred *mix*? She wondered if the ad would be so confounding no one would reply, and if this is what she'd wanted all along.

"I don't want the puppies to go," Jillie said, as she kept watch out the front window for the first of the possible owners. They'd not been able to sell them full price since the pedigree on their father's side was unclear. Still, Zoë had wanted some exchange of money. She couldn't just give them away.

"Can't we keep them? Or one of them anyway?"

"Oh, I don't know, Jillie, we already have Niki. We'll see."

"You always say that."

"I know." Zoë was too tired to think of what else to say.

Pretty soon they saw the blue truck make its uncertain way up the hill.

"Today's the big day," she said, coming out the front door. Jillie was holding onto her shirttail as they walked down the porch steps. "Jillie, this is Mr. Wyler."

"Hi," she said as she tucked her head down and scooted over to the puppy run.

"My kid's so excited he couldn't sleep all night." Mr. Wyler pointed to the little boy peeking through the window from the front seat of the truck. His hair lay in blond ringlets over his forehead. Such a child. He was an angel. His wide blue eyes were loving those puppies already. This letting go would be all right. A good lesson for Jillie too. But a lesson in what? Her eyes ached.

Jillie went over and looked in. The little boy ducked down, then peeked back up.

"What's his name?" she asked his dad.

"He's Martin," Mr. Wyler said, as they opened the gate. The pups came tumbling down the runway toward the open gate. Mr. Wyler sat down on the cement, and Zoë put Climber and Speck in his lap. They licked his ears, tugged at his shirt. Then the little boy came in and sat down, too, and pulled out a couple of dog biscuits from his front pocket. Jillie watched from the other side of the gate.

"Come on, Jillie, help me play with the other pups," she said, but Jillie just stood there.

Then it was time to say goodbye, and so Zoë picked up those two pups one last time, those two brothers, who'd slept curled up around each other almost since they were born. Max and Will came up from the gully. Their tree house was finished. Max took Climber, who snuggled into his neck and licked his face. "He was my best puppy," he said, and kissed the top of his head. Then he handed him to the little boy, who climbed up into the truck and scooted over to his side, the pup tucked against his shoulder.

Speck was asleep in the crook of Zoë's arm, so when she gave him to Will, he only sighed and went back to sleep. Will just stood there with Speck in his arms. "When he wakes up, he'll be in another world," he said. Then he handed Speck to Mr. Wyler and stepped back. Zoë caught a look of sorrow in his eyes. The thoughts of a boy are "long, long thoughts" came to mind. Longfellow. It stunned her again to see how he was growing up.

When Will turned to go, Zoë took his arm. "Wait," she said, and gathered them together and they all said, "Goodbye, Climber, goodbye, Speck. We're glad we knew you."

Jillie burst into tears and ran inside. Niki was watching out the glass window by the front door. They heard her howl from where she stood watching through the window. Zoë wondered if they should have let her say goodbye too.

"Look how happy that little boy is," Zoë said to her, as she came in the door. She was standing by the living room window, watching the truck make its careful way down the hill.

"I know," Jillie said. "He gets to have two dogs."

"But they have a big farm and lots of room."

Well, maybe they could keep one after all. She was seeing in her mind's eye the pounds of dog food, dog fur, dog shit. Still, it felt like giving your children up for adoption.

She picked Jillie up and she buried her head against Zoë's shoulder and put her arms around her neck. Niki stood there, too, her nose pressed against the glass, watching that blue truck disappear around the corner at the bottom of the hill.

"I want Daddy right now," Jillie said. Zoë stood there watching out the window, holding this starfish of a child, and thought about all the goodbyes to come.

As she came into the room, George Brazil was waving his good hand in the air. The other hand was hooked up to the IV. Zoë thought he was calling for help, but as she came closer she could see he was following along in three-quarter time to some secret music.

"Hello, Mr. Brazil," she said. He nodded as she passed his bed, and gave a short wave in benediction, or so it seemed.

"Hi, Jay," she said, pulling the curtains shut, and wrapping them up in a white gauzy circle. She didn't care what Mr. Brazil thought. "Is he okay?"

"He's out of it. They've got him chock full of drugs."

"Everybody's at a sleepover, so it's just me tonight."

"Come here, then."

She leaned over and kissed him.

"My God," he said.

"What?"

"What happened to you?"

"What do you mean?"

"Your eyelids are purple."

She reached for the compact mirror in her purse. "Well I didn't look like this in the store."

"They did this to you in a *store*? What store?"

"Nordstrom's."

"Have you thought perhaps of lawsuit?"

"You're getting awfully cheeky these days." She looked around at their fine little private room and couldn't stop smiling.

"You were at the mall?"

"Oh, I took Will's soccer shoes back, and a cosmetic person offered to give me a makeover, so I thought why not? I'd come beautiful to you for a change."

"Was she color blind or just blind?"

"All right. So maybe I'm wearing party makeup."

"So maybe we should have a party."

She looked again. He was right about the eyes—purple and pink eye shadow sort of in stripes across her eyelids, and in this light she didn't look sun-kissed like the saleswoman said, but kind of orange. "Good grief. I've got to get some of this stuff off. I'm going into the bathroom." She'd been using Jay's bathroom for the last couple of days instead of wandering down the hall.

In this light she looked even worse. Maybe it was some kind of demented sales strategy, but the saleswoman began by explaining how all the products in this new cosmetic line had sunscreen in the formula, even the eye shadow, and ended up talking about her dog, and how he'd gotten skin cancer from lying in the sun.

"I didn't know that was possible. I mean through the fur," Zoë said, sneaking a look at herself in the mirror. She couldn't exactly tell what was happening.

"He was very short-haired," she said, reaching across the counter for something. "You need to blend the purple and pink at the crease line, like this." But her eyes were shut and she could only tell what the saleslady was doing by the feel of her thumbs on her eyes. She could see that dog, though, sitting outside in the sun chewing on himself.

"He completely severed his own tail," she explained, as she began to apply the blush. "Now this works as a bronzer *and* blush. You just apply it darker under the cheekbones. Like this."

Zoë looked in the lighted mirror on the cosmetic counter but could only see the woman's white-coated arm flapping up and down.

"There." She put down the brush. "Now take a good look." Zoë looked at her white lab coat, looked at her face in the mirror, and knew she had to get out of there.

She came out of the bathroom and sat back down. "I don't know why you're in that bed." He looked so tanned and strong, lying there with his arms crossed behind his head.

"I'm not good for anything like this."

"You're good for me." She wanted to explain how frightened she was all those months of radiation, waiting for him to come home, but then he'd walk in that door, his jacket slung over his shoulder. "*Zoë!*" he'd call out, and she'd hug him and feel his back through his shirt, smell his aftershave, and that scared feeling would go right away. Or coming into this room after imagining all kinds of terrible things in the night, and seeing how crazy it was to be in that bed, the swelling all gone now.

Jay changed channels, and Zoë climbed up and lay down beside him. *Wheel of Fortune* was just beginning, but she wasn't really watching. She was thinking about Mr. Brazil on the other side of the curtain, drugged out on pain pills, his mummified feet. Mr. Brazil, who'd been strong once, too, holding his toolbox, a regular Mr. Fix-It whose shining face knew nothing of amputations or sorrow.

The curtains opened and Laura, their favorite nurse, poked her head in, looked at them lying on that bed, and smiled. "I was just wondering, Jay, if you'd like a shower."

"Oh, that sounds wonderful. It's been so long. But how would I do it?"

"We'll just put you in a shower chair and wheel you down to the shower room. You won't even have to stand up. The IV stand can wheel right down with you."

"All right," he said as Zoë scooted off the bed and sat down in the chair.

Laura looked at her. "Would you like to give it to him?"

"Really?"

"Sure. I know he'd enjoy it more than if I gave it to him. You'll just have to be careful not to trip over the IV line."

So the three of them wheeled down the corridor to the shower room at the end of the hall, Jay holding a stack of big Turkish towels in his lap. It was a private bath, so to speak, though the white-tiled walls and the bars for holding tight couldn't hide what this room was. But it looked sort of cozy in a Twilight Zone kind of way. Laura positioned the shower chair under the nozzle attached to the wall, and scooted the IV stand safely out of the way in the corner. "You can take one too," she said as she stepped into the hall. "You can lock the door, if you want." And she closed the door behind her.

"Your legs are almost the same now," Zoë said, looking down at him sitting in the shower chair in his hospital gown.

"I know."

She knew what he was thinking. It was what she was thinking too. Why not? This place had taught them a thing or two, so why bloody well not? She slipped the hospital gown off his shoulders, slipped off her shirt, too, unhooked her bra, lifted off his hospital gown, then knelt down on the tiled shower, lay her head in his lap, and loved him as well as she could.

It was becoming easier all the time now. Maybe it was a respite from the drama of her days. But she longed for the little boy dreams and was disappointed when she woke to their absence. But the dreams felt too tenuous for words. She thought about the dog and the cold and the brutal father. She wanted that dog to be safe. She knew he must be hungry. So, after supper, after his father had gone out, the boy climbed up on the counters and rummaged around in the cupboards for something that was good for dogs to eat. He mixed an old pie pan full of some raw hot dogs and last night's macaroni and cheese, poured milk over the top, then stirred it all up with the big wooden spoon that was supposed to stay on the counter by the back door. He knelt in the snow and watched the dog eat. The dog ate it all in a matter of minutes, then just licked and licked the pan. The little boy set down a saucepan of water and the dog drank all of that too. Then he began to make a funny gulping sound and arched his back and then vomited all over the snow. "Poor Piney," he said, patting him on the head. He looked back at the house, and quickly covered it with the snow he flicked up with the side of his boot. Then Dad said, "Get *in* here, boy, what're you doin' out there with that *dog*?"

The boy had gone to bed and lay there listening to the TV, hoping it covered up the sound the dog was making from time to time, but got up every little bit to see if Dad was still in his chair. Pretty soon he heard the TV go off, heard heavy footsteps coming up the stairs, heard Dad's growly cough, heard the bedroom door shut, heard the dog begin to howl again. After that he sneaked out the front door with the old woolen army blanket from the basement, and ran across the backyard as lightly as he could, afraid of the crunching noises he made in the snow.

"Here, Piney, I'm gonna wrap you up," he called in a whisper, "but you gotta be quiet." The dog was shivering and started to whine when he saw him coming across the snow. "You gotta stay here," he said, as he pushed the dog into the doghouse. He wrapped the blanket around the dog and kissed him on the top of the head and started back for the house. Halfway across the yard, he looked back and there was the dog pulling at the end of the rope. The blanket lay in a heap in the snow. He looked up at the house and saw a light go on in the bathroom and darted around the side of the house toward the front door.

He couldn't feel his toes in the old corduroy slippers by the time he crept back up the stairs to his bedroom. He wrapped up in his blanket and sat watching the doghouse lying silent under the cold, indifferent moon. Until he fell asleep, curled up himself against the window, where Zoë saw his long, sad face pressed against the glass.

Conflagration

The sun lay a golden shimmer over the water as it slipped from the sky. Zoë pulled her car over to the shoulder to watch it spread across the rim of the hills, turning them a ravishing blue. She flicked on her lights and drove on home, rounding the corner by the mailboxes, and headed up her hill in the darkening light. The bump in the road jarred her, because just then she felt something whack against the grille of the car. She sat there a millisecond, her foot fast to the brake, before she knew she had hit something. She spun into the driveway, threw the car into park, and flung open the door.

There he was, in such agony he could not quiet the high-pitched moan. It was the most terrible sound she had ever heard. For a moment she panicked that it might be Niki. But she could see Niki inside, looking out at her from the lighted front window. The dog was yelping as he tried to drag himself off the road into the bushes.

She leaned over him and thought she might be sick. She knelt down and put her head on her knees. The dog was partly in the bushes now and trying very hard to be still. Zoë leaned over to touch him briefly but took her hand back. He could fear-bite as easily as not. He tried to raise his head to bite himself to stop the pain only to flop back down into the bushes. She did not see any blood.

Now he was giving off little panting moans. His back legs were lying at a terrifying angle to the rest of him. She reached out to touch him again, she couldn't help it, but again drew her hand back. She was glad the kids weren't home. Right now she couldn't remember where they were.

"It's okay, it's okay," she said. She was pretty sure it was Roy's dog. She'd seen him come up the hill in the dark with Roy a couple of times. That low, shadowy figure rounding some corner with Roy close behind—double shadows that had frightened her since the fires had begun last summer.

Then she was running down the hill to the only place she could go. She didn't think about Roy or what he might do to her. All she could think about was that dog. She knocked and knocked, tried the buzzer, but it didn't seem to work. Then she pounded on the living room window until Roy yanked the curtains open and stared back at her. She went back to the front door and there he was, standing in the doorway with his hands on his head. She wondered if he might strike her or grab her and pull her inside.

"What's wrong?" he shouted. "What's happened? Are you okay?"

"Your dog. I'm so sorry. He's up my road. I didn't see him."

Roy didn't say a word but just took off up the hill, leaving his door wide open. Zoë was out of breath coming up behind him, as he stood in the middle of the road. "Buddy! Buddy!" he cried.

"He's right there. He's in there." Roy leaned over. The dog had managed to pull himself mostly into the bushes.

"No, no, no," Roy cried, dropping to his knees. He leaned over and touched the side of his muzzle, his head, his ears. "Buddy. Hey, Buddy. You're gonna be okay, boy." The dog tried to lift his head but now could not. Zoë could see the shape of Roy's spine through that thin, paint-splattered T-shirt, then watched his back knot up against the sobs he was trying to hold in.

"Where can I take him? I never had him anywhere."

"I know where to go. It's an ER for animals. I'm so sorry." She was crying by now. She looked at Roy for a long moment. Tears were running unabashedly down his face, but he didn't shout or yell at her.

He stood up, jammed his hands in his pockets as though he didn't know where they should go. "Once he learned how to get out, he never forgot no matter what I did. I was working. I didn't know he got up here. Can you stay with him while I go get my van?"

"Should I touch him?"

"Just talk gentle to him. He'll understand."

"Hey, Buddy, you're gonna be okay." The dog was trembling now and the panting had tamped down into a fast, shallow breathing, though he never took his eyes off her. Zoë was trembling now too. She still could see no blood.

In a flash Roy was back up the road with his brown van. He stood over the dog, who lay in such agony and despair it was hard to imagine lifting him without doing more harm.

Zoë came back with a large, candy-striped beach towel. "We could use this to help lift him."

Roy looked at it and stood up. "I don't want to hurt him any more than he already is."

"You didn't hurt him, I did."

"It wasn't your fault."

Zoë just looked at him. "It was, though."

"The towel's a good idea. We can put it under him and lift him up."

But when they tried to shift the towel under his belly, he yelped and mouthed Roy's arm. "He didn't bite me. He was just telling me to go slow. Let's use the towel for his hips and I'll carry the rest of him. Can you lift him like that? He won't weigh so much that way."

Zoë eased the towel slowly from the other side until they had slipped it all the way under him. Roy put his hands under him and wrapped his arms around his chest. The dog let out a wail, and mouthed Roy on the arm but again, did not bite him. He kept straining his neck to get up. But his back end was dead weight so Zoë lifted his hips in the towel just like a sling.

"Hey, fella. We're just goin' for a ride. We're gonna get you all fixed up." Roy kept talking to him in a slow, soft voice, and the dog quit trying to lift himself up, and finally lay his head back against Roy's chest. And like this they edged their way to the van, where Roy lifted him gently up and into the back of the van while Zoë kept hold of the corners of the towel and lifted his hindquarters. She hopped up into the van and sat down beside him.

"I'll stay back here with him. I can tell you how to get to the ER. It's not far." She didn't think of the arsonist with the can of gasoline and the lighted match, or the man with the cap outside her kitchen window, or the Hangman on the porch, or the Halloween flames against his living room window. She only thought of the dog, panting now in quick, faint breaths, with no whimper at all.

She touched his head and felt him trembling all over. "There, there, old guy," she said. A trickle of blood was seeping out his nose. He didn't take his eyes off her. They sat like that in the back of the van as Roy followed her directions.

"Is he okay back there?" Roy called, his voice thick with tears.

"He's calmed down now." No need to tell him about the blood.

"I'm drivin' as gentle as I can, but I can't help hurryin'."

There were seats for the driver and one passenger. All the other seats had been taken out. And no windows here in the back. There were ladders fastened to the sides of the van, drop cloths folded in a neat pile, buckets of paint, a big cardboard box of brushes and rollers, a smaller box of blue masking tape. But no empty candy bar or hamburger wrappers, or French fries spilled on the floor, or beer or soda cans, or plastic water bottles. She thought about the back seat of her own car.

Then she noticed the easel leaning against the ladders and the five or six canvases half-covered with tarp. And a dog's water bowl and a box of dog biscuits. She was taking it all in. She was in his van. It occurred to her in bits and pieces how foolish this was. It couldn't be much longer. Then she felt the car turn sharply, then slow to a stop, as he pulled into the parking lot.

Roy dashed around to the back of the van and yanked open the back doors. "Hey, Buddy," Roy said, and stroked his head. The dog didn't flinch. Zoë climbed out of the van and rushed through the automatic doors. She came back out with two technicians in greens carrying a blue, plastic stretcher. They slid it under the dog, who didn't make a sound. When they raised his head, you could see his neck had gone slack. He didn't move when they buckled the belts gently over him. She thought of all the possible internal injuries. Spleen, liver, kidneys, heart, aorta rupture, punctured lung.

The trickle of blood from his nose had stopped, which she took as a good sign. But his eyes had gone far away. "I think he's in shock," Zoë said. She wished Jay were here. The technicians moved on down the hall. Roy looked back at her as he followed after Buddy on the stretcher. "I'll wait out here."

Now they were punching in a code on the door lock that led to the inner sanctum. "I'm sorry, sir, you can't come back here. We need to get him in right away. Please go to the desk and they'll tell you what to do."

"But I can't leave him *alone*. He needs somebody he knows." Zoë had never seen anyone so anguished. There was that strange gesture again. His hands on his head.

"We can't let you back here, sir." Zoë could understand that. Berserk pet owners running amok, hyperventilating, passing out. It was just like with people.

She touched Roy's shoulder. "It's okay. They know what they're doing. It's better if you stay out here anyway. They want you at the desk. I'll just go and sit down."

She took a seat near the desk.

Roy was leaning on the desk now, trying to fill out some forms. "I need to explain, and I know it's hard to hear this," the receptionist was saying. "But we need to know what you want right away. Then we need to have you pay. I know it sounds like we only want money and don't care about animals. But it's the only way it can be. Most people don't have insurance for this kind of thing. You can use a credit card, or anything you want."

Roy looked over at her. "I don't know what to do. What do I do?" Zoë came up beside him. On the form were three boxes. He needed to check one:

☐ DNR $0.00

☐ BASIC CPR $800.00

☐ ADVANCED CPR $1,600.00

"They want me to say which one. But I want him to *live*."

Zoë thought of the way that dog followed him everywhere. If you had no money, would you have to choose DNR? That treacherous road. That damned bump which high-centered you, so for one blinding, tragic moment you couldn't see what must be seen. She thought about offering to help pay but did not.

Roy just looked at her then picked up the green pen in a shaky hand and checked DNR. Tears ran down his face. "If he can't be saved, no use puttin' him through more stuff than he's already got."

She thought he would be angry, that she might be imperiled, but she felt no threat. He had said it so innocently she knew there was no fury, just a great sadness at the way the world works. She only felt the suffering that was his life now.

Zoë sat down in the waiting area and watched one of the techs lead Roy to an examining room.

She saw the way he hesitated and looked down the hallway at the door with the coded lock.

"Let's go in here so you can have some Pepsi," the tech said.

Pepsi? Was this supposed to be calming? It was terrible to be waiting. Zoë went to the desk. "Excuse me, but why are you giving that man Pepsi? Does this really help?"

"Pepsi? No. We're giving him *privacy*. But he can have some Pepsi if he wants. You can get some in the vending machine over there. Is he a friend of yours?"

"He's my neighbor. But I don't really know who he is," she said. "I ran over his dog."

"Oh, I'm sorry," the receptionist said. She'd heard it all before.

Zoë sat back down. There was a television set tuned to what was going on outside. So they had security cameras even here. This place was open day and night. She'd heard that even animal hospitals were full of it on weekends under a full moon. She thought about the lock with the code on the door.

She should call home. Will would be worried. They'd be home from the movies by now. Aaron's dad was a good guy to take them all out, but he had to get up early in the morning. Jillie would be settling the pups in for the night. Zoë was going to call Jay when she'd gotten home with the groceries. He didn't like her in that Safeway parking lot at night. She thought of him lying in that awful hospital bed trying to find some television to watch, waiting for the sleeping pill that would get him through the night. She looked up at the clock. A little past nine. She found her cell phone buried at the bottom of her purse. She had no memory of grabbing it out of her car. No one answered when she called home, so she called Meghan.

"At the *vet*! Why are you at the vet? Is Niki all right?"

"I hit a dog," she whispered. "I brought him here with the owner."

"What owner?"

"The guy at the bottom of the street."

"You mean that creepy guy that's maybe the arsonist? You went in his *car*?" Meghan was practically shouting. "Well, for godsake, don't go home with him. I'll come and get you."

"I can't just leave. I ran over his dog."

"Then he might really hurt you."

"Hey, just let everybody know where I am, okay? Nobody's answering. You know what happens if Will's on the phone."

"Do you want me to run over there and check on things?"

"I just worry without Jay being there."

"Maybe I should pick you up at the vet's first. You don't want to *stay* there."

"It's okay. I need to."

"How bad is he hurt?"

Zoë remembered his eyes with the life rushing out of them. "I don't know yet," she said. "They've got him in the back."

"What about that guy? Is he mad?"

"No. He's not mad. I think he's kind of in shock. But I have to stay here."

"God, Zoë."

"I know. It's really awful." She felt the tears behind her eyes and sat down. She wanted Jay to walk in that door, wrap his arms around her, tell her what to do.

"I'll take off right now and see the kids." Meghan always knew when Zoë had made up her mind.

She looked at the vending machines. They should give him privacy. No sense in having him fall apart in front of everybody. Well, a Pepsi couldn't hurt. Or some peanut butter crackers or Oreos. On the far counter a coffee urn and Styrofoam cups. Sugar, Cremora. A water fountain. All things you'd need waiting for the long haul. She thought about waiting for Jay in Radiation, how she had thought she'd seen Roy, which of course she couldn't have. Well, she had killed his dog. She was pretty sure of it. He'd been the arsonist in her dreams for months now and here he was, just this poor guy whose dog was dying because she'd been hurrying up that hill and hadn't even thought to look out for shadows floating across the road in the falling light.

She went to the vending machine, put in her quarters, and slipped out the Pepsi. At least she could do that. Imagine waiting in that room with the door shut all by yourself. A woman in pink scrubs went in for a moment then came out. Just for a moment, through the half-open door, she saw Roy standing with his hands in his pockets. His face had changed. His long, angular face with the sharp cheekbones, the fierce eyes, which had always alarmed her in dreams, had taken on a gentleness born of anguish. His face glistened with tears. Zoë felt the grief in his eyes like a stone upon her heart.

She thought about Roy standing at the counter with those forms, his hands in his pockets, his baseball cap low over his forehead, his ponytail. It had silver in it now. He must be over forty. His face was tanned and lined around the eyes, his jaw clenched, his mouth tight. His military cargo pants, his white T-shirt splattered with paint—blue, red, yellow, work boots. She tried to imagine a house painted in colors like that. Or even rooms. She thought of the ladders and rollers in the van, but also the oils and canvases. Maybe he was an artist. Better *artist* than *arsonist* any day. Imagine such desire in someone so blighted. Of course, she was only inventing from her dreams.

She was standing in the middle of the waiting room with the Pepsi in her hand when the woman in pink touched her on the shoulder.

"I'm Dr. Guerra," she said, putting out her hand. She was a short, stocky woman with black curly hair. She looked like she could handle almost anything. "You came in with Mr. Leland?"

"Who?" she said. She'd hardly ever thought of him with his last name. "Oh. He's my neighbor." She looked at the sign on the right side of the counter. CANCER CARE. *My God.* Of course dogs got cancer too. Well, people got run over by cars. Accidents of the universe either way.

"Could you tell us what happened?" the doctor asked.

"How is he?"

"Grave." She said it with such full authority there was no need to say more.

So Zoë told the doctor how she'd been coming up the hill maybe a little too fast, and had taken the bump in the road and felt that thud against the grille of her car.

"Could I wait with him?"

"Of course. He wanted me to ask you to." So she followed the doctor back into the room where Roy sat on a chair in the corner of the room looking completely forsaken. He looked up and smiled so ingenuously Zoë could do nothing but smile back.

"I thought you might be thirsty. Would you like a Pepsi?"

He looked startled. "No," he said, then caught himself. "Sure.

Thanks. Maybe later." He took the Pepsi and held it in his lap. "He was a good boy. He was such a good boy. He's probably not gonna make it."

She started to say how vets could do amazing things these days, but the moment required the dignity of truth and so she stopped herself. She didn't believe it anyway. Roy leaned over and put his head in his hands. A little golden chain, holding what she thought was a pentagram, dangled from his neck. She thought it might be something occult or Wiccan. It wasn't the Star of David. And it wasn't a cross, that was for sure. Good or evil, dark or bright, she couldn't tell. Like so many things that were ambiguous to the end.

Then he straightened up. "I did a bad thing with that scarecrow. I always wanted to say that. I didn't know what it looked like, you know? And those lights and streamers in the window. With those fires and all. I would never do that again." He shook his head.

"Pirates of the Caribbean."

"What?"

"Disneyland." He looked at her blankly.

"It scared the kids though. The parents pulled their kids away."

"Some of the big kids liked it. It didn't do any harm."

Roy picked up the can of Pepsi and just looked at it. Zoë could tell he wanted to hand it back to her, but didn't want her to have gone to the trouble for nothing. "I don't know how to be around people," he said. He looked diminished, sitting in the chair hunched into himself.

Zoë had never seen another car in his driveway or anyone at his door. She'd slow down and look going past in the mornings on her way to work or stopping for the mail on the way home. She never stopped telling the kids to stay together and hurry past. She had demonized him enough to feel guilty, but only a little. She couldn't shake the image of that scarecrow with its head hung on its chest, the straw ready for the conflagration.

"I meant it to be a scarecrow. I meant it to scare away bad things so everybody'd be safe. But it looked like a Hangman, didn't it."

Zoë started to take a step back then stopped herself. "Well, it's hard sometimes to get things right."

"I've seen you at the mailboxes," he said. "Your little girl too. I look out for her. You and your boys sometimes. When all those fires were close by, I came up there at night to be sure everybody was okay."

"Oh . . ." Zoë said. She felt her face go hot. She should have said thank you, or at least acknowledged it, but it was too startling and too familiar, too comforting and too full of dread. It chilled her to think of that figure with the cap rustling by the window, the long shadows skirting around the corners of the house. She'd counted on it not being real. It frightened her to think of him watching them, Jillie especially. But she had just run over his dog. He was probably already dead. Her heart filled with such sorrow and fear she couldn't speak.

Then Dr. Guerra opened the door and went over to Roy and put her hand on his shoulder. "I can take you back now. You can say goodbye. He was almost gone when we got him."

"I know," Roy said softly. He didn't turn to look at Zoë, but followed the doctor out the door, down the little hallway to the door with the secret code and through the magic portal into a world of grief and loss.

Zoë grabbed the unopened Pepsi he'd set on the floor and went back into the waiting room, and threw it in the trash can. She couldn't drink it either.

She went back to her chair and closed her eyes. She could see how Roy would hug that dog goodbye, his long, thin back leaning over him. He'd bury his face in his neck, take in his smell, stroke his head, but could not say goodbye. "Take all the time you need," the doctor said. Roy shook his head and said, "Now, all I got is time," and turned and walked down the hallway through the coded door and back out into the lobby.

"You'll want this," Dr. Guerra said, coming after him. "It's good to have it." Roy took the dog's collar wordlessly, fingering it like a rosary. She gave him a hug, while he stood there awkwardly, his arms at his sides. "I'm sorry," she said. "It's sad when these things happen. Life is so fragile. And so precious."

"He was a good boy. He was such a good boy."

There were things to settle up and they'd called Roy over to the counter. Roy just stood there looking at the bill they'd printed up, fingering that collar. "I don't have my wallet or anything," he said to the receptionist.

"We don't ordinarily send bills when this happens. Some people just disappear with no way to collect."

Zoë slipped in beside him and put her credit card on the counter. "Please let me pay for this."

"Oh, no," Roy said. "No."

Zoë took the bill. "I need to do this. It would be a favor." It surprised her how much she meant it.

The bill was three hundred and seventy-four dollars. IV infusion, pain shot, emergency room fee. The bill could have been worse. It wasn't much, all things considered. All they'd done was ease him on out.

Roy stood there, looking down at that bill and the credit card, pinioned to the counter next to the flea collar ad and the ID tag brochures. Then he turned to her. "I can get the ashes next week. I didn't know you could do that," he said flatly, as though he didn't believe it himself. He slid the collar from one hand to the other and back again. "I just wanted to bring him home, you know? I didn't want to say goodbye here."

"But couldn't they just let you take him home?"

He nodded. "I don't know why, but ashes are better. I didn't want him goin' in the ground."

"Maybe it's easier this way and not so sad." She didn't know what she was saying.

Roy just looked at her.

"That was a stupid thing to say. Nothing will make it easier."

"I loved him so much," he said. She hoped he wouldn't cry in front of her. So he drew himself up and pulled his car keys from his pocket. "I don't mean to make you feel bad. It just happened. You didn't mean it."

Zoë felt her throat tighten, her face flush with heat, the ache behind her eyes. "I should probably call someone to come and get me."

"I can take you home."

"You don't need to do that."

She felt the solid thud against the grille of her car, how his head rolled to one side as they lifted him onto the stretcher. She didn't want to get into the back of that van or sit in the passenger seat.

"But we're neighbors."

"Yes we are. We're neighbors." She felt ashamed of the way she had demonized him all these months. "Is it all right for you to drive?" She couldn't imagine how they would get home. What they would say.

"I can pretend it didn't happen yet," he said. "I can pretend it's never goin' to."

"I wish it never was."

"I wish you'd known what a great dog he was." Imagine such loss with no one to tell it to.

"Okay," she said. "Thank you." He opened the door for her self-consciously, and she stepped up into the seat of the van.

Roy slipped the gears into reverse, backed out of the crazy-angled parking spot and out onto the road. "He knew things were gonna happen before I did. You know he saved my life once. He saved my life every day."

Zoë was watching his hands on the steering wheel lit by the dashboard.

It had begun to rain and Roy turned on the windshield wipers. The tires whirred over the glistening, darkened streets. Where had this rain come from so suddenly and so darkly? Zoë felt a chill but also a strange warmth. She couldn't name what she was feeling. She knew she was forever bound to him now.

"Maybe I should have buried him and not had ashes. They said this would be better, you know?" He looked away and swallowed hard. "I just want him back. I can't hardly believe he's gone. I had him twelve years. That's a long time for a dog." He couldn't stop the tears now or brush them away. "He always slept next to my bed on the floor. Now he's gonna be ashes."

Zoë felt a keening rise in her chest and knew in a moment she'd never be able to stop it.

So she shut her eyes and listened to the tires spin over the rainy street, but instead, heard the gravel under Jay's car as he slid into the driveway, the click of the doorknob, the splash of his keys on the counter, the snap of his Pepsi can, the steamy bathroom after his shower, his Old Spice aftershave on his pillow still warm with his leaving. She would rush after these sounds and smells, and then oh the surprise of it! How could he be gone? The absence of him everywhere. She would hear him whisper at the back of her neck, her hair, against her face, the tender hollow of her throat.

There would be relics everywhere—his coat over the kitchen chair, his toothbrush by the sink, his maroon parka, his blue boxers. She would tuck them under her pillow every night, her secret thing, so intimate and strange. She'd feared it for so long now, this life she knew would come someday, the birthright of her gender. Still, she would do everything she could to save him. They would go salmon fishing in a few weeks, get out on the water under that sun-washed sky.

Roy looked over at her. "Are you okay?" he said. "You better be okay."

"I'm so sorry." She felt her heart thrum.

"But you didn't mean to."

"That doesn't change anything."

"Ashes are best. They're best whether I know it or not."

In that moment she knew what she would do. She knew it absolutely. She would take his ashes to the ocean. They would float out of the silver vial into a dusky purple cloud, a lavender exhalation. In the early morning sun, the ashes would drift down through that sunlit water in little golden flecks. She would float above them until they disappeared.

"I don't want to make it worse. I'm gonna be all right, see?"

"Yes you will." She was caught by him and she knew it. Guilt and fear had become some kind of compassion or mystery that now promised safety, not dread. She could never explain it.

He turned and gave her a half-smile.

"I saw canvases in the back. I thought you might be an artist."

"I try to paint things. They got me started on it at this place I was at a long time ago and I just kept on doin' it." His eyes were shining with grief and pride. He turned to her. "I could paint his picture, couldn't I? I know him by *heart*."

"That's a wonderful idea."

"He could be standing in the snow and the sun is coming through the trees and it's on him too. He's looking right at me. I could paint his wildness. His royalty."

"His dignity."

She wanted to ask if he'd had a dog when he was a little boy. If his father had beaten him.

"There was another fire," Zoë said. She was working something out.

"Not around here though. It's farther than ever up north now."

"They still frighten me."

"Don't let that stuff worry you. You're gonna be okay." He looked at her with unwavering eyes.

"Those trash cans are a fire hazard, though," Zoë said, as if he were an old friend she was safekeeping.

"I know. I keep forgettin' pickup day."

They were rounding the corner by the mailboxes across from his house. "You can just let me out here. I can walk up the hill."

"But it's raining. I need to see you home safe. Too many bad things around."

Yes, there were. Way too many bad things. She was glad not to see the bushes or that place in the road.

"Thank you," she said formally as they pulled into her driveway. As though she were the babysitter being delivered home after the parents had come back. She slid out of the van and shut the door. She did not turn around or wave a hand in recognition, but went up the stairs and opened the door—it was unlocked—and went inside. She had been gone a long time.

Collateral Damage

There was Niki, the minute she opened the door, sniffing her wildly, her hackles raised. She was getting the whole story. Buddy and Roy in the road, the van, the ER. Niki was reading her like a police report. Zoë leaned over and hugged her as Meghan came up the stairs.

"Sorry, Sweetie, I gotta run. The kids are downstairs watching TV. They're worried about you." It was well after ten o'clock. "You okay? I'm so glad you're *back*." She gave Zoë a hug, then opened the door. "You can tell me all the details tomorrow."

"A guy, huh," Zoë said. Meghan had thrown on sweats and tied her hair back in a ponytail. Her mascara had left little thumbprints under her eyes.

When she smiled, her eyes softened. "I told him to wait up."

"Thanks, my darling. You know how much I need you."

"I'll call you tomorrow," Meghan said and turned on her heel and skipped out the door.

Zoë sat down on the couch. She was starting to tremble. She could hear the kids thundering up the stairs. "Hey, guys," she said. Jillie plunged into her lap and put her arms around her neck, then Max was hugging them both. Will was the man of the house now, standing there watching with cautious, worried eyes. Whatever they knew about all this had frightened them.

Then Will sat down, too, and they all leaned into her. She knew she was about to cry. This awful thing had happened to their mother and Jay wasn't around to gather her up like they'd seen him do a thousand times.

"Should we tell stories?" Jillie said.

"It's getting pretty late," Zoë said. She felt a wave of cool air wash over her as the fan in the corner made its turn. She hadn't realized the house had gotten so hot. She just wanted a long, cool shower and her own thoughts. But mostly she wanted these children to hold her tight. The shower could come later.

"I'll make you a Pepsi," Max said, and headed off to the kitchen before she could say no thanks, too much caffeine so late at night.

"Did it hurt?" Jillie couldn't help herself.

It all rose up before her—the wail, the trembling, his eyes locked on hers, then his head limp on the stretcher and his eyes gone—and she couldn't bring herself to say, *No, my dearest Jillie, it didn't hurt one bit.*

"Oh, I think just for a minute."

"Daddy's safe in the hospital, and there won't be blood clots anymore or any bad things, I don't think."

"No bad things. He'll be home soon and everything'll be all right again."

Zoë heard the snap of the soda can and for a second saw Jay standing by the refrigerator with a Pepsi in his hand as he turned to look at her, tender and stunned. *Why am I gone from you?*

Jay? she started to say before she heard the ice clinking into the glass from the ice maker and Max filling the glass, which overflowed onto the counter and down the cupboard onto the floor. He set the glass down and wiped up the spill before he brought it to her.

"This is so nice," she said, taking a long drink, letting the fizz hit the back of her throat. Privacy or Pepsi. Right now she'd take Pepsi. Privacy could come later.

"But what happened to him?"

"You don't have to talk about it, Mom."

"He got hit by a *car*, Jillie," Max said. Then his eyes widened. It was his mother's car, after all. "I didn't mean it, Mommy," he said as his eyes filled with tears.

"He went into air right away, I think," Jillie said. It was a concept she had been working on for several months now. The separation of body and spirit. The abiding sense of one, the finality of the other. Zoë knew what they were thinking, though. That some perilous thing could snatch their father from them in an instant. Then where would he be?

"I'm sorry, Ma," Will said. "I'm really sorry."

"His name was Buddy," Zoë said. "He was a good dog. We can just think about that."

"What about Roy?" Jillie said.

"Who's Roy?" Max said. "Oh. The Scarecrow Man."

"Roy is our neighbor," Zoë said.

"Was he too sad?" Jillie asked.

Zoë leaned back and shut her eyes. She was unbelievably tired. "He was sad. But he'll be all right," she said, straightening up. She couldn't imagine how that man would ever recover from such loss, given his life as she now imagined it.

"Maybe Buddy slept with Roy," Jillie said. She slid off the couch and crouched down beside Niki, who was lying next to Zoë's feet, sniffing her shoes. "Does he have anybody who helps him?"

"I don't know, Sweetie. I think he's pretty much by himself." Now she wanted a hot shower, not a cool one, to wash off the scent of the dying dog. Niki got up and nosed her hands. She'd forgotten to wash them.

"If Daddy gets scared, he can talk to Mr. Brazil," Jillie said. Poor Mr. Brazil, who was in far worse shape than Jay. She wondered if he were in great pain.

Cars, animals, fire, the body's mutinies inside and out. So many paths into harm's way. So many collisions on this earth.

That night she dreamed of him again. First the blue, flickering light that was both cold and hot, then the peaked roof of the house way back in the woods, and the shadow of the little boy sneaking out of the house at first light and making his way over the glittering snow. He poked his head into the doghouse and touched the dog's side. His fur was stiff and covered with frost. He tugged and tugged on the cardboard, pulled the dog all the way out of the doghouse onto the snow, and saw the cold, fixed, brown-eyed stare.

It was cold and getting colder. The wind was making that silvery sound in the trees. It was snowing now, snowing on the doghouse, on the rope lying over the frozen ground, on the blanket that lay in the middle of the yard. He just went to sleep, Zoë told him. It didn't hurt. When you're that cold, nothing hurts.

Two days later, and then there was one. Climber and Speck had gone off to the Wylers in Black Diamond; Buttercup to the large woman in yellow pants—"oh, I *love* you," she crooned as the pup licked her chin, Twinny to the photographer who wanted the pup to ride in his truck as he went from job to job. And late this afternoon, Graylie went to the woman in the Mercedes from Mercer Island. They could hear that pup whimpering all the way to the car. Jillie stared out the front window long after her black shiny car wove its way down the hill. "I loved Graylie the best," Jillie said, already speaking of her in the past tense. They tried to keep Niki from seeing the pups leave but she'd gotten back in the house and was sitting at the window next to Jillie, who knelt down and buried her head in Niki's fur.

"Don't be sad, Niki," Jillie said as Niki let out a wail. "I didn't mean it. I love *you* the best." And that left Spock, the pup with the white lightning bolt on his forehead, his mark. He was a little aloof from the rest and would often sit to the side watching the others tumble and fall before he'd dive into the roiling mix of fur. Of course, Jillie wanted to keep him, though this was the pup she had been the least drawn to.

So Jillie went out to the puppy run where Spock lay asleep in the clothes basket and sat down, tucking her feet under her, and picked him up. So many changes, so many things to worry about. A new puppy would not be one of them. Zoë thought of all the energy it would take for keeping Jay safe, all the ways she would have to be vigilant now. She'd have to watch over Niki too.

Something's coming, she thought. *Or it's already here.*

"Come on in, Jillie, it's getting dark now," Zoë said, and so Jillie came back in the house and stood by the front window where Niki sat, keeping watch.

"Roy is so sad, Mommy," Jillie said. "He's nice." A century ago, this would have terrified her and led to a stern admonition.

"Yes, he is," she said. "He's a nice man. He's our neighbor," she said again, trying out the feel of that word on her tongue.

Night was closing in now. The streetlight had come on down by the mailboxes even though it was still dusk. Zoë loved this time of day, but it never lasted long enough. It never unsettled her or made her afraid, though since the beginning of the fires, the true dark of night sometimes did. The first week of August and Zoë could imagine the turn from summer to fall. She wouldn't let herself think about that. There was safety in summer, though there were a thousand perils too—drownings in swift river currents, boating accidents, sleepy drivers coming home from summer vacations. Still, none of it touched her. Of course, her husband was in the hospital with a blood clot, and she'd just killed the neighbor's dog.

It was still light enough to see a few leaves filtering down in the little breeze that had come up. It had been so hot. It was still hot. People with their windows open, many like theirs with no screens. She'd forgotten to water the plants all week. She couldn't imagine anymore complications. Yes she could. Well, that last pup would not be one of them.

Zoë sat down on the couch and picked up a magazine. She'd have to get up to turn on a light but was too tired for that. Jillie came over and crawled into her lap. "I think we should give our puppy to Roy. He doesn't have a dog."

"That's a really nice thing to say, Jillie. You are a very kind person." Zoë knew how much she wanted to keep that pup. She knew Jillie had disobeyed the rule never to talk to him. She hugged her tight. What would it take to keep her out of harm's way in the months and years to come? The perilous years of adolescence, the tricky turn into adulthood.

She kissed the top of her head, breathed in her little girl smell, a little musky after her long day, her apple shampoo. Her very own little wood sprite.

"But he would be so happy."

She hadn't even thought of it. Now she would have to. She didn't think he even knew about the puppies, though they were half-Buddy's, after all.

"Let's get you into the shower, Sweetie. Let's wash off the day."

"Daddy's coming home tomorrow," she said, sliding off the couch and heading downstairs.

"He might. We'll have to see." Zoë wasn't counting on anything. Still, she'd have to think about Roy and the puppy. Roy and Spock. Well, they were both a little strange.

She lay there a long minute, watching the sun filter through the blinds, the dappled light of the leaves against the wall. She must have really slept in. She was glad the weather was holding. She'd told Jay nothing about Roy and Buddy and the trip to the vet. She wasn't quite sure why. She wondered what shift in their relationship had tamped her down. She'd tell him when he got home and they settled into whatever this new life would bring.

The doorbell rang, she could hear talking, and then the rush of feet down the stairs. "Roy's here," Max said.

"Roy's *here*? In our house?"

"He's upstairs with Spock."

Zoë pulled on her jeans and shirt and rushed up the stairs. In the entryway the kids were circled around Roy, who stood awkwardly in the doorway, holding Spock, who was nestled into the crook of his arm, fast asleep.

"Your little girl brought him to me. I wasn't sure you knew about this." He kept stroking the dog as he held it. He was wearing cargo pants, paint-streaked T-shirt, as before. "Here," he said, giving the puppy over.

Then Niki came in from the backyard, wagging her tail, trying to reach her pup. Zoë set her down for the reunion. The pup rolled over on his back for inspection and Niki smelled her all over. Then she smelled Roy's pant legs, his shoes, his hands.

"I'm so sorry," Zoë said. "I didn't know anything about it. Thank you for bringing him back." She picked up the puppy and shut the door behind him. She was shaking.

"Jillie?" she called. But of course Jillie was nowhere to be found.

Zoë went into the living room and stood by the window watching Roy go down the hill, his hands in his pockets, his head down, no pause at the fatal spot. She watched him walk all the way down the road until he disappeared beyond the mailboxes.

Jillie came in from outside, tear stains down her cheeks. "I said he could name him anything he wants. He doesn't have to be Spock."

"When did you do this?"

"This morning. Before you woke up."

"But you should have asked me."

"He doesn't have his dog now. He needs a dog too."

"Have you had breakfast? I'll make a nice breakfast."

She called the boys up and they all took their plates into the dining room for French toast and powdered sugar and strawberries, two pieces each. Zoë wrapped her hands around her steaming cup of coffee and stared out the dining room window. She couldn't eat a thing.

"You're right," she finally said. "Sweetie, you are completely right. We need to give him this puppy." As soon as she said it, she began thinking of the complications. He'd be over for Sunday dinners. They'd be invited to backyard barbeques. But they weren't inviting him into the family, for godsake. She hoped they would all keep their distance. But she'd said it and couldn't take it back. Better to do it now than later. So they let Niki nose the pup, then began their way down the hill. Jillie carried the pup tight against her. She didn't know what Jay would have done. She didn't even remember to think of it.

For an instant she wanted to take Jillie's hand and run back up the hill. All those months his face at their window, his breath at her ear. But there was no more time for interpretation, no more time to see the figure in the carpet.

They were in the driveway now, passing the brown van, and there were the garbage cans tightly lidded and placed side by side against the garage, and the porch—where the scarecrow man had been—a basket of red geraniums. She rang the bell.

The phone rang as she was loading the dishwasher. It was Jay. It seemed days since she'd seen him. "Hey, Zoots, guess what?"

"Tell me you're coming home."

"Yup. Later this afternoon. I'll bet I could get you to swing by and pick me up."

"I'll bet you could."

Tonight! In this very bed he would come back to her for good. Now she would have him to curl into, his arm around her, to ease her into sleep.

"You know how much I love you, don't you?" he said.

She felt the pull of tears behind her eyes. She had spent part of the week imagining life without him. Now here he'd be, safe and sound. "I know," she said.

A Clean, Well-Lighted Place

They'd probably fallen right out with the Wheat Chex, because when Will showed Zoë his bowl, there they were, seven little moths floating in his breakfast cereal. They'd probably been in the flour or sugar, multiplying like crazy, because they'd seen them flitting around the kitchen on and off all summer. Of course they should have done something right away, but they didn't connect them with the food they were actually eating.

"Why do we have to kill them?" Jillie said. "Can't we just catch them and take them outside?"

"We aren't going to kill them, we're just going to gas them. They won't even know it," Will was saying.

"Will it hurt?"

"No, Jillie, they just breathe it and go to sleep, and then it kills all the eggs they laid in our food." Will was the one who'd probably swallowed a few before he saw the rest floating around in his cereal milk.

"But what if we breathe the gas too?" Max asked.

"Oh, we won't breathe it. We'll all be downstairs asleep," Jay was explaining. "I'll open everything up first thing in the morning and by the time you guys get up it'll all be gone. It's a *bug* bomb. It's not for people."

"It just seems so drastic," Zoë said. She was much more willing to live with those little blond moths that had taken residence in their house that summer than risk anything remotely toxic. But Jay said he was sure they'd be all right, and the idea of eggs hatching in their food could not be abided. Of course, you could abide anything. You could abide radiation beams aimed at your most precious parts. You could abide radiation burning through your kidneys and pancreas and stomach and lungs and throat. You could abide anything if it let you live.

"Okay then, your time's up." Zoë wagged her finger at the moths resting on the pantry door. She knew she was a tangle of contradiction.

That night they moved the dog water downstairs. Cleaned off the counters, put all the dishes and glasses and pots and pans outside on the picnic table, and anything unopened from the pantry. They could have cookies for breakfast tomorrow. They could have whatever they wanted.

The next morning, after the bug bomb had gone off, after Jay had cleared things out and left for the doctor, they began—Will scrubbing the floor, Jillie washing down the low cupboards, Max cleaning out the pantry.

"Oh, stepmother, when can I go to the ball?" Will said from the floor.

Zoë laughed out loud. "After the floors are sparkling plenty, Cinderella."

Jillie was standing on her tiptoes over the sink, wringing out her sponge. Zoë was starting to clean out the refrigerator. None of this just sliding by. She looked over the counters littered with jars, cans, bottles, plastic containers, milk cartons, a pitcher of orange juice from yesterday, before the bomb. It was all going out. There was hardly anything left in the refrigerator. The kids weren't complaining. They were actually having a little fun. They'd get all this cleaned up and surprise Jay when he came home from the doctor's this afternoon.

"Be careful not to get water on Will's clean floor. Keep the sponge over the sink, Jillie." The dog was trying to get as much of herself as she could under the opened dishwasher door, so Jillie had to step around her. When she bumped the pitcher of orange juice, it hit the floor with a splat, splashing up Jillie's clean cupboards, all over her legs, her tennis shoes, and Niki's back, then began to fan out across the floor. Jillie started to cry.

"It's okay, Sweetie, you didn't mean it," Zoë said, gathering her up. "It's just orange juice. Just sit here on the counter out of the way."

Max turned to see what had happened and began to laugh. Then they heard something hit the floor.

"Oh no!"

"What?" Zoë took a step toward the pantry, and the next thing she knew she was sitting on the floor in the orange juice and something else. The cap to the salad oil had popped off when it hit the floor, and salad oil was oozing into the orange juice.

"Are you okay, Mom?" Before she could say *wait*, Will had slipped in it too.

"Don't anybody move!" Zoë was trying to find a dry spot for her hands so she could stand up.

"I want to slip too," Jillie said. But she tucked her feet up anyway.

"Nobody *move*." Zoë managed to get to her feet and tiptoe out of the mess. She took off her shoes and socks and raced downstairs for a stack of towels. An hour later things were pretty well back where they were when they began, but they'd made little actual progress.

"Everybody just go outside, okay? Find something to do for a while. Grab some more snacks off the picnic table. I don't care." The kids went streaming out of the house, back into summer, glad to be in the sun again and out of the kitchen.

Zoë gathered up the pile of yellow, gelatinous towels and threw them in the washer, grabbed up all the stuff from the counters and threw everything into a couple of big Hefty garbage bags, and took them outside. It was after noon by then and Jay would be home in a little while.

There must be something left in the fridge she could eat. She was hungry enough now to reach in and grab the first thing she could find. She was shaky enough to know her blood sugar was on the floor.

She thought it was the pea soup she must have made sometime during the week, but then she couldn't even remember what they'd had for dinner last night. She'd eaten half of it, right out of the jar, before she noticed that it didn't really look green enough for pea soup, now that she stopped to look at it. It looked gray, more like gravy, but when did she make gravy? They didn't even eat meat anymore, and what were those little chunks floating around in there? They looked like little bits of fat, but when did she make something like that? It hadn't really tasted bad, but then she didn't remember tasting it, exactly. And there behind the gallon carton of milk in the fridge was the pea soup. She looked down at the remaining half of what she'd just eaten.

Botulism. Paralysis of the central nervous system. They'd find her collapsed by the stove. How poetic. She didn't even like to cook. Poisoned to death by her own, inept hand. Or salmonella. Gagging, throwing up for hours, days.

The number for the Poison Control Center was printed on a green MR. YUK sticker taped to the phone. She swallowed her pride and dialed.

"Is this an emergency?" a chirpy voice said into her ear.

"I'm not sure exactly. That's what I was calling for."

"Can you hold?"

Could she hold? What did they mean, could she *hold*? "Okay, but—"

Then she heard a click and a dial tone.

She wondered if she should be kneeling on the stool like that, looking for the syrup of ipecac somewhere high up in the medicine cupboard. What if she got dizzy and fell? Ah, there it was, back behind the half-empty bottle of cough syrup and old, half-used prescriptions. So. If the directions say for a child under six to take a tablespoon, then an adult would surely have to drink the whole bottle. She peeled off the plastic safety wrapper and drank it all, then chased it down with a glass of water.

She sat on the floor of the bathroom and waited. Ten minutes. Nothing. She tried some more water. Another ten minutes. She tried a finger down her throat. And what would be the side effects of whatever she ate plus the ipecac, and then all this water? Actually, she didn't feel that bad. Maybe the ipecac was so old it wasn't having any effect.

She tried the finger again but only half-heartedly. Then she remembered the family reunion with their southern cousins when she was ten. They'd driven from southern Illinois, where they lived then, to a little summer retreat in the pine forests of Georgia—ten little cabins and the main lodge.

It began after dinner with everybody standing around a huge coffee urn on the kitchen table, waving their cups as they stood talking in that slow, sweet way she had tried to imitate the rest of the summer.

"Y'all get enough coffee now or should I make some more?" Cousin Omie said. She was the clan's matriarch. She had bright cranberry lips and eyebrows that looked like little boomerangs over each eye.

"I'll clean up then," she said, picking up the urn.

"Here, I'll help you, Omie," Cousin Joe said.

"Oh, heavens no, it's not heavy, it's empty, for goodness' sakes." Zoë watched her carry it into the kitchen, then went back outside to see what she could find to do.

She heard the scream from the front porch glider. How long that mouse had been at the bottom of the coffee urn nobody knew. It was in some stage of dehydration but had been plumped up by its sojourn in the coffee. Now it lay in the bottom of the sink, a fat, slick little thing, half buried in soapsuds. Cousin Omie was sitting on the floor, propped up against the wall, fanning herself, while everybody gathered around the sink.

After a brief family conference, it was decided that all the coffee drinkers should head for some quiet, secluded spot in the woods and stick a finger down their throats. Zoë had stood at the edge of the porch, looking into the piney forest, and listened. It came from all directions. Whoops and bellows that shook the trees, scattered the birds, routed small animals. She didn't think she could eat anything ever again.

She tried it one last time. Just an insincere little cough. She sat there waiting for her stomach to right itself. She looked up. There was an enormous cobweb in the corner by the ceiling. How long had that been there? Maybe it was the view from the floor, but she was beginning to see how dirty everything was. Like this wall—paint-chipped and streaky—and the door with little gouges toward the bottom and soap bits near the doorknob, and little splats of toothpaste on the cabinets. She should clean out those kitchen cupboards too. It was probably dangerous to keep all those half-used bottles and pills. Too easy to take something by mistake.

She forced herself up and walked into the kitchen. Everything started to spin. She knelt down on the floor, put her head between her knees, and shut her eyes. And there it was, shimmering against her closed eyelids: copper pots and pans hung from the ceiling, glinting in the sunlight coming in the kitchen window, white satiny counters edged with blue Italian tile, a fluffy ruffle fern hanging from the ceiling in the corner, oak cupboards polished smooth and warm, plates and saucers neatly stacked inside, and matching cups all in a row, their handles turned in little matching salutes.

She'd turn it into a house where nothing ever got lost or broken or spilled or stained. A pantry where you looked for the dustpan and it was always on the little hook on the left, and the brooms stacked in the corner, and the scissors right there on the hook by the light switch. There would be spices lined up in a row and not just thrown into a drawer, helter-skelter—rosemary, sweet basil, tarragon, cinnamon, thyme—all lined up on a cherrywood shelf above a stove that gleamed, and no pots ever boiled over.

She stood up again and everything righted itself. She wasn't even dizzy. She looked around for a quick little ten-minute job. She thought about the medicine cupboard. She had no idea exactly what was jammed in back there. So she swept everything out of the shelves into a big paper bag, and dumped it all out on the counter. There must have been fifteen or twenty pill bottles, and this wasn't counting the new stuff. It was their history. The dog's history too. Dog Valium for the Fourth of July, thunderstorms, and other natural disasters, drops for when the Federal Express man sprayed her eyes with Mace, ear drops for ear mites, prednisone for grass allergies, antibiotics for this awful kidney thing.

There were four empty penicillin bottles. She picked up the empty one with Will's name on it. He'd only scraped the top of his foot going off the diving board, but the next morning it was fiery and hot, and you hoped you were only imagining the red line going up the inside of his ankle. And one for Max, mostly full. *Penicillin.* That elixir of cures. Why hadn't he finished it? How neatly it fit inside her hand, like a talisman, or a rabbit's foot. The pills made a reassuring sound, tapping against the inside of the bottle when she shook it. She tucked it back in the cupboard just to be safe. It couldn't hurt to have something in reserve. Then she remembered why Max had never finished it. That sudden rash all over his chest and funny breathing that scared them to death. And she'd *kept* it? Some lesson here on the edge of life and death she had yet to learn. Zoë grabbed the edge of the counter, put her head down. This ineptitude couldn't go on. Yes it could. She grabbed the bottle back and dumped the pills down the drain.

But in all those old bottles, not one had Jay's name on it. Now there were blood sugar pills and blood thinner pills, to name two. And what do you take to thin the blood, you ask? Ah, there's some magic for you. The very stuff that's in those little blue pellets they set out for the mice in the cabin. She wondered what it felt like to bleed to death like that. Was it just a slow, cold sleep before you disappeared or blew away? She couldn't stand to think about it. But it seemed like it was either a few dead mice or *hantavirus*, which had been discovered in the Northwest last spring. She was glad Jay didn't have to have chemotherapy—not yet, anyway.

She picked up a bottle of dark red syrup. *Decadron.* That miracle sweet red syrup for the croup. The kid wakes up barking like a seal, and you can hear every breath in and out like a knife rasping against its sheath, and then you don't hear anything, so you startle from where you're sleeping on the floor by the bed, a golf umbrella positioned overhead to catch the steamy menthol vapor into a magic cloud, and you put your face close to theirs to see if they're still breathing, and they are, thank God, yes they are.

She put the rest of the stuff back in the cupboard and looked at all those bottles lined up. Now there would be order, and nobody would take anything by mistake. And plenty of room for Jay's new pills, Niki's new pills. They were giving her antibiotics and steroids and hoping for the best. Jay was taking blood thinner and blood sugar pills and hoping for the best. She read off the names like an incantation.

She could hear the wind in the trees and shut her eyes and felt the breeze coming in the open window. The kids were down in the gully on the tire swing—Jillie, too, watched over by her brothers, finally claiming it as her own. Zoë watched them flying through the noon-tide sun flickering through the leaves, childhood held forever in that circle of wavering light. In the distance she could hear a seaplane from the air harbor a couple of miles away, coming low overhead, *chugh chugh chugh chuhchuhchugh*, as it finally took the sky.

She closed the cupboard door, set the safety latch, and ran her hand down the smooth oak wood. There. She listened to the quiet of the house, and remembered their first house, when Will was just a baby and how tidy she'd kept it. They were all going to live forever and never know a day of sorrow. Everything they needed they already had.

"Well, how was your morning?" Jay said, coming in the door.

"Oh, challenging. How about you?" she asked as casually as she could manage with that catch in her throat every time Jay came home from a doctor's visit, or left for one, or got out the phone book to look up the number.

"What happened?"

"Nothing happened. We just tried to clean the kitchen and didn't get very far. What did the doctor say?" She'd meant to just ease that in, but she blurted it right out.

"Oh, not too much. Just that the pills aren't working."

"So what are they going to do, give you different pills?"

"No."

Jay had increased that dose little by little for days now and every time he tested his blood sugar it was always too high. *Too high and your cells begin to die.* It went round and round, like a wicked rhyme inside her head.

"Shots, huh," she said. "Drug paraphernalia."

"Yup. Drug paraphernalia." Alcohol swabs and little bottles of insulin stored in the fridge, needles and syringes, glucometers, sugar pills and leftover Halloween candy in the freezer, for low blood sugar emergencies.

He'd come home from the hospital weeks ago, no worse for wear, except that he was now officially diabetic, most of his islet cells officially kaput, a side effect of that first round of radiation six months ago, and the happy surprise that he couldn't jog anymore or even stand in one spot for too long without that leg cramping and swelling up like it did the night they raced to the hospital.

Thus they settled into their new summer routine, though Zoë slept on the edge of sleep most nights, listening for the sounds that said everything was all right again—Niki's sigh, the hum of the furnace fan, Jay's heartbeat, the squirrels on the deck toward morning. And Roy somewhere out there, patrolling the neighborhood. And that was all right too. She couldn't say why.

That night she lay in bed half-asleep, listening to the *chugh chugh chugh* of a plane as it clung to the treacherous sky. She lay for a long time listening to Jay's breathing. She could feel sleep coming, saw the sky on the bedroom ceiling and the plane falling through imperious stars. And dreamed she was waiting for her father to come home from the college darkroom where he'd gone hours ago to develop some photographs. No phone lines back in that little lab in the basement, and she was afraid that at last he'd had the heart attack that was his legacy from his own father. Then she was racing down a dark hallway until she came to a red light bleeding from under the darkroom door and knew this was where her father was. She opened it carefully so she wouldn't ruin the pictures. "Dad? Daddy?"

He was slumped beside one of the developing trays. But as she reached out to him, he began to fade like a developing photograph, only in reverse. She ran back down the dark hallway after the dissolving image until it faded completely, and she could no longer see his face.

She woke with her hand over her shuddering heart. Her throat ached and her face was wet.

"What is it?" Jay said, touching her hair. She scooted over and he pulled her to him and wrapped her up.

"Bad dream," she said. Her head was pounding.

She couldn't go back to that dream again. So she slipped out of his arm and felt around for her slippers next to the dog, who raised up to look at her.

"It's okay, Niki, you don't have to come. Go back to sleep." She sighed and lay back down. Zoë headed upstairs to the kitchen and flicked on the light. She leaned against the wall, rubbed her temples. Grape jelly stains like dull bruises on the yellow countertops, somebody's late night snack, splashes of orange juice on the cupboards they'd missed, and everything jammed back into the pantry every which way. She shut her eyes. No gleaming pots and pans suspended from the ceiling catching the light, no fluffy ruffle ferns, no blue

Italian-tiled counters, no spice rack with little amber bottles all in a row. She looked over the kitchen again and smiled. It was all right. It was her life.

She reached up into the medicine cabinet for the bottle of aspirin. Better to believe in that than nothing, but keep an eye out—it was nothing you could count on.

She grabbed the quilt from the chair by the back door and went outside onto the deck. She sat down on one of the deck chairs Jay had made earlier in the summer. She liked the way you could rest your head against the high back, the way the curve of the chair was a perfect fit, just for her. She closed her eyes, listened to the dark. It felt velvety and cool against her skin. She was safe, wrapped in the night. She looked up at the sky. She could see some stars drifting in and out of the clouds. You could believe in summer, in that explosion of green everywhere you turned. You could believe in that heartbreaking plentitude no matter how cruel the winter. She looked up at the sky, and watched the stars drift in and out of the clouds and knew everything would be all right.

But then the wind came up and she heard dark rustling sounds down low in the gully. She could see the tops of the trees moving in the wind against the indigo sky. The moon looked hazy and cold, hanging just above the treetops. She watched a thin layer of clouds dissolve the moon into an exhalation of light that sank lower and lower in the sky.

"I thought I could make this someplace safe," she said, getting back into bed.

Jay turned toward her from some dreaming place and held her tight.

Splitting the Heart of the Sun

The alarm went off at four thirty, but she'd been awake long before that. Her head ached and her throat hurt every time she swallowed. She'd lain there in a half-sleep most of the night, restless and achy. She'd just take some Tylenol and bundle up. She checked the kids, all fast asleep, before she headed on upstairs. After today, the season was over anyway, so this was their last chance. With the luck they'd been having lately, they'd catch their limit and be home before lunch. Actually, they'd been having phenomenal luck, considering they were using just an old rowboat without a fish finder or anything else, since the Bayliner was still in for repairs.

This summer she was the official netter. She was always afraid she'd tighten the line too soon, or yank up too hard or not hard enough, so she almost always let Jay bring them in, while she'd reach out over the side of the boat with the net in her hands and scoop the fish into the net, head to tail all in one fell swoop. The only fish she ever lost was the first one, and that was before she knew what she was doing.

Jay had worked that fish back and forth until they saw it nearing the boat just under the surface of the water. He began yelling, "Get it! Get it!" but she thought he'd said, "Hit it! Hit it," so of course she did. She hit that fish with a splat across its back, the hook jarred loose, and in a flash he'd made his getaway.

"What did you do *that* for? What were you trying to *do,* for godsake?"

"You *said* to hit it. I thought I was supposed to knock it unconscious or something before I got it in the net."

Jay couldn't stop laughing and she thought of all the endorphins and good things surging through his cells and knew if she was good for anything it was for this.

She couldn't get warm in that long dark drive to the launching dock. She'd flipped the heat up on high but she still shivered. She slid down in the seat and buried her nose inside her jacket. She could hardly keep her eyes open, still felt achy as they pulled into the parking lot by the boat launch. They slid the boat off the van, carried it to the edge of the water just as it was beginning to be light. A thin layer of fog drifted over the water. They could see the outline of other boats now, moving out from shore, slipping silently through the fog. Zoë climbed in first and Jay shoved off, then hopped in just as the boat slid out into the lake. He pulled on the starter cord till the motor caught and kicked into gear. Thus they began their dark, silent way through the fog toward their very own magic circle, where they were either floating on water or in air.

Jay knew she didn't like to talk until the sun had warmed everything up, so he just handed her some coffee without speaking. She held it between her cold hands and let the steam warm up her nose. She couldn't stop shivering.

"I'm so cold."

Jay handed her the blanket he was sitting on, pulled it over her shoulders, touched her forehead, looked into her eyes.

"You feel hot."

"It's just the steam from the coffee. I'm freezing."

"Are you sure you're okay?"

"Sure," she said brightly. "I just need the sun. You know how I am."

She could see the purple outline of the mountains in the distance. She was waiting for the moment the sun came over the crest. That moment always made up for everything. The gray became violet, and the pale rim of light turned fiery orange, igniting the layer of clouds that hung just above the mountain peak. It was an eerie beauty and always reminded her of the painting on the wall of Mrs. Poffenroth's third-grade Sunday School class, which showed Jesus stepping out of a bank of golden clouds. That picture frightened her, and so she always kept a watchful eye on sunrises and sunsets. She knew she didn't want to see Jesus coming out of the clouds because that would mean the end of the world.

There was a sign over the Gospel Light Mission in their little Illinois town that said JESUS COMING SOON in green neon letters, and that always scared her, too, though as far as she knew, Jesus had been coming soon for as long as anybody could remember. How did they know that anyway, the people who put up that sign? She knew Mrs. Poffenroth didn't know. She hated her. Ever since the day Zoë sat down at the long table in their Sunday School classroom with her box of new crayons and announced that her grandfather had died and was in heaven with Jesus.

"How do you know he's in heaven?" Mrs. Poffenroth asked.

Of course he was in heaven. Where else could he be? "He's in heaven because he's a preacher," she said, stopping her coloring.

"That doesn't mean he's in heaven, dearie." Zoë thought she could see her smirking. Even then, Zoë knew her teacher was jealous that her very own grandfather was a preacher. Maybe she'd heard of him. Maybe he was even famous. But it seemed a mean thing to say no matter what she thought. That's why she was sure Mrs. Poffenroth would never have any inside information about when Jesus was coming.

She had told their whole Sunday School class that she'd seen Jesus walking on the highway out of town, and stopped to pick him up. She knew it was Jesus by the robe and the beard and the sandals, she said, and by the way he disappeared. One minute he was sitting in the back seat of her big blue Buick and the next minute he was gone. After Sunday School, Zoë and Stanley Petrie snuck out of church to take a look at that back seat. They could hear the congregation singing the first of those five long verses of "Just as I Am," as they snuck out of the balcony pews where they were supposed to be behaving themselves during the sermon. They tiptoed down the back stairs and raced out into the church parking lot. It was easy finding her car. It was the only electric blue car in the lot. They figured they'd be able to tell whether Jesus had sat in that back seat just by looking.

They peered in through the window. The electric blue seat was covered with orange fur. They stood there a moment, just looking through the window. Finally, Stanley said, "That's Mr. Tidball's fur. He's her cat. He's got lots of orange fur. I saw it at her house once."

"He must be really bald by now."

She was trying to imagine Jesus with cat fur on his robe. "I don't think Jesus sat back there."

"I don't think so either."

She was glad. She wanted Jesus to stay up there in the clouds. She didn't want him coming down here and sitting in that horrid woman's car. She wanted him up there watching over her while she slept, so she wouldn't die before she waked. Sometimes these past months she wished she could say *Dear Jesus* in her prayers, if they were prayers, but she couldn't. Though every so often she wished they had joined a church or a prayer group or healing ritual or had consulted a shaman. The kids didn't even go to Sunday School.

The sun was glinting off the water now. Jay had let down the fishing lines, and was sitting in the bow of the boat watching the poles. Off in the distance, a salmon jumped, a silver flashing in the sky, as if to split the heart of the sun, before it dropped down and disappeared into a soundless splash. Why do they do that, so close to death? Why do they take that leap when the sun strikes the water, to hang there for a moment in the light? She watched that golden sky till the clouds melted into the blue of the day and she knew Jesus wouldn't be coming any time soon.

Jay didn't talk much when they fished. He was always busy, checking the lines, changing depths and flashers, untangling the hooks, watching the water, the sky, the other boats. But the netter got to sit back and take it easy, at least till things warmed up, or till there was something to net. She closed her eyes. Her eyes felt hot. Jay handed her a bagel with cream cheese.

"No thanks," she said, holding out her cup. He poured the last of the thermos into her cup. The sun was glinting off the lake everywhere now. She took off the blanket, unzipped her jacket. Jay had his sweatshirt off and was standing in the bow of the boat in his shorts and T-shirt.

He was looking at what the sun was doing to the lake. "I could stay out here forever," he said. Then he sat down and adjusted the lines. "I love you, Zoe." He reached over and touched her leg. "Way more fun with you here." He couldn't stop smiling. Zoë smiled back at him. She took another sip of coffee. It still hurt to swallow.

Jay stood up and took off his T-shirt. She loved looking at him. His back was so strong, and so golden in the sun. All those boyhood summers bucking bales on the farm. There was too much health in him ever to be that sick. She finished her coffee, took off her jacket, and eased her back against the stern of the boat. She could feel the sun through her sweatshirt. She shut her eyes. She hadn't felt this happy in a long time.

Jay sat watching the lines, so strangely still. Yesterday they couldn't reel them in fast enough. But it was nine o'clock already and they'd had a couple of hits, a couple of snags, but not one fish. Where was their magic circle? They'd crisscrossed that spot by the bridge a dozen times. Jay'd changed flashers, from silver to gold, changed depths and trolling speed, but without any instruments, they were only guessing. She didn't care. She didn't want to move and if they caught anything she'd have to stand up and get that net. She just wanted to float along and feel the sun on her face.

She looked around. So many more boats now, all heading south. "What's going on?" It frightened her a little. The boats were rushing past, rocking their little rowboat from side to side.

Jay looked up from the line he'd been untangling. "Hydro races," he said, as he pointed at her pole, which was bobbing up and down. "We've got one. Don't worry about the boats." But he was clearly irritated. "They should know better."

He yanked the pole out of the holder, and reeled in fast. The line stretched far out. "Look at that. He's a big one." Jay pulled back hard, reeled in some line, then let it play out again, back and forth, back and forth, as he brought the fish up from sixty feet below. Zoë thought of that fish fathoms below, with the hook in his mouth. After a while Jay would just reel him in, and he'd float effortlessly into the net. He'd have spent his fury spinning round and round, trying to shake that clawed hook from his mouth. But they always revived for one last furious moment, when you lifted them out of the water and they felt that net.

"He's coming in," Jay yelled. "Get the net!" She could see him now, a shimmer in the water twenty feet out. Jay was reeling fast, balancing himself in the rocking boat. And then that fish just coasted in like he was just along for the ride. She stood up and grabbed the net, then leaned over the side of the boat, holding the net out as far as she could reach. Her arms felt impossibly heavy. She wondered if she could hold onto it long enough to get it into the boat. She lost her balance and sat down hard. No matter what, she would not lose that fish. She'd dive in after it if she had to. Everything depended on it. She stood up and positioned the net under the floating fish, grabbed the handle with both hands, and pulled the net out of the water. The net swayed as the fish tried to leap free. Water streamed out of the net as she lifted it up and into the boat, over her legs, her shoes. She laid the net on the bottom of the boat while Jay struggled with the tangled line. The fish jerked for a moment then lay still.

Zoë leaned over to look at the fish lying inside the net, perfectly still but for its mouth, which opened and closed, opened and closed, its iridescent side heaving. *It's drowning in air*, she thought. She could hear it making a strange little sound but knew it was only the ringing in her ears.

"Hit it! Hit it!" she yelled at Jay. Jay took the fish bopper, and smacked it twice on the head. Now finally it was quiet, its secret fish eye opened wide, beholding. She saw Janet Leigh's eye in *Psycho*, as the blood swirled down the drain. She sat down, put her head between her knees. It was hard to breathe. Her throat was tightening. She shut her eyes.

Could we please go home now? she wanted to say, but thought if she just sat there with her eyes closed for a minute, the panicky, swirling feeling would go away. It was all that moving around in that rocking boat getting the fish safely netted. She'd be all right in a minute. She looked out at the water. In the distance it looked glacial. She could see the backdrop of the mountain to the south. She was starting to shiver again.

She looked up. An enormous cabin cruiser was heading right for them. Where had that come from? Jay grabbed the tiller and whipped the boat out of its path. The cabin cruiser sped on, while their little rowboat pitched from side to side as they hung on fast. Somebody sitting spread-eagled on the bow saluted with a beer in his hand.

"We've got the right of way, you jerk," Jay shouted after them, but nobody heard, nobody even looked back to see if they were all right. The wake spread out around them.

There were boats everywhere now. Cabin cruisers, flotillas of inner tubes tied together, speedboats, dinghies, sightseeing boats, all heading straight for them. They'd known the hydroplane races were today, but they hadn't really been paying attention. They hadn't figured on all this traffic hours before the races anyway. The water was all stirred up, and the rocking back and forth was making Zoë feel a little sick. She wondered if they were truly in danger. Their boat was so small. Their fishing poles bobbed up and down in the churned-up water.

Then Jay turned the boat around, and headed out of harm's way. The fishing was over. They would follow the shoreline around the lake and take the long way home. It would be safer that way. The water calmed and Jay stood up to pull in the line. Zoë leaned back in the boat and looked at him. How tall and strong and flushed with sun, and looking like he would live forever.

She looked out across the water. Everything seemed far away, pointed, sharp. She could see edges everywhere, the tree line, the whitecaps, the peaks of the houses along the shore. The sun hurt her eyes even through her sunglasses. She felt hot, sweaty, trailed her hand in the icy water. She rolled up her sweatpants, turned her face to the breeze. Something had changed. A thin, hazy layer of clouds was spreading toward them from the south. The wind had picked up and she could see the beginning of the front they'd been promised for days. You couldn't see the mountains anymore.

Zoë put her hand in that icy water and wanted the green sunlit lake of her childhood and all the years lined up ahead, tucked away for safekeeping. She wanted to float there forever in those sun-slept waters. How fearless she was, how safe in the warm shallows. Then she remembered the side of the lake where no one ever swam, that tangled far shore where water moccasins waited in the creepers and vines or swam secretly over the bottom, flicking past their toes.

The dock was up ahead now, and the little air harbor off to the right. Boats were zigzagging across their path, and jet skiers closer in, and now seaplanes coming in and out of the air harbor. She heard the drone of an engine, looked up, and saw a seaplane overhead.

"Look." Speedboats were crisscrossing the stretch of water in front of the air harbor. "Isn't that illegal?"

"Glad I'm not trying to land," Jay said, squinting off into the distance.

Zoë watched the dock come closer, could see boats lined up to launch. They were the only ones going home. Jay throttled down, turned off the engine, and they coasted in. Then he jumped out onto the dock and tied up the boat. She gathered up her sweats and the thermos and the empty bagel sack. Jay grabbed her hand and helped her up onto the dock. Clouds had drifted over, and the sun shone down through a gauzy haze. The wind ruffled the water into little waves. Zoë shivered, and pulled her sweatshirt back on. She could hear the *chugh chugh chugh* overhead.

"Are you cold?" Jay said, handing her the keys to the car. "You still don't feel good, do you."

She didn't say anything. She was watching the seaplane trying to land. It was coming in low over the water, but there was no place to land with those zigzagging boats in the way. The engine was making a coughing, sputtering sound as it tried to pull back up. Then it wasn't making any sound at all.

"Jay?" she said and pointed off to the right. They stood on the dock and watched that plane fall out of the sky and disappear into the trees.

Jay turned to look at her, and then they heard it crash. He pulled her toward him while that splintering sound spun inside her head, pounded at her temples, seized her heart.

Zoë kept thinking about the old couple in that car. She was lying on the couch, wrapped up in a quilt, watching the news while Jay made dinner. Or rather he called in for a couple of pizzas. She loved listening to everybody laughing. That poor old guy, though. They were just taking a Sunday morning drive, maybe coming home from church or Sunday brunch, and he turns to his wife to say something, and hears this scraping sound, and sees a seaplane clip the satellite dish on top of the restaurant across the street, and crash onto the pavement. Then it cartwheels across the road, and he's frantically trying to steer out of its path but it's careening right at him. He doesn't have time to touch his wife's hand, or say *I love you*, only an *oh god!* when she looks over at him, and then the car spins around into the side of the plane now stopped and jammed into the side of the auto repair shop. And miraculously no one is hurt. It's a good luck story, a fairy tale, it's a story to tell your grandchildren.

Jay came in and leaned over to kiss her, but she put up her hand. "Better not. You don't want this." He handed her another cup of chamomile tea and a couple of Tylenol.

"You were sick and you went out there anyway. What a girl." She knew what was at stake. That sun was better than any radiation machine. Joy trumped fear any day.

"Aw, shucks," she said. But her voice was nearly gone.

"You sound like Kathleen Turner."

"Lauren Bacall."

"Want a slice of pizza? Soup? Anything?"

"Nah, just you." She was remembering how fine Jay looked in that boat in the sun.

"I'd kiss you anyway."

"Just wanting to is enough." It hurt to talk. Everything hurt. But it was all right. She didn't have to be the strong one all the time. It had started to rain, and she could hear the wind blowing the rain against the window. Summer was over.

In Another Country

School had been underway for over a month now, and they hoped that the travails of last winter and spring would never come their way again. Zoë was bringing home stacks of papers to grade and half a dozen library books for her conference paper on Hitchcock's rhetoric of terror. Jillie was in second grade and reading her own books. Max was in fifth grade and a year from the anarchy of middle school. And Will, in the eighth grade, was a year from high school and the temptation of bad friends, cigarettes, sex, and drugs. Everybody was on the cusp of something. Zoë wanted to wrap them all in their sunlit innocence and keep them there forever. And Jay? He had let his assistant take over the cross-country team and was watching way too much television.

"What's this?" she said to Jay, who was stretched out on the easy chair watching *Monday Night Football* while the kids were supposedly downstairs doing their homework. They called it the Dental Chair because when you leaned all the way back you looked like you were having your teeth drilled. Zoë came into the family room holding the envelope from the Tumor Institute she'd found on the dining room table lying benignly enough in between the bills and junk mail.

"Go ahead and read it," Jay said from the chair.

The letter was just a gentle reminder for Jay to please make an appointment for a CAT scan in December. She sat down and dropped the letter in her lap. "I didn't know you'd have to do all this again."

"I told you. Every six or eight months."

"For how long?"

"I don't know, a while."

"God, Jay, how long is a while?"

"I don't know, a while. How do I know?"

"Why do they need to do this again, anyway?"

"I *suppose* it's to see if it's come back." Jay finally looked up from the TV.

"Well, you never told me."

"Sure I did. You just don't remember." He glared at her.

"You didn't, though," she said, softer this time. She was leaving in the morning for her conference in Texas and neither of them wanted a quarrel.

"And why write you this much ahead? Just so you can go crazy thinking about it?"

"I'm not the one going crazy." He was back to the game. She'd watched him all those months for signs of recovery or relapse. Now what could a test tell her that she couldn't see for herself? Tonight, though, stretched out like that, he looked like somebody's patient. They were entering that inner world again, where cells and nodes and bone and blood would rise up out of the fog, like a developing photograph to tell them either what they hoped for or what they feared.

"Jay?"

"Yeah?" His eyes were following the play on the screen.

"I wish I didn't have to go." She sat down in his lap and the chair popped back up.

"It'll be good for you to get away."

"No it won't."

"Sure it will. The sun will be good for you."

"Not good enough."

"But it will." He put his hand under her shirt.

"Okay, okay, okay. If the plane doesn't crash."

"Just be sure to take out lots of flight insurance," he said, back to the football game again. "We'll be all right."

She tucked her head in the curve of his neck. She could feel his gaze watching the game over the top of her head.

She got up and went to the refrigerator where she'd tacked up lists for everything. Dog instructions, kid instructions, vet number, emergency vet number, carpool, flight numbers, hotel number. It was all too much trouble. But she always said that before every conference. Zoë got out the Atlas and found Dallas on the map. It looked far away. In another country.

She went back into the kitchen to check the rice and hamburger she was cooking up for the dog. She wanted to make enough to last the five days she'd be gone. Niki hadn't eaten anything the past couple of days, so she thought if she made a fresh batch she might give it a try. This morning she'd had to help her off the front porch, but she took a couple of steps and lay down in the gravel in the middle of the driveway. She couldn't remember when she'd last seen her relieve herself. She knew her kidneys had pretty much all but shut down, knew that rice pottage and antibiotics twice a day weren't going to help much longer.

"I'm surprised she's still with us," the vet had said on Saturday. It'd been a slow slide all summer, then in the past weeks an inexorable rush. She'd brought Niki in for one more blood test and another bottle of antibiotics so Jay wouldn't have to do it while she was gone. They'd been standing in the middle of the waiting room, discussing what to do if Niki died over the weekend. Niki was too tired to lunge for the door these days, so she just lay on the floor trembling. Nobody in that room had to lean forward to hear it. Even the receptionist stopped what she was doing to listen.

"Do you think she can live another week? I hate to ask, but I'll be gone next weekend, and I really don't want my husband left alone with all this."

"Looking at these blood counts, that's a long shot."

What did he care? To him, all this was just the end of a long, slow process, too boring for too long.

"I just think we should find out why this happened. I mean, if she could have passed anything on to the pups."

"Then we'll need to go ahead and autopsy the kidneys."

"I know."

"So," he was explaining, "if she dies over the weekend, and I hate to put it this way, but you'll need to figure out some way to . . ." he looked away, then mumbled, "*preserve* her, then bring her in on Monday."

Zoë looked over at the little white-haired woman with half a basset hound in her lap, the other half draped across the vinyl couch where they were sitting. The woman looked at her and blinked. But Zoë just charged right on ahead.

"So how do we do that, exactly?"

"Well," he said, lowering his voice again. He'd just realized he had a waiting room full of people listening to the freakish last details of what was obviously a veterinary failure.

"You could put her *uh . . . ahem . . .*" He looked around. Then he whispered, "In the freezer. People have done that."

"But she's a big dog."

"Well, I know. But I don't know what else to tell you."

"But how would she fit?"

"Well." He glanced around the room, smiled a fast smile, and edged back toward the receptionist desk. He was almost in a whisper now. "You take out the food and a couple of shelves and then you can lift her right in." The white-haired woman was getting up off the couch and heading for the door, dragging that basset hound behind her.

It was all pretty funny that afternoon, standing in the square of light coming in through the long, curtainless window, the umpteenth bottle of antibiotics in her hand. She shouldn't have come here alone. But she didn't want Jay to have anything to do with it.

"We could put her down now. We could have done that weeks ago."

"But you said she wasn't in any pain."

He just looked at her. Who needed this extra time, anyway? Jay couldn't stand to see her like this. He'd wanted her put her down weeks ago. He'd signed a DNR when he first became ill, though Zoë didn't want Jay to ever assent to that goodnight. She wondered why Niki was holding on. Maybe she'd wanted to just wander off into the woods one night and lie down for good. Today she couldn't even get to the front yard.

Zoë was trying to hoist her back end into the car when a man came up behind her. "Can I help get her in there?" It was Roy standing there, holding that pup, who was wriggling to get out of his arms the moment he saw Niki.

"Hello, Roy," she said. Niki had turned around and was nosing Roy's legs. "Is your puppy all right?"

"He's just going to get a couple of shots. Thanks for tellin' me to come here. They're real nice to me. They're takin' real good care of him." The pup's rhinestone collar caught the sun and winked at her. In all his proclamation of manliness—the baseball cap, the camouflage pants, the T-shirt rolled up his biceps—this flash of glitz. Zoë thought of Liberace and smiled. But there was no flickering candelabra, no satire or irony. That collar seemed precious to her in some way and she felt a sudden tenderness toward him.

"Look how he's grown. He's a little man now." He was all legs and fur. No longer a little roly-poly. She was glad Roy had the pup. Still, if she'd known how things were going to turn out, she might have wanted to keep him.

"What did you name him?" she said, reaching out her hand. The pup licked her wrist.

"I thought about Buddy, you know, maybe Buddy Junior, but he needs his own name. So I named him Coyote after those coyotes in our woods. Here. You take him, and I'll lift her up for you."

"I can get one of the technicians to help."

"You don't need to do that," Roy said, and handed her the pup.

Zoë set the pup down so Niki could say hello. She sat down hard and the pup nosed her. Then she eased down onto the pavement so the pup could lick her face, climb over her back. Then the pup turned in circles while Niki put her head down, though she couldn't keep her tail from wagging even so. It had all been too much, so Zoë picked him up and held him tight against her while he licked her neck and chin. "What a big boy you are. Look at you."

Niki turned her head and tried to get back up but collapsed down hard on the pavement, her toenails scraping the asphalt as she fell. Then she let out a wail Zoë had never heard before.

"Is she okay?"

Zoë shook her head and handed him the pup. She reached down and took Niki's head into her hands. "It's okay, Niki." The sun had fallen behind the building and plunged them into shade. It was later than she thought. She looked up at Roy. "Her kidneys are failing and they can't really help her."

"Oh," Roy said. "I'm sorry."

He looked at her for a long time as he held the pup like a football, in the crook of his arm. There were tears in his eyes.

She could feel the ache of tears behind her eyes too—for Niki, who hovered over the precipice of her short, urgent life; for Jay; for her children; for Roy, so forlorn, so full of longing, so abandoned by life.

Roy saw the tears in her eyes and looked down at his shoes. "My husband is sick too," Zoë said softly. She had never said that to any-body. But she couldn't help herself. She would never have wanted to tell him that, yet here it was.

"Is it cancer?"

"Isn't it always?" she said bitterly.

"Some people don't get it. Sometimes it's something else that's bad." His eyes disappeared under the shadow of his cap. Then he looked up and tried to smile. "But some people get all better even if they have it."

She wiped her face with her hand then got her keys out of her jeans pocket.

"If there's anything you need. You know? You just gotta say."

"Thanks, Roy. That's nice of you." But she wanted to take it back. She should never say those words. She had no idea why she'd said them. It wasn't even true. She shut her eyes to stop the spinning feeling.

Roy set the pup on the front seat of his van, rolled down the window a couple of inches, and shut the door. But he was trying to get as much of himself outside the window as he could manage, which wasn't much, so he began a frantic barking.

"It's okay, boy, it's okay," Roy said, then came over to Niki, who was still pinioned to the ground.

"I'll get her in for you," he said. He leaned over and scratched behind her ears, but not before offering Niki his hand. She nosed it and lifted her head, then Roy slid his hands under her haunches and helped her stand up, while Zoë led her by the collar back to her car. Then Roy propped her front legs on the floor of the car and lifted her back end as Niki stretched out her neck and scooted forward, her front paws scrambling to take hold, until her back legs were finally under her.

"There. She's all set now." Niki lay on the back seat, panting.

"I'm glad you were here," Zoë said. She looked over at the pup, who was scratching at the window. "You know those shots don't seem to hurt them at all."

"He did real good last time. He doesn't know enough to be scared."

"Niki starts to tremble the minute we pull into the parking lot." She knew Niki was trembling even now and wouldn't stop until they were at long last home.

"Just love her best you can," Roy said. "Don't bring her back here if it won't do her no good."

Then he opened the door, grabbed the leash as the pup jumped out of the van. "Not now, boy." He turned and waved goodbye. "See you around," he said, and disappeared inside.

Zoë climbed into the driver's seat, put her head on the steering wheel. That's what they would do, all right. They'd just love her all they could. They'd never bring her back here again. No more blood tests or urine samples or X-rays. No reason good enough for all this trembling. She looked up at the sign for the last time. Kenmore Veterinary Hospital.

Zoë spooned up the rice and stuffed it into a big Tupperware container, snapped the lid shut, and put it on the bottom shelf of the refrigerator. Niki looked up at her from the floor where she was lying, trying to get as much of herself as she could under the dishwasher door, left open now most of the time because it had become her favorite place in the kitchen. It was as if she knew time was growing close and she didn't want to lose them.

"You'll be okay," Zoë said, sitting down on the floor beside her. She lifted up the door so Niki could lay her head in her lap. She nosed at the bagel she offered her then turned her head. *No thank you, not today.* Zoë picked up her front paw. It smelled like popcorn, just like always. "I'll be back soon," she said. "You hold on." Niki was watching everything with a hot, searching look.

The phone startled everyone. A gong sounded in her head. She couldn't move. "Want me to get it?" Jay said from the chair. He looked alarmed. "You okay?"

"I'll get it," she said, getting up. It was somebody saying the conference was canceled, the airlines had lost her reservations, the vet with the latest test results, her parents were ill or had fallen down or died. The kids were safe downstairs in their rooms, she was sure of it, but had the urge to go and check. Jay was right there—she could touch him anytime she wanted. She didn't want to get the phone after all.

It rang on and on while Zoë just stood there. She shut her eyes.

"I'll get it," Jay said, popping the chair back up. "It's for you," he said, not taking his eyes off the screen.

"Who is it?" she mouthed.

He shrugged and handed the phone to her.

"Hello?" Hello, hello, hello.

Roy had never called them before.

"No, she's doing about the same," she said. "Thank you. And I'm glad the pup is okay. I'm glad you had him checked out. No, it was nice that you called. It wasn't any bother."

"Who was that?" Jay said.

"Roy."

"Roy who?"

"You know, our *neighbor* Roy. I saw him at the vet's on Saturday. He was taking the pup in for his shots."

Jay just looked at her. She knew he didn't want them getting too close to him.

"Well, I'm glad we gave him the pup," she said. She saw him standing there in the parking lot with that puppy under his arm, his face half hidden under his baseball cap as shy as ever, and as sad.

Everybody had gone off to school, and she was sitting by the front window, watching for the lights of the airport shuttle coming through the morning fog. Late last night as she was finishing up in the kitchen, Will had come upstairs and given her a hug.

"Will?" she said. "What's wrong?"

"Nothing. I just wanted you not to worry about Dad. We'll take good care of him."

"Well don't let him know you're doing it," she laughed.

"I know."

"Yes you do." They smiled at each other. She reached for another hug, which he permitted.

"I hope you have a good time," he said, and slipped away. Zoë leaned against the refrigerator and watched him duck down the hall. Of course, Will knew more than he let on. She didn't know how much Jillie and Max noticed, but it seemed like they were all treading lightly across the shimmer of the day.

Then the lights of the shuttle broke through the fog as it came slowly up the hill. The shuttle pulled up into the driveway and the driver got out and grabbed her luggage from the front porch and headed back to the van.

"See you," she said to Niki. The dog turned away, and would not look back. She always knew what that suitcase meant. And after Zoë came back, she'd creep upstairs in the middle of the night in search of her overnight bag or her purse. She'd drag one or the other into the living room and shake it all out. In the morning Zoë would find the contents of her bag spread out all over the living room, and Niki outside on the back deck, in despair and ready for sentencing. Once she'd called the Poison Control Center because she'd found an empty, tooth-marked prescription bottle under the coffee table, no pills anywhere. Niki sat stoically, as close to the door as she could get, while Zoë poured half a cup of hydrogen peroxide down her throat according to the directions given by the poison control operator, to induce vomiting that never came. Later she'd be sitting in the living room, telling everybody about her trip, and Zoë would catch Niki looking at her sideways, through narrowed eyes. *I remember that you left me.*

Zoë grabbed her raincoat out of the closet and looked over at Niki curled up in the corner of the living room. "Goodbye, goodbye, goodbye," she said, and closed the door.

The wind blew hot and dry across the golf course and the patio where she was sitting next to the swimming pool. That Texas sun hung low and spiteful in the late afternoon sky, flickering in hot, wavering light off the blue-tiled swimming pool. She shut her eyes. If she had to be here, she'd just turn her face to the sun, go back a couple of months, and pretend it was summer all over again. It was still cold and foggy when the plane left Seattle. She'd sat in the airport for two hours waiting for the fog to clear before they could take off. Well, this was Texas, all right. Everything felt out of season. There was no going back, once you'd made the turn toward winter. Anyway, this was a light not to be trusted.

She was gathering the courage to go back inside and find the conference registration table, pick up her name tag, begin the wearying process of what she had supposedly come here for—panels, plenaries, keynotes. *So, what are you working on? Who? Me? Oh, well. I'm working on just holding things together. The dog is dying, and who knows about my husband. But how about you, now how are* you? Couldn't we speak our sorrows instead, she wanted to say, and offer comfort in some small way? But of course nobody ever did.

That night she lay in the king-size bed, huddled next to the edge of what would forever be her side. She'd tried the center of that big bed, but there was too much room for comfort. She'd wanted a tight little unambiguous single bed pressed against the wall. First nights away from home were always disorienting. But it was what she always looked forward to, thinking about it at home in the middle of everything. A room of her own—a bath anytime she wanted, take a book in there, hey, read the whole thing, watch any TV channel, order room service, maybe even get some schoolwork done. Nobody wanting anything. Hours stretching out easy and slow. But it never quite worked out that way. Having no practice at solitude, she always began missing everybody the minute it got dark.

She thought she was never going to fall asleep. She went to the bathroom, got a glass of water, took it back to bed, and turned off the light. She thought about everybody back home, wondered if they were safely asleep—Jay sleeping on his back, his arms across his chest; Niki curled up on Zoë's side of the bed, where she always slept when Zoë was gone; Jillie and Max and Will in a tangle of sheets and blankets, their faces warm and flushed with dreams. She'd spread her incantations over them all—a wide, drowsy net of words drifting up through the dark, silent rooftop of the hotel.

She lay there, but still couldn't sleep. She was trying to find some peaceful moment to slow her breathing. So she thought about two summers ago, when she and Jay were in Hawaii. They'd gone snorkeling every afternoon of the vacation. But she was always afraid to breathe underwater, afraid to look down and see the shadows she imagined down there, afraid of the dorsal fin cutting through the water just beyond the shallows. She'd panic and yank her head out of the water and swim straight back to shore every time.

But on that last afternoon, Jay took her hand and guided her far out toward the coral beds.

Finally, she lifted her head out of the water and looked toward shore. They were far, far out beyond the point. She leaned back and floated on the billowy drowse, her face to the sun. No fear of sea snakes, or eels coiled between the rocks, or shadowy manta rays drifting over the sand. Then she turned over and looked down and saw thousands of fish, schools of fish, darting and flitting with the currents. They floated there in the late afternoon sun like two sea creatures, fearless and full of grace. In the thinning light of the coming winter, it was a good thing to have in reserve. It was the most perfect image she could imagine, and so she tried to put herself to sleep with it on that long Texas night.

The next morning, she walked down the hall full of people like herself, wearing their conference badges, carrying their notebooks and pens, looking at their conference maps. She said hello to a few of them, hardly knew any by name. She'd go to panel sessions this morning, take notes, breathe in, breathe out, and remember who she was. She was headed to the Wrangler Room for a panel on Frontier Myths. Later this afternoon she'd give her paper on Hitchcock.

She was glad for the drama of her topic, given her panel's slot at four thirty in the afternoon. It was a miracle anybody was there to hear it at all. "Hitchcock's rhetoric of terror flips the cliché," she began. It was the terror of open spaces, not dark alleys, that held the real terror, she explained, because out in the open there was nowhere to hide.

About half a dozen sleepy souls listened politely as the four panelists ground their way through the end of the afternoon. Any questions from the audience? Not today, thank you. Polite, weary applause at the end, then everybody got up and fled the room. She went back to her room, ordered room service, and took a long, hot bath.

She could hear the phone ringing in the next room. What now? Well, she wouldn't run to the phone. That was no way to live. She slipped on her robe and walked to the bed, sat down, took a deep breath.

"I tried to get her to go outside this morning, but she wouldn't budge," Jay was saying, "so I picked her up and took her out back. But she just lay back down on the grass. She was still there this afternoon when we all got home, so I'll probably take her in, in the morning." He slipped that in like he was taking her to the vet's for booster shots or a nail clipping. "I just wanted you to know what's been going on." He said it so casually, so gently, she knew it would happen now. She looked at the clock, wondered if she could catch a flight home tonight. It was already close to eight.

"But I'll be home day after tomorrow."

"I don't think she can wait that long."

"But I wanted to be there to see her out."

"I know, Zoë, but I don't think *I* can wait that long."

She was usually the one who took her to the vet, the one Niki wouldn't look at on the drive home.

"Maybe I could get an emergency flight change or something."

"I doubt if you could do that for a dog."

"But I didn't want you to have to do this alone."

"I'll be okay."

"What'll you tell the kids?"

"The truth."

"Don't take them along, okay?"

"I wouldn't do that. They can say goodbye to her here."

She wanted to come home right then, but she was stuck there over a Saturday night with that no-changes, low-fare plane ticket.

"Well, at least this way I'll still get to see where Kennedy was shot."

Jay laughed. "That should be a real mood brightener." She'd signed up for the Saturday afternoon trip to the Texas School Book Depository Building that came along with the conference package.

"I don't like being so far away," she said, then stopped herself. No point in going any further now. So she said goodbye to Jay and turned on the first Showtime movie she could find.

The lobby was cool and dark, and just what you'd expect in that Dallas Book Depository building. She paid her five dollars for the headset and wandered over to the elevator up to the sixth floor. It felt like a mausoleum—dark, chilly, air-conditioning on too high.

She wished she'd brought a sweater. She put on her headset and began to play the tape that would take her hour by hour through those four days in November, as she wandered through a maze of photographic murals.

She turned up the volume. She could hear the commentator announce the arrival of the plane at Love Field, the crowd cheering and clapping in the background. Then there they were, coming out of the plane into the morning sun. What did they know, waving to the crowd, their faces to the sun that bright day? What did they know, stepping into that open, waiting car with the top down? Thank God the weather had cleared.

Zoë walked to the window where Oswald had stood and looked

out. If you were to stand by that northeast window, seeing what he saw, you'd want to shout *duck!* but of course nobody's listening, and nobody ducks. They're still sitting there with their smiling faces turned to the sun, about to wave at the little kid whose daddy had just hoisted him up on his shoulders. *Wave, sonny,* he said. *There's the president.* And so he did.

Zoë turned a corner and came to a section of the exhibit with chairs lined up in front of a screen. So this was the part you needed to sit down for, she thought, as she made her way to a second-row chair.

Jay was sitting on the floor of the examining room, Niki's head on his lap. He was stroking her head so she wouldn't mind the needle. How simple. How complicated.

Zoë heard the motorcade, the cheering, the commentator announcing the journey of that car down Main Street—past the jail, past the bank, then the old courthouse, now the grassy knoll of Dealey Plaza up ahead. She held her breath.

The vet was preparing the syringe into which the needle would go. Niki raised her head. "It's okay, my sweet girl," Jay said, and kept on stroking her.

Zoë leaned forward, put a hand out, but the motorcade kept on—there was no stopping it now. It turned off Main Street onto Houston, passing the intersection of Houston and Elm, then the sharp left turn toward the underpass in the distance, and looming over that funny zigzag in the road, an old warehouse, nothing to look at, with the Hertz sign sitting on top, telling the time: *12:29.*

Jay looked at his watch. Zoë would want to know. He wished she were here. He was glad she wasn't. He couldn't remember the time.

"This won't hurt her, will it?" Jay asked.

"She won't even know it."

The band-tailed pigeons on the rooftops in the sun were indifferent to the motorcade, seconds from the cool, dark, quicksilver safety of the underpass. But what was that? A thousand birds rushing skyward, a thousand birds splintering the sky. What sound had frightened those birds? Then the sudden quiet and the birds gone from that faultless, waiting sky.

Zoë saw that hot, thin sunlight, that perilous autumn sky. She saw his hand raised against the blow that had already fallen, saw Jackie's hand outstretched to pull him back before it was too late, but he was already gone. She could hear everything turning breathless and still. The man in front of her put his arm around his wife, and they leaned together as tears ran down their faces. It was *twelve thirty*.

Zoë wished Jay were here. She was glad he wasn't.

"She's gone now," the vet was saying. He leaned over, touched Jay on the shoulder, and cleared his throat.

"Goodbye, girl," Jay said, burying his face in her neck. He stroked her one last time before he got up for good. They let him out the back door. It wouldn't do anybody any good to have him walk through the waiting room looking like that.

The flight home was over in seconds. She sat huddled against the window, looking out at the sky. She cried all the way home.

Her seatmate kept shooting her glances over his half-glasses. She could tell he was just pretending to read. Her dark glasses and lap full of shredded Kleenex were a dead giveaway.

"A death in the family?" he finally asked.

"Oh, no," she said. "Just the dog."

They landed as the trip had begun—in a rainy mist. But on the drive around the lake coming home, Zoë could see the sun catching a little wave here and there, and those gauzy clouds beginning to dissolve.

All the way home the kids kept exchanging secret glances. And lots of whispering and shushing she wasn't supposed to notice coming from the back seat. They drove up their little hill, and the first thing she saw was the living room window and the face that wasn't there. Then something shimmery waving in the breeze out of the corner of her eye. She turned around as Jay pulled into the driveway. It was an old *Happy Birthday* banner wrapped around the wooden marker where Pecky lay buried, as well as three or four white rats, goldfish too many to count, a couple of lizards, an entire ant farm, one well-loved stuffed animal who had died in the washing machine, and most recently Niki's very first pup.

The kids carried her suitcase and overnight bag into the house and set them down in the living room. She was looking out the living room window at either Mardi Gras or Christmas, or Halloween, it was hard to tell. There were streamers and ribbons and banners over every piece of standing vegetation. They'd wanted to bury Niki at home, but as it turned out, medical science kept her. The kids wanted to have the funeral anyway, and this was it. She wondered if all this was real to them. But the kids were old hands at it.

"I let everybody do exactly what they wanted to out there," Jay said, shrugging his shoulders, suppressing a smile.

Zoë put her arms around his waist, tucked her head under his chin, breathed him in, before she kissed him. "It was great that you did all this," she said, looking over at the cake on the dining room table. *Happy Birthday Irene.* She looked again. "Who's Irene?"

"I have no idea," Jay said.

"Dog cake?"

"Of course."

"No dog."

Jay just looked at her and plowed on ahead. "Anyway, the kids thought they might get the dogs from down the street to come up. Don't worry, we've got an ice cream cake in the freezer." They'd always celebrated dog birthdays by getting an abandoned cake at the supermarket. That was part of the pleasure—finding the most disgusting cake in the store, then feeding it to the birthday dog and any other dogs that might be passing by.

Zoë wondered about good old Irene and why somebody would order a birthday cake for her and then never pick it up. Maybe it was Irene herself. Maybe she changed her mind about having a birthday. Zoë sat down at the dining room table and stared at that cake. Jay'd gone outside.

The voice on the answering machine had been whispery and tremulous. It was a couple of weeks ago when she'd been cleaning up old messages. "This is Irene" . . . something or other. She was trying to reach the surgeon who'd removed part of her colon a month ago because she was sure it had spread to her breast, for when she woke up this morning her breast was aching, or maybe it was her heart, she couldn't tell. She'd probably been sitting in her rocker by the phone since yesterday, twisting the handkerchief in her lap, and patting her chest, and trying to take long, slow breaths, because she couldn't bother him *again*, he was so busy, otherwise he'd have called her back, but oh my, she couldn't wait like this much longer.

Zoë knew by that voice she'd wait days before trying him again. What was she, a conduit for pain? She seemed to gather it up like a human lodestone. Well, she certainly wasn't going to call her back.

"You called the wrong number," Zoë said as gently as she could. "You called me by mistake. But I really don't think it spreads like that. I'm sure the doctor will tell you that. You should call him right back." So Zoë wished her well, and erased her from the machine. Now here was Irene, again, back on this birthday cake for the dog funeral. Of course there were a million Irenes in the world. Still, Zoë wondered about this Irene and why she never got her birthday cake. Well, it was fit for the dogs, now.

She looked at the cake again. *Happy birthday, Irene, it's good to be home.* Sitting there in the dining room with the late afternoon sun coming at last through the cathedral window, it was good to be home.

The kids kept running in and out of the house, carrying things. The sun was going down, and Jay told them it was now or never. Soon it would be too dark. So they called her outside and they gathered around the marker with the silver birthday banner and said goodbye.

The kids were getting ready to bury an old metal chest they'd found in the garage. They'd collected Niki's things and laid them one by one in the bottom of the chest—her collar; her red leash; her dish with *NIKI* in big, gold, stick-on letters; Squeaker, her favorite chase toy; her half-chewed dog pepperoni stick.

Will began. "Everybody needs to say something funny about Niki."

Jillie raised her hand, according to the script they'd written. Zoë could see her behind the scenes, battling to go first. She cleared her throat. "I remember that time Niki barfed on Daddy when he was in bed." *Come here, Niki*, Jay'd said, patting his chest. And so she did. It was the funniest thing any of them could remember, except for Jay, of course, who still didn't think it was very funny. You didn't see canine projectile vomiting every day.

"It splatted all over Daddy's face," Jillie said, "like it came out of a fire hose!"

It had indeed splatted all over his face, his chest, and down his arms. "Oh, shit!" he'd said, jumping out of bed, and racing to the bathroom and into the shower. Niki watched him run down the hall, walked over to the edge of the bed, and unceremoniously did it again.

They stood there with the sun going down, trying to remember how funny it was, and how much they had all laughed. Nobody said anything. Then Max told the story of Niki climbing onto the roof from the back deck. They looked up from dinner and there she was, looking back at them through the window. And so it went.

The light was almost gone now. The trees near the edge of the gully rose up against the purple sky. They could see the moon coming up from behind the hill. "You guys better skip the long part," Jay said. "It's getting too dark to see." They were going to read some poems.

"I don't have to see. I know mine by heart," Jillie said.

"Go ahead," Will said, putting his arm around her shoulder. Then she read *Goodnight Moon*. She loved the old lady bunny who whispered *hush* as she sat rocking by the fire, who watched over the baby bunny in the big bed, and the kittens and the mittens and the mouse in the corner. That book always comforted her some way and settled her into sleep.

"Goodnight kittens, Goodnight mittens
Goodnight nobody, Goodnight mush.
Goodnight to the old lady whispering *hush*."

And there was Irene herself, sitting in the rocking chair by the phone, by the moon coming in the window, by the kittens and the mittens, and the socks hung by the fire. *Goodnight, Irene*, Zoë thought. *The song is for you, it was always for you.*

Jillie finished the story and laid the book in the chest. "Goodnight, Niki, whispering *hush*."

Jay switched on his flashlight while the kids planted sunflower seeds, the biggest flower they knew. Zoë thought about spring and what the yard would look like with all those sunflower stalks pushing their way into the world, grinning and nodding their approval all summer long.

The flashlight spread its light in an arc that caught Roy's shadow just for a moment, before he stepped back into the woods. The bushes shivered faintly. She knew he was there. Sometimes she believed she was the only one who saw him. It was all right, even if it couldn't be explained without giving people the creeps. She had told no one, not even Jay.

"Okay, guys, it's getting cold out here," Jay said, aiming the flashlight through the sword ferns, and pointing the way back.

"I'm not cold," Jillie said. "I want it to be longer."

"Dad, you never get cold," Max said. For a second his eyes flickered with alarm. "Are you okay?"

Zoë reached out for him. "Jay?"

"Max, it doesn't mean anything to be cold," Will said. "I'm cold."

Jay looked stricken. He knew what Max meant. When he turned to aim the flashlight home, his laugh caught in his throat. He dropped the flashlight, making the sword ferns tremble before it went dark.

"Daddy, I can hold your hand. I'm warm."

They remembered who took Niki in. It was only yesterday. Anybody would be cold after that.

Will picked up the flashlight and shook it, but it had gone dead. "Let's go in."

So they silently made their way inside and had their ice cream and cake instead of dinner. The house grew dark and quiet. Somebody needed to turn on a light, or the television or the radio. But the kids had all gone downstairs, where it was also too quiet. Zoë went into the living room and sat down on the floor by the coffee table. There was her overnight bag in the middle of the room. No need to worry about putting it away now. She picked up the picture of Jay and Niki hiking the Pacific Crest Trail. The sun was shining down on everything—the snow, the mountains in the distance, shining down on Niki, shining down on Jay.

Zoë sat there for a long time, listening to the quiet. No toenails skidding around the corner, no tail thumping against the wall, or chink of her collar, or the sound of her yawn, or her sigh as she settled in to sleep. What was sorrow anyway but this? The sound of absence everywhere.

Long Shadows of Winter

D ays followed days like rows of tumbling dominoes, and before they knew it, October had vanished into the foggy chill of November. Halloween had come and gone with only a couple of pumpkins, and Jillie and Max in no-nonsense white sheets with eye-holes, and Will staying in. Roy had left a big sack of candy by his door, with a sign that said, *HELP YOURSELF,* which was just as well, all things considered.

One day Zoë walked through a fiery cloud of leaves caught by the wind, a radiant blooming against the blue heartbreak of the sky. A week later those same trees were forlorn and hung with grief, unyielding sculptures against the ashen sky. The few sunny days they had were so piercing, so unexpected, they turned away and shut their eyes. Those days kept them off balance, all right, and they did their best to believe in everything they could.

She thought of this time last year and the fires that had raged. Yet here they were, safe in an innocence of darker things. They drew in early, sat around the fire after dinner without a thought, buttoned up wool sweaters under their rain slickers, put extra blankets on the beds. The wind blew the leaves against the house and they flickered past the windows, collecting in soggy, dirty piles. Next week would be Thanksgiving. What would they have to be thankful for? Everything.

—

It was raining hard. She'd managed to get in with the grocery bags before it had become a torrent. Where was everybody? She was glad she'd gotten home before this downpour. She'd done it all. No need to bother Jay. The kids could help her put away the groceries. The rain was pelting the side of the house, and the skylight was getting a real drumming. They'd already bought the turkey and it was thawing in the kitchen sink. Tomorrow would be Thanksgiving.

She thought about Roy as she passed his house, how he'd spend Thanksgiving. If anybody ever invited him. Or if he ever had a guest. She wondered if they should ask him over. She was just beginning to imagine it when the doorbell rang. Who would be at her doorstep in this weather?

The man looked startlingly ordinary. He could have been a salesman, except who would be selling things in this rain? He was standing there in his gray raincoat, shaking his umbrella. She might have expected a square jaw, strong forehead, steely blue eyes. But this guy's glasses were slipping down his nose with the rain. He wasn't much taller than Will. His black car had pulled up behind hers. It frightened her. She wished Jay were home.

She couldn't really see his badge, though she'd taken his word that he, indeed, was an FBI agent. She stood there with her hand on the doorknob. She didn't feel like inviting him in. Of course he would be with the Arson Unit.

"I've been checking with your neighbors, and I'm just wondering if you've ever noticed anything odd or out of the ordinary around here."

She knew what was coming next.

"Some of your neighbors are concerned about Mr. Leland down at the bottom of the hill. Do you know him?" She knew they'd called the Arson Hotline on him. Probably many times.

"Sure. He's just the guy down the street."

"Well, we're looking at everybody again." His eyes were wide and stunned behind his foggy glasses. "The arsonist has got to be *some-body's* neighbor." He sounded a little despairing. He'd probably been at this stretch too long. Or maybe it was the rain.

"But there haven't been any fires for weeks now. They're not really around here anymore." She could feel herself tighten against him.

"Mrs. Penney. How well do you know Mr. Leland?"

She had no idea what to say. But she would not let him in her house. He could just stand there on the porch in the rain. "How well does anybody know their neighbors?"

"I mean just generally. Your main impression. We don't have any proof of anything, but he's a 'person of interest,' as we say." She could imagine what he was thinking, each thought darker than the next. "Have you seen him out at night, maybe prowling around?"

"Prowling around what?"

"Oh, just in the neighborhood."

"But we're up the hill. What would he be doing up here?"

"Well. We're just trying to rule some things out. Some of the neighbors . . ." He looked like he was a moment from stepping inside. "Have you noticed his van gone at night sometimes?" He turned to look down the driveway, where she had a clear view of Roy's house.

"I don't think people really keep track of things like that," she said, but knew her neighbors might be. "I know some of the kids made things up about him. They like to think he's the boogeyman. You know how kids like to scare themselves to prove how brave they are. He's just different. There's nothing wrong with that." Once she'd started, she couldn't stop talking. She was afraid of what she'd say. "I know he hasn't always kept things tidied up. I think he sometimes forgets about garbage pickup days. It just gets away from him."

She was making it up as she went along. She hadn't known how strongly she felt. Or maybe she'd just never understood what the talk of ignorant neighbors could do. She thought about that Halloween night last year and the way he'd scared everybody, how she had hated him for it.

She saw Roy's gray eyes, how they could smile even when his face was shy of smiling. "Why are you talking just about him? There must be lots of people who are a little strange in their lives." She remembered how anguished he was at his shyness, his awkward ways.

"Well. We've had quite a few reports about him from your neighbors." He turned and pointed toward the woods. "Living so close to the forest. You've got kids. You must worry about that. An arsonist is the most lethal criminal of all. A house can go up in an instant."

Her heart was racing. The words tumbled out on the rush of breath building inside her. "He was new and his Halloween decorations were kind of over the top and people started all this crazy talk."

"We're very interested in that."

"Really? Why would his Halloween decorations be interesting to you?"

She hadn't meant to sound so challenging and couldn't believe how flushed she felt, how her heart was pounding against her chest.

"Fires. Fascination with fires."

"He likes dogs," Jillie said from behind her. How long had she been standing there?

"Yes. Yes he does. He's careful with them. And very loving."

"Well, hello, little girl. What's your name?"

Jillie darted back behind her mother.

"It's all right, Sweetie. This man is just about to leave."

Then Jillie stepped out from behind her mother and gathered him up in her eyes. "He's my friend."

"Well. Thanks for your help now." He put out his hand, then

quickly withdrew it. "Cute kid. I'd like to talk some more. When it's a better time. If you think of anything, you can give us a call," he said, handing her his card.

Zoë shut the door and locked it. "Here, Sweetie, throw this away," she said, handing her the card. But she wouldn't invite Roy for Thanksgiving. She didn't realize how much she had wanted to until then.

The hard rains of winter kept on well into December. It looked like the sky had vanished for good, covered over with an unrepentant, hovering gray. The trees were ominous figures that broke through the fog in sudden, rangy gasps. Jay was too tired to put up outside Christmas lights, and nobody wanted Will and Max anywhere near the roof or that ladder. They settled for the largest Christmas tree they'd ever had. It sent them to the store for boxes of extra lights and bulbs. At the top was the red and gold steeple that was Jay's favorite. She thought it looked like it belonged in a brothel. Jay'd also come home with an electric Santa that sang "Jingle Bell Rock" while it did a version of the twist but was recalled due to an electrical malfunction that could cause it to melt. So it was dubbed Melting Santa and kept safely unplugged on the window ledge by the tree. As presents materialized under the tree in the coming days, they all waited for the new CAT scan results that would tell them where they had been, where they were going.

"So it's not gone after all," Zoë said darkly as they settled into bed. She was angry at him for letting all this happen. She was ashamed and hoped it hadn't shown. He should have taken better care of himself. He should have taken better care of them.

"I don't know how to answer that." He'd turned his face from her.

"It wasn't a question."

"What is it then?"

"Our apocalypse," she said in a whisper. She couldn't touch him.

"Probably." He reached out for her, but she just looked at him. "But we made it through the Millennium. The year 2000, come and gone."

Finally she turned toward him and touched his face. "Our bank didn't fail."

"Our clocks didn't stop."

"Plane didn't crash."

"We didn't run out of food."

"Or water."

"Or love," he said.

"Or hope." September 11, 2001, was only nine months away, and light-years from anyone's darkest imagining. She sat up, peeked out the blinds. All quiet and still, the woodpile safe as ever.

"What do we tell the kids?"

"We could mention the new treatment."

"You know it's kind of a long shot, don't you?" Jay rolled over and burrowed his head into the pillow.

"Well it's something. It's more than something."

They had come late in the day from the oncologist—God how she hated that word. So now it was ionized air and Mexican peach pits. And whey protein. Coconut milk. Seaweed extract. Prayers and chants. Still, he didn't feel too badly, and you couldn't tell any of this by looking at him from a distance. And there was this new biologic set to begin in a couple of weeks.

Neither of them could say anything more, now that it all had been said. Soon Zoë could hear Jay's breathing and knew he'd fallen asleep. That was Jay, all right. He could sleep through anything. Soon she'd have to be mother and father, and something else—a third thing she couldn't name.

But when was *soon*? Soon was right around the corner. But maybe not! In minutes or hours, a year would be a lifetime. She'd take it. Zoë moved over as far onto her side of the bed as she could. Soon it would all be her side. Well, it was better to know than not. But how could you really believe such a thing? A year to live! How could a doctor say something like that? It was almost malpractice. And how could a person really believe it? She felt black, frantic wings whirring against her face. Bats swooping overhead between the trees.

"Who are those dogs?" Jillie said one morning that second week in January. She was kneeling on the couch, her nose pressed against the living room window.

"What dogs?" Zoë said, coming into the room with Jillie's coat and lunch pail.

"Those dogs." She was pointing out the front window at two enormous dogs, sitting in the middle of the front lawn in the fog. You couldn't see the mountains or the sun, but those dogs were impossible to miss—two retrievers, one golden, one red, looking through the fog back up at the house.

"Well, we can't think about those dogs, we're already late." Will and Max had already caught their bus. Zoë was driving Jillie to her new school—a private school with a second-grade teacher not in the middle of a clinical depression and bursting into tears five times a day. "Just ignore them, Jillie, we don't want them hanging around here." No more pets. No more hostages to fate, big or small.

But it was an old story by now. Every now and then some poor, confused dog wandered up their hill or down from the top, got all turned around on their little dead-end road, and then couldn't find its way back home. They'd hang around for a day or two, then finally figure it out. People too. They'd have too much to drink and then crawl up the hill, hanging their heads out the car window. Then they'd turn around and drift back down.

But when Jillie opened the front door, there they were, sitting on the porch, waiting to be let in. "Oh shit," Zoë said under her breath. Their tails banged against the side of the house as they tried to nose their way through the door.

"Go away," she said, and pulled the door halfway shut. They were wet and muddy, with huge wet and muddy feet. They were young, maybe a year or two, one male, one female. Jillie reached through the door to pet them.

"Don't do that, Sweetie," Zoë said. "We don't know who they are. We want them to go home where they belong."

Zoë looked back as they edged out of the driveway. There was the sagging Happy Birthday streamer in Ferny Land. And on the little patio outside the downstairs slider, their two pumpkins beginning at last to cave in on themselves. The kids had had a bet to see how long pumpkins could last if you kept them outside. They drove down the hill and Jillie turned around to look back. The dogs had followed the car out the driveway and were chasing down the hill after them. When they turned the corner by the mailboxes, the dogs had stopped halfway down the hill and were standing in the middle of the road looking after them.

She turned past Roy's house. The curtains were drawn tight, but many of the curtain hooks had gone missing and the curtains looked like they might fall down any minute. The big brown van was gone. Zoë wondered about the pup, if he were locked in the house or tied up out back. Roy wouldn't risk him getting out like Buddy had. She hoped he was riding around with him. She hoped he was out on a job and not out setting any fires. She didn't really mean it. Roy would never do something like that.

She thought back to the dogs and wondered if they were truly lost or if they'd been dumped here sometime in the middle of the night. That happened too.

"But what if they're starving?" Jillie said, as they turned onto the highway.

"They're all right. They look like someone's been feeding them just fine." The whole morning had gone wrong, and now they were later than ever.

"I really like those dogs."

"I know you do."

She'd rushed everybody this morning. Max and Will had already gone off to the bus stop, angry at her for making them wear their winter coats. She'd stuffed some lunch money into their pockets and told them to get some pizza. But then they were on their way—books, lunches, coats all packed in, seat belts on, doors locked, as they sailed on down the highway. It looked like the sun was going to break through the fog any minute now. Already she was feeling better. She turned on the car radio, found the sweet spot against the seat. Jillie sat in the middle of the back seat in her booster chair, looking at her new red shoes. "9 to 5" by Sheena Easton was playing on the Golden Oldies station, and though Zoe cranked up the volume, Jillie refused to sing along.

"All right, start watching for the lake," Zoë said, glancing at her through the rearview mirror. It was their old game, a contest to see which one could see the lake first, as they pulled out onto the highway. It was the first part of the script they'd made up to get them through their morning leave-taking. It was like ritual in the true sense, safekeeping against certain unspoken things, and now she had resurrected it to get through these first weeks at her new school.

"When will you pick me up?" she said. It was part of the litany of separation.

"Right after my classes are done and your school is out and you're looking at books in the library."

"Yesterday I thought you weren't coming and I started to cry." Zoë had been twenty minutes late. Jillie had been sitting in the reading corner of the library on the bean bag chair, her knees tucked up under her chin, watching the door.

"I might cry today if you don't come," Jillie said. She was getting back at Zoë for yesterday.

"But you know I'll always come and get you."

They drove on down the road. Jillie was leaning forward, trying to see the lake. They passed a group of apartment buildings and then things opened up.

"I see it!" There was the lake, glinting through the vanishing fog in between the trees lining the road.

"Oh, you won again! How do you *do* that?" Everything would be all right now.

She looked on down the road at the long line of traffic bunching up ahead. Traffic was backing up way past the stoplight now. "Maybe the light's broken." They moved closer. They were really going to be late now.

"What are those ducks in the road for?" Sitting high up in her booster seat, Jillie could see everything.

"Maybe they got turned around or something." They edged closer and coasted to a stop.

One of them was bloody on the road, neck outstretched, bloody feathers scattered everywhere. The other one was in the middle of the road, hunched down into itself against the cars going by.

"Did a car hit it?"

"Uh-huh." So much for the one duck, but the other one was trying to get across the highway to the grass by the side of the road. Its wings or legs must have been broken because it was scooting and flopping its way across the pavement. Everybody was looking out their windows at the ducks. Except for the people a few cars back who couldn't see what had happened and were sounding their horns.

"Did we hit the ducks?"

"Oh no, Sweetie. The car probably didn't even know what happened. It probably didn't even see the ducks." She wondered if those in the car would have even felt them, all feathers and air under the wheels.

The white duck had made its way to the edge of the road onto the grass where it just sat, a little tilted, its bloody chest heaving. Cars were beginning to move out again.

"See how pretty the lake is?" Zoë said as they passed the bloody place on the road.

"What's going to happen to the ducks?" Jillie was looking back at the duck on the grass. She put her thumb in her mouth, something Zoë hadn't seen her do for a long time. "I don't want to go to school today. I want to stay with you," she said through her thumb.

"That duck will be all right. Somebody will find it and take it to a hospital." Jillie didn't say anything for a long time. They were moving away from the lake and toward the city now. She couldn't see the water anymore; there were too many buildings in the way.

"That other duck is dead."

"It's sad when this happens. But ducks can't just come onto the road without cars hitting them."

"They better build a fence so ducks can't go on the road."

"Oh, I think ducks hardly ever come onto the road."

"Well, they better build a fence so they can't, even if they want to."

"That's a really good idea, Jillie."

"It wasn't the duck's fault."

"No, it wasn't. It's too bad when animals get in the way of cars."

"Why do bad things happen?"

"I don't know, Sweetie. Most of the time just good things happen."

"Not to Daddy. Bad things happen to him all the time."

Zoë's eyes filled with tears and blurred her way. She wiped them with the back of her hand, hoping Jillie hadn't seen, but she had. Zoë couldn't think of a thing to say.

"Bad things happened to Niki too." Zoë caught her daughter's eyes in the rearview mirror. It was the saddest thing she'd ever seen.

"When somebody dies, we wouldn't be sad if we didn't love them so much." She should never have said it like that.

Now Zoë didn't even lift her hand from the steering wheel to wipe her tears away. She took the next turn off the highway into the Safeway parking lot. She turned off the engine and just sat there. Both of them knew that something important had been said and could not be taken back.

Finally Jillie said, "I'll bet Roy really loves his new dog. I'll bet he loves him so much already. We could already love those dogs in our yard."

"How about we just go inside and not worry about being late? Cupcakes or doughnuts or maybe pistachio ice cream? You can have anything you want." She might as well pick up a few things that could stay in the car all day as long as they were there.

Jillie held on tight as they walked down the aisles. Then there they were in front of what Zoë most wanted to avoid. "We should get some food for those dogs."

"Oh, they'll probably be gone by the time we get home."

"But I really want them to stay."

"I know, Sweetie, but they already belong to somebody."

Jillie touched the golden cocker spaniel on the dog food bag. "I don't want anything to eat."

"Well, I'm going to get a coffee with whipped cream and chocolate sprinkles on top."

"My tummy hurts," Jillie said. Her cheeks were flushed and Zoë felt her forehead. No fever. But none of this was working. So Zoë bent down and scooped her up, and Jillie wrapped her arms and legs around her, her own little starfish, as always. They stood there like this next to the dog food, while Zoë rocked her gently side to side and nobody ate anything at all.

Traffic was smoother now, but still slow. It seemed important to get to school for both of them. She looked back at Jillie, who was sitting so still, rubbing her cheek with the corner of her jacket, since she was too big to take her blanket.

"When are you going to pick me up?" Good. They were back to the script. They would get through it now.

"Right after school's out, just like always, when you're in the library waiting."

Zoë slowed as she neared the corner. There were always school patrols on that street, standing on the corner, crossing children. But today she was so late there were no children in the crosswalk. No patrols anywhere. She pulled up in front of the school, signal light flashing.

She got out of the car and opened her door, but Jillie didn't move. "I don't want to go."

"I know, but the day will go by fast and then I'll be right back to find you."

"Okay." Jillie unfastened her seat belt and grabbed her backpack and slid across the seat. She crossed her heart as always, and slipped out the door. "Bye, Mommy," she said, and was gone.

"See you," Zoë said after her. "I love you." But Jillie didn't turn around. "I love you," she tried again. She wanted to run after her and scoop her up and never let her go.

They were both quiet coming home in the car. Zoë offered to stop for ice cream on the way, but Jillie said she wanted to get home to see if the dogs were still there.

Zoë most fervently hoped they were not.

Jillie didn't seem to remember where the ducks had been. She was concentrating on the dogs.

The clouds had rolled in again, and the sun on the water seemed distant and long ago, as they drove on around the lake, gray and sullen under that comfortless sky. It was beginning to rain. Zoë turned on the wipers and thought about those dogs. She had no idea what they would do if they were still there. She knew they couldn't keep them but knew what pressures would build if they did not. She was sure they were only lost anyway, sure the owners would be as glad to get them back as she'd be to get rid of them. They were probably wearing ID tags. In the rush she hadn't even looked. They'd call the owners and what a fine reunion that would be. But she also knew those dogs couldn't stay around too long or that reunion would be too hard on Jillie.

She flicked off her belt so she could jump out of the car the minute they pulled into the driveway. "Put your belt back on, Sweetie." Now they could see the edge of the yard. No dogs. No dogs in the driveway either, as they turned in. No dogs on the porch. No dogs anywhere. Gone, thank God.

"See? They were just visiting. They've gone on home." Jillie climbed out of the car and ran into the house, leaving the door wide open.

Zoë gathered up her books and Jillie's coat and lunch box. But she could see everything.

All over the entryway rug, the floors down the hall, the stairs—muddy paw prints—a couple of sacks full of wadded-up paper towels, and a pile of wet, muddy bath towels next to the door. Zoë could hear Will and Max laughing downstairs. She could hear Jillie squeal. Then the kids came racing up the stairs right along with the dogs.

"Look, Mom!" Max knelt down between the dogs, who began licking his face until they tipped him over. Jillie stood off to the side, trying to read her mother's look. The hope in her face broke Zoë's heart.

"We cleaned them all up and fed them," Will said, pointing to the plastic bowls sitting in the middle of the hallway.

"No, no, no! They can't be in here."

"Why not?" they said, standing there all lined up against her.

"Because they don't belong to us. They need to go home where they belong."

"But what if they're lost and they don't know the way home?" Max said.

"I think they're starving." Jillie leaned over to pet the red dog who'd collapsed onto her feet.

Will glared at Jillie and shook his head. He was clearly taking the lead in this choreographed entreaty. "We couldn't find any dog food, so we fed them hot dogs and lots of bread. They loved it."

Zoë had thrown out all the dog food over a month ago. And all the toys, leashes, and collars they had not buried. She'd even moved the couch in front of the window so there would be something in that window when she drove up the hill. The dogs had gotten up and were turning in circles, banging their tails against the door, the wall, their legs, their toenails skidding over the floor as they took off down the hall.

"We gave them more milk and the rest of the doughnuts." Max looked uncertainly at Zoë, then at the dogs. Zoë hoped they hadn't overdone it. It wouldn't do to have them throwing up on the living room rug. "Here, doggies," Max called. They came racing back down the hall, as if he'd said their name.

"Well, we need to get them back outside. They're probably not used to being in the house."

"Then why did they run inside when we opened the door?" Will said.

They all stood there by the open door and watched those dogs dash back into the living room and jump onto the couch. "Shoo! Shoo!" She'd never said those words in her life. The kids just stared at her. But the dogs jumped off the couch and sat down in the middle of the room, looking back up at her.

"You know we can't keep them."

Nobody said anything. They just gave each other secret, sideways looks.

Now the dogs were lying side by side in the middle of the living room. She'd just lean over and check to see if they were wearing collars or IDs. She would not touch them. But no tags. No collars.

"They like you already," Jillie said. The dogs were licking her shoes.

But then Zoë managed to get the dogs out the door, though clearly they did not want to leave. "Go. Go on home," she said, and slammed the door.

Zoë turned to look out the window. There'd been too much of everything. The rain was coming down hard now and she could see it would be dark before long. The streetlight by the mailboxes had come on. Then there was Jay, coming up the hill in that little blue

car. She always loved the way he took the hill, like he couldn't wait
to get home. But today he eased over the bump in the road like any
jostling would hurt all over. Today he didn't come bounding up the
stairs and into the house. Today he took a long time getting out of the
car, and when he came through the door the light from the hall cast
his face in deep shadows. She hugged him long and hard, and for the
first time she thought she could feel his shoulder blades through his
jacket. She knew not to help him out of it. He laid it over the railing
and made his way toward the couch in the living room.

"You know the dogs are right outside the door, I suppose."

"Don't even talk about it."

Jay just looked at her. Then he lay down on the couch and shut his
eyes.

"Can I help?" he called after her, as she headed to the kitchen to
start dinner.

Zoë leaned her head against the refrigerator. "Nah. But thanks.
They better not be petting those dogs," she called out as an
afterthought.

Soon she called everybody to dinner and the kids came up the
stairs in a tight little knot of solidarity.

Nobody felt like talking. They were listening for the thump of a
tail against the wall, a scratch at the door, the chink of a collar, a
sigh—sounds they'd kissed goodbye over two months ago. But they
were already moving on. It was too late to go back now.

"Jillie, come back and eat your dinner. You're just encouraging
them. If we let them alone, they'll just go on home."

They listened to the rain drum against the window.

After the kids were in bed, Zoë and Jay checked the paper's Lost
Pets section. Such an accumulation of grief: lost Labs, cockers, poo-
dles, Dalmatians, one lost horse, a pet chicken, and one lost bulldog

puppy in need of medication. Beloved family pet. Reward. Children heartbroken. All lost and gone a day, a week, a month. Where did you go? They called the Humane Society, they called PAWS, nobody missing two retrievers, one male, one female, one golden, one red. Nobody to say, *This time I will be more careful. This time I will keep you forever.*

They drew the curtains and turned out the lights. "Go away," Zoë whispered through the door. She opened it an inch. They were sleeping head to flank against the front door. The rain kept on. The wind came up and drove the rain against the house. She lay in bed listening to the rain, and the sound of bedroom doors opening and closing all night long. She knew what those kids were up to.

The next morning, Jay woke her up and said, "I want you to see this." He'd gotten up to take his early morning meds.

She threw on her sweats and came upstairs. It was just beginning to be light. She opened the front door a couple of inches. There were the dogs, curled up against the house, covered with blankets.

She thought of distemper and rabies and canine diseases of unknown origins, and how one way or the other those dogs would only get lost or stolen or hit by a car or grow old in an eyeblink, seven years at a time. "I can't do this."

"Okay," Jay said. "Do what you have to do. But it's okay with me, you know?"

"Look," she said to the kids that morning when they'd all come upstairs, "we'll build them a little shelter outside till their owners find them." She'd already called in an ad to the Found Pets section of the paper.

They just looked at her.

"But what if they can't ever find them?" Jillie said. "They could sleep with us like Niki did. We could name them."

"Don't do that, Jillie. Don't give them names."

A few days later, Zoë was sitting on the couch by the window, watching Jillie and a little friend of hers from down the hill chasing the dogs from one end of the lawn to the other. It was late in the afternoon and the fog was moving in from the lake. The red dog had picked up one of the old pumpkins and was racing across the lawn, carrying it by the stem. The golden dog ran after him, until the pumpkin vanished into a blaze of orange light.

Next week the new treatment would begin, though they still could not speak of it. Something old, something new, something borrowed, something blue. Now they would have tried it all. This last one would come in a clear tube that would dangle from a bag that hovered overhead. She thought back to last winter and how she had looked for signs everywhere she went. The ghostly old woman in periwinkle blue, the little old Devil in her dreams, the black bird outside their bedroom window—portents, omens, apparitions, as unreadable then as now. And what of her incantations to ward off the curses she saw everywhere she turned? All those words offered up in terror and rage to the blinding sky. And now here they were, breaking through the fog in flashes of red and gold, signs without translation, the very thing itself.

That night they lay in bed a long time before either of them went to sleep. Tomorrow would be just another day, like many other such days. There would be no end to them. She would believe in this new treatment for as long as she could. She moved over next to him and thought of how they had floated in that wide, gentle sea. But then the old dread returned, as it so often did, and she got up to sit in the chair by the window. She pulled a blanket around her shoulders and lifted the blinds. They had made it through Christmas. They had made it through the Millennium. She sat there for a long time, watching the moon drift in and out of the clouds. It was snowing lightly. She wondered if it would be there in the morning. It was so cold.

The dogs lay by the foot of the bed curled up against each other, like spoons. These golden dogs, lost or found, reclaimed or not, gift or sorrow, theirs for the hour. Soon she, too, would believe in them, to love them as best they could for however long they could, this strange and sudden emblem of hope. Their good luck charm after all.

But the following morning came the phone call Zoë had feared. She wanted to shout at the woman on the phone. *You should have taken better care of them. You shouldn't have lost them. They were almost ours.* Now her children had another loss. They stood in a knot in the corner of the living room admitting no smile. Their hearts were not moved by the glad reunion before them. The late afternoon sun slanted across their faces as they watched those dogs circle their owners, jumping up and licking their faces, batting the walls, the furniture with their wild and extravagant tails. They raced down the hall and back, down the stairs and up again.

"They shouldn't get to take them back," Max said as he turned to watch their pickup truck make its way down the hill, with the dogs staring out the back. They all watched from the window. And there at the bottom of the hill, Roy was getting the mail, the dog at his heel. He looked up as the truck went on by. Then he stepped into the road and stared up the hill, his hands on his head in that familiar gesture of despair. He stood there for several minutes before he turned back toward his house, the dog leading the way.

Zoë watched from the window and wondered if Roy could see her looking back. Then she turned and said, "I know it's sad, but they didn't belong to us."

"They did, though," Will said bitterly. "They did once."

"We loved them," Jillie said, burying her face in Zoë's sweater. Then she pulled away and rushed downstairs. "Now we don't have any dogs," she cried over her shoulder.

The sun had gone and the trees cast their thick, dusky shadows across the snow.

"What do you want for dinner?" Zoë asked as she headed toward the kitchen. "I'll make you anything you want."

Nobody could think of anything to eat.

I Will Leave You Never

She was drifting deep inside the night, so warm, so still, such pleasure and delight. The blinds permitted no light or sound, save a single expiration that wrapped them all in a net of dreams. Then into the dark, he called her name. Only the tightness in his voice betrayed how he'd tried to say it as softly as he could. She was so deeply asleep she didn't rouse. She hardly ever slept like this. He said it again, a little louder this time, though he couldn't touch her yet. Still, through the dark, she heard him call her name. *Jay?* She sat up sharply.

"I'm so sorry to wake you, but my breathing's kind of funny."

"What do you mean *funny*?"

"I don't know. It kind of hurts to breathe."

"Christ, Jay, what hurts?"

"My chest. Just a little."

"Down your arm?"

"No. I don't think so. Maybe a little."

The furnace fan whirred in the air like breathing.

It couldn't be his heart. Of all the things wrong with him, it was never his heart. *Strong heart, brave heart,* she said to herself as she dialed 911. No need to wake the kids. The sirens and the red flashing lights across their windows did that. They'd been sleeping on the edge of sleep for weeks now anyway.

Something had been missed. The stress of all that radiation on his heart? Her cobalt blue shield had slammed down into place the minute she'd heard him say her name. She couldn't feel a thing. Every catch in his breath, every sneeze, every sigh was a harbinger of the end unless she stayed put behind that shield. All these new treatments were set to go next week. It would be their last chance. But a chance, nonetheless. She'd tucked all the bad things somewhere in the future. Now here it was.

She followed the red lights through the night fog as they floated down the road. They'd turned off the siren, which she took as a good sign. She turned the corner into the emergency room lot. There were ambulances and aid cars angled every which way near the Emergency door. Some terrible thing had just happened. She couldn't catch her breath. She skidded into the only parking place she could find and rushed inside after him. He tried to grab her hand as the gurney slid into the lobby. Where was everybody? No one at the desk, no one in the waiting room. Zoë couldn't stop touching him. She held onto his shoulder as they wheeled him through the double doors and down the hall, into a cubicle of his own. She held his foot through the sheet, as they laid him slowly onto the bed.

"Not a pretty picture," Jay said, looking away. She knew he'd tried a dark-humored joke but the tears in his eyes gave him away.

"We'll get you squared away in a minute," someone said, and left in a rush. Zoë wanted to grab her arm and pull her back. He was already hooked up to the heart monitor and an IV. He'd come in that way. Something terrible was going on. She could hear the rush of gurneys down the hall, a clanging, shoes pounding the linoleum, a woman crying in gulps of air. A terrible car accident. Multiple cars, multiple wounds. Zoë peeked down the hall. "All hell breaking loose."

She was glad she wasn't that woman. It was probably only indigestion. Just a little pressure from something of no consequence, like those ice cream spasms he'd had last spring.

She looked back at Jay. It was as if he didn't hear any of this.

He didn't take his eyes from her face. "You know what this means, don't you? You know where we are now, don't you?" He was looking at her fiercely.

"Well, it can't be your heart. It just feels like it. Like those spasms during radiation." She was sitting on the bed now, stroking his arm.

"Yeah. It's kind of like that."

No one had explained the effects of radiation on the heart.

Jay lay his head back, shut his eyes. "I really don't want to be here."

Zoë's eyes were swimming with tears. "I know. Should I go out and find somebody? It's taking too long."

"I feel kind of funny," he said. "I think I pulled a muscle getting onto the gurney, or maybe getting onto the bed."

"Do you feel short of breath?"

"Yeah. A little. Not much."

"I should go get someone."

"No. Don't leave."

Zoë bent over and put her face next to his. Her cheek came away wet.

"I don't want to leave you." He was panting now.

"You're not going anywhere." She took his face in her hands and would not forsake his eyes. "You promised."

"You'll never know"—he had to catch his breath now—"how much I love you."

She could only whisper, "But I do."

Now he was grabbing the sides of the bed. His breath was rapid, shallow.

She lay her hand on his chest. "Keep still if you can." She looked past the curtained cubicle. Somebody would be in any minute now. If they didn't come in a second, she'd run out and grab the first person she saw no matter what was happening out there.

They had been there for hours. They had been there for minutes.

"My chest," he whispered.

"I'm going to get somebody."

"Don't go." He reached to touch her but his arm fell back onto the bed. He was looking at her so deeply she couldn't move. There must be a button to press but she couldn't leave him to look for it. There was no death in his eyes, she was sure of it. But it was something she'd never seen before. All the life he had gathering into his eyes. He was becoming translucent. His face was full of radiance, his eyes were full of light. *We are memorizing each other,* she was thinking. His eyes were clear, crystalline. They could find no words, but even so, something was being said. She could feel it shimmer between them. Later, she would want words that could be taken up in her hands for safekeeping.

Then she watched his eyes grow wide, looking beyond looking, staring at something too far for her to see. His breathing changed. Just two little puffs of breath, then a pause, then two more quick little commas of breath. Then three breaths without sound, just a gentle lifting of his face to catch the last of all the air there was. He'd said no intubation.

She yanked open the curtains and rushed down the hall. She heard herself yell *Help!* She thought she had shouted it but maybe she hadn't. But someone must have seen the look on her face because in an instant she was surrounded by people touching him, his leg, his arm, his head, his chest, his face. She should have said, *No, don't.* But she couldn't. She looked at the clock. It hadn't moved. Of course it had. Then she put her hand out, shook her head. But there was no need. They already knew he'd signed a DNR.

Then he tried once more to catch a puff of air that could not be caught. The pause went on, and still his chin rose though his breath was gone and there was nothing to catch, just this urgent, valiant effort to take in all the life that could be until the very last. No one moved.

She didn't watch the monitors. She only turned when the line that moved across the screen, with no peaks or valleys, began to pronounce its deadly hum. Then she turned back to his eyes, still his own, but seeing nothing of this world. Then she watched as they slowly closed, a choreography of love and death.

"Come back," she said. "Don't go."

Finally they took her to a little room with a leather couch and a TV down the hall from him. A chaplain was on his way. She wanted to go home. She wanted to stay. What she wanted she would never have again.

Still, some explanations were in order. His heart stopped beating and he died. That's what happens when you die, for godsake. Her bitterness rose up. She was on fire with it. She felt a keening rise into her throat but stopped it with a hand across her mouth. She would not cry out. A doctor she didn't recognize came in and sat by her on the leather couch in this TV room—or was it a prayer room?—and explained it well enough. A blood clot had traveled from somewhere to his heart, that's all. *Coup de coeur.* An arrow to the heart. Of course, this wasn't the real translation. Well, that's the French for you when it came to love. All or nothing. The literal French translation was closer to falling in love than a blow to the heart.

She swallowed the words as a stone, which lodged in her throat. She knew she could die from it. Then she felt it slide farther down, and she tried again to swallow it, but it lodged there, and she could feel her throat tighten around it—before it dropped into her stomach, where it lay smooth and still, and not as bad as you might think. Which is just as well, as she imagined it would lie like that forever. But it was nothing like falling in love. She had already done that.

Fire and Ice

In her dream she didn't hear the doorbell, or the wild pounding on the front door or the shouting from the front lawn. She didn't smell the smoke. Then she heard the fist against their bedroom windows and saw Roy, lit by the motion sensor light. She reached for Jay, but he was gone. She could see the flames rush across the glass, and now she heard it gnawing at the branches that snapped then crashed to the ground. Treetops exploded into balls of flame that jumped from tree to tree in a shower of sparks and smoke. The moon was blood red.

Zoë flew down the hall, grabbing the kids out of their beds and out the rec room door at the far end of the house. Where were the neighbors? If the whole woods caught fire, they'd need to run for their lives. They stood in the driveway wrapped around each other, watching the moon vanish in a cloud of black smoke, then reappear, dark and heavy with sorrow. Molten stars fell through the air and covered the lawn.

"It's beautiful," Jillie said. "Stars are falling on our grass."

"Like snow," Max said, "only it's red." The embers flickered and pulsed across the lawn, edging toward where they watched, holding hands. *Be ready to run*, Zoë thought but didn't say, because she couldn't stop watching. "You're right. It's beautiful."

"Mom? We should leave. I could drive us."

Zoë fumbled in her pajama pocket. "The keys are gone." She couldn't seem to move.

Will pulled Jillie and Max close.

But then the fire truck was coming up the hill, making its treacherous way over the bump in the road, stopping beside the house.

"Where's Daddy?" Jillie said, tugged from sleep.

"Jillie," Will said softly. "He died."

"Oh." She looks stunned. "I forgot." Then she turned around and pointed to Ferny Land, dark and green and backlit by the coming fire. "He's here."

And there he was, just at the edge of sight, standing with his arms crossed, watching over them, and then he was gone, vanished into the smoky night air.

"It was Daddy," Jillie said.

"Where?" Zoë said, waking herself up to the dark. She yanked up the blinds. There was no fire, no motion sensor light, no Roy, no Jay, and no sounds but the furnace fan gently insisting that all was well, which she didn't believe for a minute. She looked out at the woods and the moon filtering through the trees. There was the woodpile, so diminished and benign. She'd used wood from that woodpile every night this week for fires that held her to the moment in its comfort and dread.

But the dream terror remained, so just to be sure, she got up to check on them. She envied their sleep, resisted the temptation to crawl into bed with Jillie, and made her way up the stairs. She was testing her mettle. A walk through the house in the dark was as good a place to start as any. Who had turned out all the lights? She had turned out all the lights.

It was a week after the service, and finally all the company was gone. Her parents, her cousins, Jay's sister. She should be doing better than this by now. But she couldn't stop her darkest thoughts. She should have been able to save him. There must have been some cure out there beyond flaxseed oil and cottage cheese. Ah, the Budwig diet—the final dissembler. Jay'd had to gag it down. There could have been more praying. Her prayers were always desperate and illiterate. Often she was afraid of them.

Of course, the kids needed her now more than ever. But she was only half there most of the time. They couldn't stop touching her. Sometimes Zoë didn't know she was crying until she heard one of the kids say she could stop now, it would be all right. They wrapped themselves tightly around her and wouldn't let her go. They patted her and brought her tea and opened cans of chicken noodle soup. They spread soda crackers with peanut butter and bread with jam. They ate ice cream for breakfast and stayed home from school. They played *Monopoly* all day and let her win every time. "It's only two thousand dollars, Mom," they told her when she landed on Boardwalk with a hotel. "We'll give you a loan." Anything to keep her in the game.

She thought about turning on the lights but stood there listening to the sound of the dark instead. She thought it was death. But death had no sound. Death was a smell. The cloying, earthly sweet smell of decay. The lilies. She could hardly breathe. The lilies had wrapped her in a dream for three days. Once she had been glad for lilies. The smell of Easter morning, the way they had filled the church with their airy, powdery sweetness. But now when she came up the stairs their smell assaulted her. It reminded her of those Halloween vanilla candy skulls.

So many flowers. She hated them all. She had always hated gladiolas. That alien, showy flower which filled out a funereal spray and gave such false surprise. There was nothing glad about them. It was the first thing she saw when she walked in and took her seat in the first row. She had said no gladiolas. But there they were.

And the bitter smell of chrysanthemums. Even the baby's breath haunted her. So feathery and light. Their delicacy carried no smell. They were just an accent or filler, but she'd always loved them for themselves, even so. She thought of Jay's breath. Two little puffs, a whisper of a breath, a baby's breath, his last. And his face, his beautiful face, and his blue eyes reaching for what was already lost. The carnations were barely a whisper now. She'd remembered one Mother's Day from her childhood, when the minister said if your mother were alive you wore a red carnation, and if she were dead a white one, and how she'd looked at her parents' white carnations and then down at the red one she was holding tightly in her hands. This house had white carnations everywhere she turned.

Well, they all had to go. She was going to put them in the trash, but then she had a moment of remorse. She'd give them back to nature.

It must be past midnight. Her watch had stopped days ago. It was all right. All she had now was time. She'd toss them all into the gully. She couldn't do it fast enough. It took her four armloads, ribbons and all. She stood there for a long time, letting the dark wrap around her. She'd turned out the back porch light because even then she knew she'd look like a crazy person, her parka thrown over her nightgown, her bare, pale legs and scruffy slippers. The bulb on the motion sensor light by the back garage door had gone out long ago. These past days the fires had seemed remote, dreamlike. She felt like laughing at all the outrageous precautions she had demanded. She thought the danger was outside, when it was inside all along. So why would she dream of those fires now?

She couldn't save anybody from anything. Least of all her children. She was no good for them now. All the vitamins, seat belts, soy

milk, green tea, the double-locked doors, lights here, lights there—
how stupid to think you could keep the people you loved all safe. She
thought of how she had kept her hand on Jay's chest as he slept, to feel
his slow, steady breath.

In the morning she'd see all those flowers and ribbons spread out
over the blackberry bushes and ferns down the hill into the gully,
crazy spots of color against the deep brown and green of winter. She
laughed out loud at the thought of it. Her neighbor would think she'd
lost her mind. Well, she had.

She was standing on the edge of the woods now, looking down
to the floor of the gully. There was something wild down there that
waited for her. The wild thing she was seeking was down there, next
to the tree house and the tire swing. She wanted something to happen
but didn't know what. Maybe she could go back into the house now
that the death smell was gone. She'd open a couple of windows to
be sure. She didn't know that the ground right here was just grass
clippings and autumn leaves and nothing to stand on.

As she tossed the flowers, her feet slipped out from under her
until she finally caught hold of some sword ferns and blackberry
bushes with thorns as sharp as ever. She cried out but knew no one
had heard her. She turned over carefully and pulled herself back up
onto solid ground. She sat on the deck and wiped her face. She knew
she was crying but felt nothing. She had wanted some strange pun
ishment and here it was. Her hands throbbed with all the anger and
sorrow and pain she knew were coming. She wanted to see if she
could stand it. Anything was better than this crushing despair. So
what if 90 percent of people who got it were cured if he wasn't one
of them?

She stood up and looked down at her bleeding hands. There were
gashes over her palms, at her wrists, her fingertips. She wiped them

on her coat. They throbbed more than ever. She wanted to hold suffering in her hands. Now she understood cutting—that terrible thing that cursed some of her students, their suffering disguised by an extra-long T-shirt or sweater. She might need medical attention.

She could hear the silvery trembling of wind chimes as the wind moved through the trees, the moon a pearly light behind the clouds. Then it appeared magically, only to rush across the sky and into the clouds and disappear again. Somewhere between light and dark there was something she had to know. She looked out into the woods for the flickering blue light. Why else had she come out here?

Jay could never talk about Roy because he had feared him more than he was willing to admit. But when everything began to take on such urgency, he'd tried to warn her about Roy without frightening her. Zoë knew how much the thought of Roy skulking about and Zoë all alone worried him. "He thinks he's saving us, Jay. He thinks he's protecting us."

"From what?"

There was no answer she could say.

She sat on the edge of the deck, catching her breath. It was so dark. And it had grown so cold so quickly. She could feel the fog before she saw it. She would just sit here for another moment or two.

"Come back to me in the night," she said out loud, "like you said you would." The moon had gone under a cloud and she could no longer see her breath.

The fog had crept in completely now and she couldn't see across the backyard at all. The deck was covered with frost, so she'd have to be careful getting up. No motion sensor light by the garage, no light on the front porch either. When did it get to be so dark inside? Weren't the kids always turning on the lights? So what was she trying to do, turning out all the lights before bed? But these days daylight

was more terrifying than any night. Jay's absence in the light was
unbearable. No jacket slung over the kitchen chair, *Dad's home!*, no
keys in a jumble on the counter next to the pile of accumulating mail,
his shoes on the floor of the closet, reading glasses on top of the TV,
his latest book, *Love, Medicine and Miracles*. She should have thrown
that out days ago. What miracle could possibly matter now?

At least the detritus of illness had been swept away. The pill bottles,
the cases of coconut milk, their latest elixir of health—nutrients that
go right into the bloodstream and bypass the liver. Getting rid of all
that had been easy. That had taken one violent moment. But his keys?
Where should they go now? And his reading glasses! Or his watch.
Someone had hung his jacket back in the hall closet out of plain sight
as if it might, if you wished hard enough, conjure him out of thin
air when you came upon it, and then such surprise when it did not.
Better not to see things by day. Better to float in this silky dark where
they could meet just on the edge of dreams.

Then she remembered the other thing she'd come outside for.
She'd left the automatic garage door wide open. She couldn't remember why she'd opened it in the first place. It had been acting funny
for weeks and she'd told the kids not to go near it. She got up slowly
and walked carefully over the frosty deck to the back garage door,
unlocked it, and looked inside—there it was, cavernous, the door
open for the asking, lit for a moment by the thin, amber light of her
flashlight. And things she could not bear to see by daylight lit enough
to catch her by surprise—Jay's golf clubs, his fishing gear, the lawn
mower, skill saw, the workbench, his bike.

They were always going to get that wacky door fixed. But it had
been a crazy year. A heartbreak of a year. She still couldn't believe it.
He'd just gone off fishing in the Straits or maybe Alaska. He'd been
gone ten days, so he'd be back any time now. But his fishing poles

were stacked against the wall, and his tackle box and downriggers were right there on the shelves, plain as day.

She thought of all those fires the arsonist had set with old rags and wood and kerosene he'd found waiting in garages just like this one. Jay had disabled the outside automatic door button, at her insistence—otherwise, anybody at all could get in. So you had to use the button just inside the back door of the garage to open that automatic door. But it was so wide and unsteady, you had to dash from the back of the garage to the front in time to grasp it in the middle and help it along.

Zoë pushed the button to close that ancient, oversized garage door, ignoring the usual groans and shimmies as the door struggled mightily to close itself. Then she zigzagged through the garage and grabbed the center of that big door and gave it a tug. But it jerked—it had never done that before—and seemed to be on the verge of slipping off its tracks. It was coming down too fast and she couldn't slow it down. She was afraid to let go, afraid it would just come down in a crash upon her. Then she lost her balance and found herself on her hands and knees in the gravel, the door pinning her underneath. But it had stopped that grinding noise.

"*Help! Help!*" she said to the night. But there was no help. She wondered if she could edge her way out from under the door before it collapsed to the ground. It was holding so far. She wasn't ready to try it yet. So she crouched there, the door against her back, her hands pressing into the gravel. She shut her eyes. "Jay," she said out loud. She knew he was near. She knew he hadn't left her yet. She couldn't feel the gravel digging into her palms anymore. "Jay?" she said again. She could feel his smooth, strong back, his arms, his breath on her neck. *I'm still here*, he said across her heart. She felt light. She could almost touch him now, he was so close.

And then someone beside her, lifting the door. She felt no pressure now and so she edged her way out from under the door and stood up. A shadowy figure stepped back into the dark, though she could feel his presence just out of reach. She stood with empty arms. "Jay?" She knew it wasn't Jay. Still, the air had moved as if in a breeze.

A figure shuffled in the gravel toward her. "It's just me. It's just Roy. I didn't want to scare you."

"What are you doing here?"

"I was walking my dog and I heard your garage door. It's pretty loud, and it's so late I thought something was wrong."

"Oh, it was." She was trembling and couldn't catch her breath.

"I like to walk him at night and check on the neighborhood, you know? Be sure everybody's okay." She had never seen him walking the dog by day, but she knew if he did, he'd feel the neighbors' eyes from an upstairs window, or a gap in the curtains, or from the edge of the porch, maybe saying something in dark, grating syllables, as he tucked in his chin and hurried on.

"I saw all the cars and the florist vans coming up the hill last week. I'm really sorry." She felt her chest give way. Everything was spinning and she reached out her hand. He stepped forward and put his arms around her so tentatively, so gently, she hardly felt it. She leaned against him, felt his flannel shirt against her cheek, and started to cry.

"It's okay. It's okay. It's okay," he whispered. They stayed there while the fog wrapped them in a secret tenderness. You couldn't see to the road.

She felt something nuzzle her hand.

"He remembers you," Roy said.

There was the pup, so big now. Almost full-grown. Zoë knelt down and the dog licked her neck. She put her arms around him and buried her face in his soft, thick fur and breathed in his smell. She shut her eyes again and there was Niki come back to her.

Then she stood up and felt a cold wind across her face. The fog spun itself into the trees, catching in the branches.

"We should get that garage door down. Let me see if I can get it back down." So he jockeyed it back and forth, then pushed down hard, and the garage door let go of its hold on the kink and he eased it on down.

"Roy," she said. "Thank you."

He nodded but didn't say anything. Then he picked up something from the gravel wedged under the garage door. "Better use it if you come outside." It was her flashlight. "You never know what could be out here. I'll see if it works." But when he flicked it on, it worked only too well, and for one shocking moment, it caught his face in an arc of light.

He looked like he had been beaten. He flicked off the light and handed it to her. But there was no need for a flashlight now, because the moon had been working its way out of the fog all this while, until there it was, unbelievably white and full to bursting. It washed the gravel white as snow and the frost on the road. Suddenly they were in another country. The moonlight was like rippling water across his face. The swollen eye with the cut above the eye still fresh. The bruise on his cheek, the cut on his lip. Roy flinched, knowing she had seen everything.

"What happened? Who did this to you?"

He stepped back and turned his head. "Just kid stuff. Come here, boy," he said, and the dog came right to him. "Nobody did nothing. I fell down my very own stairs."

"That's a *beating*. That's not kid's stuff. Was it those boys down the street?"

"Oh, I'm used to it. They don't really mean no harm. You know, ringing the doorbell and running away. Eggs on the window." The scarecrow like a crucifix chalked on his door after Halloween. Other things.

"You should call the sheriff. I'm sorry nobody's done anything to stop it. I've just been so busy lately and I'm tucked away up here. But I should have done something."

She knew where most of it had been coming from. That tortured house down the hill next to the bus stop with the father who beat his boys with a belt. No wonder they had turned so mean. Will said Danny Ferguson, the oldest boy, had organized some of the other kids for pranks. She could hardly call them pranks. Then a couple of weeks ago, *Hangman Go Hang Yourself* in red paint on his driveway, which he'd tried to wash off but only turned it into a pale red smear, though the letters showed through.

She was hoping the winter rains would take care of the rest.

"I've had that kind of stuff my whole life."

It hurt her to hear it. Even her kids were bothered by it. "Nobody should be treated like that," Will had said. They'd gotten that moral compass from their dad. She didn't know what they'd gotten from her.

"Well, you get used to it," Roy said, but with such despair she knew he'd never gotten used to being a throwaway person like that. She knew in that moment like never before what that dog she'd run over had meant to him.

"You really saved me," she said. She wanted to do something for him but hadn't the slightest idea what.

"It's good to do something that somebody needs. It's hard to find things like that." He picked up something from the ground. It was a dog dish and long leash. The pup sat quietly next to him. "See, I'm not so good around people. I was always doing something wrong without even knowing it." A life like that could make you into anything. She could still see his eye so swollen and bruised.

Blighted. That's what he was. She thought of The Old Lamplighter, making his rounds to light up the night. *Nine o'clock and all is well,* he calls, as his lamplight swings back and forth. She hoped most devoutly that's who he was.

"Best be getting home now."

She wanted to touch his arm or hand but was shy of the distance coming between them.

"Those were great-looking dogs you had. I was hoping you could've kept 'em."

Zoë didn't know what to say. It startled her how much he knew.

"You take good care of yourself now."

"I will. You too."

In that moment she knew, her throbbing hands notwithstanding, that she was standing on sure ground and would not fall again. She could feel her back straighten and no pain anywhere. She was glad the flashlight didn't show the gashes on her hands.

"Thanks again," she called after Roy, who was making his careful way down that frosty road into the white-spun moonlight. The leash was rolled up in one hand and the dog dish in the other, while the pup followed close beside. She wanted to call after him but did not. She wondered about the dog dish. She should have asked him why he'd brought it. Or the leash. You could see that dog needed no leash at all.

The Lark Ascending

The next morning she rolled over and reached for Jay, then pulled her hand back from the empty pillow, like it had been slapped. How many mornings would she wake to his death all over again? Where was he now? In the dream Jay was reaching for her, but she kept slipping out of his hands. In the distance she saw his face, luminous in the moonlight. Then a moon-driven shadow darkened as she watched him go. She shut her eyes and smelled Old Spice—ambergris, vanilla, cinnamon. That heartbreak of a scent. She sat up and rubbed her neck. She'd slept with her face in the pillow again. She knew she wouldn't go back to sleep, so she might as well get up. She slipped off her nightgown, pulled on her sweats, and came slowly up the stairs to an early morning, dark as night. She heard a whimpering and pawing on the other side of the door. Now what was that? She opened the door slowly, and the dog put his nose against her legs and licked her hand. She stepped outside, and knelt down.

The leash was tied around the railing, so there was no chance he could escape. He was looking at her with such hope and expectation she thought it was Niki and gasped at the resurrection. But the rhinestone collar was unmistakable. And the dog dish with the gold letters, COYOTE, filled with water, the dog bed and the rawhide bone.

A piece of folded-over yellow notebook paper was taped to the railing: *Love him best you can.*

She stepped off the porch onto the driveway. "Roy?" She looked back at the dog, who was straining at the leash, but making no sound. "Roy?"

There was Roy's driveway but no brown van that she could see. She took off down the hill to Roy's front door. She didn't think of all the ways she could fall. The driveway was empty. The red smudges were still there. She wondered how much winter rain it would take to erase them. What a terrible message. It hurt her to think of it: *Hangman Go Hang Yourself.*

She rang the bell. She rang it again. "Roy? Are you home?" She knocked tentatively, then forcefully. She stepped off the porch and walked around to the front window. There was a gap between the curtains. She tapped on the glass, pressed her face close. She thought she could see something, a shadow, a figure. The wind sifted through the fir trees and made tears come to her eyes. She went back onto the porch and said to the door, "Why did you leave your dog with us?"

The streetlight had gone out and she turned toward the sudden darkness. Something white was floating toward her led by an arc of light. Who was this man coming to her in a white terry robe, his shock of white hair catching first light?

"I went out to get the paper and heard you calling," he said. His arm was reaching out to her, or so it seemed.

"Mr. Merwin?"

"Are you all right?" he said, as he stepped onto the porch.

"I don't know. I don't think so." She put her hand on the railing, leaned against it. Moments ago she was asleep. Now here she was. She could hear the dog beginning to bark. "He left his dog on our porch."

"Well, he's a strange one, isn't he," Mr. Merwin said.

"I wondered if he were home. People around here, in the

neighborhood . . ." She couldn't quiet her wild and frantic heart. "These boys down the hill. Sometimes they did bad things to him."

"I've heard that. You know, I'm sorry to admit I never did anything about it. That's why I came over when I heard you. I thought I might help."

"Last night he was so despairing. He helped me with my garage door. His face. Someone had battered his face. These boys down the street. I know I told you that." She had reached out to touch his arm then took her hand back. She began to shiver. Her breath was coming in startled little knots.

"He gave his puppy to us. I think something's wrong." She wondered if he'd come to her house last night to give up the dog. She didn't remember taking the note but here it was in her hand.

Mr. Merwin took the offered note and read it out loud. "*Love him best you can.*"

"I see what you mean. Well, it's odd, don't you think?" He handed the note back to her. "Should we see if the door's locked?"

"We could go in together."

Mr. Merwin turned the doorknob, nudged the door open. It was so dark. "Hello?" Zoë said to the dark. "Is anybody home?" Her voice came back to her, hollow and thin. She felt around the wall for a light switch. There it was. She flicked the lights, but it was darker than ever. "I thought I saw something inside. Maybe someone's in here," Zoë whispered.

"Can we come in, sir? I've got your neighbor here." Mr. Merwin reached out to touch Zoë's arm. "I've got my flashlight. My eyes aren't so great, so I carry it to get the newspaper."

The flashlight spun in an arc down the hall. Then there it was, caught in Mr. Merwin's flashlight. "I'll be damned."

Zoë's heart thundered.

"It's that scarecrow from Halloween." Mr. Merwin's hand was shaking, turning the room into a chiaroscuro of light. "Good Christ! He's sitting in a chair. He's got his legs crossed."

Zoë felt light-headed. "Like he's a friend. Or company."

"Oh my. We're talking about a dummy, you know. I need to sit down." He started to laugh. "But he's got the only chair."

"It is kind of funny," Zoë said, but the laugh stopped in her throat. "It's not funny, is it." She looked hard at the scarecrow, watching over everything. She felt the sting of tears.

"Maybe he had a good laugh," Mr. Merwin said. "Maybe it comforted him some way."

"So he might be all right then?" Zoë felt her breathing settle into a soft desire.

"But you know when that scarecrow was hanging there on the porch, I thought he looked crucified. It unsettled me."

"People are crucified by lots of things." Roy's battered face in the moonlight rose up before her. And *Jay*. She couldn't think of Jay. She felt a little sick. She reached for the wall but there was nothing there. When she grasped Mr. Merwin's arm, he dropped the flashlight, and it skittered across the floor and went out.

"It's so dark in here," Mr. Merwin said. "We'll never find it. We'd better go."

"I'm so cold." She couldn't remember being this cold. How long had the power been out?

They didn't know what else to do but to just close the door behind them. "Nights are so long," Zoë said. "Like there's no end to them. I'm sorry about the flashlight." They stood on the porch, watching the day breaking over the treetops. She had never been so glad of the light.

"I met your children on Halloween. Lovely children."

"Jay told me. My husband told me."

"You're very lucky, you know, to have children."

"Oh," she said. "Yes I am."

"Call me Will," he said. She wanted him to put his arms around her. And then for a moment he did.

His back was warm through the terry robe. She could smell his shampoo.

"I'm Zoë," she said, trying not to cry.

"I know," he said as he stepped back. "You all right now?"

"He was never the arsonist, was he."

"No, he wasn't."

Mr. Merwin turned to look back at that empty house. "They caught him, you know. The goddamned son of the editor of the *Everett Herald*. Can you believe that? The dad turned him in. He confessed like he was proud it had taken so long." Mr. Merwin drew his hand through his hair.

Zoë hadn't watched the news or read the paper for days. Maybe weeks. She knew if she started crying, she'd never stop. But she knew he could see her eyes were full of tears even so.

"I know what you're thinking," he said. "That poor guy. All that pain for nothing. Now he's gone. You going to be all right?"

She could only nod. She couldn't tell him that her husband had just died. That there must have been something she could have done to save him. *If you wanted it more than your very heart, you could have found something no one had ever thought of before.* She knew how hard she'd tried and look how things turned out. She'd be half of a whole the rest of her life.

"I just have to walk up the hill and then I'm home."

He took her hand like he was going to shake it and then clasped it in both of his. "Your hand is so cold." He rubbed it for a moment and then held it a moment longer. She saw a distant, familiar sadness.

"Do you have people?" She couldn't help herself. "People that love you?"

Mr. Merwin looked stunned.

"I'm sorry. I didn't mean to pry."

He waved her away. "Well. I'd better go on in and get dressed. I guess the day's started."

She watched him make his slow, determined way across the street. Then he turned back around. "What will you do with the dog?" he called.

"Keep him. Love him."

"That's good. You should do that. I'll be seeing you," he said as he waved goodbye. She watched him walk up the driveway in his white terry robe, his crown of white hair. He picked up the newspaper and tucked it under his arm. And then he was gone.

Dawn was filtering through the trees as, for the moment, her heart quieted into a whisper. She stood by the gate as this newborn light worked away at the early morning scrim of fog. She looked everywhere but at that porch and front door. She hardly knew Roy, but she knew there must be a prayer to be said. *Godspeed*, she thought. She saw a bird rise up in annunciation or alarm as the sun ignited the treetops.

She couldn't go home just yet. She'd have to pull herself together as if she had no fierce-beating heart. Her children were still asleep up the hill—how could she see them through this? She imagined them growing into their lives afraid of everything. How could she explain it? She imagined the conversation.

She would have to tell them Roy was gone now. That people drove him away.

No, I don't know why he'd leave his dog, she'd say to the children. *Maybe he wants us to know he is a good person.*

Maybe he knows we don't have any dogs, Jillie would say. *But he loved him so much.*

Yes, he did. And now we can love him too.

She thought about scarecrows and how they weren't scary at all but angels in disguise, protecting them against dark and rapacious things. She looked at the yellow paper again and felt something touch the back of her neck like a whisper or a kiss. She turned around but no one was there.

She could hear the chimes again as the wind moved through the trees. She looked up. But there was no wind. She was traveling fast now. Then there he was, the little boy with the long, serious face, the sad gray eyes. She knelt down in the snow and blew on his cold, cold hands. She led him through the woods until she came to the little hill with the wooden marker. That poor child she'd called Roy in her dreams had grown up into this blighted, damaged man. She believed it now for good but knew she would always keep that dreaming child to herself.

She stood just at the edge of the yard, holding tightly to the wrought iron spears of the gate. All the people she tried to help and could not. She looked up at her house. To live with such absence, such missing to the bone. She could feel Jay's arms safe and warm around her, his kiss on her face. "Come back," she said. She should never say this. It would be the final cheat of her heart. "Well, Jay is an angel now too," she said again.

There couldn't be enough living things to fill this house. She saw herself in the middle of that king-size bed with Jillie and Max and

Will and this pup who was Niki herself, reclaimed from death. She came up the hill and onto the porch. The kids had taken everything inside. She imagined the reunion.

She stood for a long time with her hand on the doorknob. It was all before her. You could learn to love anything, even terrible things, if you could love them for what they are teaching you. She could not do this, of course. But she would go in. It was her life. It was what came next. She went in and closed the door behind her.

Author's Note

I Will Leave You Never wove its way in and out of my life for many years. Other books and essays took its place in my mind and heart, while it waited patiently, or so I thought, in the dreaded, proverbial drawer. And then it rose up and took its rightful place as book number three. So it's hard to know where it truly began, though now I know where and how it ends.

But with so many shifts and turns along the way, it's curious to me how a book finds its final shape and timbre and color.

Is it true? I had a husband, a father, a mother. I have three children, as does the main character of this book. However, I must confess that although it is indeed true, it is also completely made up. All I can say now is that this book came from the mysterious, sacred alchemy that occurs when memory and the imagination finally meet completely and utterly outside words. And that this book was fueled, miraculously, by love.

So the story that began the summer we took the kids to Glacier Park, just after a grizzly bear mauling, has no bear in it at all. How that story became another and another, and finally this one, is a mystery, even to me.

But. I am at work on book four, in which a bear makes a wondrous and unexpected appearance—along with my grandmother's near-drowning, a wily cottonmouth snake, and Virginia Woolf's Clarissa Dalloway. I don't know how all these things came to be in the same book. All I can do for now is say thank you.

About the Author

photo credit: Jeannine Pound

A nn Putnam is an internationally known Hemingway scholar, who has made more than six trips to Cuba as part of the Ernest Hemingway International Colloquium. Her novel *Cuban Quartermoon* (June 2022) came, in part, from those trips, as well as a residency at Hedgebrook writers' colony. She has published the memoir *Full Moon at Noontide: A Daughter's Last Goodbye* (University of Iowa Press), and short stories in *Nine by Three: Stories* (Collins Press), among others. Her literary criticism appears in many collections and periodicals. She holds a PhD from the University of Washington and has taught creative writing, gender studies, and American literature for many years. She has also bred Alaskan Malamutes, which appear prominently in *I Will Leave You Never*. During COVID, she completed another novel, which features a drowning, Virginia Woolf, bears, and snake handling in the Deep South. Just goes to show what happens when you never get out of the house. She lives in Gig Harbor, Washington.

SELECTED TITLES FROM SHE WRITES PRESS

She Writes Press is an independent publishing company founded to serve women writers everywhere. Visit us at www.shewritespress.com.

Appearances by Sondra Helene. $16.95, 978-1-63152-499-8
Samantha, the wife of a successful Boston businessman, loves both her husband and her sister—but the two of them have fought a cold war for years. When her sister is diagnosed with lung cancer, Samantha's family and marriage are tipped into crisis.

Other Fires by Lenore H. Gay. $16.95, 978-1-63152-773-9
Joss and Phil's already rocky marriage is fragmented when, after being injured in a devastating fire, Phil begins to call Joss an imposter. Faced with a husband who no longer recognizes her, Joss struggles to find motivation to save their marriage, even as family secrets start to emerge that challenge everything she thought she knew.

Bridge of the Gods by Diane Rios. $16.95, 978-1-63152-244-4
When twelve year-old Chloe Ashton is abducted and sold to vagabonds, she is taken deep into the Oregon woods, where she learns that the old legends are true: animals can talk, mountains do think, and deep in the forests, the trees still practice their old ways.

Return of the Evening Star by Diane Rios. $16.95, 978-1-63152-545-2
In this second installment of the Silver Mountain Series, Chloe Ashton and her friends race to protect the people and animals of Fairfax, who have come under attack from speeding ambulances that prowl the land, mowing down anything in their path and dragging their victims to a mysterious hospital deep in the woods.

Clara at the Edge by Maryl Jo Fox. $16.95, 978-1-63152-250-5
Seventy-three-year-old Clara, a stubborn widow, must finally reconcile with her estranged son and face the guilty secrets tied to her daughter's death—with the help of a rowdy spirit guide in the form of a magic purple wasp.